Prince of
Shadow and Ash

PRINCE OF SHADOW AND ASH

SELINA R. GONZALEZ

Cover Design by Deranged Doctor Designs

Paperback ISBN 978-1-7344676-1-1
Ebook ISBN 978-1-7344676-2-8

Published by Wyvern Wing Press
www.WyvernWingPress.com
www.SelinaRGonzalez.com

To Mom:
This book would not exist
without you for so many reasons.

WORLD MAP

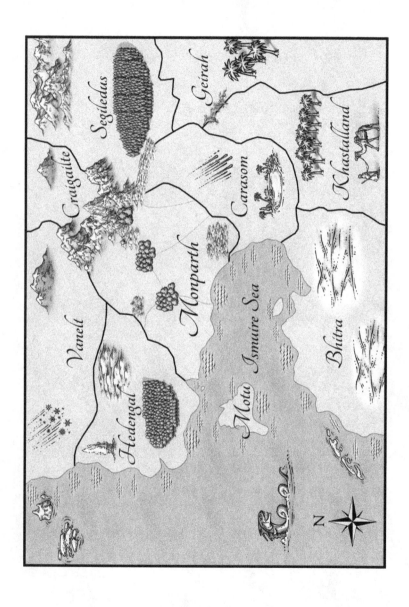

MAP OF MONPARTH

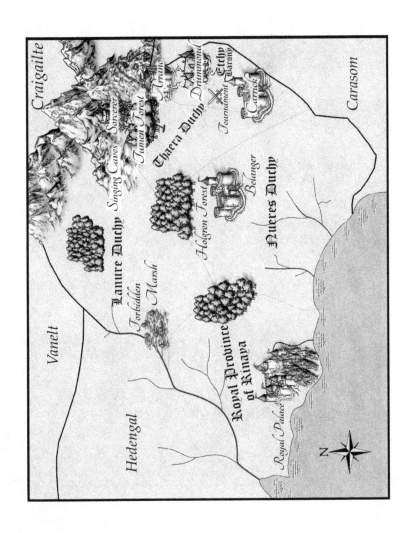

CHAPTER 1

THIS QUEST FOR A MARSH FLOWER WOULD BE EASIER WITHOUT the hulking black armor and oversized black sword.

Regulus tried to stretch his neck, but his helm and the bulky pauldrons impeded the movement. Curse the sorcerer and his driving, inexplicable need for theatricality. At least Regulus had the more practical hunting knife across his lower back.

Not as if he needed the heavy armor, anyway. The sorcery inside him kept him alive, and without the armor, his progress would have been faster. With an agitated groan, he gripped his helm by its decorative metal horns and removed it. Instead of the usual relief of fresh air on his face, humidity clung to his skin.

The marsh stank like rotting carcasses. His damp hair stuck to his forehead and neck and the sweat made the old scar that traced across his right cheek through the corner of his mouth to his chin itch. He turned his head, working out the tension in his neck and scanning for potential enemies. Muddy water—or maybe it was watery mud—stretched in every direction, broken up with patches of marsh grass, green-tipped cattails, and tangled briars. Fog drifted over everything, diluting the sunlight into a drab gray and providing cover for any lurking beasts.

Regulus had grown up near the Forbidden Marsh, and he'd heard all the stories. Stories of people who entered and never came out. Tales of screams carried on the wind that rustled the cattails. Rumors claimed monsters lurked in the Marsh. Human-hating centaurs, devious fairies, even the last of the redclaws—gaunt, tall, pale creatures with strange long limbs and six-inch-long claws stained permanently red by the blood of their victims.

He had dismissed them as tall tales, designed to frighten children into compliance. That was, after all, how his cruel childhood guardian had used the Marsh and its monsters. As a threat. But now, with the marsh grasses and cattails rasping around him and the unnatural gray mist, his nerves were on edge.

And yet, after over an hour of wandering wild, untamed growth and solid-looking moss that gave way beneath his boots, he had found nothing. Not a single monster, and no sign of the magical flower he hunted. He pulled the drawing of the starshade plant out of his belt and studied it. A short black plant with thick stalks and small black flowers that the sorcerer said should glow blue.

He refolded the parchment, pulled the helm back on, and trudged onward. The black helm had wide slanted rectangles for eye openings and fine holes to allow airflow over the mouth. Two long, thick horns curved from the top like the horns of a bull. His master got some twisted pleasure out of scaring anyone Regulus might encounter on his missions. He would have left it off, but he needed his hands free to draw his sword.

As he continued his search, the desolation of the marsh seemed ominous. As if something out there watched him, unseen in the gray haze. The muck of the marsh squelched under his boots. Each footstep sounded like a blade being pulled from a wound.

He shook his head. Maybe monsters prowled the Marsh, maybe they didn't. He had no reason to fear monsters. He was one of them. All that mattered was finding the flower as commanded and getting back home.

Home. Regulus smiled. Poor Harold would faint when he saw the state of the armor. The boy had adjusted well from the life of mercenary baggage boy to squire. Better than Regulus had adjusted to the life of a lord. His smile faded. *Harold is a far more loyal and dedicated squire than a slave like me deserves.*

The sharp snap of a breaking twig interrupted his thoughts. He drew his sword, turning slowly. The ebony-black blade glinted. The four-foot-long blade was nearly as wide as his palm at the cross-guard and narrowed down to a sharp point. He surveyed the marsh grasses and brush. Nothing. To his right, he heard what sounded like...muttering?

Regulus spun to face a dense stand of marsh grass. The grass mumbled in a quiet, scratchy voice, "Smells like venison. Venison is tasty, yes."

"Who's there?"

With a squeal like an injured piglet, a pale green hobgoblin with a long pointy chin and nose, wearing what looked like dead vines as clothes, leapt up at him. Cursing, Regulus swung his sword, but the hobgoblin was too small, maybe as long as Regulus' forearm from its webbed toes to the mossy-looking hair on its head. The creature grabbed onto his breastplate and scrambled around.

"Get off!" He swatted at the hobgoblin with his right hand, still awkwardly holding his sword in the other. The menace scurried down to Regulus' right hip, toward the satchel looped onto his belt, muttering about venison.

"Don't you dare!" He seized the vines around its torso. The hobgoblin screamed and flailed. Regulus tried to throw it away, but it grabbed onto his gauntlet with unexpected strength. The vines in his hand broke, and the creature jumped onto his side again.

With an irritated growl, Regulus drew his hunting knife. The hobgoblin yanked on his satchel and gnawed on the loops, trying to free it. Regulus stabbed at the creature, but it moved as if it sensed the knife coming. The blade glanced across Regulus' armor and sliced through part of his satchel.

The hobgoblin grunted as it tugged, and the fabric ripped. Dried venison and an apple went flying. The hobgoblin hooted in victory, catching most of the meat midair. Desperate, Regulus swung his arms, trying to catch the green-skinned menace. To his surprise, it worked. But now he had an angry hobgoblin pinned between his chest and forearms and a weapon in each hand. *Idiot.* At least his men weren't there to witness his humiliation.

The hobgoblin screamed and wiggled, and Regulus realized he didn't have any other options. He dropped his arms, and the little beast scampered off with a gleeful squeal. Regulus sheathed his dagger and his sword and checked his torn satchel. Empty. He groaned and looked around his feet, but the mud had swallowed any food the hobgoblin hadn't stolen.

He kicked at the muck then grabbed for the parchment at his belt. Gone. He cursed. Well, he had looked at it a dozen times, he didn't need it. Besides, there couldn't be that many glowing flowers. He checked the water horn on his left side—at least that was still there. Nothing to do but press on.

The thick clouds made judging the passing time difficult. Why did the sorcerer send him, anyway? He could probably use some spell to lead him right to the stupid plants. *And I know he could hover over this filth.*

A faint blue shine on the other side of a tangled mass of briars caught his eye. Hope sparked as he cut his way into a small clearing. A ring of sludge surrounded a raised patch of grass-covered ground, no more than two paces wide. And interspersed over the miniature island—starshade plants. Relieved, Regulus drew his knife and knelt next to the nearest plant.

After digging up ten of the plants to collect their roots, he tied them together using strips of fabric from his ripped satchel. He tied the roots to his belt and stood. Now to find his way back out of the marsh.

An hour later, he trudged on, lost and starving. *Is anything in this Etiros-forsaken marsh edible?* A bramble bush covered in juicy-looking red berries drew his attention. He scrambled for them, then stopped. They could be poisonous. *Can poison kill me?* He shrugged. What did it matter? Dresden would scold him for such thoughts— but Dresden wouldn't know.

He picked a berry and tossed it in his mouth. It tasted tart yet sweet, and not bad. He ate berries as quickly as his gloved hands allowed. Once he had eaten several handfuls, he took a long drink of water from his horn and looked around.

The marsh stretched on forever. The large standing stones that marked the entrance and where he had left his horse were nowhere to be seen. He squinted at the sun, trying to judge the time and the direction he needed to go. Finally, he decided it must be around two in the afternoon. *Based on that, I need to go…* He turned to his left and pointed at nothing. *That way.*

Before long, he felt a painful twinge in his stomach. Then another. His gut twisted violently, and his vision blacked out. He blinked and stumbled forward as his eyes cleared, wrestling his helm off and dropping it into the muck. Pain wracked his body and heat radiated from his stomach. He fell onto all fours and vomited.

Red marsh berries: poisonous.

Sorcery: expels poison.

The muscles in his abdomen contracted, and he groaned as bile burned his throat. He reached up to wipe sweat off his forehead, but mud coated his gloved hand. The foamy vomit had a stench different from the stench of the marsh. He moaned and clutched at his stomach as he vomited a third time, his whole body shaking and achy. *Times like this, I wish I could die.*

He heard a new sound among the quiet rustling of the marsh. Clomp, squelch, clomp, squelch from every side. He blinked back the sweat running into his eyes and looked up through the mud and hair sticking around his face. Tall marsh grass blocked his view. His hand shook as he drew his sword and used it to push himself to his feet. His vision blacked out again and his head spun. He closed his eyes, steadying himself.

He opened his eyes to a towering centaur staring down at him. The horse half was the size of a destrier, with a dark brown coat the same shade as the human half's skin. A large broadsword gleamed in the centaur's hands, held in front of a leather breastplate. The centaur stomped a hoof, and the muscles in his bare arms bulged as he pointed his sword at Regulus.

Great. Regulus had only had the misfortune of crossing a band of centaurs once, and he and his men had barely escaped alive. On the bright side, his stomach was unclenching, the burning in his throat subsiding, and the light-headed feeling receding.

"You have stolen from the Forbidden Marsh." The centaur's voice was commanding and deep. "You cannot leave the marsh with the starshade roots. Surrender them or die."

Regulus counted six other centaurs surrounding him. Three men with swords, two women with drawn bows, and a smaller male centaur whose human half looked to be maybe fourteen. The young centaur gripped a spear and swayed, his eyes wide. *Not a child. Etiros, why?* Regulus swallowed, his anguished heart crying out in the hope that somehow, after all he had done, the creator-god still heard his prayers. *Not a child.*

Regulus looked back at the centaur who had spoken. "I don't want trouble," he said slowly. He raised his sword and assumed a defensive position. "But I'm afraid I can't give up the roots."

"Starshade roots are only good for poison and sorcery!" A female centaur to his right eyed Regulus down the shaft of an arrow.

Of course they were. Why else would the sorcerer want them?

"We are the protectors of the Forbidden Marsh," the first centaur said. "You will leave the roots or die."

If only. Regulus rolled his shoulders, his strength returning. He took a step back. "Please. Don't attack me. I *really* don't want to hurt anyone."

The centaur frowned. "You are a very good liar."

"It's the truth." Regulus eyed his helm lying in the mud. "I wish you no harm. But I have no choice. I have to take the starshade roots. And you won't kill me. You can't."

"Jaresha." The centaur stomped a hoof.

He heard the twang of a bowstring and dove for his helm. An arrow flew over him as he replaced his mud-covered helm on his head. Another arrow pinged off his armor. He bolted for the space to the brown centaur's right. These centaurs weren't evil. They didn't deserve to die. He wouldn't kill them unnecessarily. The power of the sorcerer's mark lent speed to his legs, giving him a slim chance of outrunning the centaurs.

Pain burned from the mark hidden under the gauntlet on his right arm. He groaned and skidded to a stop, remembering the sorcerer's directions. *"Kill anyone or anything that tries to stop you."* He turned and the pain faded. The brown centaur charged.

The centaur slammed his broadsword into Regulus' chest, knocking him onto his back. Regulus swung at the centaur's forelegs and the centaur screamed as the massive blade cleaved through bone. Regulus winced at the sound. One of the female centaurs shrieked while the wounded centaur collapsed.

Regulus scrambled to his feet and turned to go. The pain in his arm redoubled. *No. I don't want to do this.*

"Don't try to stop me!" Some part of his mind whispered it wouldn't matter, they had already tried, the mark wouldn't let him leave until they were all dead, but he had to hope. He had to try.

An arrow found the gap under the side of Regulus' helm and buried in his neck. He choked and swayed as his vision spotted from the pain. He ripped the arrow out. As he fell forward, he jammed his sword into the ground and used it to remain standing. An agonizing prickling sensation pulled at the hole in his neck until it closed. He took a deep breath and straightened.

A female centaur with a white coat and golden hair gaped, her face pale. Her bow trembled in her hands. The lead male centaur had fallen on his side and was hyperventilating between shrieks. Both human and equine lungs heaved. Regulus looked at the hacked-off end of the centaurs' leg. *At this point, it's a mercy.* The mark on his arm burned and ached, goading him on. He raised the sword and swung. The other centaurs screamed. He looked away from the headless body.

"I'm leaving. You're not stopping me," Regulus said. He turned away and bit back a cry as pain sliced up his right arm from the mark to his shoulder.

"He must have a bond," a male voice said behind him. Disturbed wonder laced the centaur's strained voice. "He can't die."

Regulus took another step. *They're letting me go,* he told himself. As if maybe he could convince the mark. Pain spread over his shoulder and reached into his chest, clawing across his skin and grinding through his bones. His heart ached, but he turned back around. *Maybe if they say it...*

"Say you're not stopping me. You're letting me go."

The centaurs shuffled and glanced at each other. Muck flew up from the boy's frantically tapping hooves. The boy glanced at the dead centaur and whimpered. His spear shook in his hands.

The pain stopped. Regulus felt a tickle at the back of his head, like something wiggling into his brain. He barely had time to think *no, not again* before he lost all control of his body. He could still sense everything. His hands gripping the sword. The sharp tang of centaur blood. He still stared at the group of frightened and uncertain-looking centaurs. But he couldn't so much as blink. The sorcerer's presence in his mind felt like a tiny piece of sharp, cold iron lodged in his head.

His mouth moved at the sorcerer's command. Regulus' voice came out, but the words were not his. "What is going on?" He looked down at the dead centaur as the sorcerer controlled his body, looking through his eyes.

No, stop. He tried to close his eyes, to look away, anything. But he couldn't. The sorcerer gazed at Regulus' bloody handiwork, meaning Regulus did, too. He looked at the centaurs who were still alive. Regulus' consciousness felt trapped in someone else's body. His mind screamed. His body didn't care.

Regulus sighed, but the sigh wasn't his. "First, I feel my power draining away to heal you twice in rapid succession, then I sense you defying me. I'm trying to decipher this ridiculous code. I don't need distractions."

Regulus' arms raised his sword, and his legs moved him forward. The centaurs backed up, their faces contorted in horror. Regulus mentally begged them to run.

"What is so difficult about following instructions, boy?" his mouth said. "Kill them and get back here, or we'll have a conversation about your friends." Regulus' mind shuddered and protested, but his body didn't respond. "And be quick about it!"

The feeling of cold iron slipped out of his brain. Regulus teetered forward as control of his body reverted to his own mind. The mark burned faintly. The centaurs stood frozen. One of them muttered something in a language he didn't understand and drew a strange symbol in the air.

Regulus steeled himself. *At least they're not human. Most centaurs don't even like humans.* The thought didn't bring comfort. *At least they're not my friends.*

He let his instincts and training take over and lunged. Years of sword fighting experience and every ounce of magically enhanced strength, agility, and speed powered his blade. He aimed a thrust at the golden-haired female's equine ribcage. She gasped and reared back, but that just allowed him to bury the sword straight up through horse and human. She was dead before he pulled his blade free.

Regulus turned and slashed across the hind legs of the second female as she turned to flee, then drove his sword through her back. He turned and found himself staring at the young centaur. The boy stood shaking, rooted to the ground, like a sapling shuddering in a strong wind.

"Run," Regulus rumbled. He turned from the boy and blocked the sword of a male centaur with a white-and-brown coat. Within moments, the centaur was dead. Regulus spun, looking for the remaining two adult males. Hooves pounded into his chest and Regulus fell backward, gasping for air.

The centaur raised his sword and aimed for Regulus' neck. Regulus rolled and scrambled to his feet. The centaur turned, his face red. "Sorcerous abomination!"

The centaur swung wildly in his rage. Regulus easily parried the attack and drove his sword up under the bottom edge of the centaur's leather breastplate. The centaur screamed and toppled over as Regulus pulled out his sword. He looked around. He stood surrounded by centaur corpses, watery mud stained with red swirls, and cattails that rasped against each other, making a sound like mourning. The boy and the last male centaur were gone.

He waited for the mark to burn, to tell him to hunt them down. But it didn't. He sobbed with relief and left the centaur bodies before his stomach tried to force up nothing. He cleaned some of the blood off his blade with marsh grass. It took him a couple tries to sheath the oversized sword; his hands shook so badly.

Better them than Dresden or Harold or any of the others. Better centaurs in a marsh than my friends in my castle. Still, the screams of the centaurs echoed in his ears. Killing wasn't difficult—in fact he was good at it. But he had always followed a strict no-killing-innocents policy. Until the sorcerer.

He double-checked the roots tied to his belt. After redetermining his direction, he trudged on. Guilt dragged him down more than the mud and water clogging his boots as the day wore on.

The sun had dipped low to the horizon when he spotted the standing stones. He picked up his pace, eager to be out of that dreadful marsh. His black stallion, Sieger, was waiting where he had left him, munching grass. He mounted Sieger with ease despite his heavy armor and the exhaustion and blood loss. His blood-soaked tunic had dried into stiff, uncomfortable folds beneath his neck.

Regulus made camp after midnight. Increased abilities and healing or no, he still needed rest. Time to recover. Not that he slept well. By himself, he couldn't remove most of his armor. He slept for a few hours before waking to a pain in his back. Moonlight shone through the trees. With a groan, he stretched as best he could and staggered to his feet. *Can't die, but can still feel like death.* He put his greaves, gloves, and helm back on.

"I'm sorry, Sieger." He rubbed the stallion's neck, coaxing him awake. "It's time to go again."

Sieger nickered and shook his mane.

"I know, I know." Regulus rubbed Sieger's muzzle. He would have given almost anything to be asleep in his own bed. But such was not his lot. He removed his helm to take a drink of water and was disappointed to find only one gulp left in his horn. Now he was out of food and water, and with little time to spare to get more. The sorcerer expected him back soon. Begrudgingly, he turned back to Sieger and gripped the pommel of the saddle.

He froze as a branch snapped behind him.

SELINA R. GONZALEZ

CHAPTER 2

REGULUS INCHED HIS HAND TOWARD HIS SWORD. RUSTLING AND
the crunch of last autumn's leaves sounded some five paces behind
him. Someone or something lurked in the bushes. He focused his
hearing as he wrapped his fingers around the sword's grip, his mind
racing to rule out possibilities. No heavy breathing, and the intruder
had gotten quite close before he heard them. Ruled out anything as
big as a bear or troll. No creak of leather or clink or scrape of metal,
so it wasn't armored. No clomp of hooves, so neither centaur nor
minotaur.

He tried to think of where he was, what sort of creatures lived
here. Goblins? Unlikely this far from any caves. Monparth had
driven most monsters into uninhabited areas, but there were
periodic incursions. Could be something as harmless as a satyr or
dangerous as a thike, a medium-sized lithe feline with poisonous
barbs on its long tail. Or a human, which were best not under-
estimated. He turned, bringing his sword into a guard position.

Nothing.

His eyes strained to peer into the shadows. Only moments had
passed, whatever or whoever had been there must still be there. He
moved toward the bushes. There, in a small clearing. A humanoid
shape, hidden in a dark robe. The person or creature appeared to
be facing away from him. Maybe they weren't even aware of his presence.

Regulus leapt through the bushes at the figure. It started to turn
at the sudden noise, but he pressed the point of the sword against
the figure's back. "Who are you?"

"Wh-what?" a normal-sounding man stuttered.

"What are you doing out here in the middle of the night?"

The man quivered. "I—I'm just—"

"Spit it out!"

A woman's scream ripped through the night. Regulus whipped his head up. A woman in a dark cloak stood in the clearing, her hands covering her mouth. Moonlight glinted off the whites of her wide eyes.

"Carolyn, run!" the man shouted. But Carolyn stood as if frozen in place.

Regulus looked down at the man, then back at the woman. Back and forth. Heat rushed to his cheeks. "You're just... meeting..." He moved his sword away from the man's back. "Sorry."

The man staggered forward. He looked over his shoulder at Regulus. "You mad..." His jaw slackened. "What...who are you?"

Oh, you had to ask. A burning sensation emanated from the mark on Regulus' forearm and he gritted his teeth. "I am the Black Knight. And I serve the Prince of Shadow and Ash." He sheathed his sword as the pain in his arm vanished. "Go. Now."

The lovers hurried away, their faces drawn and pale. This was why he preferred traveling at night and avoided roads. Every disputed sighting of the now legendary Black Knight made him more nervous he would get caught.

Monparth's laws forbade the use of dark, corrupted magic. And after over twenty years without mages, wielders of pure magic, people were extra wary of any hint of sorcery. The authorities would consider Regulus the sorcerer's accomplice, and his men guilty by association. He couldn't die, but his men could. At least the loathsome horned helm protected his identity.

Regulus rode all day, keeping Sieger at a trot as much as possible and stopping only to steal a couple apples as he passed an orchard. Despite the days growing longer as summer approached, the sun set too soon. He stopped and managed to sleep for a few hours until a pinch from the mark on his arm woke him.

"I can only cross the kingdom so fast," Regulus growled under his breath as he slammed the helm back on and rode into the night.

Around midday, he neared the sorcerer's tower in the Tumen Forest. He always knew when he was close.

The bark on trees turned black. Dead, midnight-colored leaves clung to lifeless ebony-shaded branches and covered the forest floor. Brittle tangles of dead wood vine made a pale contrast where the vines wrapped around branches. As the tower came into view, the trees became white, skeletal. All their bark had fallen away, revealing wood drained of all color and life. Barren fir branches stuck out like spikes, while naked deciduous boughs reached out like bony fingers.

Not even grass grew this close to the tower. The only thing that did grow were mushrooms. Velvety purple mushrooms shaped like thimbles, bright red domed mushrooms, flat round mushrooms as yellow as a daisy's center. A faint glow emanated from underneath some. Regulus assumed all of them were poisonous.

Two years ago, when he was first bound to the sorcerer, there had been only a small circle of blackened trees. Sometimes obviously, sometimes imperceptibly, the decay had spread. Now the deathly forest stretched a ten-minute ride in every direction around the sorcerer's tower.

Built of reddish brick darkened by time and sorcery, the tower itself stood around four stories tall, topped with narrow crenellations and covered in layers of dead wood vine. Yellow light filtered through the rough grayish glass of the single gothic window in the top level. Regulus used to wonder why someone who called himself a prince would live in such a drab old tower. He didn't care anymore. Although, he suspected the Prince of Shadow and Ash simply liked dead, creepy things as much as he liked torturing Regulus.

Sore, hungry, and exhausted, Regulus dismounted with difficulty. He stuffed the helm in his saddlebag. The iron-latticed oak door opened, and the sorcerer stepped out.

A man of below-average height, the sorcerer's physique belied his power. A wide, dark leather belt set with polished obsidian secured a long black tunic over his stomach paunch. Crimson accents edged the tunic. The hood of a gold-stitched sable robe shadowed his face, hiding his eyes above a pinched-looking nose. A graying brown beard fell in waves down to his chest. But he walked and spoke with the authority of the prince he pretended to be.

"You're late." The sorcerer's dark tone chilled Regulus' blood.

He untied the roots from his belt. "I got here as quickly as I could, my lord."

"After trying to disobey." The sorcerer strode forward and snatched the roots from Regulus with pale, knobby fingers. "Do we have a problem, mercenary?"

Regulus swallowed and bowed his head. *Don't take the bait.* "No, my lord." *I'm not a mercenary anymore. And yes, we have many problems.*

"Kill all the centaurs?"

"Yes." *No.* He kept his expression calm and neutral.

"Good." The sorcerer counted the roots under his breath. "Ten," he muttered. "Good thing, too. Room for error. Tricky business, breaking an enchantment." He looked at Regulus. "I need one more thing."

Regulus stopped himself from protesting. He needed to rest and eat. He wanted to go home, even if only for a couple days. The sorcerer never sent him out again immediately after returning. But it was no use arguing. The sorcerer got want he wanted. Always. "Yes, my lord?"

"Wait here." The sorcerer took the roots inside the tower and returned with a tin goblet and a small carving knife. "Take off your glove and give me your arm. I need your blood."

"What?" Regulus gaped. "Why?"

The corners of the sorcerer's mouth turned down. Tendrils of pain, like red-hot vines growing under his skin, shot up Regulus' right arm. He grunted and used his teeth to pull his glove off his right hand.

"Yes, my lord." The pain faded as he held his arm toward the sorcerer.

"Better." A momentary flicker of a smile made the sorcerer's beard twitch. "You should be thanking me. I thought about making you bring me the blood of one of your friends. Maybe the one with the beard. Or the boy."

Regulus flinched. "I've been obeying you, my lord," he said, choosing his words carefully as the sorcerer grabbed his hand. "I only hesitated today, and I did as you commanded and slaughtered the centaurs. There's no need to harm my men." *Please, Etiros. Let him be forgiving.*

The sorcerer pulled down on Regulus' hand so he could see the underside of his wrist beneath his gauntlet. "Mm, yes. You've become such an obedient pet. Almost a pity. I did so enjoy making you hurt them." The sorcerer sliced the knife across Regulus' wrist. Regulus drew in a sharp breath that hissed between his teeth. "But hesitate again, and I'm going to lose my temper."

Regulus stared at the dead wood vine and hoped his master wouldn't notice his rage. Any defiance always ended in pain. If he was lucky, only his own. The sorcerer let his blood drain into the goblet until the bond linking his life to the sorcerer's closed the wound, preventing him from bleeding out.

The sorcerer waved Regulus away as he walked back inside. "Run on home. I have important matters to attend to." The door slammed shut, leaving Regulus and Sieger alone with the dead forest.

Shoulders sagging, Regulus remounted. "Let's go home, Sieger."

The stars had been out for hours when he arrived at Arrano castle. It was an old castle, long out of style, but it was his. The

25

square central tower and surrounding four-story wall stood atop a hill. A flag bearing the Arrano crest—a red rose over crossed white swords on a field of black—flew from the north wall turret. The barren hill rose in a gradual incline to the front of the castle.

Regulus didn't follow the road up the hill. Instead, he struck out around the castle. Far downhill, with enough space around the hill to ensure a clear line of sight in case of attack, the woods began again. A massive willow tree grew at the edge of the woods. Regulus scanned the surrounding area, ensuring no one was near, then led Sieger under the swaying curtain of the willow's hanging branches. The stallion whinnied, protesting what came next.

"I know." He patted Sieger's neck. "I know."

Near the tree's trunk rested a large boulder. Regulus picked it up, the strength the sorcerer's mark granted him making the task easy. A large chunk of grassy ground pulled away with the stone— a dirt and grass-covered wooden panel cemented to the boulder's base. A hole appeared where the panel and boulder had been, with dirt steps leading into the earth.

He set the boulder down so the edge of the panel jutted out over the opening. He descended halfway, turned to his right, and felt for the hole in the dirt wall. His fingers found the torch, flint, and an apple where he had left them, and he set about lighting the torch. With the apple and lit torch in hand, he went back for Sieger.

The stallion shook his head, pawed the ground, and snorted. Regulus sighed. "Come on, boy."

He held out the apple, and Sieger reached for it. Regulus pulled it back a little and backed down the stairs. With a snort of frustration, Sieger followed. Once down the steps, Regulus gave Sieger the apple. While Sieger crunched the apple, Regulus stuck the torch in an iron rung in the dirt wall. He returned to the steps and pulled the panel and boulder back over the tunnel entrance. Maneuvering it into place over his head by holding onto the handles on the bottom was awkward, but he'd done it enough times it didn't take long.

The tunnel, which was just tall enough and wide enough for Sieger, sloped upward. He led Sieger until they reached another set of packed dirt steps. Another wooden panel blocked the exit, this one covered with stones to make it blend in with the floor of the stables and to give it extra weight. He deposited the torch in an iron ring in the wall and heaved the trapdoor aside. He extinguished the torch and led Sieger out of the tunnel.

It took a moment for his eyes to adjust. Stalls abutted the outer castle wall to his right, and to his left stretched a wooden wall with shuttered windows. Narrow bands of moonlight streaked across the hay-strewn dirt floor. The smell of horses and manure filled his nostrils, and the quiet, steady breathing of horses provided a backdrop to the muffled stomp of Sieger's hooves. He led Sieger to his stall and returned the cover to the tunnel entrance. He left Sieger, still wearing all his tack, and headed through his private hedge-protected lane from the stables to a side door in the castle. All part of preventing his few servants from knowing about the Black Knight. He pulled off his helm, closing his eyes as welcome night air cooled his skin.

A lamp and flint stood on a pedestal near the castle door, waiting for him. With the lamp in one hand and helm in the other, he crept up the stairs, his armor echoing. He knocked on a plain wooden door near the top of the stairs and waited. Nothing. He couldn't blame the boy, but he also couldn't get out of his armor unaided. He knocked again, harder, and opened the door.

"Harold."

The young man sat up in his bed. "Wha…my lord?" Harold rubbed his eyes. A lad of sixteen years, Harold was lanky and a touch fidgety. His dark blond hair was a mess, and he had drool in the scraggly beard he was so proud of.

"Yes. Get up, I need help with my armor."

"Of course, my lord." Harold teetered out of bed and toward the door, blinking. Regulus suppressed a smile. "I'll carry the lamp, my lord."

They continued up the winding staircase, went through a door into a hallway, and walked down to Regulus' room. Harold unlocked and opened the door.

A giant mass of dark fur bolted through the door and jumped on Regulus, knocking him back. Despite his exhaustion, Regulus grinned.

"Hey, Magnus." Regulus scratched the dog behind a floppy ear as its giant pink tongue licked his face. Standing on his hind legs, the massive dog was almost as tall as Regulus. "All right, down boy."

Magnus trotted back into Regulus' room, wagging his fluffy light brown tail, and jumped on the bed. His fur—of which he had a copious amount—was black on his face, chest, and haunches, and the rest was brown, getting lighter to the pale fur on the underside of his tail.

The curtains on the wall-length window were open, and dim moonlight illuminated the room. A large four-poster bed, currently occupied by Magnus, took up most of the room. Next to the bed, a nightstand just big enough for a food tray stood empty. A massive fireplace filled most of the wall opposite his bed, with a small armchair and footstool placed in front of it. Other than his large oak dresser, and a small desk and chair, the only other furnishing was a couple of large trunks, one padlocked shut, and a large rug. Harold set the lamp on the nightstand and headed for the fireplace.

"Armor first, Harold," Regulus said, unwilling to stay in the heavy, stinking armor any longer.

"Of course, my lord."

Regulus stared out the window at the stars while Harold removed his armor piece by piece, tutting at the muck covering it. "Did you go for a swim in a giant mud puddle?"

Regulus chuckled half-heartedly. "More or less."

"I think you'll be needing a bath, my lord."

No argument there. "Tomorrow, Harold." Regulus peeled off his blood-encrusted tunic. "For now, I need sleep. No, leave that," he added as Harold moved to collect the armor for cleaning. "Go back to bed."

Harold nodded. "Thank you, my lord."

The young man slipped out, and Regulus went to his bed. Magnus shifted over just enough to allow Regulus to crawl under the covers, then burrowed against his side.

The sun had passed its zenith when Regulus awoke to Harold hauling his armor out of the room. Magnus placed his head on Regulus' chest, panting happily. Harold offered to draw a bath and bring food, which Regulus gratefully accepted.

As he waited, Regulus rubbed his thumb over the mark on the underside of his right forearm. Although the mark itself was smooth, the skin around and under it was rough from repeated scarring. The product of too many failed attempts to remove it. The black mark looked like two hollow diamonds connected to a V, with the open side toward his wrist. Despite the scarring, the mark remained, clear as when it first appeared. He stood and walked to the window.

Best not to dwell on what you can't change. His father's cousin had said that when Regulus went to live with him at six. *"Make the most of your lot in life,"* Lord Kimberly would say, usually after punishing Regulus for some minor infraction. *"It could be worse."*

Except nothing could be worse than this.

No, he chided himself. Dresden's voice replaced Kimberly's in his mind. *"You're my brother."* He could be alone. *All* his friends could be dead. Or they could have abandoned him any time in the two years he had borne the sorcerer's mark. They probably should have. Things could be worse. But that knowledge did nothing for his aching soul.

After food and a bath, Regulus strapped on his sword and headed out to the courtyard. Not the oversized black sword. He hated it, and the armor. Both given to him by the sorcerer. No, this was one of his own standard steel broadswords. He didn't need it within his own castle, but after years as a mercenary, he felt exposed without it. Magnus loped beside him. Even down on all fours, the dog's head came up nearly to his waist.

A couple servants nodded at him deferentially as he walked to the stables. Something after two years, he was still getting used to. He only had eight servants running the entire castle, plus a handful of guards. The gardens were overgrown and the extra rooms dusty and generally everything was shabby, but he couldn't risk more watching eyes. He found Sieger groomed and chomping on hay in the stable. The stallion nickered at Regulus.

"Good boy, Sieger." He scratched Sieger's neck.

"Glad to see you're up, Reg," a voice said from behind him.

Regulus smiled and turned around. "Hey, Drez."

A little shorter than Regulus and a year younger, Dresden Jakobs was muscular with a constant low-level energy. Thick black brows shadowed his dark eyes, and he kept his thick black hair and beard short and well-groomed. He had a long, angular nose and a dark olive complexion, like most Carasians. Twin scimitars criss-crossed his back as usual.

Dresden was silent for a moment as his piercing gaze bored into Regulus. "Maybe you wouldn't come back so tired if you let me help."

"No. If one of you died, what would be the point?" Regulus stroked Sieger's neck. "I'm not discussing it again." By the hurt look Dresden gave him, Regulus must have slipped into his captain voice again. "We agreed," he added quietly.

Agreed I need your support here more than out there.

"I know." Dresden's brow furrowed as he scratched behind Magnus' ears. "What was it this time?"

"Roots of some glowing plant in the Forbidden Marsh guarded by hobgoblins and centaurs."

"I *hate* hobgoblins." Dresden spat.

"I'm aware, old friend." He didn't bother to hide his amusement.

"Nasty, troublesome creatures."

"Apparently they like venison, not just your collection of lucky rabbit feet."

"I maintain their theft is linked to our getting trapped for two days in that ravine."

Regulus laughed. "I maintain that link is completely circumstantial."

"Whatever you say." Dresden stopped petting Magnus. "Oh, almost forgot." He pulled a crumpled letter out of his belt and handed it to Regulus.

Regulus glanced at the broken red wax seal on the parchment. A raven's head over an axe. *Drummond.* "Reading my missives again, Drez?"

Lord and Lady Drummond cordially invite you to join them on Springtide the 26th, at 6 in the evening, for a supper party to honor the visit of Lady Jamina Belanger and her daughter, Lady Adelaide Belanger.

"Only the interesting-looking ones." Dresden leaned back on his elbows on the door of an empty stall across from Sieger's. "Plus, we never know how long you'll be gone. What if it's pressing?"

"I suppose that's fair." Regulus read over the letter.

He frowned. He hated these parties. Dresden loved them, but Drez flirted with every unmarried woman who would talk to him from the serving girls to the guests.

"Are you going?" Drez asked. "If Adelaide is as pretty as her sister, might be worth it for once."

Regulus folded the invite and looked at Dresden. "And when have you met her sister?"

"Lady Minerva, Sir Drummond's wife." Dresden shrugged. "That's why they're visiting, because Minerva Drummond is pregnant."

He raised a brow. "You know as much gossip as a barmaid."

"How else am I supposed to amuse myself while you're off fighting centaurs? So," Dresden pressed. "You going? It'll be good for you. Drink some wine, talk to a pretty girl."

"Assuming I'm not called away," he said grimly. "And only because it's the polite thing to do. But I doubt I'll be talking to any pretty girls." He elbowed Drez. "You coming along?"

"Obviously. If you're too stoic and frowny-faced to engage Lady Belanger, you can bet your immortality I will."

"Frowny-faced? Really."

Dresden pointed at Regulus' face. "Exactly! Just like that."

Regulus realized he was right and rolled his eyes. "Okay, okay. But I'm not looking for a wife—"

"Yes, you are. You're nearly thirty, a lord with enough land and income to live comfortably, and no family. Your bachelorhood is an affront to common decency."

"What?" Regulus blinked. Sure, Drez had hinted in the past he wanted Regulus to marry. Even as mercenaries, Dresden had sometimes tried to play matchmaker, despite Regulus' protests. A wife was impractical for a mercenary, and he'd had no interest in casual romance.

"You need somebody other than Magnus, Reg."

Regulus bent down and covered Magnus' soft, floppy ears. "Hey, you'll hurt his feelings. Besides, I have you."

Even as he said it, he knew Drez had a point. He scratched Magnus' head. Okay, yes, sometimes he envied his married knights. Sometimes he not only wondered what it would be like to have someone look at him the way Sarah looked at Jerrick, or to hold someone the way Perceval held Leonora, but wanted that. Sure, he wouldn't mind having someone waiting for him at home. But he couldn't have that. Not right now. He sighed and straightened.

"Look, maybe if things were different. But with the sorcerer—"

"To hell with the sorcerer."

Regulus flinched. Even though the sorcerer couldn't have overheard, Regulus almost expected the mark on his arm to start burning. Nothing happened.

Dresden cursed and shook his head. "See, this is my point! You need a distraction. You need something to get your confidence back."

"A wife isn't a distraction, that's a commitment." A commitment Etiros knew he couldn't make while the sorcerer's slave.

"I'm not asking you to carry the next eligible noblewoman you meet straight to a chapel." Drez looked down and kicked at the dirt. "I'm asking you to live your life. I'm asking you to find some joy." He looked up, his brows pinched. "You might not be free yet, but that doesn't mean you have to live like a slave. I'm asking you to live like you're going to be free. Because you will be. Has…he given any indication of how close you are?"

"No." *Sometimes I'm not sure he actually plans to let me go.* But he couldn't think like that. The sorcerer had given his word he would release him when his debt was paid. He had to believe that was true, or he'd lose his mind.

"Well, he will, eventually." Dresden smirked. "And then you're going to have no idea what to do with yourself after spending all your time moping. Besides, the moping is insufferable. And this lone wolf act doesn't suit you. So go meet a pretty girl. Fall in love. Be happy."

Regulus stared across the courtyard, watching a sparrow flitting through the flower-covered apple trees. All he wanted, all he had ever wanted, was a normal life. But he didn't want to play pretend. "Not yet. Maybe when—"

"No!" Drez clenched his fists. Magnus whined and licked Dresden's hand. Dresden relaxed, but he fixed Regulus with an intent glare. "No excuses. We agreed. What's our mantra?"

Regulus rubbed his forehead. "My circumstances don't define me. I choose who I am. Not the sorcerer." The words had helped once. A reminder that his worth, his identity, were not dictated by the sorcerer, or anyone else. That even when his options were limited, his choices still mattered. After two years, the words felt hollow. But to tell Dresden that would feel like letting him down.

"Don't let him take your life," Dresden said. Magnus tried to weave between Dresden's legs, and he pushed the dog aside with an affectionate smile. "So you're going to be friendly and at least consider getting to know the lovely, eligible Lady Belanger. Do it for me."

He rubbed the side of his neck. "Drez, she won't look at me twice."

"Why?"

"This, for one." He pointed at the scar stretching down his right cheek to his chin. "Second, even I have heard of Lord Alfred Belanger. He's wealthy and knows the king. I'm a—"

"Lord," Dresden cut in.

"Bastard."

They glared at each other. It shouldn't matter. He *was* a lord. But it did, and they both knew it.

"And a mercenary."

"Former." Drez scratched his beard. "And a good, honorable, kind man. You're talking to her." He nodded once, as if that settled it.

Regulus frowned. "Last I checked, I give the orders around here." Dresden's jaw tightened and he wished he could take it back. Guilt twisted his gut. He hung his head. "Okay."

Dresden grinned, his anger and concern vanishing. "You have to at least try to engage her in conversation. Promise me."

"Fine." Regulus gave a terse nod. "But give me a chance. She sees you and your beard first and she won't want anything to do with my scarred face."

Dresden stroked his beard. "Ha! I knew you were jealous of my beard."

SELINA R. GONZALEZ

CHAPTER 3

THE KNIFE SPUN THROUGH THE AIR, THE SHARP EDGES REFLECTING the cloudy afternoon sunlight as it arced up and back down. Adelaide caught the blade between her fingertips and absent-mindedly flipped it back up. It cartwheeled up and back down, the hilt landing in her palm. She leaned on the pommel of her saddle, holding the knife out to her side, and stared at the back of Sir Ruddard's helm, glinting silver above his maroon cloak, as if he wasn't there. She heard the clomp of hooves on the packed, uneven dirt road as if from a distance. Two long days of riding, from before the sun cast its warm glow until the moon cooled the land, had driven her past boredom until her mind—and her legs and rear—felt numb.

Ahead, a large, half-dead walnut tree stretched barren branches over the road. Adelaide moved her fingers down to the smooth, rounded end of the knife's flat hilt. She raised her arm, and with a fluid motion, straightened her elbow and released the knife. The blade made a soft thunk as it stuck into a low branch just as Sir Ruddard rode under the bough.

"Adelaide!"

Adelaide jumped at her mother's voice. She looked back over her shoulder at Mother. The breeze teased fly-away hairs from Mother's crown of dark brown braids. Her skin, a burnt umber a few shades darker than Adelaide's, had a warm glow from riding all day.

Mother frowned. "What if you had hit Sir Ruddard?" Her Khastallander accent made her vowels sound exaggerated.

"Me?" Adelaide chuckled. "Miss? Not in ages."

"*Garhaa soondir haninai,*" Mother said, slipping into Khast as she often did when rebuking her children or when her emotions ran high. *Haughtiness is unbecoming.*

"Yes, Mother," Adelaide replied in Khast. She turned as she approached the branch. As she rode beneath the dead limb, she reached up and pulled the knife free. "But even if I *had* missed, he's wearing armor," she said, subconsciously switching back to Monparthian. "He would have been fine."

"And your blade might have been dulled or chipped," Mother chided, also switching back to Monparthian. "A *hamila* takes care of her blade." *A lady.*

Adelaide leaned over and slipped the knife back into her boot and adjusted her skirt. "It's just that the time is going so slowly!" A raindrop fell on her nose, and she glowered at the gray sky. Thunder rumbled in the distance. "Beautiful weather for two days, and in late Springtide, no less. So naturally it would rain the last day."

Mother laughed. "That should be reason for gratitude, not grumbling."

She shifted in her saddle. "It seems worse, somehow. Like nature is laughing at us. 'You thought you could make it all the way to Etchy without getting wet? Let me send a rainstorm your way.'" A big raindrop fell on her forehead, and she wiped it away.

"We could make camp until the rain passes, my ladies," Sir Ruddard called over his shoulder. Ruddard had taken up the vanguard today. Sir Charing and Sir Hayes rode behind Adelaide, her mother, their two handmaids, and two pack horses. Like knight bookends, Adelaide thought.

"Nonsense," Mother said. "If it gets too bad, we can stop. But Adelaide has a point. I am tired of traveling. We press on."

"Yes, my lady."

Nothing sounded better than finishing this journey, even if Adelaide was unsure about staying with her sister's new family. Getting off horseback would be welcome, as would sleeping in a real bed again. More importantly, the sooner they arrived at the Drummond's, the sooner she saw Minerva. Two years felt like an eternity, and the occasional letter did little to ease her loneliness.

Adelaide pulled the hood of her cloak over her head as the rain fell faster. Why did they have to be riding across pastureland instead of through a forest when it rained? Some trees between her and the sky would be wonderful. She prodded her blue roan gelding, Zephyr, into a trot and moved next to Ruddard.

The rain formed little rivulets down Ruddard's helm. Droplets clung to his scraggly gray beard. Even though his horse was taller than Zephyr, he was still shorter than her.

"If we don't stop, when do you think we will arrive?"

Ruddard pulled his cloak tighter around his shoulders to protect his chainmail tunic from the rain. "Midevening, optimist-ically."

That left at least four more hours of riding. She let Zephyr fall back into line. *Don't get me wrong, Zephyr; I love you. But I'm tired. I'm sure you are, too.*

About an hour later, hail drove them to a small stand of trees a short distance out of their way. The trees, their leaves still small, provided little protection. Worse, they had to share the space with three cows that refused to move.

While they waited, they ate the last of their food. They started out again as soon as the rain subsided to a light shower. Darkness fell, and a waning crescent moon glinted between clouds. Ruddard slowed his horse and signaled for them to stop as they approached a pass between a couple small wooded hills. The knights behind them pressed in, forcing their caravan into a tighter group. Adelaide eyed the trees. Had he seen something? She leaned forward, pulled her dagger from her right boot, and two throwing knives from her left. Steel scraped against leather as Ruddard drew his sword. Her heart rate increased as her gaze darted from shadow to shadow.

"Is someone there?" Mother murmured.

"Not sure." Ruddard prodded his horse forward. "Best to be cautious."

Behind them, Sir Charing drew his sword. Adelaide glanced back as Sir Hayes nocked an arrow. Moonlight glinted on the blade of Mother's dagger. The maids' eyes were wide in their pale faces. If anyone attacked them, the handmaids would be useless. Not for the first time, and doubtless not for the last, Adelaide mentally chided the entire kingdom of Monparth for teaching its daughters to rely on men to defend them. As if there would always be a good man available. All the same, she would rather not have today be the day she had to put her training to the test.

They were halfway through the pass when torches lit on either side of them. A dozen or so men dressed in dark, ragged clothing stepped out of the trees. Handkerchiefs hid the lower half of their faces, and they carried an array of battered swords and spears. A large, muscular man bearing a longsword stepped closer.

"My, my. What have we here?" His deep voice carried a note of amusement. "Don't you know robbers roam these roads after dark?"

"You are bold," Ruddard adjusted his grip on his sword, "attacking travelers so close to the Drummond Estate."

"Drummond?" The man laughed. "Nearly an hour away. And we haven't attacked nobody." He ran his hand along the flat of his blade, admiring the weapon. Even in the faint light, Adelaide could tell it needed sharpening. "Yet."

Adelaide prepped the throwing knives, keeping one in her palm while she gripped the other between her thumb and the side of her forefinger. Still, she prayed to Etiros that she wouldn't need to use them. As her pulse rose, the magic inside her stirred, a constrained energy coursing through her veins. But she had years of practice keeping it hidden.

"Look, this is simple," the man continued. "You hand over your valuables, no attacking necessary."

Adelaide snorted before she could stop herself. She didn't have any driving desire to fight them, but she wasn't about to hand over their bags like a beat dog abandoning its bone.

The man looked at her. "You think your big, strong knights will protect you, pretty lady?" He gestured to his companions. "They're outnumbered. Three to twelve."

The bandit stepped closer to her horse, and Ruddard held out his sword. "Stay back," Ruddard warned.

The man ignored him. "See, lady, just give us your jewelry, and you don't have to watch us kill your brave knights."

"Three to twelve, you say?" Mother mused.

"That's right." The leader shifted his attention to Mother. "It'd be a shame if something happened to you lasses while your knights were engaged."

"A foreigner," another bandit said. "To come this far, they must have something valuable."

Adelaide gripped her dagger tighter, ignoring the sweat making the hilt slick.

"I question your math." Mother urged her horse closer to Adelaide and the bandit. "I count five on our side. I like our chances; don't you, Sir Ruddard?"

"Aye, my lady," Sir Ruddard said.

Adelaide's breathing became faster, shallower. She glanced from bandit to bandit, wondering if she would have to fight them. Would she have to kill one? A chill ran down her arms, followed by a rush of energy. She focused on keeping the thrumming magic inside. The last thing she needed was for bandits to spread word of a brown-skinned female mage to every corner of the kingdom. All her years of hiding would be for nothing.

The large man guffawed. "Oh, are the lovely ladies armed? How adorable." He sauntered up to Zephyr and held his sword a few inches from Adelaide's neck. She stiffened. He was within her reach. "We'll be takin' our payment for your travel through our pass now. In gold or blood. Your choice."

Adelaide batted the man's sword aside with the flat of her dagger's blade. Just as she had drilled, she stabbed into the base of his neck, driving deep above his clavicle and the neckline of his loose chainmail. The bandit screamed and staggered back as she ripped the blade away. Blood erupted after it and her stomach twisted, but she didn't have time to be repulsed. Another bandit charged her, brandishing a spear.

She arced her left hand forward and threw a knife. It buried deep in his throat, and he fell. She vaguely noted the *whoosh, thump, whoosh, thump* of Sir Hayes shooting arrows and the clang of swords, but she focused on the bandit coming toward her from behind. She threw the other knife. He dodged—not fast enough. It struck his right shoulder, burying into his arm to the side of his leather chest-plate. He yelped, and his sword fell from his hand. He yanked the knife free as Adelaide pulled her last throwing knife from her boot. Before she even had finished drawing it, another knife slammed into the bandit's forehead. His eyes glassed over, and he collapsed forward.

Adelaide looked over at Mother, but she had turned to a bandit on her other side. The man tried to pull Mother off her horse. Mother stabbed without hesitation. The man clutched his neck, stumbling back as Mother withdrew her blade.

It was over. The bandits all lay dead or dying. Adelaide's heart raced as she scanned the dark trees. *Never let your guard down until you are certain the fight is won.* Nothing but the gentle creak of trees and the panting of horses reached her ears.

Years. Years of practice. Of training. Of preparing but being told to hope killing was never necessary. Thousands of times stabbing mannequins of straw and dirt. But stabbing a real person felt different.

Killing felt different.

She didn't care for it.

Not that death was foreign. In her twenty-one years, Adelaide had heard about and seen her share of the violence in Monparth. She had seen Father's knights return from run-ins with brigands, blood staining their clothes. Years ago, she had traveled through the remains of a village destroyed by a horde of goblins driven from their caves by a mining operation. The blood had dried all over the cracked bricks and collapsed wood walls. She'd witnessed a hanging. Seen a murderer's head on a pike. But death at your own hand… She looked down at the dagger in her hand. Blood dripped from the tip, staining her skirt. Her hand shook. She took a deep breath and dismounted.

Mother walked up next to her and placed a hand on her shoulder. *"Kiah tuhn theack hi?"* *Are you all right?*

"Yes." Her voice cracked, betraying her.

To her surprise, Mother pulled her into an embrace. "Oh, Adelaide." Her tone was soothing. "They were murderers, robbers, and villains." Adelaide nodded into her mother's shoulder, breathing in the smell of cinnamon.

"I'm sorry, Ad. I was younger than you are when I first took a life. But I remember." She stroked Adelaide's hair.

The shaking eased. Adelaide's breathing leveled out. Mother broke the embrace.

"Come, *Tha Shiraa,*" Mother said. *Little Tigress.* For once, the nickname made Adelaide wince. Mother lifted her chin with her forefinger, forcing her to make eye contact. "A lady cares for her blade. Clean your dagger. If you can, collect your knives."

Adelaide nodded. She couldn't seem to get her tongue working again. Numbly, she used her already blood-stained dress to clean her dagger then returned it to her right boot. The maids still sat on their horses, the whites of their eyes shining in the starlight. Sir Hayes walked from bandit to bandit, confirming they were all dead.

She walked toward the first man she had thrown a knife at. He lay sprawled on his belly, his neck twisted with his head looking to the side at an odd angle. The flat handle of her throwing knife protruded from just beneath his collarbone in a pool of blood. Her stomach roiling, she retrieved the knife. *Etiros, forgive me.*

She moved to the next bandit. Sir Charing rolled the dead man onto his back while Mother stood by. Mother pulled her knife from his head and walked away. Adelaide bent down, averting her gaze from the wide eyes in his blood-stained face as she pulled her knife from the dead man's arm. Sir Charing watched her stand back up.

"You did well," Charing said, his voice quiet, respectful. "Although I shouldn't have allowed him to get so close in the first place."

"What? No." Adelaide shook her head.

Despite the heaviness in her limbs, the clenching in her stomach, and the headache forming behind her eyes, she had to disagree with Monparthian culture. She may have been born to a Monparthian father and raised in Monparth, but Mother had taught her the same beliefs she had learned from her mother. Men should protect, yes, but women had every right to defend themselves.

"You were waiting for a command. I would have asked for your help if I needed it."

Sir Charing knit his brow. "I have watched you train, my lady. I am not sorry I did not protect you. I am sorry I did not save you from taking a life."

Adelaide busied herself cleaning her knives. But as she remembered the scream…the glassy, vacant eyes of the last bandit…her hands shook again. She knew what would happen when she chose to act. Mother had told her often enough. *"Blades are for hurting and killing. Using them is a grave responsibility."* Adelaide had thought she understood that before. Now she actually did. She exhaled, trying to get her muscles under control. Her hand slipped, and the blade nicked the fleshy part of her hand beneath her thumb. She winced and turned away.

"The first battle, the first kill…if a knight tells you it was not difficult, that it did not take time for them to…forgive themselves," Sir Charing said, his tone somber, "they are either lying or monsters."

She nodded and released a little of the magic pent up inside her into her palm. Warmth radiated across the cut, numbing and healing. A soft blue light shone between her fingers in her clenched fist, but she kept her hand close to her stomach and cupped her other hand over it to hide the glow. Mother would have a fit if she saw Adelaide breaking their no-magic rule.

There had once been mages in Monparth. Now, so far as Adelaide knew, she was the only one. A couple years before her birth, every mage in Monparth was massacred. Then the killer vanished, just like shadows. So that's what people called the unknown murderer, when they spoke of the massacre at all: The Shadow. And Adelaide hid her magic so a decades-old threat wouldn't re-emerge to ensure her magic-infused blood soaked the ground.

But the cut was small, healing it wouldn't take long. No one would see. The light faded. She opened her fist. All healed. She returned her knives to the straps sewn into her boot and turned back to Sir Charing. "Does it get better?"

Charing frowned. "This feeling will fade, yes. You will feel better, in the sun of another day, when this is in the past, yes. Does killing get better? No. Easier? Regretfully…yes."

Adelaide returned to Zephyr as Mother and Sir Charing also remounted. As they continued toward the Drummonds, Adelaide's thoughts wandered.

She appreciated Sir Charing's honesty. Of all her father's knights, only Sir Charing and Sir Ruddard had never disparaged her or Minerva for learning to use knives and daggers. Only Sir Charing had ever helped. The others, Adelaide knew, spoke disapprovingly behind their backs of Mother continuing the Khastallander tradition of mothers teaching their daughters to defend themselves. Father hadn't minded. He adored Mother and usually agreed with her.

Her half-siblings, however, were as disdainful about Adelaide keeping blades in her boots as they were about...pretty much everything else about her and Minerva and their mother. Never in front of Father, of course. At least since four of her five half-siblings had moved away, she no longer had to deal with them. Father's eldest son was more dismissive than outright antagonistic, but she was still glad to leave him and his snobbish wife behind.

Finally, they arrived at the Drummond estate. Firelight flickered from various windows in the three-story stone mansion. A guard paced the crenellated roof. Adelaide thought the combination of villa and castle looked strange and boxy. The Drummonds had no personal chapel, like the small, plain stone structure within Father's castle walls. But Minerva had said in her letters they attended the parish chapel a half days' ride away if they needed the council of a priest or to pay the gratitude tax to Etiros after the harvest. The party dismounted in the courtyard as servants rushed to take care of their horses and trunks.

Minerva and her husband, Sir Gaius Drummond, met them at the entrance. Minerva was shorter than Adelaide, making Min just above average height for a woman in Monparth. She had a slender build Adelaide envied. Her stomach had an almost imperceptible bump, but she was just over four months pregnant. Wisps of her dark hair, piled in braids on her head with silver pins, framed her soft features and round cheeks. Like Adelaide, she had a deep tan complexion and brown eyes, although Minerva's eyes and skin were lighter. Of the two of them, Minerva had gotten more of their father's Monparthian looks.

Sir Gaius was barely taller than Adelaide, with an athletic build. Strong, but lean. Neatly combed reddish hair and a short red beard framed his ruddy face. His blue eyes sparkled as he greeted them with a warm yet nervous smile.

Minerva ran up to their mother and hugged her, planting a kiss on her cheek. "Mother! I'm so glad you could come!"

"As am I." Tears glistened in the corners of Mother's eyes. "Your father regrets he couldn't join us, but he felt he couldn't leave in the middle of the renovations."

Minerva turned to Adelaide, her smile wrinkling around her eyes. "Ad!" Her expression changed from delight to horror. "Is that... blood?"

"I'm fine," she said in a rush. "It's not mine."

"What happened?" Minerva demanded.

"Bandits." Sir Ruddard spoke up from behind them. "Everyone is safe and unharmed."

Gaius looked alarmed. "Where? Do we need to send men?"

"No, no. There were only twelve, and they are all dead."

Gaius ushered Minerva deeper inside. "Perhaps we should finish discussing this alone, sir." He smiled at Minerva. "You ladies go upstairs."

Minerva cocked an eyebrow. "If you are concerned about us *ladies* hearing about fighting, you should take another look at my sister's dress."

The muscles on the back of Adelaide's neck knotted. She chased away the tension with an uncomfortable laugh. "Come, Sir Gaius, you've been married to my sister long enough to know we have claws."

"I only..." Gaius flushed. "You shouldn't need to fight. It is our duty to protect as far as we are able. And it is my honor to protect you." He kissed Minerva's forehead. "But mostly I think your mother and sister look ready to sleep."

Part of Adelaide wanted to argue, but she couldn't disagree with him on the ready for sleep part. She wanted nothing more than to lie down on a nice, comfy bed. Two days on the hard ground was not her idea of a good time.

"Of course!" Minerva grabbed Adelaide's hand and led them into the manor. She linked one arm with Adelaide's and the other with Mother's arm. "I'll take you to your rooms."

Gaius bowed as they passed, the stiffness in his smile making him look uncomfortable. Adelaide and Mother's handmaids followed a short distance behind them, while the knights helped the servants with the horses and their belongings. As they walked up the stairs, Adelaide admired the intricate knots carved on the wood paneling lining the walls.

"How are you feeling?" Mother asked.

"Oh, better now," Minerva said. "I was ill most mornings for a while, but lately I've felt much better and less exhausted. Gaius' mother has been very kind and helpful." She leaned her head on Mother's shoulder. Her voice softened, a warm whisper. "But she's not you."

Minerva led them to a wooden door carved with peacocks and led them inside. "This is your room, Addie."

Adelaide half smirked, half scowled. "You know I don't answer to that."

Minerva winked. "As your *older* sister, I can call you whatever I choose."

"Be nice, *Tha Lonri*," Mother said with a smile. *Little Fox.* Mother always said Minerva was playful like a fox, and Adelaide was bold like a tigress.

Minerva kissed Adelaide's cheek. "See you in the morning, *Adelaide.*"

CHAPTER 4

THE NEXT FEW DAYS WERE HEAVENLY. ADELAIDE HAD MISSED her sister even more than she'd realized, especially laughing together. The Drummonds were amicable. Minerva convinced Adelaide and Gaius to play checkers, and her victory in the first game sparked a competition. They played a few rounds each night. By the end of the fourth day, she was up by three, and Gaius had relaxed into the friendly, if serious, man she remembered from his visits during Minerva's courtship.

Lady Drummond recruited Adelaide and her mother into helping with a tapestry depicting Saint Melvius' taming of jaguars. Adelaide was a fair embroider, but it wasn't her favorite hobby. She preferred sewing clothes to embroidery. Far more exciting, Lord Drummond granted her unrestricted access to his library.

One cloudy afternoon, Adelaide ran her fingertips over the book spines. The scents of old parchment, worn leather, dusty tapestries, cold stone, and old ash in the fireplace combined into a comforting musty smell. She sank into the large leather chair in front of the fireplace and looked around at the four large bookshelves, all lined with books. So much knowledge. So many stories. She grinned to herself. What would she find? What did she want to read? Where to start?

She turned and surveyed the three floor-to-ceiling walls of books, enjoying the silence as motes drifted in the muted sunlight slanting through the window. Finally, she began perusing the books. Some were stiff and old. Some new. A prayer book sported a gold-overlaid cover. She took a bestiary featuring color paintings. A book of heraldry caught her eye, and she flipped through the colorful illustrations before returning it to the shelf. She found a collection of romance poetry and added it to the bestiary. Only the crinkle of parchment and muted protest of leather and the shuffle of her bare feet on the carpet broke the silence. She bent down to a bottom shelf and pulled out a book with an iron-bound cover. Something shifted behind it.

Down on her knees, she peered into the empty space on the shelf. She could just see a worn leather cover. She moved some other books out of the way and freed the trapped book. The plain leather back had been facing her. She flipped it over and ran her fingertips over the embossed metal image of a man enwreathed in swirling flames. He held his hands out to his sides, his expression calm.

She opened the book and read the blue ink of the title page. *A Compendium of Known Magical Abilities and Tales of Mages of Legend.* She gasped. A book on magic? She clutched the book to her chest, looking around furtively. No one watched her. She was as alone as she had been when she first entered. Still, her ears burned, and her spine tingled with anticipation at the discovery of her new treasure.

After all these years…finally. Mother would return home in a week, leaving Adelaide unsupervised. She could read this book and learn how to *use* her magic. To be a real mage. She did feel a little guilty. Mother and Father just wanted to protect her, and she used to agree with their reasons for keeping her abilities secret and inactive. She didn't *want* to be murdered. Even if she often wished she hadn't spent three years of her childhood alone with Mother in a cottage learning to hide her magic, she never blamed her parents for their protectiveness. But over twenty years had passed since mages were eradicated from Monparth. If The Shadow still hunted mages, wouldn't it have found her by now?

A few years ago, Adelaide had tried to argue the threat was in the past. She had never seen Mother so angry, ranting in Khast about murder and foolish risks. Even if The Shadow didn't find her, did she have any idea how many people would want to use the only mage in Monparth for their own ends? Did she want people to view her as a commodity, a weapon? Adelaide had learned several new Khast curse words that day and didn't use her magic for months. But the energy inside her begged for release. So she practiced in her room, with the curtains drawn and the door locked. And she tried not to think about getting murdered by an unknown threat.

If she could learn to control her power, she could protect herself. Right? Unwanted images of bloody, glassy-eyed bandits popped into her mind. She pushed them away. Maybe she could defend herself without killing. It might be easier with magic. And she might not always have her dagger and knives. Now she had a way to learn. So far, she had managed to create blue-tinted light, fire, and on a few occasions, a solid blast of light capable of knocking over a heavy object, like a full trunk. But she had no idea what else she was even *capable* of doing and finding time to test herself when no one would catch her was difficult.

Mother wouldn't approve. But…it was part of her, wasn't it? Mother taught her to use daggers and throwing knives, just like every other Khastallander mother, all the way in Monparth, because Mother was Khastallander. Mother would not deny her culture, her identity, even after marrying Father and moving to Monparth. *And I am a mage. Whether or not my parents like it. Whether I am the last mage alive in Monparth or not.* Etiros had seen fit to make her a mage. How could she deny a part of herself?

She looked at the book in her hands. Just parchment, leather, metal and ink. Like any book on the shelves. But so much more. Knowledge and power and more control of her life. She smiled and added it to her small pile.

The fourth day after their arrival, the Drummonds hosted a supper party in their honor. Adelaide tended to dislike these social gatherings. People hid behind carved smiles and pleasant lies. Plus, Lady Drummond had requested she recite. A common enough request. Adelaide had been to many feasts where a member of the nobility would recite a poem or ballade—usually a legend of Monparth, sometimes a romance. It was an accepted way of thanking your host. But she had never volunteered.

What would people truly think as they watched her? Would they see her as any other noble performing a recitation? Or would they focus on the warm brown of her skin? The occasional Khastall-ander roundness of a vowel that always seemed to appear when she got nervous? Minerva said she was too self-conscious, but then, Minerva wasn't as tall as most men, and blended in better with the Monparthians than Adelaide. But it would be rude to refuse. And if being Khastallander didn't bother Mother, it wouldn't bother her, either.

The day of the party, Adelaide wandered into the sitting room where Minerva and Mother were discussing pregnancy and babies. She joined them on the sunlit couch and hugged a pillow edged in aqua tassels to her chest. "Anyone interesting coming tonight?"

"Don't be in too big a rush to find a suitor," Mother said without looking up from stitching a baby blanket.

Adelaide blushed. "That's not what I meant!" *Although, I'm not uninterested...*

There were many reasons Adelaide wasn't married, why she had never had a proper suitor. Several older siblings, for one. For another, noble Monparthian men showed less interest in a half-Khastallander with brown skin. She knew her half-noble blood made some see her as an inferior choice. Other times she suspected the men who flirted with her simply found her foreign appearance intriguing. Minerva had experienced the same issues, although her marriage to Gaius had given Adelaide hope again. But there were other reasons.

One main one.

Courting was difficult when she had a secret to keep. She couldn't court someone she didn't trust, but how could she know if she trusted someone enough to tell him the truth about her magic until she courted him?

"Let's see…" Minerva said. "Baron and Baroness Carrick. Maybe their eldest son, Lord Carrick and his wife? I'm not sure if they could make it. I believe the baron's youngest son is coming, Sir Nolan." Minerva gave her a saucy grin. "That reminds me, Lady Drummond says to tell you he's twenty-seven and very eligible."

"Oh, really?" Adelaide smirked back.

"Yes, but also a flirt and a scoundrel, I've heard. So…be careful, I suppose." Minerva thought for a moment. "Lord and Lady Russelthorn. Several other knights and ladies. Lord and Lady Drummond took care of the invites and all the planning." Her fingertips traced circles on her stomach. "I am immensely grateful. Having to deal with these social niceties and remember everyone when some mornings I couldn't stand up straight would have been a nightmare."

"I wish we didn't have to meet everyone." Adelaide rested her chin on the pillow. "We're here to see *you*, not strangers."

Mother frowned. "And I thought I taught you better manners."

"Oh, don't worry, I'll be perfectly polite." Adelaide fiddled with the tassels on the pillow. "I just hope the conversation is more interesting than," she went into an affected falsetto, "yes, the weather *has* been lovely. I understand the tournament in Red Falls is spectacular, I may go this year."

Minerva chuckled and Mother shook her head, smiling.

"Well, the tournament in Red Falls *is* spectacular."

Adelaide jumped at the sound of Gaius' voice behind her. She looked back and spotted him standing in the doorway. "Ah…how long have you been standing there?"

Gaius laughed as he walked over to Minerva. "Long enough to know you have low expectations for the conversation this evening." He kissed the top of Minerva's head. "Mother sent me to let you all know the guests will start arriving in about two hours, and to recommend you get dressed."

"All right." Minerva stood. "I'll see you in a couple hours." She winked at Adelaide. "And I promise I'll bring my best conversational skills."

Adelaide fidgeted with the azure silk scarf. Nothing she did with it felt right. Draped in front? No. In back? No. Over her head…? Definitely not. Wrapped around her shoulders? Too slippery. In the crook of her elbows? Too awkward. What was she supposed to *do* with it? But Lady Drummond had given it to her as a gift, so she couldn't go without it.

"You look fine, dear." Mother whispered as they stood in the foyer waiting for the guests to enter. "Stop fidgeting."

Various knights and ladies whose names she would never remember greeted her and Mother in the entrance hall. Adelaide smiled and curtsied and fussed with her scarf. She had moved it down to her elbows when one end slid out and fell behind her. She curtsied to a Sir Mowbray and Dame Mowbray, ignoring the trailing scarf. After they passed by, she looked down and behind her, searching for the end of the scarf and losing the other end. *Darn slippery thing.* She stepped to the side, trying to spot the scarf on the ground.

There. All right. I need to find a way to retrieve it quickly when no one is looking—

A man's boots appeared on the other side of the scarf, and Adelaide's eyes widened. The man crouched down and picked up the scarf. *Oh, the embarrassment.* Her cheeks burned as the man held the scarf out to her. She reached for it, looking up at the man who had retrieved it.

He was tall. *So* tall. For the first time, she felt almost...diminutive. She guessed he must be nearing thirty years old. He wore a black jerkin over a dark green long-sleeved tunic with sleeves that pulled across his muscles. Thick black hair hung in loose curls around his ears and neck. He was clean-shaven, with a sharp jaw and high, angular cheekbones. A rough pinkish scar ran diagonally across his right cheek, from under the outside corner of his eye to the corner of his lips before it curved down his chin to his jawline. His brows furrowed together. But her gaze fixed on the way his light gray irises caught the fading sunlight, almost seeming to have a light of their own. Dark lashes framed his eyes, drawing attention to the piercing ferocity behind them.

"I believe this is yours?" His voice was clear, deep, and warm.

She gingerly took the scarf, her stomach twisting. "Thank you." The words came out in a horrifying squeak and the heat in her face spread to her ears.

"Pardon *me*," a man's voice said behind him, brimming with condescension. "But you and your man here are blocking the way."

Adelaide hadn't even registered the man standing to the scarred man's left. He had a deep olive complexion, aquiline nose, and thick, dark beard trimmed close to his face. The bearded man frowned at the impatient guest behind them.

The handsome man with the scar looked over his shoulder. "Apologies." He looked back to Adelaide and nodded. "My lady." He turned into the great hall, followed by the bearded man.

"Wait!" Adelaide's chest tightened as she realized in a panic how loudly she had spoken. The men paused and looked back. "I..."

Now is not the time to get all tongue-tied! "Um, that is… I apologize, I didn't hear your name."

The man's scarred lips turned up in a slight smile. "Oh. Lord Regulus Hargreaves of Arrano, my lady." He inclined his head to her. "And my lieuten—um, one of my knights, Sir Dresden Jakobs." He gestured to the man with the beard, who bowed.

"Pardon me, my lady," interrupted the same male voice, but in a much warmer tone. "Sir Nolan Carrick, at your service."

Adelaide looked over in surprise as Sir Carrick snatched up her hand and kissed her fingers. She curtsied, trying to mask her confusion. She glanced toward Lord Hargreaves, but he and his knight had disappeared into the main hall. "Adelaide Belanger."

Sir Carrick gave her a crooked smile. "I know. I am honored and most pleased to make your acquaintance, Lady Belanger."

Nolan Carrick looked younger than the man with the scar, and far less battle-worn. He wasn't much taller than her. A crimson doublet with ostentatious silver stitching covered a black shirt that clung to strong arms. He had a square face, with a clean-shaven, defined jaw. With his blue eyes and well-combed light brown hair, he was fairly attractive. But Adelaide was so distracted thinking about the gray-eyed Lord Hargreaves of Arrano, she didn't care.

Nolan moved on, and Baron and Baroness Carrick entered next. A few more nobles of varying status arrived, and they all entered the dining hall. To Adelaide's disappointment, Lord Hargreaves sat at a distant table. She wanted to ask Minerva about him but could hardly do so at supper.

Finally, the fish, fowl, bread, and pudding courses were all finished. Lady Drummond invited her to recite. Nerves knotted her full stomach, but she curtsied and stood on the dais at the end of the table with Lord and Lady Drummond and Baron and Baroness Carrick. Adelaide recited the Ballad of Elwynn and Leander, star-crossed lovers who died trying to bring peace to a kingdom torn asunder by war. The assembled nobility applauded daintily when she finished. Now the difficult part of the evening: mingling.

SELINA R. GONZALEZ

CHAPTER 5

REGULUS KEPT LOOKING OVER AT ADELAIDE DURING SUPPER. His distraction prevented him from engaging in conversation, but no one at the table seemed interested in talking with him, anyway. Dresden elbowed him in the side.

"She's going to catch you staring," he whispered. "Ease up a little. You don't want to scare her."

As if that mattered. He glanced across the hall at Sir Mowbray. A little over two years ago, Mowbray had hired Regulus as a mercenary. Now Regulus was a lord—Mowbray's superior. The pointed way Mowbray ignored Regulus at social events made Mowbray's feelings on the matter clear.

Everyone seems to either fear or hate me. Certainly no one trusts me. I'm just the bastard mercenary to them. These people will tell Adelaide what they think of me, and then she won't so much as look my way. Like everyone else. Not to mention that while the sorcerer's mark marred his arm, he shouldn't want her to look his way. But he did.

He couldn't help himself—she was lovely. He hadn't expected to find her so attractive. Her height surprised him. Fine, it was superficial, but he liked a tall woman. Most women looked small and fragile; like he could accidentally crush them even without his enhanced strength. He didn't get that feeling from her. She felt solid and...magnetic. Her thick black hair escaped from her hairpins, wavy strands brushing against her round face and cheeks. Her complexion was darker than Dresden's, and even if he hadn't met her mother, he saw the Khastallander in her. He'd enjoyed his time in Khastalland. By and large, he had found Khastallanders to be a sincere and passionate people.

After supper, Adelaide stood to do a recitation. Her gray-blue dress had a wide, scooping neckline that showed off her shoulders and collarbones without being showy, but still hugged her figure. A wide V-shaped brass belt accentuated her waist. She kept fiddling with the bright blue scarf she had dropped earlier as she recited a poem whose words Regulus barely comprehended. He was too busy telling himself *stop thinking about how beautiful she is. Stop. The sorcerer won't care if she's angelic or a hag, he'd just care if hurting her would hurt me.* But as Adelaide spoke, saying something about lovers and sacrifice, her gaze momentarily met his. *What was I thinking about again?*

Her clear, low voice washed over him, releasing tension in his muscles. He had never been so relaxed when surrounded by other nobles. He could have sat there and listened to her all night. *No.* He was doing this to please Drez, nothing more. When she finished and people rose to move around and socialize, Dresden punched him on the shoulder.

"So, are you going to sit here frowning, or are you going to go talk to her?"

Regulus forced his face to relax. He felt uncomfortably warm. "I'm not frowning."

"You're always frowning." Drez gestured in Adelaide's direction. "Go. You gave your word."

"Hmph." But he stood and walked toward where Adelaide stood near the dais. He kept his word. And he owed Dresden.

Regulus was acutely aware of the nobles watching him and whispering as he passed. He swallowed back the urge to leave. If only she weren't standing at the head of the room. To his relief, she stepped over toward the corner after ending her conversation with an older couple.

Adelaide stared up at a stained-glass window with a floral vine design. With the sun set, the details of the design were difficult to see. Flickering orange light from a nearby tall iron candelabra reflected in the glasswork, but that didn't seem worthy of her undivided attention. Perhaps she didn't want to talk to anyone. He glanced at Dresden, who held up his hands as if asking *what are you waiting for?*

"Lady Belanger?"

She turned toward him and smiled. At *him*. Like she was *pleased*. "Oh. Lord Arrano. Or is it Lord Hargreaves? I…um…thank you. For saving my scarf." She blushed and waved the end of the scarf in his direction, looking about as awkward as he felt. He smiled in amusement.

A little flirting *would* please Drez…

"Of course. And it's Hargreaves. I'm just lord of Arrano estate." Regulus cleared his throat. "Your recite…reciting…you have a lovely voice for recitation." *Oh, this is going so smoothly.* He clasped his hands behind his back. Sweat tickled his neck. "One of the loveliest things I've ever heard."

She blinked. "One of? I've already had four people tell me it was the most beautiful thing they've had the pleasure of hearing."

Regulus glanced away. For once, he wished he knew how to talk like the nobles.

Adelaide laughed. "Of course, every one of them was lying."

He looked back at her and furrowed his brow, surprised both by her relaxed laughter and her bluntness.

"I mean, really. The way some people go on, you would suppose I was an angel, which is ridiculous. So. What was it, then?" She pulled her scarf up over her shoulders.

"What was what?" His mind raced to catch up, still stuck on the possibility of Adelaide being an angel.

"The most beautiful sound you've ever heard?"

He paused. He didn't need to consider the answer, but whether or not to share. "It's a long story, but laughing while crying. Joy overpowering sorrow." He stared into the distance. "I'll never forget that sound. The relief, the happiness. That's what I think freedom sounds like."

"That's...beautiful." She looked thoughtful, her lips turned up in a slight smile. For a moment, they just looked at each other.

"So..." He laughed nervously. *So what, Regulus! Where were you going with this?* Why couldn't he think straight? *This is your fault, Drez.*

"My father and mother laughing."

He blinked. "What?"

"The most beautiful sound I've ever heard. My parents giggling like newly-weds when they don't know anyone is around. Because it's the sound of how much they love each other. It sounds like freedom—not caring what anyone else thinks." She glanced away, then studied the scarf in her hands.

"My father met my mother when he was away, fighting in the Trade War. His first wife had died a couple years prior. I'm glad they found each other." Adelaide looked up at him, a stray curl of hair falling over her eye. She watched him as if weighing his reaction. "Whenever my stepsiblings or snobbish nobles look down on my mother because she's the daughter of a traveling merchant from Khastalland, that sound gives me hope. None of that matters to my parents."

Regulus' heart lurched in sympathy. "The nobles, they can be..." He trailed off before he said something he would regret. "People matter more than lineages. What's the point in judging someone for something they can't control?"

"You sound like you mean that." She tilted her head, her brows knit in contemplation and a slight smile on her pink lips.

"Of course..." *Ah. She doesn't know what I am.* How to tell her? Perhaps, of all people, she wouldn't judge him for his bastardy. But a rich merchant's daughter was a far cry from an unwed serving girl.

Adelaide pulled her scarf tighter around her shoulders. "Earlier today I was complaining no one ever says anything interesting, and certainly never anything true, at these parties. I'm glad to be wrong."

He smiled, searching for something to say to keep the conversation going—and interesting, even though part of his brain warned him not to go getting attached. He couldn't court her, regardless of what Dresden said. *Right?* But he was actually enjoying himself for once. "Your mother is Khastallander?"

"Yes." Adelaide's face clouded.

Idiot, she thinks you're judging her. He rushed on. "I visited Khastalland once. I loved it. So vibrant. Hot as—" He coughed, narrowly saving himself from slipping into the vulgarity he had picked up as a mercenary. "Very hot. Even the food."

"Oh, I love Khastallander spices," Adelaide exclaimed. "My mother brought a cook with her. She does what she can with what she can get here, but I love when she makes Khastalland recipes. My favorite is this flaky dessert pastry with chocolate that's a little bit spicy, they call it—"

"Nalotavi," Regulus said at the same time as Adelaide. They laughed. "You know it?"

"Know it, it's my favorite!" He grinned. "Sarah—that is, the wife of one of my knights—she's a baker, and she makes excellent nalotavi for someone who has never been to Khastalland."

"Hmm, I may have to borrow this Sarah's services. I'd love to surprise Minerva. I'm certain she hasn't had nalotavi since she moved here."

"I'll have to send you some." *Was that too forward?* He shifted uncomfortably as the conversation stalled. *It was too forward. Pull it together, Regulus!*

"Is Sarah married to the knight who came with you? Sir—what was his name again? Sorry, I met so many people tonight."

"Dresden Jakobs." He chuckled. "And no, Dresden's unmarried."

Adelaide nodded. "Did you knight him?"

"Yes?" He hadn't meant it to sound like a question, but he didn't understand why she was asking.

"How long has his family been in Monparth? He's not Monparthian by blood, is he?"

Wait, what? "No, he's Carasian." Why the sudden interest in Dresden's family history? "Just his parents. Moved here from Carasom before he was born."

"Nobles?"

"No…" Suddenly, he understood. She found Dresden attractive. Girls always found Dresden attractive. He was probably right about the beard. Regulus had to fight the impulse to touch his scar. Worse, she wanted to know if Dresden was suitable marriage material. *I guess I misjudged her. Lineage matters to her.*

Adelaide tilted her head to the side. "And the one who married the baker. Noble?"

His mood soured. *Oh.* "Most of my knights were not noble-born, Lady Belanger."

Regulus braced himself for the inevitable look of distaste, the questions about why or casual judgment. He should just admit his bastardy and mercenary past now. Maybe she would walk away, and he wouldn't have to see her lovely face twist into disgust.

"So it's not empty talk." She beamed, sounding delighted. "You don't just say things, you do them."

He rubbed the back of his neck, off kilter and unsure what to make of the direction of this conversation. "I'm not sure—"

"People matter more than lineages." Adelaide nodded, like a judge making a ruling. "You believe that."

"Of course I do." He dropped his hand to his side, relief and surprise flooding him. "I don't say things I don't mean."

Her eyes glinted, teasing and slightly dangerous. "And what do you think of me, Lord Hargreaves?" Her bronze skin took on extra color as she blushed.

"Ah…" His throat seemed to close up and heat flared over his face. *I think I'd like to get to know you better.* He wished he had a glass of water. *What?* his mind screamed. *Get to know her better?* His heart screamed back, *yes,* silencing thoughts of the sorcerer. What was the question again? What he thought of her? How was a gentleman supposed to answer a question like that?

Before he could answer, a man with perfectly combed dark blond hair stepped partly between them. Baron Carrick's youngest, Nolan Carrick, again.

"Begging your pardon, my lady," Carrick said, his back to Regulus. "I *must* congratulate you. I have never heard anything so beautiful in my life."

Adelaide raised an eyebrow and glanced at Regulus. Regulus stifled a snicker, despite his irritation at the interruption.

"Please," Carrick offered her his arm. "My parents would *love* to speak with you."

"Oh." Adelaide nodded, but didn't take his arm. "I was in the middle of a conversation with Lord Hargreaves, but I will be sure to speak with them after."

Regulus suppressed a grin. She would rather talk to him than a baronial family? Maybe she didn't realize Carrick was a wealthy bachelor. Or maybe—and his heart leapt at the thought—she just didn't care.

"I'm sure Hargreaves can wait, and I did tell my parents I'd bring you over." Carrick moved his arm, inviting her to take it. "Barons do hate to be kept waiting."

Adelaide glanced at Regulus apologetically, but took Carrick's arm. "Of course."

Regulus' spirits fell as they walked away. He turned and scanned the crowd for Dresden. He spotted him talking to a young noblewoman standing against a wall. Drez leaned toward her with a teasing smile as he spoke, and the girl blushed and laughed and rolled her eyes. Regulus shook his head. Did all his knights have to be ladies' men, while he couldn't manage one full conversation without a blunder? He spotted Adelaide conversing with the baron and baroness. Carrick stepped closer and placed his hand on Adelaide's lower back, and she didn't move away.

Who am I joking? If Dresden saw him, he would doubtless point out he was frowning again. *She's perfect, and I'm...* He swallowed down his self-loathing. *No woman would want me over a Carrick. And they'd be right, too.* He hated he'd let Dresden's nonsense get into his head. To think he could be just a man who liked a girl, not a scarred slave who shouldn't even be here. Stupidity. The worst kind, too. Felt amazing in the moment, but left you aching.

Dresden now leaned against the wall next to the young lady and had a strand of her hair curled around his finger. With a sigh, Regulus made his way to the door. He wouldn't pull Drez away when he was enjoying himself. He retrieved his cloak from the page at the front entrance, and headed home.

CHAPTER 6

AS SIR NOLAN CARRICK LED HER TOWARD HIS PARENTS, ADELAIDE glanced back over her shoulder. Lord Hargreaves was already looking away. *I thought our conversation was engaging. Perhaps I was wrong.* She looked forward again. *Maybe I don't want to know what he would have said.* She didn't know why she'd asked. He'd handed her an opportunity to ask someone's honest opinion. The way he'd turned red and looked like a cornered rabbit left only two choices. In the moment, she had thought he intended to say something complimentary and was embarrassed. But maybe he was trying to figure out how to avoid telling her a harsher truth.

Sir Nolan leaned toward her, his voice low. "I apologize if that came across as rude, but the code of chivalry leaves me honor-bound not to leave a maiden in distress."

"Distress?" Adelaide frowned and shifted her hand on his arm so they weren't walking so close. "I wasn't in distress."

"Oh?" Nolan raised his brows. "I couldn't imagine you were talking to that bastard mercenary willingly."

Her mouth fell open in shock. "I *beg* your pardon?"

"I mean, sure, he's not a mercenary anymore." He shrugged. "Supposedly."

She didn't try to mask her shock and disgust. "That is hardly a civilized way to discuss a nobleman."

"You clearly haven't heard about Hargreaves." He smiled slyly. "I'll tell you the abridged version—he's not to be trusted. Ah, here we are." He leaned close and whispered, "They didn't actually ask to speak to you, but it was the best excuse I could think of."

Adelaide swallowed back her disdain and plastered on a smile as they stopped in front of the baron and baroness. She used the opportunity to curtsy as a pretense to release Nolan's arm.

"A splendid recitation, my dear." The baroness smiled. A few short, wispy white-gray strands of hair peeked out from her wimple. *How old fashioned.* She was short and had a full face etched with smile lines.

"Thank you, my lady." Back to boring niceties.

"Indeed," Baron Carrick raised his glass of wine toward her, as if offering a toast.

"Tell me," the baroness said, "what are your interests? Hobbies?"

"Oh." Adelaide moved the scarf to her neck. "Calligraphy, sewing. I love reading." *Probably best not to mention the ancient dagger technique of Khastalland. Obviously can't mention the magic.*

"Do you enjoy dancing?" Nolan inquired.

"Of course."

"Brilliant." Nolan stepped closer to her and placed his hand on her lower back.

A knot formed in Adelaide's throat and her whole body tensed. But stepping away would appear insulting.

"I was thinking, Father, that it has been far too long since a proper dance has been held in Etchy Barony." Nolan's tone was too sweet, taking on a pleading, manipulative edge. He smiled at Adelaide. "You *would* join us, wouldn't you?"

She mustered her politest tone. "Certainly, Sir Carrick."

"Please." Nolan rubbed his thumb against her back, and she straightened uncomfortably. "I do hope you will call me Nolan."

"Oh, we hardly know each other, Sir Carrick." She looked to his parents. "That hardly seems appropriate at this time."

The baron chuckled. "You could learn something from her, Nolan."

"Well, I'll certainly do my best to remedy that and get to know you as soon as possible, Lady Belanger." Nolan smiled coyly and moved his hand to her hip. Heat rushed to her face. Worse, heat was building in the palm of her right hand. She clenched her fists. *Control it.*

Adelaide cleared her throat, every fiber of her body on alert. "Forgive me, Baron Carrick, Baroness." Her words came out in a rushed gasp. "But I..." She couldn't come up with a reasonable excuse to leave. "I...need a moment. To freshen up." She bobbed a half curtsy. "Thank you for coming," she added breathlessly before hurrying off.

She darted into a parlor off the main hall and leaned on the back of a couch, her right hand still clenched. Faint rays of moonlight crisscrossed the floor following the lattice-work on the window. Her chest heaved as she realized she'd been holding her breath. *"He's a scoundrel."* That's what Minerva had said. *"Be careful."* She stared at the logs stacked in the cold fireplace. *The nerve...* Never had a man dared be so forward with her. She exhaled slowly, trying to steady her breathing. *It was nothing. He just put his hand on my back.*

Unexpectedly.

For no reason.

She groaned and opened her clenched fist, letting the warmth grow as magic flowed into her palm. Her skin glowed sky blue. She thrust her hand toward the fireplace, directing her energy into a stream of yellow-orange fire that hit the logs with a crackling roar. She let the energy wane, the magic recede. The extra warmth and the light in her palm faded away. With a sigh, she sank down onto the couch. Nolan hadn't done anything terribly wrong. But she'd still felt trapped. *I've never liked being trapped.*

The door opened and she darted to her feet. "Oh—Minerva." She sat back down. "I know; I should be out there. I just...needed a moment."

Minerva eased the door closed. She looked at Adelaide, at the lively fire and back again. "Some servant is going to take the fall for that, you know."

Adelaide blushed. "I'll put it out before I leave."

Minerva sat next to her. "Is everything all right? I saw you walking away from the baron and baroness in a hurry." She paused. "Did they say something...unkind?"

"Oh, no. Nolan Carrick is—friendly. I wasn't sure how to react." They sat in silence for a moment. "Do you know anything about Lord Hargreaves? Sir Nolan said some odd things."

Minerva leaned back against the couch. "I know he's illegitimate and because of that was sent away when he was very young. It's why he's Lord of Arrano, not Lord Arrano."

No wonder he doesn't care about lineages. Adelaide's heart wrenched. *But being treated differently for something that's not your fault...sent away from the people you love. The life you know.* She clutched the pillow tighter. *I understand how that feels. Even if not that extreme.*

Minerva must have known what she was thinking, because she put her arm around Adelaide's shoulders. "He worked as a mercenary until he inherited Arrano when the legitimate heir died childless. Other than that, only rumors."

So he was a mercenary. Adelaide tucked an escaped strand of hair behind her ear and turned so she could see Minerva's face. This hairstyle was *not* cooperating tonight. "What sort of rumors?"

Minerva shifted, her hand resting on her stomach. "When he arrived to claim Arrano, his step-mother was still alive, as was his half-brother's wife. They put forth a champion to challenge him. People say he won the duel too easily. No one has heard from the Arrano ladies since. Rational minds say they went to family in Craigailte. But between that and the fact he often disappears alone and has never once invited anyone into Arrano castle, it's led to some wild speculation." She chuckled. "My personal favorite is he's a vampire."

Adelaide laughed in disbelief. "He's hardly pale enough for that."

"There are other stories. He's a sorcerer. He made a deal with a demon to get his father's estate and title. He's hiding something terrible in his castle. Some say he's still a mercenary."

Adelaide frowned. None of this lined up with the sweet, slightly awkward man she had talked to. "If people think he's so horrible, why did Lord and Lady Drummond invite him?"

"Oh, it would be terribly impolite not to," Minerva said matter-of-factly. "So most people invite him, although he doesn't always come. I suspect some nobles do so out of fear. If he is a supernatural being or demonic servant, they fear offending him." She shrugged. "But mostly people are curious. They hope one day he will observe proper social protocol and return the invite, and they can see inside Arrano."

Adelaide stared at the dancing flames. "Do you think he's dangerous?"

Minerva thought for a moment. "Possibly. He doesn't look particularly friendly. But I have never seen him be anything but polite and reserved. Maybe if he smiled more people would be willing to give him a chance."

"He smiled tonight." *He smiled for me.*

"Well, he left, so you don't have to worry about him. Your blades can stay stowed in your boots." Minerva stood and held out her hand. "Come on. Our guests are waiting."

"Humph." Despite how much she wanted to continue avoiding said guests, Adelaide took Minerva's hand and they headed toward the door. "Oh—wait. Nearly forgot." She turned toward the fireplace and held out both hands, concentrating. Her palms glowed as she slammed her hands into fists. The fire collapsed on itself, going out with a *whoosh.*

"Adelaide!" Minerva's eyes widened. She peered around, as if afraid someone could have seen. "Did Father and Mother change their minds?"

Adelaide's heart beat faster. "Please don't tell—"

"I see." Minerva sighed. "I won't. But you have to stop."

"It's not that easy." Adelaide fiddled with her scarf. "It's part of me."

The deep shadows on Minerva's face in the moonlight made her look extra afraid and disapproving. "I don't want to lose you."

"I'm being careful. No one knows. Besides, I have my daggers." She smiled, but Min's frown deepened.

"The Shadow killed warrior mages, too." Min took a deep breath through her nose and exhaled. "I've always admired your courage, Ad. But you know it's safest to hide." Minerva turned toward the door. "Just…don't do anything stupid, all right?"

"I won't," she said as Minerva opened the door. *But I still hate hiding.*

Adelaide managed to avoid Sir Nolan for the rest of the party, although he seemed to keep appearing nearby. To her disappointment, Lord Hargreaves had disappeared. Guests flowed out, with gracious but empty well-wishes for her and Mother and gratitude to the Drummonds for hosting. Lord Hargreaves' knight, Sir Dresden, lingered in front of her.

"Lord Hargreaves asked me to tell you he enjoyed your conversation and regrets he had to leave early to attend to other business. He hopes your paths cross again soon." Sir Dresden smiled, more of a charming, playful smirk. "Might I bring him a message from you, my lady?"

"Oh." *So he was interested?* She glanced at Mother, but she was busy talking to a woman with silver-streaked blond hair. Dresden waited expectantly. What on earth was she supposed to say? She didn't want to be too forward, but she also didn't want to appear uninterested. "I wish Lord Hargreaves hadn't left so soon. I would have liked to continue our conversation. It was the only real conversation I had all night."

Dresden bowed, his eyes dancing. "Excellent. I wish you the best, Lady Belanger."

"Wait!" She pushed a strand of hair away from her eye as Dresden's brows pinched. "Can…can you tell him I know? And I don't care about lineages, either?"

The corner of Dresden's mouth quirked upward. "I will, my lady."

Adelaide felt flustered for the next several farewells and hoped it didn't show. Eventually the line of guests ended, and Lord Drummond closed the door, but she was certain the Carricks hadn't passed her. How did she completely miss them?

Looking more relaxed with the guests gone, Gaius leaned over to kiss Minerva's cheek, but she turned her head and kissed him. Adelaide grinned. Lady Drummond breezed past with a broad smile.

"Thank you for waiting, Baron."

Adelaide turned and her eyes widened. The Carricks stood at the back of the small foyer, near the staircase leading up to the residential floors. Nolan leaned against an oak table bearing a marble bust of one of the previous Lord Drummonds, looking right at her. He smiled when he caught her gaze.

"Your trunks were already brought up. If you will follow me." Lady Drummond turned and headed up the stairs. The baron and baroness followed. Nolan languidly pushed off the table, his gaze never leaving her. He winked before following his parents.

Adelaide whirled back toward Minerva and Gaius, who were laughing with Mother. "The Carricks are staying the night?"

Gaius nodded. "It's a day's ride from here to the Carrick's castle. Offering them accommodation to thank them for making the trip is proper. They'll breakfast with us in the morning and return home."

"Breakfast?" Adelaide started pulling half-fallen hairpins out of her hair. "Min, you didn't warn me?"

"I didn't know." Minerva looked apologetic. "As I said, Lady Drummond took care of all the arrangements."

"Oh, right." *Great.*

That night, Adelaide lay awake in bed. Sir Nolan's playful wink had left her unsettled, and his rude interruptions irked her. Lord Hargreaves, however, had been so pleasant and friendly and… genuine. That might have been the only honest conversation she'd ever had at a party. He had opened up to her. *How could he possibly be as horrible as people think?* But then why did he keep to himself in his castle?

He was a mystery, and her brain couldn't leave the puzzle alone, even though she had no way to discover the answer. She wished he had stayed longer. Maybe she'd see him again while she stayed with Minerva during the pregnancy. She hoped so. Even after she fell asleep, Regulus Hargreaves' pale gray eyes haunted her dreams.

CHAPTER 7

THE NEXT MORNING ADELAIDE SKIPPED DOWN THE STAIRS TO breakfast, wishing she could have asked Regulus Hargreaves about his time in Khastalland. Did he know any Khast? She'd have to ask him the next time she saw him. As she careened around the corner into the landing to the second floor, she nearly collided with Baroness Carrick. Baron Carrick and Sir Nolan stood just behind the baroness, Nolan with an amused expression.

"Oh, pardon me, my lady!" Adelaide curtsied as her pulse spiked and a string of Khast curses went through her head. *I forgot.* She smoothed her lavender-gray skirt and took another step back, hoping she hadn't offended them. If she'd remembered, she wouldn't have worn a sleeveless dress with a low neckline and would have done something with her hair beyond brushing it. She'd been thinking of going riding in the summer sun, not looking proper in front of a baronial family. "I apologize; I should have been paying more attention."

Baroness Carrick's eyebrows lifted. "Ah, well." Her face relaxed into a small smile. "No harm done."

The baron looked at her appraisingly. "It's good to see a young lady with both beauty and energy. You must have many suitors."

Her cheeks burned. "N-no." She fiddled with her hands. *Why couldn't Minerva be here? She's so much smoother with the nobles.*

"Shall we continue to breakfast?" Baroness Carrick took her husband's arm and headed downstairs.

Nolan's gaze swept over Adelaide and she combed her fingers through her hair. "You have a unique sense of style, Lady Adelaide."

"Khastallander based—that is, its pattern…my mother." *Stop stammering.* "My mother taught me to sew using Khastallander patterns."

"Well, you look lovely." Nolan chuckled. The grin on his face suggested he thought her stammering indicated his attentions pleasantly flustered her. If anything, she felt the opposite. He offered her his arm. She didn't want to accept, but she wouldn't be impolite to her hosts' guest and a baron's son.

They followed his parents. A servant directed them to the smaller dining hall, used for the Drummond family's private meals. Lord and Lady Drummond and Mother were already in the hall, but not yet seated. Gaius and Minerva entered after them. Once the baron and baroness had taken their seats, Lord and Lady Drummond sat down. Nolan pulled out a chair for Adelaide and sat next to her. *Grand.*

Lord Drummond, Baron Carrick, and Gaius jumped into a discussion about rumors of goblins spotted at the distant Vanelt-Monparth border. Lady Drummond pulled Mother, Minerva, and the baroness into discussing newborns while servants carried in trays of place settings and delicious-smelling food.

"I had hoped to speak more with you last night, but you always seemed to be otherwise engaged," Nolan said quietly. "I must have seemed a cad for interrupting your conversation with Lord Hargreaves and didn't want to repeat my offense. But I assure you, I acted out of concern."

Adelaide watched a maid pour water into her goblet. "Sir Carrick—"

"Nolan, please. I much prefer it." He gave her a saccharine smile.

"Sir Nolan," she amended, hoping this compromise would keep him distant but placated, "has Lord Hargreaves done something to offend you?"

"Other than claiming a title he doesn't deserve and running innocent, noble ladies out of Monparth—assuming they are even still alive—no, I suppose not." He turned toward her as he piled eggs and roast duck on his plate. His knee bumped hers under the table and she twisted her legs away. "But I wish to talk about you, Adelaide." His voice dipped as he spoke her name, becoming low and husky.

She gulped down water. "There isn't much to me." *Not much I can or want to tell you, anyway.* She spread jam over a piece of toast, wishing Minerva wasn't focused on Baroness Carrick.

"Oh, that seems unlikely." A touch at her shoulder startled her. Nolan trailed his fingertips down her arm with a sly grin.

"Don't," Adelaide whispered, her thoughts snapping to the blades hidden in her boots. *My bare skin is not an invitation.*

"Sorry." He pulled his hand away, looking sheepish. "I got carried away. You're hard to resist."

She took an unladylike, large bite of toast she hoped would discourage further conversation, at least until the uncomfortable feeling in her stomach faded. She turned her attention to the other conversations at the table.

"The Black Knight has been spotted again," Gaius said. "Near the eastern marshes, according to Sir Tobias."

Adelaide swallowed her toast. "Who's the Black Knight?"

All four men looked at her.

"Who's the Black Knight?" Gaius lowered his fork, his raised eyebrows pinched together. "What do you mean, who's the Black Knight?"

Lady Drummond clicked her tongue, looking uncomfortable. "Gaius, dear, this is hardly a topic of conversation for gentle young ladies."

Baroness Carrick chuckled. "Young ladies love stories of terrifying monsters. It gives them a reason to seek comfort from a strong young knight." Her eyes danced as she glanced between Adelaide and Nolan.

Adelaide ignored her insinuation. "So is the Black Knight a monster or a man?"

Lord Drummond tapped his fingers on the table. "The Black Knight is a legend. Nothing more."

Gaius rolled his eyes. "He's real, I'm sure of it. Sure, no one can prove he exists, but enough people claim to have seen him he must be real. It's this knight dressed in all-black armor, from his helm to his greaves. Hulking armor with horns on his helm." His voice was eager. "He's tall as an ogre, strong as a troll, quick as a nymph and deadly as a viper. He shows up in different places, slaying monsters and killing anyone who gets in his way. It's said he can't be defeated."

"Gaius thinks he's a hero of old legend, come back to life," Minerva said with a laugh. "Here to rid the world of monsters."

"That's ridiculous." Nolan reached for his goblet. "If a hero of legend came back to life, they wouldn't parade about looking like demon spawn."

Gaius raised a brow. "I have a bet with Flynn Greensburg. I think the Black Knight's a hero. Flynn thinks he's a malicious spirit that kills for fun. Hunts down magical creatures for the thrill of the fight."

"What of the rumors he's told people he serves a Prince of Shadow and Ash?" the baron asked. "That hardly sounds heroic."

"Peasants," Gaius said with a dismissive wave. "Probably made it up for attention."

Adelaide placed a piece of fish on her plate. "And how will either of you win this bet?"

"If the Black Knight is real, eventually someone will see something or talk to him even." Gaius shrugged. "Or he'll go berserk and start killing everything and then Flynn will be right."

Adelaide shuddered, but Baron Carrick laughed. "I think your friend has the better odds," the baron said, "although I certainly hope he's wrong."

Adelaide tried to picture this hulking knight in black armor wearing a helm with horns. "Has anyone seen him in Thaera?" She shouldn't want someone or something so menacing to be in the duchy she herself was in, but she couldn't help her curiosity.

"Not just in Thaera Duchy, but in Etchy Barony." The baron's countenance darkened. "I don't like these rumors. They make my people uneasy."

The Drummonds lived within the Carrick's barony. That was uncomfortably close. Nolan patted her thigh under the table. "Don't worry. You're perfectly safe."

She shifted farther away from him and focused on her breakfast. *Safe from the Black Knight? Or safe from you?*

Thankfully, the Carricks left after breakfast. Adelaide forgot all about Nolan Carrick until a messenger arrived with a letter addressed to her two days later. She worked a knife under the gryphon-stamped wax seal and eased the letter open, considering tossing it without reading. Mother and Minerva watched from across the drawing room while a small fire popped in the fireplace and cloudy afternoon sunlight angled across the wood paneled floor. A pressed navy-blue flower fell out of the letter onto her lap.

> *Dear Lady Adelaide Belanger,*
>
> *I greatly enjoyed spending even such a brief time in your presence. I hope soon to have the opportunity to get to know you more intimately. Until then, accept this flower as a token of my regard—a dark and lovely bloom that, I fear, cannot come close to equaling your beauty.*
>
> *Affectionately,*
> *Sir Nolan Carrick*

"Etiros spare me." Adelaide rolled her eyes.

"What does it say?" Minerva asked.

Adelaide scowled at the letter, resisting the urge to ignite it in her hand. "I am a dark and lovely flower, and Sir Nolan Carrick wishes to know me more," her upper lip curled in distaste, "intimately."

Mother huffed and muttered something under her breath in Khast about daggers and pretentious boys' faces. Minerva chided Mother while Adelaide laughed and tossed the letter and flower into the fireplace. Later that afternoon, another letter arrived, this one addressed to both Mother and Adelaide. Mother showed the wax seal, imprinted with a rose over crossed swords, to Minerva.

"Do you recognize this?"

Minerva frowned. "It's vaguely familiar. I'm not sure."

Adelaide snatched away the letter, opened it, and read it aloud—which she immediately regretted.

Dear Ladies Tamina and Adelaide Belanger,

I was honored to make your acquaintance. I wish to apologize for abandoning the festivities early and assure you I meant no disrespect. I hope our paths will cross again—preferably when other duties do not draw me away prematurely from the pleasure of your company.

Sincerely yours,

Lord Regulus Hargreaves of Arrano

Adelaide blushed when Mother frowned and said, "Who is Lord Hargreaves?" The letter was addressed to both of them, but it was obvious its message was for Adelaide. She wanted to respond, but Mother wouldn't hear of it.

"It's acceptable for him to apologize for an impolite exit," Mother said. "But you are a lady and will not write a man letters unless he is formally courting you."

That only made Adelaide more embarrassed. As if she could think about courting him after one conversation. But that night, as she thought about Regulus Hargreaves' note and the look in his gray eyes as he talked about his favorite sound…she wondered what it would be like to court him.

Over the next days, Adelaide perfected the art of avoiding Lady Drummond and her tapestry. Gaius got ahead of her in checkers, but she had her revenge and regained the lead. Mother thought their rivalry had grown out of control and wasn't very lady-like, and Lady Drummond agreed. Adelaide didn't care. Gaius felt like the brother she had never had, and she *did* have two half-brothers. But neither of them had ever had much interest in her.

When it came time for Mother to leave, Adelaide couldn't believe they had already been at the Drummonds for nearly three weeks. Minerva tried to talk her into staying longer, but Mother said she missed Father, and needed to get back so she could resume overseeing the household. As previously agreed, Adelaide would stay to support Minerva through the pregnancy.

The day after Mother left, the Drummonds and Adelaide received invitations to a dance to be hosted in a week's time by Baron and Baroness Carrick. It would be quite the affair—supper, entertainment, dancing, and a grand breakfast for all attendees who stayed the night. Lady Drummond declared they would most certainly stay the night.

Adelaide didn't share Lord and Lady Drummond's enthusiasm over the invitation. Something about Nolan Carrick made her uncomfortable. Beyond his rude attitude toward Lord Hargreaves, even beyond his uninvited touches. *Trust your woman's intuition*, Mother always said. Well, her intuition said not to trust Nolan Carrick. She put the invitation on her vanity and stared at it, wishing she could decline. But it would be unthinkable to refuse a higher-ranking noble's invitation without the excuse of another engagement.

Hmmm. Adelaide smiled to herself. *Which means Lord Hargreaves will likely be there.* Her mood lightened. If she could talk to Lord Hargreaves, maybe get a chance to satisfy her curiosity and learn some of the truth about him… She could endure an evening with a smug, spoiled show-off like Nolan Carrick. She stared at the quill and ink pot on the back of the vanity. Her fingers twitched. *Mother will never know.* She smiled to herself as she penned a quick note.

She sealed the letter and set it aside. Her gaze moved to the stack of books she had borrowed from Lord Drummond's library. Right now, she had more important things to occupy her thoughts than men. Mother had left. Adelaide had locked the door to her room. Her maid Giselle was out doing laundry and wouldn't be back for a while. Adelaide sorted through the books. *A History of Monparth, Part III. Saint Kardeman's Bestiary and Herbal. The Life of King Saewyne the Magnificent.* All interesting titles, but not what she wanted just now.

She pulled out a volume whose dark leather binding displayed cracks from getting dried out and leaned forward in her seat in front of the vanity. The pages crinkled as she opened it. *Careful. Don't break it!* She ran her index finger over the title on the first page. *A Compendium of Known Magical Abilities and Tales of Mages of Legend.* No author was listed.

She could imagine Mother's disapproving voice as she began reading. *"You don't want to make yourself a target."* Well, if simple farmers and even children weren't spared, her level of knowledge wasn't the issue. And if whatever dark force was behind The Shadow came after her, she would need more than knives to defend herself. She took a deep breath and turned the page to a list of subjects, broken down by category: light, fire, horticulture, healing, combat, bindings, and storing magic in objects.

"In the beginning, Etiros imbued all living things with magic." Adelaide skimmed the preface. Generalities on magic being a pure form of energy that Etiros used to give life, but that an excess of this energy in a person resulted in a mage. It said magic could be *"corrupted into sorcery by malicious intent or when used to take instead of give."*

It also gave a sobering warning; one her parents had never given. *"Because magic is inextricably tied to a living thing's life energy, use of magic wearies the mage. Over-exertion of magical ability can cause long periods of slumber, fainting, and on occasion, death."* Adelaide couldn't imagine the desperation a mage would have to feel to push their abilities so far they killed themselves. She hurried on.

Each category in the *Compendium* started with basic, boring abilities. Although, stories of mages forming a free-floating source of light, erecting a solid barrier, and maintaining a constant heat of flame in a furnace were interesting.

Mages supposedly could force plants to grow faster and fruit to ripen, and calm animals. She marveled at descriptions of mages healing broken bones, curing illnesses, and a rumor a mage had reattached a severed limb. Adelaide had figured out basic healing early, as receiving your first dagger at age five resulted in many cuts. If only the *Compendium* explained *how* to do all these things. She fanned through the pages.

An illustration caught her eye, and she flipped back. A man held a gigantic white sword that appeared to be emitting flames. She looked at the facing page and read under her breath.

"Substantive magic. Subset: Conjure weapons of light and flame.

"Mages can shape the light they produce to form a weapon which, while composed entirely of light and sometimes of flame, is none-the-less material..."

Adelaide looked up and stared at her reflection in the vanity mirror. "Form a weapon of solid light. I can do that?"

The rest of the entry detailed the history of the technique and variations on weapon types. No instructions, other than "shape the light they produce." She slumped back in her chair.

"Maybe if I just concentrate..." She stood and moved away from the vanity. The curtains were drawn, no one would see. She raised her hand, palm up, and let the tingle of energy flow to her hand. A soft sphere of periwinkle-tinted light ignited above her outstretched palm. It had taken months of secret practice to form that sphere, instead of releasing a burst of flame. She stared at the sphere, willing it to become a sword. Nothing.

Okay...start smaller. A dagger?

Her mind ached from the concentration. The sphere elongated, became rectangular, then narrowed. "Yes!" She grinned, and the rectangle of pale blue light vanished like water from a burst skin. "No." She rubbed her forehead and rolled her shoulders back. *Come on. You can do it.*

Once again, she conjured the light and focused on shaping it. She practiced for over an hour. Finally, the light took the shape of a crude dagger. A plain, round hilt as long as her palm was wide, attached to a long, thin blade. It looked soft around the edges, but the center appeared solid.

Her pulse racing, she reached for the handle. *The moment of truth.* Her fingers closed around the hilt—

Knocking echoed from the door, and Adelaide jumped. The dagger vanished. She threw her head back and groaned. *No! I was so close!* She placed the *Compendium* back under the other books and unlocked the door.

Giselle walked in carrying a basket of clean clothes. "Everything all right, m'lady?"

"Of course. Just doing some reading."

CHAPTER 8

THE DAY WAS CLOUDY BUT WARM, AND THE SMELL OF EARTH and new leaves and grass filled the air. Regulus adjusted his back against the tree trunk. Above him, the oak leaves stood out bright green against the pale gray clouds.

"If I were you, I'd call on her." Jerrick slouched against the rail fence encircling the archery range behind the castle and bit into another bread roll. A dull thunk sounded as Dresden threw another knife at the archery target.

Originally from Bhitra, Jerrick Faras' accent made his vowels sound long and his consonants hard. He was about average height and muscular and could wield a battle-axe with deadly precision. His short black hair clung to his head in tight curls. He favored brightly dyed fabrics because of how well they contrasted with his dark skin. Today he wore a yellow tunic Regulus would never dream of attempting to wear.

"Call on her?"

"Yes," Jerrick said around a mouthful of bread. "Go visit her at the Drummonds' like a man."

"That's what I've been telling him!" Dresden threw his hands up in exasperation. He stood on the other side of the fence, inside the archery range. He didn't have his bow today, though, just the knives stuck in the top rail of the fence. "I told you, she wants to talk to you!"

"Because you lied to her. I didn't ask you to say anything. I didn't even speak to you before I left!"

"Ah, but was I wrong?" Dresden pulled another throwing knife out of the top rail of the fence. "You enjoyed your conversation and regretted leaving early. That's not a lie. And she *likes* you. I'm sure of it. So do something."

"I sent her that letter you forced me to write." Regulus pulled at a handful of grass.

Dresden rolled his eyes. "Which you also addressed to her mother like a dunce."

Regulus threw the grass over the fence at Drez, his irritation rising. What did it matter? Romance wasn't his lot in life. Servitude was.

"Drez knows what he's talking about," Jerrick said. "I'd know. *I* have a wife."

"See?" Dresden slapped Jerrick's shoulder and turned back toward the canvas-covered wooden target. He threw the knife in a swift motion, and it buried at the edge of the red center of the target near three other knives.

Regulus nodded at Dresden's target. "I see Estevan's lessons are paying off."

"Yes, just don't tell him that. He already walks with enough of a swagger." Drez pulled out another knife and shook it at Regulus. "But you're trying to change the subject. Do what Jerrick would do."

"If I recall, Jerrick, your courtship, for lack of a better term, consisted of you claiming you visited the same baker every day because he had the best bread you'd ever tasted when you were actually trying to seduce his daughter." Regulus grinned, propped his hands behind his head, and leaned back against the oak trunk.

"Hey." Jerrick pointed at Regulus, still holding a half-eaten roll. "He did have the best bread. He also had the most beautiful daughter. Now I have the best wife *and* the best bread." He bit into the roll and wagged his finger at Regulus. "Don't underestimate the power of freshly baked bread."

88

"There you go." Dresden spread out his hands. "Send her Sarah's rolls. You'll win her heart in no time."

"Let's not get ahead of ourselves." *Although, sending Adelaide some nalotavi might not be the worst idea.* He swatted a beetle off his pant leg. *No, sending her anything is a bad idea.* "We barely spoke."

"And yet you can't stop thinking about her," Drez teased.

Regulus closed his eyes, picturing Adelaide's brown eyes, her soft-looking dark hair. The way she smiled at him. He remembered Nolan Carrick, standing close to her, his hand on her back... He opened his eyes. "So? I'm sure she's forgotten all about me."

"Well, you haven't done much to keep yourself in her thoughts," Jerrick said. "It's been two weeks since the letter. At this point, sending her rolls *would* be an improvement."

Footsteps from the opposite side of the garden drew Regulus' attention away from Jerrick. Perceval Williamson clomped toward them, scowling. He was older than Regulus by a few years, and his repeatedly broken nose had odd bumps. Perceval must have been working the fields around his and Leonora's cottage again, because his face sported a light sunburn under his short, stiff brown hair.

Regulus stood. "What's happened?"

"You've been snubbed, Captain." Despite no longer being mercenaries, and despite the fact he'd asked his friends to call him Regulus, Perceval still insisted on calling him Captain. Perceval waved a folded letter. "The Carricks are hosting a party next week, and it doesn't seem you're invited."

"Etiros above, I thought we might have a problem on our borders or something serious." Regulus shrugged. "So? The Carricks never invite me. Carrick's a baron, he can choose not to invite a lesser noble. Besides, I hate parties."

"True." Perceval grinned, his eyebrows lifting like he had a secret. "But those parties usually don't have a certain dark-haired lady in attendance."

"Adelaide will be there?" Regulus regretted how eager he sounded as Drez smirked. He reached over the fence and smacked the back of Dresden's head.

"Indeed." Perceval handed Regulus the letter. *Lord Regulus Hargreaves of Arrano* was written across the front in curling script.

"I thought you said I *wasn't* invited?" Regulus flipped it over and sighed when he saw the broken seal. "Is it so hard for you all not to read my personal correspondence?"

"Didn't recognize the seal," Perceval grunted. "Precautionary measure."

"What can a letter do to me, Perce?" Regulus eyed the rearing unicorn impressed on the torn red wax. He didn't recognize it, either. He unfolded the parchment.

> Dear Lord Regulus Hargreaves,
> I apologize I did not write sooner. I hope you don't think I bear you any ill-will for needing to leave early, although I wish you'd said goodbye. I hope to continue our conversation at Baron Carrick's party.
> I do hope you'll stay longer. Perhaps I can discover if you are as good a dancer as you are a conversationalist.
> Signed,
> Lady Adelaide Belanger

Regulus' heart about stopped. As he reread the letter, his emotions jumped from elated to defeated. Adelaide wanted to see him again. She wanted to talk to him. She wanted to *dance* with him. But he had received no invite. He stared at the gentle curves of her signature. *Wait.* He jerked his head up and glared at Perceval. "You read this?"

Perceval held up his hands. "How was I supposed to know it was from Lady Belanger?"

"Wait, what?" Dresden leaned over the fence, trying to read the note. Regulus shoved the letter into his belt.

"Lady Belanger wants to dance with the Captain," Perceval said with a chuckle.

Regulus' face heated. "It doesn't matter. I can't show up un-invited." *And she'll realize what a poor choice I am when she knows I wasn't invited.*

"Can't you though?" Perceval grinned, a manic light behind his eyes. "It's so fun to rile the nobles. You should have seen the look on my father's face when I showed up to a supper party drunk."

"And to think you didn't do well at university," Jerrick said with mock amazement.

"No," Dresden said, turning the throwing knife over in his hand thoughtfully. "But, when the Carricks host a party, the other nobles feel they have to reciprocate. You should get invited to at least a couple of those parties. This is excellent. Oh, you'll get another chance to woo the lovely Adelaide."

"I'm not going to woo her, Drez."

"Then by Hallilek," Jerrick invoked the Bhitran deity with a perplexed expression, "why are we having this conversation?"

Dresden leaned his hip against the fence. "And why not?"

"You know why not." *Because I'm a monster.*

Jerrick and Perceval shifted and glanced at each other.

"We talked about this, Reg," Drez said quietly. "Perce, Jerrick, back me up. He can't hide here forever."

Perceval grunted. "You need a wife."

"Might give you something to look forward to," Jerrick said. "Make life more bearable."

"Or someone else to hurt." Regulus shook his head. "I shouldn't have written that letter."

"Then why'd you do it?" Dresden snapped.

Regulus poked his finger in a knot in the fence and avoided Dresden's intense regard. *Because I like her; because I wanted to. Because she said she didn't care about my bastardy. Because, for a moment, I pretended I was normal, and it felt good.* "Moment of weakness."

"Doing something because it brings you joy isn't weakness." Drez sighed and scratched his beard. "It was one time. The sorcerer controlled you once in two years. And you know how to avoid it happening again."

Regulus snorted. *If only you knew.* "One time, but I still almost—" He stopped as the mark on his right arm tingled, like the gentlest touch of the points of a thousand needles. He grabbed his arm and grimaced.

"The mark?" Dresden murmured.

Regulus nodded. His men watched him leave in silence. There was nothing to say; nothing they could do. Nothing that wouldn't make things worse, anyway. Up in his room, Regulus unlocked the chest that housed the black suit of armor and a bronze mirror. The rectangular mirror was just larger than Regulus' head, with a plain frame. He hesitated before he picked it up and placed it on a nail on the wall.

"I'm here, my lord."

The mirror shimmered and an image of the sorcerer replaced the burnished surface. "Excellent." Deep shadows hid the sorcerer's eyes beneath his ever-present hood. "I need you to go to the Singing Caves. There's a cave marked by a white elm with golden leaves. Enter it and retrieve a relic from the dragon's horde."

"The what?" Regulus gaped at the sorcerer.

"The dragon, the dragon!" The sorcerer waved his hands. "Kill the dragon if necessary, find the relic it is guarding, and bring it to me."

ast Columbia Branch
10-313-7700
ttp://hclibrary.org

onday, November 29, 2021 1:06:22 PM
73522

Item: 31267419435464
Title: Shroud of Eternity
Call no.: F GOO
Due: 12/20/2021

Item: 31267507716429
Title: Prince of Shadow and Ash
Call no.: F GON
Due: 12/20/2021

Item: 31267505916385
Title: Death's mistress : sister of darkness
Call no.: F GOO
Due: 12/20/2021

Item: 31267507722617
Title: The scribbly man
Call no.: F GOO
Due: 12/20/2021

Total items: 4

Self-pickup of holds now available.
Check out your own items using a
SelfCheck or HCLS CheckItOut app.
New hours are M Th 10am - 9pm,
          F Sa 10am 6pm,
   Sun 1pm 5pm (as of Sep 12).

Regulus massaged his temples. An actual dragon? "But—"

Pain sliced up his arm from the mark.

"Question," he gasped. "Not—defiance." The pain vanished. "Don't dragons usually have piles of treasure, my lord? How will I recognize the relic?"

The sorcerer harrumphed. "It will be separate from the other treasures, perhaps even displayed in a difficult-to-reach area. And, it looks like this." He held a parchment in front of the mirror. A drawing of what looked like a hollow oval composed of thick wire swirling into a rounded point at each end filled the mirror. The sorcerer waited a moment, then pulled the drawing away. "It shouldn't be hard to find, if you have half a brain."

Regulus' shoulders tensed as he tried to hide his indignation. He could not afford to anger the sorcerer with his men so close. "Anything else I should know?"

"Just that it's powerful, so if you let that dragon destroy it, I'll destroy you. And I want it quickly. It will take you a couple days to ride to the Caves. Best leave now." The image shimmered and reverted to a dull mirror. Regulus' hazy reflection stared back. Judging him.

A powerful relic guarded by a dragon sounded ominous. Evil. Giving the sorcerer more power seemed a mistake. But what else could he do? *I can't resist him.* Regulus rubbed the mark through his sleeve. *I've tried.*

He sank onto his bed and pulled out Adelaide's letter. He touched her signature and let himself imagine dancing with her, holding her. It was flattering she thought he would be invited. Would she mind that he wasn't? He looked up at the mirror. It didn't matter. No woman deserved a sorcerer's slave. Regulus' heart clenched as he ripped the letter in half.

Selina R. Gonzalez

CHAPTER 9

ADELAIDE LEANED OUT OF THE CARRIAGE WINDOW AS THEY approached the Carrick's massive castle. Fading daylight cast an orange glow over the long, wide drive lined with chestnut trees and filled with other carriages and riders. The deep, crenelated wall encompassing the castle, extensive gardens, and courtyards stood three stories tall. Towers emerged above the wall about every fifty paces. The bottom of a portcullis peeked out of the archway above the towering iron-covered front gates. A water fountain depicting a mermaid holding a giant shell over her head dominated the courtyard.

The castle itself was four stories tall and square, with large, round five-story-tall towers at each corner. Crenellations wrapped around the entirety of the castle. Pale limestone formed the edifice, including the gargoyles and grotesques depicting mythical creatures spaced along the top of the castle. Not for nothing were the Carricks known as the wealthiest baronial family in Monparth. Rumor had it their wealth approached that of the ducal families.

Carriages, horses, and servants filled the courtyard. The sound of creaking carriages, hoof-beats, neighs, bubbling water, and chatter echoed against the walls of the castle. Smoke from the myriad of torches arranged around the courtyard wafted in the air. A servant greeted their party, directing others to see to their mounts and baggage. Adelaide turned around, wide-eyed, taking in everything. And she thought Father's castle was impressive.

Minerva shook Adelaide's shoulder, diverting her attention from the displays of power. They were being escorted inside.

Inside was just as grand. The foyer sported vaulted ceilings and brightly colored tapestries covered stone walls. Coats of armor and bronze statues stood guard in the halls. A marble statue of an embracing woman and man on the brink of sharing a kiss stood on a large limestone pedestal in the center of the foyer. Adelaide slowed to a stop, marveling at the intricate detail on their simple, draping clothes. They even had fingernails.

"It's a beautiful piece," a male voice said near her shoulder. Adelaide jumped and turned toward the speaker. Nolan simpered. "Apologies. I didn't mean to startle you, Lady Adelaide."

"Sir Carrick." She smiled and curtsied, but her pulse hammered behind her temple.

"I thought we had agreed on Nolan?" He looked up at the statue. "My father acquired this when he was fighting in the Trade War. I understand your father won a good deal of his fortune in that conflict."

"Yes." Adelaide fixed her gaze on the marble curls of the woman's hair. "King Olfan was generous in rewarding his bravery." She hated when people made it sound like her father was a mere robber warrior, even if war spoils had added to his wealth.

"He met your mother while in Carasom, is that correct?"

"Yes. She was traveling with her father." Adelaide braced herself for the inevitable casual judgment of her mother's non-noble lineage.

"She must have made quite an impression. You take after her—impossible to ignore."

Wait...what? She glanced sideways at Nolan. His mouth curved up in a slight smile and his eyes glinted as his gaze wandered over her. Her cheeks flushed, and she looked back to the statue.

Nolan laughed. "Don't be shy." He gestured to the statue. "Beautiful things are meant to be admired."

"Pardon me, Sir Carrick." Adelaide was relieved to hear Lady Drummond's voice. "But I'm afraid I must steal Lady Belanger. We were just on our way to our quarters."

"Ah, forgive me." Nolan bowed and swept up Adelaide's hand, brushing a kiss against her fingers. He smiled as he released her hand. "I look forward to seeing you at supper."

As they followed a maid down the hall, Lady Drummond smiled conspiratorially. "I believe Sir Nolan has it in mind to court you, dear girl. Lucky you!"

"Yes," Adelaide murmured. "Lucky me."

They had just enough time to get dressed and freshen their hair before heading down for the banquet. Adelaide wore a light blue dress with fitted sleeves under a sleeveless silk overdress of dark blue, comprised of two long pieces of fabric sewn together at her shoulders and laced together at her sides with a thick crimson satin cord. A braided crimson and gold belt tied in front, the long tails hanging down almost to the bottom of the dress. A single teardrop-shaped sapphire hung on the end of her thin gold necklace. The outfit had been a gift from Lady Drummond, made for Adelaide expressly for the Carrick's party. She could only guess Lady Drummond worried she would choose something too Khast-allander and embarrass the Drummonds.

As the guests entered the great hall, servants showed them to their seats. To Adelaide's confusion, a page beckoned her in a different direction than her sister and Lady Drummond. "Pardon me, are we headed the right direction?"

The boy looked over his shoulder. "Yes, my lady. This way, my lady." They walked toward the head of the hall.

"I think you may have me confused with someone else. Lady Adelaide Belanger. I'm here with my sister, Lady Minerva

Drummond, and the Drummonds?" She looked around for them, spotting them moving to their seats at a long table on the side of the hall. "I think a mistake has been made—"

"No mistake, Lady Adelaide." Nolan flashed a cavalier smile as he walked up beside her. "You are seated next to me."

Adelaide blinked, trying to hide her surprise. Nolan had changed as well. He now wore a royal blue knee-length tunic lined with crimson and pale blue stockings. A sword hung at his hip from an intricately engraved leather belt with a gold buckle. A gold brooch of a gryphon, the symbol of the Carrick family, secured a blue half cape to his right shoulder. He offered her his arm.

"Wonderful," she managed. Gingerly, she tucked her hand in the crook of his elbow. Only when she glanced down did the truth hit her. They were dressed to match. Too much so to be a coincidence. Heat rushed to her ears. *I could slap Lady Drummond! When did she tell him what I was wearing?* If Adelaide had known, she would have worn tomorrow's traveling dress. Now she stood in a room full of nobles, her clothing screaming *I am courting Nolan Carrick* against her will.

"You are breathtaking." Nolan's voice was low, personal.

Somehow, she managed to respond. "Thank you, Sir Nolan." *Be polite. Return the compliment.* "You look handsome yourself." It wasn't untrue. He did look fetching. But she couldn't seem to relax around him. *It's just nerves. I've never had a proper suitor.*

"Well, Sir Nolan is an improvement over Sir Carrick, so I'll take it." He winked.

Nolan led her to a seat at the table below the dais. Food already covered the table on the dais like all the others, but the four chairs behind it were empty. Nolan pulled out a chair at the lower table for her, and Adelaide sat down, aware of the many eyes around the room watching her. She wondered how much of the low hum of conversation was about her. She searched the crowd for Minerva. Even a quick smile from her sister would calm her nerves. Unfortunately, Min sat with her back toward Adelaide, and she was deep in conversation with Lady Drummond.

"I knew blue and crimson would suit you." Nolan sat next to her. "I hope finding the fabric wasn't too much trouble."

"What? You requested this?"

He frowned. "Yes... And you...accepted?"

"No. I had no idea."

They stared at each other. Nolan cleared his throat. "I sent a messenger to the Drummonds, asking you to wear these colors. The messenger said you'd accepted."

"Lady Drummond must have accepted on my behalf," Adelaide said flatly. She fiddled with her silver utensils as anger heated her skin. "And didn't tell me."

"I'm sorry." He sounded genuine. "Do you...mind, though?"

She stared at the ceramic plate and silver goblet in front of her. "I was unprepared," she said carefully. She didn't want to make this evening too miserable. *Please let supper start soon.*

Adelaide surveyed the room. Nobles were still entering and being seated. So far, no sign of Lord Regulus Hargreaves. *He's quite tall, you'd think he would be easy to spot.* The influx of guests slowed, but even as her disappointment grew, she felt relieved he wasn't there. She didn't want him to see her with Nolan like...this.

A servant showed a man to the empty seat on her other side. The woman next to him must have recognized him, because they struck up a conversation.

Nolan's warm hand covered hers. "Will you attend the tournament next month?"

"Tournament?" She smoothed her skirts as an excuse to remove her hand from under his.

Disappointment flickered over Nolan's face, but his usual self-assured smile returned. "Yes, the Etchy Tournament? My father hosts it every year."

She forced herself to look at him, to be polite. "Will you be competing?"

"Oh, of course!" He reached over and brushed a strand of hair behind her ear. She managed not to grimace. "I was rather hoping I could compete in your honor."

Her cheeks flushed as panic crippled her mind. "I…um…" A trumpet flare mercifully interrupted, and silence fell over the room.

Baron and Baroness Carrick entered, followed by a man who was clearly Carrick's eldest son and a woman who seemed to be his wife. They moved to their seats, and the baron welcomed the guests and sat down.

Cupbearers moved among the tables bearing large containers of wine. A group of minstrels entered and played in a corner. A juggler and two acrobats leapt into the open area in the middle of the hall. Adelaide had never been so thankful for the distraction of entertainment and the excuse of food to avoid conversation. The nobleman to her right, Sir Morris MacCombe, son of Baron MacCombe, was friendly. Their conversation, while comprised of standard supper party small talk, was amiable. MacCombe, in fact, seemed eager to engage her. Nolan and MacCombe never acknowledged each other, at times outright ignoring each other when the conversation could have included both. It made her even more uncomfortable, but at least MacCombe was kind and didn't flirt with or touch her.

Part of her felt foolish and guilty. Nolan was handsome, with his silky chestnut hair, merry blue eyes, and square jaw. He came from a wealthy, powerful, and respected family. A small part of her relished the flattering attention, the knowledge that many young noblewomen would swoon for Nolan. However, he had done nothing so far to impress her, to set him apart from any other young nobleman with too much time and money. Besides, she had always fancied taller men, like Regulus Hargreaves. The ease of the thought surprised her, and she choked on a sip of wine.

"Are you all right?" Nolan asked.

"Oh, yes." She dabbed her mouth with a cloth napkin. Her tongue seemed to get ahead of her brain. "I notice Lord Hargreaves is not in attendance."

"The mercenary?" Nolan rolled his eyes. "Of course not."

Adelaide looked at him, her brow furrowed. "I understand he used to be a mercenary, but he is a nobleman now, isn't he?"

"He's a petty lord of little account. And the only reason he's a noble at all is because his philandering father was so taken with his peasant mother he added their mongrel son to his will. Arrano even buried her under a statue of an angel. Disgraceful." He plopped a grape in his mouth.

"You're saying Lord Hargreaves wasn't invited?" Her heart twisted. *Oh, no. My letter...* She felt horrible she'd assumed and hoped Regulus hadn't taken it as an insult.

Nolan cocked an eyebrow. "Why should the Baron and Baroness Carrick invite the son of a washing wench into their home?"

She stared at him as she clenched her fork in a white-knuckled fist. "That's unfair and uncalled for."

He shifted and glanced about. "I'm sorry. Some people are best avoided, and Hargreaves is the worst of them. He may hold the title of lord, but it's not who he is. He could have been knighted, but he took off and became a mercenary. Mercenaries are not men of honor. Hargreaves only left the life because he inherited Arrano's land and title. He likely killed Lady Arrano and her daughter-in-law. Then he had the audacity to knight his mercenaries. Three of them aren't even Monparthian."

"Have something against non-Monparthians?" A hard edge crept into her voice.

Nolan reddened. "No, of course not." He cleared his throat. "Hargreaves keeps mostly to himself and often disappears alone for unknown reasons. But I have a theory: once a mercenary, always a mercenary. I suspect he misses the life and runs off to satiate his blood-lust." He rested his hand on her arm and looked into her eyes. "Hargreaves is not to be trusted. I advise you keep your distance, for your own safety."

"I can take care of myself." She looked away. "Can you prove all this?"

"Unfortunately, no. But a knight's intuition is never wrong."

Adelaide stifled a snicker. It hardly seemed chivalrous to be hasty in judgment. But perhaps she was doing the same with Nolan. *No. He has proven himself to be prejudiced, condescending, and a flirt.*

"But enough of such talk." Nolan grabbed his goblet. "It's a party, after all."

Adelaide stared past the acrobats, wishing Minerva would turn around. This party couldn't end soon enough.

CHAPTER 10

ADELAIDE DID HER BEST TO TRY AT LEAST A BITE OF EACH course, but her appetite had vanished. She couldn't decide which bothered her more: the idea of Regulus Hargreaves being a blood-thirsty, self-serving villain, or Nolan Carrick's crass haughtiness. She had difficulty reconciling the kind laughter, easy conversation, and apparent humility she had seen in Regulus with the murderer Nolan described. And yet... What did a person truly know about another after one brief conversation?

Nothing.

She would have given anything to retire after supper, but her parents had raised her to be decorous and respectful, and leaving before dancing would be insulting to the Carricks.

Nolan wasted no time asking her to dance. As the lute players and pipers began to play, they joined other couples in a stately dance. The way Nolan's piercing gaze did not leave her face made her far more uncomfortable than his warm fingertips underneath hers. Every time the steps of the dance dictated that they part or turn away from each other was a short reprieve from his intense and undesired attentions. The dance ended, and she curtsied as best she could with Nolan's fingers still curled under her own. He bowed, bringing her fingers to his lips, his eyes fixed on hers.

The air in the room was far too hot. Adelaide forced a smile and inclined her head. "Thank you for the dance, Sir Nolan. I fear I need to sit down for a while."

"You're not feeling unwell, I hope? The night has scarcely begun." He rubbed his thumb over her knuckles.

Perhaps she was projecting her own urgent desire to escape, but she thought she detected a hint of panic in his words. She shifted and pulled her hand away. "Just...a little lightheaded."

"I'm sorry to hear that." Nolan moved to her side, wrapping an arm around her shoulders.

This is the opposite of what I wanted!

"Here." He guided her to some chairs near the wall. "Wait right here. I'd like to introduce you to my brother."

"Oh—" But Nolan darted away before she could protest. He returned a couple minutes later with his brother. The elder Carrick was just shorter than Nolan, with similar light brown hair and blue eyes. He sported a neatly trimmed mustache.

"Lady Adelaide, this is my eldest brother, William. Will, this is Adelaide."

William bowed and Adelaide moved to stand and curtsy, but William held up his hand. "Please, sit. I understand you're not feeling well."

She shifted. "I needed a moment to breathe and cool down."

The corner of William's mouth twitched. "Yes, Nolan can have that effect."

She rubbed the side of her neck, unsure what to say, since *I'm not all warm and breathless over your brother's charms* seemed a bit... antagonistic and forward. "Don't you have another brother?" she asked, desperate to change the subject.

"Yes, Michael," Nolan said. His eyes narrowed.

William clasped his hands behind his back. "Michael married Baron MacCombe's daughter, Elaine, a few years ago. They live in a castle along the Monparth-Carasom border that Baron Mac-Combe gave them."

"How generous." Adelaide slipped into the small talk expected at these gatherings. "I spoke with Sir Morris MacCombe over supper. He was friendly."

Nolan's jaw tightened. "Yes, well, he's likely to announce an engagement to Duke Randall's daughter Elizabeth soon." The irritation in his voice was unmistakable, but the cause baffled Adelaide. *Is he irritated MacCombe was friendly to me, or irritated he's marrying Elizabeth Randall?*

William cast a sidelong glance at his brother, but his expression remained serene. "Elizabeth is my wife's sister. But Sir Morris and Nolan had a bit of a…quarrel last year."

"Bygones." Nolan glared at his brother as Adelaide fidgeted with her skirt so she wouldn't have to look at the brothers.

"Yes, well." William slapped Nolan's back. "Nolan has matured in the last year. He's a bright, talented young man. We expect him to do well at the Etchy Tournament. He marginally lost the joust last year. But I'm not competing this year, so his chances are good." She looked up in surprise at William's teasing tone. Nolan looked like he'd tasted something sour.

"Joking aside," William continued, "I wouldn't place any bets against him. Not that you would gamble, of course. But I fear I have other guests to see." He bowed. "It was an honor and a pleasure to make your acquaintance, Lady Belanger. I expect I'll be seeing you again. Soon and often."

"The honor was mine, Lord Carrick."

William nodded, then turned and ambled away. *Soon and often.* The Carrick family *expected* her to court Nolan. *Perfect.*

Nolan recovered his composure and looked unbothered by his brother's teasing. "Feeling any better?"

"Actually, I'm developing a headache," she lied.

Nolan sat next to her, his forehead wrinkled. "Shall I send for the physician?"

"Oh, no, I think I need to sleep." She stood. "I'll just go to my room—"

"Then I will accompany you," he declared as he stood. "It's a large castle, I'd hate for you to get lost."

She stiffened. "Thank you, but I can find my way on my own. I won't tear you away from your party—"

"Adelaide, please." Nolan placed his hand on her shoulder and stepped in closer. "There is no party with you gone."

She willed herself not to laugh or gag. *Etiros, spare me.*

"*You* are the reason for hosting this event; the only reason I care about this party at all. Please." He looked like a puppy begging for scraps from the table. His hand slid down her arm and he took her hand. "I don't need to dance. Just…sit with me. Stay with me."

How in Monparth was she supposed to respond to *that*? Especially when all she could think about was getting some space to herself?

Nolan took another step closer and placed his free hand on the side of Adelaide's neck. Her heart leapt into her throat. "Don't leave," he breathed. His gaze fell to her lips as his thumb caressed her cheek.

"I…I'm sorry." Adelaide yanked her hand free and made as hasty a departure as possible without sacrificing all decorum.

Once in her room and dressed in her nightgown, she found sleep evaded her, so she paced. Too many thoughts swirled in her mind—most related to the fact every noble at the party would suspect an impending courtship.

She despised Nolan's cockiness and disregard for her personal space. And his vehemence toward Lord Regulus. It didn't seem Nolan had ever even *tried* to get to know Regulus or hear his side of the story. He just hated Regulus because his mother was a peasant. Didn't Regulus deserve a chance to defend himself and his own honor?

As Adelaide paced, her irritation mounted. Her palms warmed as magical energy coursed through her. She needed a distraction. Something to do, something else to focus on. She held her hand out and her palm filled with eggshell-blue light. She focused on the light, drawing it out of her palm and into a tight, dense orb. She expanded the orb, letting it grow until it was as large as her head, but still hovering above her palm.

"Now the real test," she murmured. She raised her palm and concentrated on sending the orb up. A grin spread over her face as the orb floated above her, illuminating the entire room.

But could she do something else now? Walk away? Do other magic, even? She conjured a dagger—a trick she had been practicing every chance she got ever since she first tried it. The solid light dagger now materialized as desired about eighty percent of the time. She gripped the simple dagger in her hand and laughed in delight when the orb stayed in place.

Oh, yes! Her spirits fell as she looked around the empty room. *If only I could share this with someone.*

The first time she had hit the bullseye on a target with a throwing knife, she was seven. "That's my little tigress," Mother had said in Khast. Father had kissed her forehead and said he was proud. Minerva and Adelaide then spent the afternoon competing to land more bullseyes. Minerva was only a little disappointed when Adelaide won. But practicing magic? That earned her the opposite reaction. Dread and reprimands instead of pride. Like when she quenched the fire in front of Minerva.

The dagger faded, and the orb flickered out. Adelaide flopped onto the bed and stared at the dark green canopy above her. Keeping secrets made her feel so alone. But did she have a choice?

"It's too dangerous, *Tha Shiraa*," Mother's warning to her at age five had been seared into her mind. "No one knows who or what was behind The Shadow. We don't want them to come for you, too."

The Shadow. Most people didn't talk about the massacre of the mages, but when they did, it was with terrified reverence. Mages had never been abundant in Monparth, but Father said mages once did everything from farming to working as healers to leading warriors in battle.

Then mages started turning up dead. Murdered. Killed in their sleep. An arrow through their neck as they went about their daily tasks. Poisoned in their own homes. Some were found dead with no visible cause. Within weeks, every single mage within Monparth, from infants to the elderly, was dead.

Initially, some had thought the killings ordered by King Olfan, the current king's father, to prevent sorcerers. Olfan's eldest son had been a mage, but Monparthian law forbade mages from inheriting the throne. Too much power for one individual, too much risk of a mage becoming a sorcerer—and the history of sorcerer-kings was written in blood. The prince had disappeared for several years only to reemerge as a sorcerer and attempt regicide—or patricide. The court mages drove him out, hunted him down, and killed him. A year later, mages started being murdered. Then the court mages were slaughtered, and people stopped blaming the king. No one was ever caught.

A few years later, Adelaide's magic escaped for the first time. She was three. And she'd been hiding ever since. If the worry The Shadow would kill her wasn't enough, the only living mage in Monparth would be valuable—for healing, for protection, for war. And as Father said, above all else, men with power crave more power. Her parents insisted she not practice magic and tell no one. Not even her half-siblings knew.

That was the real reason she wouldn't court Nolan, beyond his prejudice against Regulus. Something deep in her gut warned her she couldn't trust Nolan with her secret. And if she couldn't tell him the truth, she couldn't marry him. Again she wished Regulus had come. She wanted to talk to him, find out if he seemed trust-worthy, or if Nolan was right. She made a face at the canopy. *Why, so you can court him? Stop being ridiculous.*

Someone knocked on the door and Adelaide jumped.

"Adelaide?" Minerva's voice.

Adelaide answered the door, and Minerva entered, a deep furrow between her brows. "Are you all right? Sir Carrick said you weren't feeling well."

Adelaide slumped against the door as she closed it. "I'm fine. I just…needed some space." She looked at Minerva accusingly. "Did you see his clothes? Did you know—"

"Heavens, no!" Minerva's eyes widened. "Lady Drummond is very proud of herself. She thinks you'll thank her later. I was horrified and told her as much. I'm so sorry, Ad."

"Well, good." Adelaide forced herself to keep a straight face. "Because I had sworn to never speak to you again if you had any-thing to do with it." She smiled, and Minerva laughed.

"I take it you don't care for him?"

Adelaide twirled a ribbon on her dressing gown around her finger. "He's…haughty. Self-absorbed. I think he hates Lord Hargreaves simply because he's illegitimate, which is ridiculous." She let the ribbon unravel and fall off her finger. "Maybe it's unfair of me, but I don't trust him."

"Thank Etiros." Minerva's relieved tone surprised Adelaide. Min sat on the edge of her bed. "I honestly don't like him, either. I overheard some ladies claiming Nolan Carrick's charm has…undone a few women. I hate unsubstantiated rumors, but it makes me uncomfortable."

"You're uncomfortable? I don't want to know what rumors they'll spread about me now." She slouched on the bed next to Minerva.

"Are you sure you're fine?" Minerva stroked Adelaide's hair. "You know you can tell me anything, right?"

"I know." *Do I?* They sat in silence until Adelaide couldn't take it anymore. "I found a book on magic in Lord Drummond's library."

Minerva's hand froze on Adelaide's back. "Ad…"

"I know, I know. But…it's been twenty-three years. Surely it's safe by now."

"You don't know that. You can't know that."

"If someone was still hunting mages, why didn't they find me as a child?" Adelaide stood. "Do you have any idea how difficult it is to keep this power inside me? It's this constant pressure, begging for release."

Minerva dropped her gaze. "Ad—"

"Just…look." Adelaide formed a dagger. The blue light of the blade cast odd shadows on Minerva's face as she held the magic weapon out to her sister.

"Oh," Minerva whispered, her eyes wide and jaw slack. She reached out and brushed her fingers against the hilt. "It's…solid. That's…" She shook her head. "You *have* daggers, Adelaide."

"But what if sometime I don't? And what else could I do? I can help people!"

"With a dagger?"

Adelaide groaned. "All right, look. Mother panicked when she caught me doing this, so I've never told you I can. But watch. And don't panic." She drew the blade of her magic dagger across her palm and winced from the sharp pain.

"Adelaide!" Minerva gasped.

"It's all right!" Adelaide vanished the blade and healed her hand. A comforting numb sensation spread over the cut, and the skin pulled back together. The blue glow of her palm illuminated Minerva's horrified expression. The light dimmed, and Adelaide rinsed her hand in the water bowl on the dresser. She turned back to Minerva. "See?"

Minerva grabbed her hand and ran her fingers over the smooth skin. "It's…like it never happened," she breathed.

"Exactly!" Adelaide smiled broadly, excitement making her heart race. "Mother and Father want to keep me safe; I *know* that. But…isn't magic a gift? It's a natural part of the world. The priests say Etiros imbued all living things with magic. Isn't it a source of goodness Etiros gave me access to for a reason?"

Minerva's sad eyes filled with pity. "And what about all those mages who died? What good did their gift do them?"

"Just because they died doesn't mean they had done nothing good with their magic before that," Adelaide countered.

"Ad…" Minerva massaged her forehead. "I can't stop you. And I won't try. But I don't want to lose you, either. And what if it's not only your own life you put in danger?" She rubbed her growing belly protectively.

Adelaide's posture fell. Maybe her sister was right. But maybe she wasn't. "I'll be careful."

"Thank you." Minerva held out her hand, and Adelaide helped her stand. "Get some rest. I'll see you tomorrow."

In the morning, Adelaide faked illness as an excuse to avoid breakfast. Gaius and Minerva stole a few indulgently sweet fruit-filled pastries, which Adelaide devoured as she waited for their carriage in the bustling courtyard. She spied Nolan wandering the chaos of departing guests as if searching for someone. Their carriage pulled around, and she rushed inside. Relief filled her when Carrick castle faded from sight.

CHAPTER 11

REGULUS REINED IN SIEGER AT THE CREST OF A HILL COVERED in tall grass. A wide valley that deepened and narrowed into a ravine stretched out ahead of them. Beyond, the spur of the Pelandian Mountains known as the Barren Range rose behind a blue-gray haze. Oaks, maples, and juniper bushes grew scattered near the valley entrance, and the mouths of caves yawned dark in the ravine walls. A strong breeze tugged on his cloak and carried the scent of apple trees. The gust moved across the cave mouths, creating a faint sound somewhere between a whistle and a soft cry.

The famous Singing Caves.

He clicked his tongue and Sieger started forward again at a gentle trot. At the entrance to the valley, he tied Sieger to a low branch of a young maple, tight enough the horse wouldn't wander off, but loose enough if something came at Sieger and he tried to run, he could pull free. He removed his cloak and hung it over another branch. A cloak was a liability in battle, and anyone who happened by would assume the owner was nearby and likely leave Sieger alone. Before setting out, he double-checked his gear and supplies. He had the massive black sword from the sorcerer, a hunting knife across his lower back, and a dagger and water horn on his right hip. Blackened iron covered the front of a kite-shaped shield, its wooden back wrapped in hardened leather. He slung a bag of miscellaneous supplies over his shoulder and started out.

Regulus chewed on dried venison as he walked, savoring the salty, smoky flavor. Only the rustle of grass, leaves, and the sighing of wind in the caves reached his ears. He hadn't seen a living thing since before the last hill. He peered into each cave as he passed, listening and watching the shadows. Nothing moved in the valley or the caves. The valley deepened, the hills on either side rising the closer he got to the Barren Mountains. Gradually, the ravine narrowed. The sides became more uneven, with more caves and craggy spurs of rock. More places for things to hide.

At last, he spied the white elm with golden leaves. It grew so close to the mouth of the cave the trunk had melded with the stone. The branches spread over the entrance, deepening the shadows within. The mouth of the cave stretched over twice as tall as Regulus, and nearly as wide. *Okay. The dragon's no bigger than the entrance, right? Big, but not as big as I feared.* The golden leaves of the white elm rustled in the breeze while the caves moaned and whistled. Wind snuck between his helm and the back of his breastplate, chilling his neck. His instincts told him not to enter that cave. He ate a last bite of venison, pulled a torch from his bag, and lit it. He held it at arm's length and peered into the darkness filling the cave. With a deep breath to steady his nerves, he headed in.

As his eyes adjusted to the gloom of the cave and the torchlight, Regulus scanned the shadows. He kept his right hand on the hilt of his sheathed sword. Breezes swirled past, occasionally whistling in the caves. His footsteps echoed, every clank of his armor magnified as the sound bounced. After a while, he heard the trickle of water. Rivulets ran down the sides of the cave. The cave widened and curved as he progressed, making it difficult to see into the dark shadows. All sunlight had long since disappeared. The air grew dank, heavy, and stale as the wind stopped. A rotten and burnt smell became more apparent. After walking for around half an hour, he heard a new sound. Like the sighing, whistling wind, but different.

Several minutes later, the cave forked. To his right, the roof of the cave sloped down, and the cave narrowed. To his left, the cave widened. The noise, which sounded uncomfortably like breathing, came from the left.

Why are you hesitating? You know the dragon's to the left. He took a deep breath. *Well, yes, that's why I'm hesitating. I've never faced an actual dragon before.*

He stretched as much as his armor and the shield strapped to his left arm would allow and double-checked his weapons. "Here goes," he said aloud. His voice sounded hollow in his helm. Head held high and every muscle straining with nervous energy, he strode into the left passage.

After a couple minutes, he had no doubt the sound was breathing. He passed a pile of bones. A deer, maybe. More unsettling was what looked like massive troll bones. A slight, warm, fetid breeze rushed toward him in time with the breathing. The stench worsened, and the cool dampness of the cave transitioned into warm humidity. Sweat rolled down his forehead under his helm. He rounded yet another curve. *Where is that infernal—*

Dragon.

The beast slept on a mound of gold, silver, jewels, and bones, curled into a ball like a gargantuan cat. It looked like an oversized lizard, covered in dull scales the color of dried sage. The dragon's head, longer than Regulus' height, rested on a front foot the size of Regulus' torso and legs, with five claws the length of his forearm. Dull black horns curled back from the crown of its head. Its nostrils flared as it breathed out, its breath sulfuric and hot. The tip of its tail, shaped like a barbed arrow as wide as Regulus' chest, twitched in front of its snout. It had no wings, just four legs like oak trees.

Regulus swallowed and looked around for the relic in the dim light. His torch sputtered in the dragon's breath, making the shadows in the cave flicker. As quietly as possible, he walked around the dragon. He saw nothing that looked like the drawing in the pile under the dragon, but that didn't mean it wasn't there. Hopefully the sorcerer was right, and it was somewhere else in the cave.

Technically, the sorcerer had told him to kill the dragon *if necessary* and take the relic. If he could skip the fighting the dragon part, he would do so. True, the dragon couldn't kill him. But it could burn him, cut him, scar him. Dying was still painful. The feeling of death without the release of dying was a hellish experience, one he tried to avoid.

He proceeded cautiously, holding up his torch to illuminate as much of the cave as possible. The dragon's breath vibrated the floor. Behind the dragon, near the back of the cave, a white stone caught the torchlight. The square pedestal stood about as tall as Regulus' waist. A faded, repulsive gray-brown rotting pillow rested on top. Cradled on the pillow lay an object made of thick gold wire twisted into the shape of a hollow egg and coated in dust.

The relic was about half a foot long and slightly narrower, with a short rod in the hollow center that looked like a mount for something that was missing. He picked it up and shook off some of the dust, but with the humidity of the room, most of it stuck. He shrugged and deposited it in his bag, then froze.

The rhythm of the dragon's breathing had changed. *Clink. Clink.* Metallic rustling and clattering echoed in the cave. Regulus pressed his eyes closed. *You couldn't stay asleep, could you?* He adjusted his grip on his shield, set the torch down on the pillow, which caught fire, and drew his sword. A low growl reverberated around the room and resonated in his chest. He turned, praying dragons didn't really breathe fire.

The dragon, now towering over him, its red serpentine eyes flashing, snarled. Its mouth glowed orange. Regulus yanked his shield up, hiding as much of his body behind it as possible. Fire pummeled the shield. The heat was terrible, the roar of the flames loud, the force of the blast startling. He leaned into the shield, pushing hard against the rock floor to brace himself. Without his enhanced strength, he wouldn't have withstood the onslaught. The stream of fire ended, and Regulus blinked sweat out of his eyes.

The dragon roared, the sound deafening in the cave. Regulus straightened and ran forward, keeping the shield between him and the dragon. He swung at the dragon's neck. The blade met scales with an echoing clang as a shock ran up his arm. He yanked the sword down, leaving only a scratch. Regulus gulped. *This is not good.* The dragon snarled again, baring sharp, yellowed teeth.

Regulus blocked a swipe of its huge front foot with his shield, but the force knocked him sideways. Its claws dragged against the front of the shield with a piercing grating noise. The weight pulled his arm down. He dropped his sword, drew his dagger, and reached over the shield, stabbing into the dragon's foot right between two black-clawed toes. The blade slipped between scales and Regulus pushed it in to its hilt. The dragon roared. It yanked its foot back, tearing the dagger out of Regulus' hand. As the dragon howled, Regulus spotted a small, lighter area unprotected by thick scales at the top of its neck, under its chin. He snatched the sword back up and lunged toward the dragon's neck, breathing hard.

The dragon recovered, and Regulus narrowly dodged another swipe of its foot. But now the dragon had tucked down its head, and rows of pointed teeth were between him and his target. He spun to the side, trying to disorient the creature. The dragon dove, and he ducked. Teeth as big as his hands clamped onto the shield. Frantic, he pulled his arm out of the shield. His gauntlet caught on the first strap. *Too tight!* His heart raced as he fought against the dragon's pull and the strap.

He had barely freed his arm when the dragon forced its jaws closed. The shield bent, the metal making a piercing grinding sound as wood splinters flew everywhere. The dragon spit the shield away, flames curling around the crushed metal and remaining fragments of wood. Regulus scrambled back. *Focus.* He had found a potential striking point. He just needed to get close enough. Curse the sorcerer's showy armor. What he needed was maneuverability, not a dramatic appearance.

Something slammed into his stomach, throwing him back against the cave wall. His sword fell from his hand with a clatter. Whatever had hit him tore through his armor with a metallic rending that tormented his ears. Regulus screamed as pain flared. He grabbed for whatever had lodged itself in his torso and found the barbed arrowhead tip of the dragon's tail buried in his abdomen. His blood flowed between dark scales. He choked as blood forced its way up his throat. He couldn't. Breathe.

His chest tightened and his neck stiffened as he attempted to cough up the blood gagging him, but the dragon's tail had destroyed his abdominal muscles. The dragon yanked its tail away, and Regulus collapsed to his knees. Pain turned the world white. His own rumbling pulse filled his ears.

He could breathe again. Pulling and pinching added to his already immeasurable pain as dark magic coursed through his body. He rolled onto his side, screaming, unable to even think about the dragon. He felt the gash mending back together; like millions of white-hot needles stitching him together from the inside out with thread laced with poison ivy. He looked up and saw the dragon's wide-open mouth careening toward him.

On instinct, he rolled to the side. The dragon slammed its snout into the cave floor as Regulus struggled to his knees. *There.* His sword lay only a few feet away. The dragon growled and shook its head. It raised a massive forefoot to step on him. Regulus waited as long as he dared before darting forward, his gut wrenching.

The claws hit the cave floor with a sharp clack. Dust and pebbles flew. Regulus crawled forward and grasped the hilt of his sword. He rolled onto his back as the dragon lunged again, its tongue flicking between its teeth. From his back, Regulus thrust his sword up as the dragon's open mouth descended. He looked away, clenching his eyes shut and grimacing. Some part of him wondered whether he would finally die if the dragon bit him in half.

Sword met flesh. The dragon's growl vibrated his arms. The force of the dragon's attack drove the sword down, but Regulus pushed up, his eyes still pressed closed as the dragon's breath scorched his skin. His sword pulled to the side, and he lost his grip. He opened his eyes to the dragon staggering and pawing at the sword buried deep in the roof of its mouth. Smoke curled from its flaring nostrils and its eyes rolled, turning white. He staggered to his feet while drawing his hunting knife. The dragon roared and flailed, sending gold and jewels flying.

Regulus jumped forward and skirted a blindly thrown foot. He stumbled over the whipping tail. Coins pinged off his armor. His wound had closed. It still throbbed, but it was healed. The dragon, still holding its mouth wide open, looked up at the cave ceiling. Regulus jumped onto the monster's leg, clutching the knife with both hands. He pushed off the leg with a shout and leapt toward the dragon's throat, his gaze fixed on the paler, less scaled patch.

With every ounce of his strength, he thrust up into the dragon's throat. The knife dug into the center of the spot. The dragon screeched. Regulus pushed the blade in deep. The momentum of his jump spent, he fell. With a grunt, he yanked the knife back out and bubbling deep green blood flowed out, splattering over his armor.

He landed hard on the ground as the dragon stumbled. Regulus scurried back. With a crash, the cacophony of treasure being scattered, and the scrape of scales on stone, the dragon fell. The cave shook and Regulus stumbled. Its eyes rolled around in its head, then went still. A great sigh rushed through the cave like wind, and the dragon stopped breathing.

Regulus watched, unmoving. His nerves buzzed and his muscles twitched. He crept forward and nudged the dragon's muzzle with the tip of his boot. *Dead.* He exhaled heavily, wrenched off his helm, and tossed it away with a clatter. His hands on his knees, he gulped in putrid air as if he had been drowning. Which, he supposed, he probably *had* nearly drowned, choking on his own blood. With a shudder, he vomited. Bloody bile splashed onto his dragon-blood flecked greaves.

All this pain. All this suffering. Being dragged back from the brink of death. For *what?* What was so Etiros-forsaken important to the sorcerer about these artifacts and relics? Why did the sorcerer make him do all this? And why wouldn't it just end?

Some part of him whispered he could have let the dragon eat him. Couldn't be brought back from digestion, right? Then again, sometimes the power of the sorcerer frightened him.

But no. He wouldn't give up, not now. Not this close to being free, not after he'd fought for so long. Not after everything his friends had done for him; after he'd promised to keep going. He thought of Dresden. *"You'll get through this. I'll help."* They stayed for him; he could stay around for them.

As the burning in his throat and mouth subsided, leaving behind a sour taste, Regulus straightened. He eyed the dragon. He'd killed countless dozens of violent beasts over his years as a mercenary. Gryphons, ice serpents, manticores, therarns—creatures of the deserts like great cats but covered in scales, and more. He'd never felt remorse for any of them. They had terrorized innocent people. But this dragon's only offense was being in the sorcerer's way. He shook the twinge of pity for the beautifully fearsome creature away. It had attacked him. Still, part of him whispered it hadn't needed to die.

He reached for the bag and realized it had fallen off. *Wonderful.* His boots clacked on the cave floor as he circled the dragon's head.

Its mouth was open, and Regulus struggled to force it open further. His muscles strained as he pressed on its lower lip, the dragon's body already hardening. He had to crawl on its massive, serpentine tongue to reach his sword. It took a bit of effort to dislodge it from the back of the monster's mouth. Then he moved the dragon's jaw again to retrieve his hunting knife.

Wonder if my dagger's still in its foot. Sure enough, it was. He pulled it out, and hands full of green dragon blood-soaked blades, he began looking for his bag. Gold and silver coins, goblets, jewel-encrusted necklaces, and even a couple crowns were strewn about the cave. He searched in the fading light of the dying torch, which had been knocked to the ground during the brawl. He spotted the bag and reached in, holding his breath. His fingers closed around thick metal wire. He closed his eyes and released his breath.

He pulled out a handkerchief and wiped off his blades before he returned them to their respective sheaths. Riches glittered in the torchlight. He paused, then added a few jewel-covered gold trinkets to the bag. If he was going to play mercenary for the sorcerer, he might as well get paid. His weary steps dragged as he picked up the torch, fetched his helm, and left the dragon behind.

The torch didn't last long, and he had to make his way based on where the air smelled freshest. After running into a couple walls, he walked with his hands held out in front of him. *Etiros, please. Get me out of here.* Eventually, he spied a faint light, and made for it. The light grew blinding. As fresh air blew into his face and he glimpsed green, he sighed in relief.

Thank you. If Etiros still heard him after all he had done, Regulus didn't know. But he needed to believe he wasn't alone.

CHAPTER 12

THE CORRUPTION AROUND THE SORCERER'S TOWER HAD spread again. The dead trees started sooner. Charcoal leaves, as if they had been scorched, littered the forest floor and maintained a fragile grip on blackened branches. The white branches closer to the tower swayed, dead fingers clawing the sky. Sieger whinnied and snorted, tensing beneath Regulus.

"I know, boy." He rubbed Sieger's neck. "I don't like it, either."

Could air smell…lifeless? Not musty with the stench of decay. Just…empty, lacking vibrancy. Leaves made a dull rustle beneath Sieger's hooves. Sieger stepped on a twig, and a sharp snap interrupted the eerie silence.

The sorcerer waited in front of his tower, arms crossed, mouth pressed into a tight line. "I told you to *kill the dragon*, not *get killed* by the dragon!" His beard twitched in rhythm with his rapid, sharp speech. "It's exhausting keeping you alive!"

Then why bother? And try dying, that's not a leisure activity! But Regulus kept his tongue in check as he dismounted and removed his helm. He pulled the relic out of his bag. "I did kill it, my lord. And here's…whatever this is."

The sorcerer snatched the hollow gold egg out of his hand. "Doesn't matter." He looked it over, inspecting it. Apparently satisfied, he tucked it under his arm. His lips curled downward as he looked at Regulus. "This won't do."

The sorcerer held out his hand. Ivy-colored light emanated from his palm toward Regulus' abdomen. The first time Regulus saw the sorcerer flashed through his mind. Shards of green light. His men dying. Irrational dread coiled in his chest, but he shoved aside the painful memory. *He isn't attacking.* The torn armor screeched and groaned as the sorcerer mended the jagged hole left by the dragon's tail. Once done, the sorcerer turned toward the tower.

Regulus stared at the relic in the crook of the sorcerer's arm. Two years of service, and he still had the same questions. *Why do all this? What is so important? What's he doing?*

"Why are you still standing there?" The sorcerer looked over his shoulder, pausing at the door. "What do you want? A biscuit? Go away!"

"I fought a dragon." Regulus rubbed the back of his neck. Asking was a bad idea. But… "A *dragon*. Nearly died, again. And I wondered—"

The sorcerer laughed; deep, coarse, and mocking. "No. You still have plenty of debt to pay off." He smiled, a patronizing flash of white teeth. "I'm keeping track. But this piece is a good step. You're getting close. I'll release you as soon as we're even."

"Actually, my lord," Regulus took a deep breath, "I just wondered why."

The sorcerer's amused smile vanished. "Slaves don't know their master's business. You don't need to know what it's for to retrieve it, any more than a dog needs to know anatomy to chew on a bone."

Regulus' jaw tightened. He turned back to Sieger.

"Hargreaves."

He closed his eyes, then faced the sorcerer again. "Yes, my lord?"

"I don't like intrusive questions."

Anger and trepidation squeezed his chest. It wasn't fair. A question didn't demand an answer. A question wasn't dangerous. But he knew better. He bowed his head and braced for the pain. "I apologize, my lord."

The sorcerer tapped his forefinger against the relic. "Are you forgetting your place?"

"No, my lord. I apologize. I had no right to ask." He stared at the ground, outrage battling against fear the sorcerer's anger wouldn't be satisfied with hurting him. "Forgive me."

"I think your title has gone to your head. I was planning on a mercenary, not a lord."

Regulus gulped, unsure how to respond. Safest to say nothing. The pain would come. The sorcerer would let him go. He just needed to avoid angering the sorcerer into taking control of his body. *I can't hurt my friends again.*

"Do you need reminded how powerless you are?"

"No, my lord." Desperate, he knelt and bowed his head. He would suffer any humiliation to spare his men. "You are the Prince of Shadow and Ash. I am...nothing." Silently, he prayed to Etiros for mercy. Mercy for his friends. "I won't question you again, my lord."

The sorcerer was quiet. Regulus tapped his toes inside his boot, panic rising as he cursed his own stupidity. He bowed until his hot forehead touched cool earth. *Please. Please.*

"You've irritated me, Hargreaves. Between taking all my energy to keep you from dying, asking impertinent questions, and wasting my time, I'm feeling the need to hurt someone. Choose."

Regulus raised his head, the blood draining from his face. "My lord?"

"You, or one of your friends. Choose."

He didn't hesitate as relief flooded him. "Me."

"Predictable and boring. Suit yourself."

Searing heat and the sensation of thousands of tiny cuts raced up Regulus' right arm from the mark and spread over his chest before covering his whole body. He bit back a cry. The pain intensified, and a strangled scream caught in his throat. He fell forward on his hands, his arms shaking. He dug his fingers into the blackened dirt as darkness pressed in on the edges of his vision.

The pain pushed deeper, through his bones and organs, beyond bearing. His scream scraped his throat raw. The pain faded back toward his mark and stopped. Sweat rolled down his face, and he hung his head, his body still trembling.

"Next time," the sorcerer said as he headed into the tower, "you won't get to choose."

Regulus slept for a day and a half after arriving back at his estate. When he emerged from his room, he headed to Arrano's overgrown garden. Dresden appeared out of nowhere, waving a piece of parchment in the bright sunlight.

"I come bearing good news!"

Regulus eyed the parchment and grunted. He turned down another grass-infested path, his sword bumping a stone bench. As ever, Magnus followed close behind, his shaggy tan tail wagging leisurely, large pink tongue hanging out of his black muzzle.

"Oh, cheer up." Drez propped his arm on Regulus' shoulder and leaned on him, holding up the parchment. "'To Lord Regulus Hargreaves of Arrano,'" he read aloud. "'Sir Thomas Glower and Dame Isabelle Glower cordially invite you to join them for a feast to be held on their estate a week hence on the eleventh of Verdanmunth at six o'clock in the evening.' I told their messenger you would attend."

"Great. This is meant to cheer me?" Regulus shrugged Dresden off his shoulder.

"That's only half of the good news." Drez pulled another letter from the back of his belt and held it out, the unbroken seal toward Regulus. "I even had the courtesy not to read this one, despite my curiosity."

The wax bore an impression of a rearing unicorn. Regulus' breath caught, but he wouldn't give Dresden the satisfaction of admitting it. Unfortunately, he grabbed the parchment too eagerly, and Drez laughed.

Regulus turned away and opened the letter. The words indented the parchment and globs of ink marred the letters, as if she had been pressing too hard.

Dear Lord Regulus Hargreaves,

I apologize for any offense I caused. Please forgive my impertinence. I had no idea the Carricks were so prejudiced as to not invite you. If it helps, it was a miserable party. I hope I'll see you at some other party. I've had my fill of shallow nobles, and your honesty and acceptance are refreshing.

Sincerely,

Lady Adelaide Belanger

Regulus leaned against a tree, willing his heart to stop dancing. He should put the letter down. He should burn it. Instead, he read it again. And again. And again.

"Well, is it good news? Because you're clutching it like you're afraid it will turn to ash in your hands, and your expression keeps flickering between pleased and confused."

Regulus hesitated, then handed the letter to Dresden. Dresden read it and grinned as he handed it back. "I'm so glad I told the Glowers you're going. She'll likely be there."

"You're incorrigible." *And irritating. I can't see her again.* Because he knew, deep down, he wouldn't be able to stay away from her.

"Pick a good outfit—"

"Drez." Regulus rubbed Magnus' head. "The sorcerer says I'm getting close, but… I killed a dragon, and even that's not enough."

"You killed a dragon?"

"Did you say *dragon*?" a voice asked from Regulus' right.

Two of his knights, Caleb and Estevan, walked toward them. Both men wore swords at their sides. As usual, Estevan was playing with a knife. This one had a round hole in the end of the hilt, and he was spinning it around his forefinger and catching the grip. Spin, catch. Spin the opposite direction, catch.

Regulus didn't know where Estevan was from, because Estevan himself wasn't sure. His family were gypsies, and his accent was a strange amalgam of places he'd lived. A liberal sprinkling of freckles covered his tan face. His thick, curly brown hair refused to be tamed. The wing of a tattoo of a gryphon on his back peeked out from under his shirt collar at his shoulder. At twenty-two, Estevan was the youngest of Regulus' knights, and accordingly, the cockiest.

"Dragon," Regulus confirmed.

"Like, big, scaly, horned, fire-breathing, winged dragon?" Estevan pressed.

"Yes to everything but the wings."

Estevan whistled. "You kill it?"

"Barely."

"It kill you?" Estevan grinned.

"Hey!" Caleb smacked Estevan's shoulder. "Show a little respect."

Caleb was in his mid-thirties but liked to act much younger. He had a lanky yet strong build, as light and deadly as the long bows he favored. His unkempt dark blond hair hung around his pale face, and a scruffy short beard covered his cheeks and chin.

Estevan nodded. "Of course. We must always show proper respect for the dead." Both men put on melodramatically somber expressions and bowed their heads in mock respect.

Regulus rolled his eyes but chuckled. "Yes, it probably killed me." He grimaced at the memory of the dragon's sharp tail sliding out of his abdomen.

Estevan flipped the knife again. "Not an experience I envy. Still. Would've been something to see a real, live dragon."

"Something terrifying," Dresden said. "What would you do, throw a knife at it?"

"Of course." Estevan sighted down the blade. "Right at its eye. Blind it. Then when it tries to spit fire, throw one down its gullet."

"Hm." Regulus nodded. "Not a terrible plan. I'll keep that in mind. Maybe I'll use a bow, though."

"Yes, your knife-throwing skills are...non-existent." Estevan threw the knife past Regulus' head. It whirred past his ear, and Regulus turned as the knife stuck into a tree a few paces behind him. He turned back toward Estevan, who bowed with a flourish.

"Show-off."

"The words of the dead can't hurt me." Estevan strode past him, his posture self-assured. "We're headed to town and the tavern, if anyone is interested. Grabbing Perce and Jerrick, too."

Dresden snorted. "It's barely past three."

"By the time we arrive, it will be quarter to five," Caleb said.

Estevan retrieved the knife and stuck it in his boot. "Gives time to get a nice steak pie, down a few pints, flirt with a few barmaids, smoke a pipe, and get back at a decent hour."

"Well," Caleb grinned as he followed Estevan, "the hour we get back depends on how well the flirting goes."

A smile betrayed Regulus' amusement. He looked at Drez. "If nothing else, I better go to keep an eye on them."

"On one condition." Drez crossed his arms. "You promise to go the Glower's banquet and talk to Lady Belanger."

"I thought you'd be pleased I'm going with them, the way you go on about leaving the castle." Regulus headed toward the stables. "You going to stop me if I say no?"

He *did* want to go to the party. He wanted to see Adelaide. But he couldn't. The abomination who didn't die when a dragon ripped open his gut didn't deserve her. And when a misstep with the sorcerer endangered his loved ones, he couldn't put her in danger. *Not that the sorcerer would know about her. I could keep the relationship secret. I could be free soon.*

"Stop you? No." Dresden strolled next to him. "I'll get Caleb to sing and play his lute at the tavern, which will make Perceval drink more. Which will make it easy to trick Perceval into starting a brawl that Jerrick will join. Then I'll tell Leonora and Sarah you started the fight. Or at least didn't stop them."

"You wouldn't."

"Would. They'll let loose on you, then on their husbands, and then Perce and Jerrick will complain to you...it'll be a nightmare."

"Drez." Regulus ran his hand through his hair and rested it on the pommel of his sword. "I don't deserve Adel—"

"No." Drez shook his head, his eyes flashing. "I won't have it. You're more than good enough, and you deserve to be happy."

Arguing would only make Dresden more stubborn. Besides, he would like to believe Dresden. Regulus switched tactics. "It's too danger—"

"No. No excuses. Look at us." Drez spread his arms out. "We're all fine. You'll be free before long. You've managed not to anger the sorcerer in over a year and a half."

That I've told you. Still, Regulus' resolve was crumbling. He never would have guessed she would write him again, and it only heightened his curiosity and interest. Would she consider him as a suitor? It was a foolish thought, but he stubbornly wanted to know.

"I'm not kidding about Sarah and Leonora." Drez winked.

"Aw, fine." Regulus pushed Dresden away, frowning to keep from smiling. "I'll go! Barring any sorcerous intervention, I'll go."

Drez rubbed his shoulder, even though Regulus hadn't shoved him hard enough to warrant such drama. "Excellent." Dresden stuck his thumbs in his belt and whistled as he headed to the stables. Magnus bounded after Drez. Regulus followed, wondering if Adelaide liked dogs.

CHAPTER 13

THE DOOR CLICKED SHUT AND THE PRINCE OF SHADOW AND Ash leaned against it, allowing himself to catch his breath. Curse it all. He would never let on to Hargreaves that torturing him wasn't effortless. It wasn't terrible—already most of the expended magical energy had returned—but how often he needed to divert power into controlling Hargreaves made him irritable. At least it had some benefits.

He smiled, cherishing the agony on Hargreaves' face, the scream his slave had tried to suppress. A welcome diversion from the monotony of planning his vengeance.

He had known Hargreaves would choose pain for himself before he allowed any of his men to be harmed. However, torturing Hargreaves through the bond was far less draining than taking control of his body—especially with the fight Hargreaves put up. The man's mental thrashing whenever the Prince took over gave him a headache for hours afterward. He would rather not spend the requisite energy to force Hargreaves to hurt his own friends. But Hargreaves needn't know that. The threat was enough.

Fear was a powerful motivator.

The Prince ascended the stairs that wound around the interior of his tower, the top piece of the staff tucked under his arm. Willing slaves were considerably easier to control. He had required someone with a good heart to get past the magical enchantments around one of the other pieces, but he hadn't expected a mercenary to be so stubbornly moral. The ones he had sent to slaughter Monparth's mages had been bloodthirsty and grateful for the bond that let them dole out violence without risk to themselves. They had begged him not to release them, but he'd had no reason to let them leech from his sorcery after the mages were obliterated. Meanwhile, Hargreaves was desperate to lose his bond.

The Prince snorted. *Idiot.*

He set the gold oval topper next to the three rods that formed the rest of the staff. Only one piece left. He was close to deciphering its location. Some of what he'd discovered made him nervous, though. Potential complications to retrieving the final piece. Ah, well. He would solve that riddle when he heard it. Nothing would stop him from achieving his goal. Not this time.

The Prince sat at his desk and opened a faded leather-bound journal, marked with water stains and discolored with age. The brittle pages crackled. He laid his new journal open next to it, dipped his quill in ink, and returned to the arduous task of translating the old Monparthian.

He had work to do before he could unleash his vengeance on Monparth.

CHAPTER 14

SWEAT TICKLED THE BACK OF REGULUS' NECK AS HE ENTERED the Glower's banquet hall. Two rows of tables ran the length of the long hall, decked with candles and tin place settings on navy blue tablecloths. Tall candelabras lined the stone walls, positioned between large vases stuffed with fragrant flowers in bright colors. Some nobles sat at the long tables; others were being shown to their seats. He scanned the room for Adelaide but didn't see her. He couldn't decide if that made him more anxious or less. *This is stupid. It's just supper.*

"Good evening, Lord Hargreaves, Sir Jakobs." A servant stepped toward them and bowed. "This way."

"Pardon me," Dresden said, surprising Regulus. "Have the Drummonds arrived yet?"

"No, sir."

"Might it be possible for my lord to be seated next to Lady Belanger?"

The servant looked over his shoulder, forehead creased. "I fear the seating has already been arranged—"

Dresden pulled a pouch of coins off his belt. "I would gladly compensate you for any inconvenience."

Regulus stiffened. *A bribe?* What was Dresden thinking? But sitting next to Adelaide *would* make supper more interesting. The idea both excited and terrified him.

The servant's eyes darted around in mild alarm, but he discreetly took the pouch. "I've just remembered, you're seated over here, my lord." He made an adjustment in his course and indicated a couple seats. "I would take the seat on the left, my lord," he added.

Regulus nodded and he and Drez took their seats. "The hell, Drez?" he muttered.

"Breathe," Dresden whispered.

"I *am* breathing."

"You look like you're holding your breath."

He forced himself to relax. "This is a bad idea." His stomach roiled.

Dresden turned toward him, leaning his forearm on the table in front of the delicate tin plate. "What have we talked about?"

Surely Drez wasn't going to do this right here, right now.

"You need to *live* your life and stop moping over things you can't control. Choices, Regulus. Choose some joy." Dresden smiled. "Get to know her."

Regulus fiddled with his spoon, watching the flickering candle-light reflect in its dull surface. Fine, he wanted to get to know her. Didn't mean he should. Sometimes he wanted alcohol before noon. Didn't mean that was a good idea.

"Lord Hargreaves?"

Regulus snapped his head up and found himself looking into Adelaide's rich brown eyes outlined by dark lashes. His mind seemed to break. *Etiros, she's beautiful.* For a moment, he couldn't find his voice. "Lady Belanger." *How articulate.*

"It appears we are seated next to each other."

"Are we?" Regulus bolted to his feet and pulled out her chair. Next to her, Sir Gaius was helping his wife, with her now visible stomach bump, into her chair. Lord and Lady Drummond sat on Lady Minerva's other side. Adelaide sat and Regulus pushed her seat forward before retaking his own.

She smirked. "What a fortunate coincidence."

Regulus' jaw went slack, and Dresden stifled a chuckle. "I…"

"I'm sure our hosts won't notice." She laughed, and he calmed.

"Allow me to explain, my lady." Drez leaned forward, looking around Regulus at Adelaide. "Regulus mentioned wishing he could get to know you better, so I persuaded a servant to seat you together. Please forgive my minor transgression of protocol. I hope you don't find me impertinent."

Adelaide raised a brow, looking positively regal. "Sir Dresden Jakobs, right?"

"Yes, my lady."

"It sounds to me like Lord Hargreaves is fortunate to have you as a friend." Her eyes shone playfully.

A friend. As if two words could sum up their complicated relationship. All the times Regulus hadn't been a worthy friend to Dresden threatened to overwhelm him.

"Drez is a better friend than I deserve," he admitted. "He's had my back for years. We've been through everything together. There's no one I trust more or owe as much to."

Dresden laughed, but it sounded uncomfortable. "He owes me nothing. I'm far more fortunate to have Regulus as a friend."

As if that's true. He knew Drez meant it. He just didn't agree.

Adelaide didn't respond. Was she judging him for being too familiar with one of his knights? Or wondering about his past? She watched him, her head tilted, gaze intense. Heat crept up his neck and he looked away.

Across the room, a man stared at him. He looked closer. Nolan Carrick stood rigid, glaring. Without breaking eye contact, Carrick moved his hand to the dagger at his belt and gave the smallest shake of his head. Carrick smiled, as if nothing had happened, and followed a squire to a seat next to Sir Glower.

Regulus shifted and looked back at Adelaide. She watched Carrick take his seat, and his chest constricted with disappointment.

But her eyes narrowed, and her jaw tightened. She shook her head and her features relaxed. He recalled her letter. *"It was a miserable party."*

"Does this mean I didn't offend you?" Adelaide's quiet voice interrupted his confused thoughts. "You never wrote back."

His face burned. "No. I'm sorry I didn't respond. I've been traveling on business," he faltered, "for a friend." And he hadn't known what to say.

She traced a slender finger over the edge of her plate. "I'm truly sorry."

He grasped for a proper response. "I'm sorry you suffered a miserable party. Although, I assumed the Carricks would host extraordinary parties."

"Oh, the party was spectacular." Her hand curled into a fist, her voice dark. "The company was miserable." She darted a glance at Regulus, then fixated on her plate. "Have you…heard anything? About the Carrick's dance?"

"Should I have?"

"No." Her posture relaxed as she exhaled.

The gentle clanking of a fork against a goblet drew their attention to the head of the room. Sir Glower welcomed everyone and thanked them for coming and Etiros for providing for their safety and health.

As servants filled their goblets with wine, Adelaide spoke. "According to Sir Jakobs, you wanted to get to know me. What do you want to know?"

"Oh." His mind blanked. "I…well, I don't know much about you. What would you want me to know?"

"Hm. No one's ever asked me that." She smiled at a servant as he set a basket of bread in front of them.

Regulus studied Adelaide while she buttered a roll and thought. Her round cheeks and slender nose. The dark brown of her eyes. Her soft pink lips. Her hair, tumbling about her shoulders in black waves. Like a calm sea on a dark night. The wide collar of her crimson dress hugged her upper arms, leaving the top of her shoulders exposed. Her black hair against the rich brown of her skin and the vibrant contrast of the red nearly took his breath away. He forced himself to stop staring. A servant set down a roast duck and began carving it in front of them.

"I speak Khast," Adelaide said between bites of roll. "My mother taught Minerva and me, although I'm more fluent than Min. Mother always says, 'I may have left Khastalland, but I am and always will be a Khastallander. It is part of me, and it is part of you, even though you have never seen it, *Tha Shiraa*.'"

Regulus inclined his head, trying to remember the few Khast words he had picked up, but he hadn't had reason to think of them in years. "Thah Sheer-ah?"

She blushed and tucked a strand of hair behind her ear. "My mother's nickname for me, in Khast. *Tha Shiraa*. Little Tigress." She pulled a comb from the other side of her head and showed it to him. An ivory carving of a sleeping tiger curled into a ball, delicately painted in striking orange and black. "It's why she gave me this." She returned the comb to her hair.

"*Tha Shiraa*," he repeated. "Why tigress?"

"Too many times testing the limits, pushing the bounds of safety. And a penchant for speaking out of turn. Father said I was bold, and Mother agreed."

"Bold like a tigress." Regulus chuckled as he cut into the roast duck the servant set on his plate. "That's wonderful."

"Really?" Adelaide looked at him.

"Of course," he murmured, transfixed by the intensity of her eyes.

"Many find boldness…unfeminine," she said, not breaking eye contact.

He couldn't suppress a snort. "Many people are fools."

"Indeed." She finally looked away.

After a moment, she continued. "I have five half-siblings, my father's children with his first wife. The youngest, twins, were two when their mother died. The oldest was only eight." She poked the roast duck with her fork. "My father went to war shortly after and met my mother. He returned with a new wife who soon was pregnant. It was hard on them. Not as much when they were younger, but the older we got... We were different." She shrugged. "It didn't help I spent several years away as a child because I was—sickly." She cleared her throat. "Thank Etiros for Minerva, or I might have lost my mind."

Even as he empathized with her lack of connection with her half-siblings, he latched onto her mention of Etiros. Until that moment, he hadn't considered that most Khastallanders venerated the pantheistic god Prakasroht, not the creator-god worshiped in Carasom and Monparth. At least religious disagreements wouldn't be an issue, especially if they had children—*wait, what? Slow down.*

She gave him a weak smile. "So that's Adelaide Belanger. Half-noble daughter of a lord's second wife who speaks Khast and barely knows her half-siblings."

The loneliness and rejection in her words cut his heart. He had the sudden and strong urge to take her hand or caress her face. That would be wildly improper. A voice in the back of his mind urged caution, reminding him of the dangers of getting too involved, but he wasn't listening.

"What a strange way to describe yourself."

"What?" Adelaide glanced at him askance.

"If I were you," Regulus smiled, "I would say, 'Adelaide Belanger, daughter of a war hero, woman of intellect who speaks Khast and Monparthian, paragon of honesty and grace with the heart of a tigress.'"

She stared, and his palms grew slick. He sounded like an idiot boy, writing atrocious love poetry. Adelaide grinned, and the embarrassment faded. "I like your version better, too."

"Wait until I tell the men about this…" Drez whispered, so low Regulus barely heard him. Regulus stomped on his foot, and Drez jammed his knee into the table. A servant came by with a wine jug, and Regulus held up his goblet, ignoring Drez's glare.

"And how would you describe yourself, Lord Hargreaves?"

He swirled the wine in his goblet. *Bastard son of a lord of little account who became a mercenary, swore an oath that made him an evil sorcerer's slave, and has too many deaths on his conscience.*

"I'm afraid Regulus has never been good at self-praise." Dresden leaned around him. "Allow me. Regulus Hargreaves, a strong leader, a good man, and a selfless friend who needs to take better care of himself."

Regulus took a long drink and swallowed hard. *And a fool.* A fool who wished he hadn't come and wished the night would never end all at once.

Adelaide leaned on the table. "Tell me, Sir Jakobs—"

"My friends call me Dresden, my lady," Drez interrupted. "Or even Drez."

"All right, Dresden." Her smile looked full of mischief. "Be honest with me."

"On my honor."

She squinted and dropped her voice in a fake whisper. "Is Lord Hargreaves a vampire?"

Regulus' eyes widened. "Wh—"

"Oh, no," Dresden said, his tone serious. "He's a shape-shifting spirit."

Adelaide and Dresden both laughed, and Regulus realized how tense his shoulders were. He took a deep breath. "Hilarious."

She turned back to her food. "Tell me, Lord Hargreaves, what do you want me to know about you?"

What *did* he want her to know? What did he dare tell her?

Dresden elbowed his side. "Speak up, man, or I'll tell her every dirty prank you've ever pulled." Regulus suppressed his scowl.

"I wouldn't have thought you the prankster type." Confusion and amusement mixed in Adelaide's expression.

He wasn't sure what to make of that. "To be honest, Dresden is the prankster. I just sometimes helped. What type *do* you think me?"

She studied him, lips pursed. "Strong. Serious. Observant. Diligent." She paused. "Kind." She returned to her food. "But you still haven't answered."

He laughed nervously. "Right." He poked at the peas on his plate. So many things he could tell her. So many he couldn't. He recalled her teasing question, *is Lord Hargreaves a vampire?* Which rumor to address? "I didn't send my father's wife and my sister-in-law away. Or kill them."

Adelaide paused and lowered her fork, watching him.

"I offered to let them stay at Arrano, even after they challenged me, and I won against their champion." He couldn't take her unwavering regard any longer and traced his forefinger over the vine pattern in the tablecloth. "I hoped my father's wife might forgive me, but…" He shrugged. "She always hated me." *She wanted me dead.* "So they left. Wouldn't accept any help from me. I don't even know if they made it to Craigailte as they had planned."

Adelaide's fork rested on her plate with the same bite of food as she listened.

"I was a mercenary, but I believe in honor." He met her eyes. "I may be a killer, but I'm not a murderer." *Not by choice, at least.* "That's what I'd want you to know. To believe."

"Oh, Lord Hargreaves." Her sad smile made him feel uncomfortably vulnerable. "I'm sorry about the vampire comment.

I didn't mean… I never believed you killed them." They looked at each other for a long moment. She picked her fork back up.

"Well," Dresden said. "The prize for terrible supper conversation goes to Regulus bringing up murder."

Adelaide laughed, and Regulus' stomach unknotted enough for him to continue eating.

"Don't think you get out of sharing, Dresden," Adelaide said as she picked up her goblet. "What should I know about you?"

"Oh." Dresden shifted. "I fight with scimitars. I'm Carasian, although I grew up in Monparth, so I consider myself Monparthian. And… I am drawing a blank on things that are both interesting and appropriate to say."

Regulus snorted. "I wish I was surprised."

"All right, then…" Adelaide chuckled. "So you moved here with your family? I'd love to hear about them."

A burning coal settled in Regulus' stomach. He opened his mouth to shift the conversation, but Dresden answered, his tone casual.

"My parents moved before I was born, but I left my family to join a nobles' household when I was very young. Not far—a day's travel. Apparently, that was still too far to visit. I didn't really blame them, but I couldn't leave." Drez shrugged.

Regulus hoped his guilt wasn't written all over his face. His childhood guardian didn't let him or Dresden wander that far, but it still felt like Dresden's estrangement from his family was Regulus' fault. And the careful way Dresden chose his words, telling the truth while hiding he had left his impoverished family to be Regulus' servant, just reminded Regulus how much he was hiding from Adelaide.

"You don't talk to someone for years, they become strangers." Drez prodded the carrots on his plate. "By the time rejoining them was an option, I doubt they would have recognized me. It was easier not to go back. So Regulus got stuck with me." He clapped his hand on Regulus' shoulder and grinned. "We were a couple hot-headed boys without close family, so we became mercenaries and traveled the world."

Adelaide's soft eyes looked between Regulus and Dresden, compassionate, but also curious. "I'm glad you two found each other."

"Wait." Dresden sat up straighter. "I've got it. I dislike rules."

"Really?" Sarcasm dripped from Adelaide's voice. "I never would have guessed, sir bribed-the-servant." Regulus flushed.

Dresden choked. "I never said—"

"*Persuaded?* Mm-hm." She lifted a brow, a poorly suppressed smile twisting her lips. "Was it worth it?"

"You tell me," Drez said. If Regulus didn't know better, he would have called his tone flirtatious.

Adelaide cocked her head, her gaze flicking from Dresden to Regulus. Regulus' heart about stopped. He swore her cheeks pinkened. "I'm glad you dislike rules."

The conversation turned to less personal matters—hobbies and interests and likes and dislikes. As they ate and chatted, Regulus' nervousness abated. For the first time in his life, he didn't feel out of place among the nobles, didn't feel like an unwanted intruder. He felt like he belonged.

CHAPTER 15

ADELAIDE COULDN'T REMEMBER A BETTER BANQUET. NOT that the food itself was special. The Carricks, with their great wealth, had provided better. But the company... Regulus Hargreaves was a tantalizing mystery. A little awkward, but she found it authentic and endearing. He clearly didn't judge her for her bloodline, nor did he seem superficially attracted to her Khastallander features. And he hadn't tried to touch her once. She still knew precious little about Regulus, but what she knew, she liked.

As he described places he'd visited in Khastalland, sights and sounds and tastes, she studied him. He had a smile that crinkled his eyes. A deep, hearty laugh. He radiated an acceptance and understanding she found rare. Dresden grabbed Regulus' arm, laughing as he reminded Regulus of a humorous anecdote from their travels. A simple gesture, one between friends, not lord and vassal. Their easy rapport spoke volumes about Regulus' character and humility.

The rough, shiny scar that ran from the outside of Regulus' right eye through the corner of his mouth to his chin gave him a roguish quality. His eyes were sharp, his movements controlled but energetic. He seemed on alert, taut, like a drawn bowstring. He felt dangerous yet not threatening, like a friendly wolf.

Perhaps his frank admission to being a mercenary, a killer, should have bothered her. But Father had found Mother while fighting a war, and bandits' blood had stained her own weapons, so she couldn't fault him. Everything about his earnest and quiet demeanor indicated he wasn't a blood-thirsty savage without honor any more than her own father was.

Supper ended; servants cleared the tables. Minstrels played, the notes of the flute and lyre drifting over the sound of multiplying conversations. Minerva and Gaius wandered away. Even Dresden left with a remark about a pretty girl that made Regulus sigh and roll his eyes. But neither of them made any move to leave their chairs.

"Have you heard of this Black Knight?" Adelaide asked. "Sir Gaius told me some strange rumors."

"Yes." Regulus cleared his throat and worked his jaw as if the question irritated him. "I've heard of him. Often."

"Do you think he's real?"

"Yes. I'm afraid I do."

She turned and wrapped her arm around the back of her chair. "You haven't seen him, have you?"

"No." He shifted in his seat. "Drez did. From a distance. Not recently."

"Really?" Adelaide made a mental note to ask Dresden about his sighting later. "It's said someone killed a dragon in the Singing Caves. Some are claiming the Black Knight was seen in the area. Lord Drummond says dragons don't exist in Monparth anymore, and neither does the Black Knight. But people are selling dragon scales." She rested her chin on the back of the chair. "What do you think?"

He went pale and closed his eyes as sweat gleamed on his forehead.

"Lord Hargreaves?" Adelaide reached for his arm, alarmed. "Are you all right?" He looked at her hand on his arm. She snatched it back. *Too forward, Adelaide!*

"I'm sorry." He sighed. "I've fought a dragon before. It brought back some...painful memories."

She gasped. "You...you've fought a dragon?" Words tumbled out of her mouth. "When? Where? How? Did you kill it? Did it breathe fire? What did it look like?"

Regulus massaged his forehead, his expression pinched.

"I'm sorry," she blurted. "I didn't mean to pry."

"No, no." He smiled, but it didn't reach his eyes. "I can't blame you." He chuckled. "Even if I wasn't prepared for so many questions on the subject from a lady."

"Oh." She snapped her mouth closed and angled away.

"No, I didn't mean that negatively!" Regulus said quickly. "I appreciate that you're interested. I just wasn't expecting it—I have little experience talking to ladies."

Her heart softened and she turned back toward him. "It must have been horrible. You don't need to tell me."

"And disappoint you?" He shook his head. "Let's see... Yes, a real, live dragon. Not terribly long—"

"You have some nerve, Hargreaves," Nolan's voice interrupted at Adelaide's shoulder. She looked up to see him glowering as if Regulus had insulted the entire Carrick line. His casual stance and crossed arms relayed a haughty and careless belief in himself, likely in his own superiority. His short, light brown hair had been perfectly combed.

"Pardon?" She looked back at Regulus, who glared at Nolan.

"Should you even be here?" Nolan asked, ignoring her. "Let alone talking with someone of Lady Belanger's quality."

"I was invited," Regulus said evenly. "Same as you."

"Same as me?" Disdain rang in every word Nolan spoke. "Not even close. I didn't need to bribe a servant to avoid sitting at the end of the hall." He stepped past Adelaide's shoulder, closer to Regulus. "It's not safe to let a mongrel wolf into the house with the dogs. The Glowers should know better."

Adelaide gasped and stood. "Sir Nolan!"

Nolan put an arm around her shoulders protectively—no, possessively. "Don't worry. He won't bother you any longer."

She shoved his arm off. "Bother me? Lord Hargreaves isn't the one bothering me. He has been nothing but a gentleman all evening. The only wolf here is you and your insolent pride. You owe Lord Hargreaves an apology."

"I—what?" Nolan lowered his voice as he grabbed her arm. She stared at his hand, dumbfounded. "Hargreaves is no gentleman, I don't—"

She yanked her arm away. "Touch me again without my consent and I will stab you."

"*Stab* me?"

In a swift, fluid motion, Adelaide bent down and drew the dagger out of her boot. She pointed the dagger at Nolan. "Regulus is no threat. And if he were, I can take care of myself."

"I meant no offense to you, Adelaide—"

"But you caused offense. And you certainly meant offense to Regulus." Warmth spread through her body as her magic kindled. She took a deep breath, forcing herself to be calm and keep her power in check. "You should leave before you make things worse."

A vein in Nolan's forehead bulged. He looked at her, then behind her, eyes flashing. He bowed curtly. "Forgive me, my lady, for having your best interests at heart." He opened and closed his mouth a few times before giving the most forced smile Adelaide had ever seen. "I spoke out of concern for a lady's wellbeing, safety, and reputation. I beg your pardon, Lord Hargreaves." He strode away.

In the wake of his departure, she realized several nearby nobles were staring and whispering. She dropped her hand, hiding her dagger in the folds of her skirt. At least the interaction might end any rumors she was courting Nolan.

She turned back to Regulus and almost bumped into his chest; he stood so close behind her. The skin around his long scar pulled tight and puckered around his deep frown. His features softened as he lowered his gaze to her face.

"Bold like a tigress," he murmured, smiling.

Adelaide hid her smile by sheathing her dagger and retaking her seat. "I apologize. He—"

"I've heard worse." Regulus rubbed the back of his neck. He sat without looking at her. "What he said…about your reputation." His throat bobbed. "He's likely right."

"What?"

"My blood is…tainted. My past—"

"I told you, I don't care."

"They do." He motioned around them.

She hesitated, then spoke quietly. "I only know from accidental eavesdropping, but my half-siblings resent our mother for…sullying Father. And for replacing their mother." She bit her cheek. "They said Minerva and I would make better servants than nobility."

Regulus winced.

She indicated the room. "So, I don't particularly care what *they* might think, Lord Hargreaves."

"A minute ago…" His posture relaxed as he glanced at her. "You called me Regulus."

Heat rushed up her neck to the tips of her ears. "I…did I?"

"You don't have to stop. If you like." Regulus reddened. "May I call you Adelaide?"

"I'd like that." Her voice came out soft. His piercing gray eyes glittered as the corner of his mouth quirked upward. Her stomach fluttered.

Oh. Oh, no.

I like him.

CHAPTER 16

THE BARRIER OF BLUE LIGHT STRETCHED FROM FLOOR TO ceiling down the length of one side of her bed. Adelaide smiled to herself. She had lost count of how many times she had attempted conjuring a barrier. Only two days prior—the day after the banquet, in fact—had she managed to get a barrier about the size of a small shield to stay up after she broke the link between the barrier and her hands. She walked around the edge of her bed, examining the thin barrier of shimmering, near-transparent azure light.

Now for the real test. She picked a throwing knife up off her desk and threw it at the barrier. It hit the barrier, and a ripple of energy pulsed out from the point of impact as the knife bounced back and fell onto her bed.

"Yes!" She clapped her hands over her mouth. Her heart hammered as she listened.

No one came knocking.

The barrier held.

Adelaide giggled and tried throwing the knife again. Same result. "I wonder…"

She walked around to the other side and raised her glowing palm. A point of light appeared over her outstretched hand and exploded into small ball of flame. She launched the small fireball at the barrier.

The barrier absorbed the fire with a sound like distant wind.

Adelaide gave a little jump. She rubbed her hands together, pondering what to try next.

Someone knocked on the door of her room and she nearly jumped out of her skin. "Just a moment!" She waved her hand, and the barrier wavered then disappeared.

After taking a moment to collect herself and slow her panicked breathing, she unlocked and opened the door. One of the Drummonds' maids stood at the door, holding a short, square wooden box.

"A messenger just delivered these for you, my lady." The maid offered the box and a letter with a slight bow of her head. "From Sir Nolan Carrick."

Adelaide rolled her eyes. "Thank you." She closed the door and sat on her bed. The letter bore her name in a neat, flowing script. She broke the crimson wax seal of a gryphon on the back and read quickly.

Dear Lady Adelaide Belanger,

I pray you will forgive me for my inexcusable behavior at the Glower banquet. I admit I had drunk too much wine, and I am not ashamed to admit that I acted partly out of jealousy for your attentions. You are a rare and incomparable lady of good name and angelic beauty, and you deserve the affection of a man of similarly good name and appearance. I acted rashly, not as a gentleman, I fear, but as a man blinded by his admiration for you and a desire to see you unsullied by the dark forces of this world. I urge you, as a man of chivalry and honor, and as one who cares for you, not to trust Regulus Hargreaves. Please accept this humble token of my sincere apology and my admiration for your strong spirit, kind heart, and indescribable beauty.

Yours in heart and soul,
Sir Nolan Carrick

Adelaide made a disgusted sound and tossed the letter aside. More out of curiosity than anything else, she lifted the lid off the box. Inside, on a blue velvet cloth, lay a necklace. It was a collar, really, formed of solid, flat silver wire, shaped to fit around the neck, with an elegant swirling design framing either side of a large, oval moonstone she guessed would rest between her collarbones if she put it on. She had no intention of ever doing so.

"Forgive me, and love me, because I'm rich!" she muttered. She replaced the lid and stuck the box and letter in a drawer in the vanity desk. She rolled her neck, pushing thoughts of Nolan's stubborn pride and selfish behavior away. Back to practicing magic.

Another knock on the door, and Adelaide stifled a groan. The same servant held a basket covered with a rough brown cloth with another letter resting on top. The maid giggled and smiled. "Just delivered for you, from—"

"Nolan Carrick, yes, yes." She halfheartedly reached for the basket.

"No, my lady." The maid winked. "From Lord Regulus Hargreaves of Arrano."

An unexpected catch in her breath. Adelaide grabbed the basket with a little more intensity than necessary or proper. "Thank you." She slammed the door shut as she hurried to her bed. The letter had her name on the front, although not in as precise and elegant of a script. A red seal on the back was imprinted with a rose over a pair of crossed swords. She broke the seal and fell back on the bed, holding the letter above her as she read.

SELINA R. GONZALEZ

Dear Lady Adelaide Belanger,
I greatly enjoyed your company at the Glowers' feast. Your conversation turned an evening that would have been long and trying into an enjoyable night that passed far too quickly. I am impressed by your wit, your honesty, your thoughtfulness, and your bold heart. I hope I am not being too forward in sending a small token of my admiration. I hope my little gift reminds you of home—and keeps me in your thoughts, as you are in mine. I look forward to when our paths cross again. Until then, I shall have to settle for fond memories of your gentle face framed by silky black hair and the deep warmth of your dark brown eyes.
Sincerely yours,
Regulus

In a different, more curving script at the bottom, was a postscript.

P.S. Regulus threw this note away because he feared it was too sentimental and forward, but I switched out the letters because this one is a more accurate representation of his heart. Perhaps it can be our secret? I should very much like to live.
—Dresden Jakobs

Adelaide chuckled and reread the note. It was sappy, yes. But it felt honest. Real. She rolled over and pulled the cloth off the top of the basket and gasped.

Nalotavi. Four large, perfectly flaky, chocolatey and spicy smelling nalotavi rolls. She tossed the cloth back over the basket

154

and raced down the hall to Minerva's study. She didn't even bother knocking, just walked in, basket in hand.

Minerva looked up in surprise from her needlework. "You startled me. Is everything—"

"Min, look!" She held the basket in front of her sister and yanked off the cloth.

Min's mouth fell open. "Is that…"

"Nalotavi, yes!" Adelaide grabbed one out of the basket and took a bite. "Mmm." She let the flaky, buttery, chocolate-laced pastry dissolve in her mouth and savored the gentle kick of the ginger and cinnamon at the end. Minerva didn't wait for an invitation; she took one of the other rolls and bit into it.

Contented ecstasy spread over Minerva's face. "Where did you get this?" she asked after several bites.

Adelaide finished chewing and swallowed. "A gift. From Lord Regulus."

"Mm-hmmm." Minerva winked.

"Stop it." She took a large bite to signal she wouldn't answer any more questions.

"Oh!" Minerva gasped and waved Adelaide over. "Come here, hurry!"

"What's wrong?" Adelaide set the basket and her roll on an empty armchair and rushed to kneel next to her sister, her insides knotting.

"Nothing, here!" Min grabbed her hand and pressed it to her round stomach. "Right…" She shifted Adelaide's hand over the soft fabric of her dress. "Hm…"

Something jabbed against Adelaide's palm. "Min! Was that—" The baby moved again.

"Mm-hm!" Minerva laughed, still holding Adelaide's hand on her belly.

"Oh, Min." Adelaide beamed, her throat tight and eyes moist.

"I've been waiting for the little one to move when you're in the room." Minerva chuckled. "Gaius is going to be jealous. He keeps falling asleep with his hand on my stomach; he loves feeling the baby move. I think he's more impatient for him or her to arrive than I am."

"Well, over halfway there." Adelaide pulled her hand away, as the baby seemed to have gotten comfortable.

Minerva pointed to the basket. "Might I steal another nalotavi roll? I think the baby likes them." She winked and Adelaide laughed.

"Fine. For the baby." She handed Minerva another roll and picked her own back up.

"I have to admit," Min said between bites, "this is working well in Lord Hargreaves' favor."

Adelaide didn't respond, but she had to agree.

CHAPTER 17

REGULUS SAT IN A LARGE ARMCHAIR IN HIS ROOM ACROSS FROM the small fire crackling in the fireplace, feet propped up on a cushioned stool. The orange light of the fire provided the only illumination now that the sun had set. He rubbed his thumb over the mark on his arm. Nearly three weeks had passed since he had returned from killing the dragon, and he hadn't heard from the sorcerer. In the two years since receiving the mark, there had been times he had gone three months without the sorcerer contacting him. Still, if the sorcerer was too busy to bother him, what was he busy with?

The sudden appearance of Magnus' large head in his lap pulled him out of his gloomy thoughts. "Hey, boy." He scratched under Magnus' chin. Magnus licked the rough, scarred mark on Regulus arm. "I'm afraid you can't clean that off, buddy." He pulled his sleeve back down and massaged Magnus' big, floppy ears. Magnus stood with his head resting on Regulus' thigh. As Regulus massaged his ears and the side of his head, Magnus closed his eyes and panted. Someone knocked on the door.

"Come in."

Dresden walked in, his face like stone. "Care to explain this?" He held up a piece of parchment. Magnus left to rub against Dresden's legs.

"Explain what?" Regulus knit his brows. "Is that a letter?"

Drez strode over and shoved the parchment in his face. "You left this in the dining hall."

As Regulus' eyes focused on the writing in the dim light, he recognized it as the letter confirming his entry into the Etchy Tournament. "Oh. That. I was going to tell you about that."

"When? It's in four days! We'll have to leave the day after next!" Dresden dropped the letter in Regulus' lap as Magnus curled up on the rug in front of the fireplace. "'Oh, Drez, get ready for a trip. Where? The Etchy Tournament, time to go, no time to talk.'"

Regulus ducked his head. "Something of the sort did cross my mind."

"Reg, there's a reason you don't do tournaments!" With a groan, Drez sat on the end of Regulus' bed.

"I know—"

"Then explain! Did the sorcerer tell you he won't need you for the next week?"

"Well, no—"

"So you could have to up and leave with no explanation?"

"That wouldn't be so strange—"

"And has your superhuman strength disappeared recently?"

"No—"

"Are you still healing supernaturally quickly?"

"Drez—"

"Is sorcery still a capital offense? What changed, Regulus? What?" Dresden looked uncharacteristically tired as he drew his hand down his face. "You're going to get caught."

Regulus stared at the fire. Every objection Dresden raised and more had already occurred to him. He knew he was being foolish; he just didn't care. Because for once, something was going right.

"I can be careful. I can hold myself back. I've practiced, you've seen it."

"When have you ever cared about tournaments?" Drez walked over to the fireplace. He knelt and scratched Magnus' head. "You told me you didn't want to take part in the nobles' games of vanity and posturing, regardless of the danger of doing so with your… Condition."

"Things change."

"What changed?" Dresden leaned against the wood-paneled wall next to the fireplace and crossed his arms. "Based on the checklist I went down, nothing…has…" A stricken expression came over his face. "Don't say it. Don't you say it."

Regulus offered a guilty half smile. "You wanted this."

"Oh, for the love of…" Drez rubbed his forehead. "Do you even know if she will be there?"

"She asked if I'd be there. I couldn't tell her no." *The yes was out of my mouth before I could stop myself.* He couldn't disappoint Adelaide now. And even though it was dangerous—for himself and Adelaide—he wanted to go. After she pulled a dagger on Carrick, Regulus knew he was a lost cause. He would do anything she asked. The way her eyes lit up when he said he'd be there… *She's making me reckless.*

"You're an idiot."

Yes, probably. "I'll be careful. I won't be found out." He looked down at his hands. "But if something goes wrong…well, same plan. None of you knew anything."

"I'm not abandoning you, Reg." Dresden's voice was tight with anger. "The others won't, either. Don't you get that yet?"

It's the only reason I keep coming back. "I'm not letting any of you die because of me."

"You're only in this mess because of me and the others," Dresden said quietly.

He took his feet off the stool and sat forward in his chair. "No. This was my choice. Something goes wrong; you swear on everything you can think of you didn't know. Or what is the point of what I've done?"

Dresden glowered at the floor in silence. "Well...don't get caught and it won't be an issue." He straightened. "So, you really like her?"

No. I think I might love her. "I know I shouldn't—"

Drez cursed. "Stop. You don't have to be afraid of being happy."

"I'm not afraid of being happy. I'm afraid of hurting her." Regulus rubbed the tension building in his shoulder. "When I'm here, it's easier to tell myself it's dangerous. But when I'm around her..." He shrugged, his face heating. *I believe in a better life.*

"You're more yourself." The corner of Drez's mouth pulled up in a bittersweet smile. "You better win. Make this ridiculous risk worth it."

Regulus smiled wryly. "Obviously."

CHAPTER 18

THE TOURNAMENT GROUNDS WERE ALREADY BUZZING WITH activity as Adelaide dismounted. She held her hand up to shade her eyes from the bright afternoon sun as Gaius helped Minerva out of their carriage. Lord and Lady Drummond had decided not to attend the tournament as Lord Drummond had sprained his ankle. All the better for Adelaide, who could get away with riding Zephyr instead of being trapped in the carriage. Since Lady Drummond wasn't around to purse her lips at Adelaide's fashion choices, Adelaide wore a comfortable riding dress.

The close-fitting bodice of the gray-blue dress had long, fitted sleeves. The skirt, split beneath a wide black belt, parted when she walked to reveal a dark blue, smaller skirt that came to her mid-thigh. While still Monparthian and conservative in style, the split skirt would have scandalized Gaius' prim-and-proper mother.

Adelaide wandered toward whatever caught her attention. She admired a fine bay stallion here, looked at the archery field being assembled there. Gaius and Minerva followed as she wove between tents and rushing servants and squires leading enormous destriers. Dust coated everything, and the air smelled of manure, cooking food, and sweat.

As they walked, Adelaide spotted a large group of men. They wore clean but plain clothes, and most had a sword on their belt, but none wore armor. Probably knights there serving their lords and not competing; a few of the younger ones might be squires. A glint of sunlight on flying metal caught her eye, and she looked closer, slowing. Another glint of metal. Knives. They were throwing knives. A thrill went through her, and she sped toward the group.

Several knives with red handles were embedded in a large, sprawling beech tree a few paces away from the group. A few of the red-handled knives had blue-handled knives near them. Sometimes the red and blue were right next to each other, sometimes they had a good bit of space. Plenty of holes showed where knives had been thrown and removed.

A stocky man with a balding head and bushy black beard threw another blue-handled knife. It scraped across a branch, just below a red-handled knife, but fell to the ground. Several men groaned. The thrower stood next to a post with three more blue-handled knives stuck in it. Adelaide watched with interest as the man threw the remaining knives with no better luck.

"Not bad," a thin man with salt-and-pepper hair said. "But Estevan wins another round." Several men grumbled while others gloated as money exchanged hands. A boy of about ten ran out to the tree and pulled all the knives free.

"Any other takers?" Salt-and-Pepper asked.

"What exactly is going on?" Adelaide asked a lean man with a weathered face and blond hair.

He looked at her in surprise. "Oh, just a bit of fun, m'lady. That there is Estevan." He pointed at a young man of average height and a thin but muscular build with tan skin and thick, curly brown hair. The dark edge of a tattoo showed just above his collar. "He's about one of the best knife-throwers there is. He gets the first throw. His opponent throws second. If he can get all of his knives within four fingers' breadth of Estevan's, he wins. If not, Estevan wins."

Adelaide nodded, as Salt-and-Pepper kept asking for volunteers. "I take it Estevan hasn't lost yet."

"No, m'lady."

"Come on," the older man crooned. "Is no one bold and skilled enough to knock this upstart down a peg or two? Someone must want to try their hand at it."

"I'll throw." Adelaide said it before she even realized she was speaking. Minerva sighed behind her and Gaius choked.

Amusement, shock, and confusion showed on the men's faces. Adelaide cleared her throat. "I'll throw," she repeated. No way would she back down now.

"With all due respect my lady," Salt-and-Pepper said, looking uncomfortable, "this is a gambling game—"

Adelaide reached into the purse at her belt and pulled out a few silver coins. "Is this enough?"

"Um…" The man looked lost and confused, so Adelaide smiled sweetly at Estevan.

"Won't you let a lady have a little fun?"

Estevan chuckled. "I'm not going to make it easy for you."

Adelaide grinned. "I should hope not. Fair's fair."

"All right… I guess the lady throws." Salt-and-Pepper shrugged.

Estevan stepped forward, and the boy stuck the red-handled knives into the post. Estevan threw in rapid succession, each knife burying deep into the oak in different places and angles. Adelaide studied him, noting his ease, balanced stance, and excellent follow-through. Once he'd thrown all eight knives, he stepped back. "My lady."

The men whispered to each other and a few sniggered, but she ignored them and handed the man in charge her silver. As she walked to the post, she studied the position of the knives in the tree. All right. A few tricky angles and a couple thinner branches. But not terrible. The boy stuck the blue-handled knives into the post and stepped away.

Adelaide pulled the first one free and held it for a moment, judging its weight and balance. She tossed it in the air and caught it a couple times. She took a deep breath, stood as near as she could to where Estevan had stood, and threw the knife.

CHAPTER 19

"OKAY, BUT DO YOU *NEED* TO DO THREE EVENTS?" DRESDEN asked as they walked across the dusty tournament grounds.

People were everywhere. Noblewomen cast furtive glances their way and noblemen poorly hid their surprise at seeing Regulus. Young men caroused and winked at giggling young women. Servants hurried to do their masters' bidding and freemen shouted to each other as they finished constructing rough arenas and stands with benches for the audience. The air was rank with the smell of horses. A lord whose name he'd forgotten cast a suspicious glance his way, but Regulus squared his shoulders. He had every right to compete.

Regulus stepped around a pile of horse manure. "Define *need*."

Dresden rolled his eyes. "I get the joust. What's the point if you enter a tournament and don't joust, right? Sword makes sense, even if it's a touch risky. Archery, though?"

"I've been practicing so much, I'd like to see how I do," Regulus said, a little defensively.

"Archery has never been your strongest point."

"Then there's room for improvement. If nothing else, watching the others will give me some ideas."

"You are a strange man."

"I suppose you would know, wouldn't you?"

Dresden snorted. He pointed at a group of men. "Looks like Estevan is getting up to mischief already."

"Oh?" Regulus looked as Estevan threw a knife at an oak tree and stepped back. "Should have known we'd find him throwing knives. Likely gambling, too." They ambled toward the group to see how his opponent would fare. Regulus stumbled.

"Is that—"

"Adelaide," Regulus breathed. Adelaide strode to the post were Estevan had stood moments before. Her blue dress parted as she walked, revealing black boots and fitted breeches. A boy stuck several knives in the post.

"She's not…throwing knives…is she?" Dresden asked.

Adelaide pulled out one of the knives, hefting it in her hand.

Regulus waved his hand. "Khastallanders teach women to use daggers and throwing knives. So…"

"So she thought she'd compete against Estevan?" Dresden shook his head as they stopped at the edge of the group of bystanders.

Adelaide adjusted her stance, raised her arm. She threw the knife. With a flash of reflected sunlight, it arced through the air and buried in the tree with a soft thud, less than a palm's breadth from one of Estevan's knives. She tilted her head to the side, then grabbed another knife. The onlookers, most of whom had been talking and several laughing, had fallen silent. She threw the next knife, then threw the rest as quickly as she could pull them from the post, which was impressively fast. When she finished, she leaned back on her heels, crossed her arms, and grinned at Estevan.

All her knives had landed close to Estevan's. Three of her knives were practically touching his. Estevan stared at the tree, jaw slack. Silence. Regulus looked back and forth between the knives and Adelaide's jubilant expression. Her eyes sparkled over her confident smile. Regulus' heart squeezed strangely. *Etiros, I'm in love.*

"Let's hear it for the lady," one man shouted. The rest of the congregated men cheered, and Adelaide blushed and gave a small curtsy. A few of the men looked downcast as they handed over coins to jubilant friends.

"We have a new winner," said a man with gray-flecked black hair. He handed Adelaide a handful of coins. "Most impressive, m'lady."

Adelaide pocketed her winnings and crossed over to Estevan with a smile. "Excellent throwing."

"You too," Estevan said slowly, jaw still slack. He shook his head and smiled. "I'm sorry. That was...spectacular. Congratulations, Lady...?"

"Belanger."

"Lady Belanger." Estevan's eyes went wide. "B-Belanger?" Regulus watched in amusement as terrified realization dawned on Estevan's face.

"Yes...?" Adelaide chuckled awkwardly.

Regulus walked up to them. "Lady Adelaide."

She looked up and beamed. "Lord Regulus!"

He smiled. "I see you've met another of my knights, Sir Estevan Wolgemuth."

Estevan bowed, although his face was red. "It's an honor to meet you, my lady, even an honor to lose to you. Reg—Lord Hargreaves speaks highly of you."

"Does he?" She pushed some of her hair back behind her ear, momentarily hiding her face.

"Never letting you live this down," Dresden whispered to Estevan. Estevan scowled and went to retrieve the knives from the tree.

Sir Gaius and Lady Minerva came up next to Adelaide. Sir Gaius chuckled and shook his head. "I knew you threw knives, but by my sword, that was something to watch." Minerva elbowed him. "What? Swearing? Your sister just gambled and threw knives against a man she didn't even know, I think I can be forgiven for an innocent oath."

Regulus bowed. "Sir Gaius. Lady Minerva."

"Lord Hargreaves," they said in unison as they bowed and curtsied.

"Dresden and I were on our way to see the jousting arena." He looked at Adelaide. "Perhaps you all would walk with us?"

"We would love to," Adelaide said.

Regulus smiled. "Excellent." For a moment, he hesitated. He offered her his arm. She placed her hand in the crook of his elbow and stepped closer to him. Close enough her skirt brushed his leg. He cleared his throat and started toward the jousting arena.

Dresden and Sir Gaius and Minerva fell behind them. Regulus suspected this to be on purpose, probably a design of Dresden's. But he couldn't think of anything other than Adelaide's hand on his arm.

"I thought Estevan was the best knife-thrower I'd ever met." He chuckled. "I may have to re-evaluate."

"That wasn't exactly ladylike, I suppose."

He looked down at her in surprise. "What? Why not?"

She looked up, brow creased. "Gaius is right. I gambled *and* threw knives in competition against someone I didn't even know. Not things ladies are supposed to do."

"Why?"

Adelaide wrinkled her nose. "I don't know why. I've been asking for years and no one will tell me!"

They laughed and Regulus felt warmth spread through his chest.

"It truly doesn't bother you?"

Regulus shrugged. "Can I be honest?"

"All right…"

"It was beautiful."

Adelaide tripped forward and he caught her shoulders. She leaned into his side for the briefest moment, and his lungs squeezed. She steadied herself, returning her hand to the crook of his elbow. He swallowed hard. Forced himself to breathe.

"There was a rock," she muttered.

After a moment, Regulus continued. "I saw beauty. Confident dignity in your posture. Sophistication in your movements, grace in the arc of the blades. I saw nothing unladylike. Just elegant, mesmerizing strength. You know your own capabilities, and that confidence is attractive."

Adelaide looked at him sideways, a smile dancing at the corner of her lips. "Attractive?"

His face heated. "I…um…" Panic rose in his chest. Had it been too forward to say that?

"I suppose you called my *confidence* attractive," Adelaide said, her voice thoughtful. "So, there's room for debate on whether *I* am attractive."

Their eyes met. In unison, they just…stopped walking. Stood there. So close together. Her lips parted slightly, and he felt the sudden, strong urge to lean down and kiss her.

"No," he whispered, his voice hoarse. "No debate. Not from me."

"If we're being honest," she murmured, "you're pretty good-looking yourself."

His heart thudded. "Better without the scar, I'd imagine," he said without thinking.

She cocked her head to the side and grinned. "I like it."

He ran his free hand through his hair, then rubbed the pommel of his sword. His scar? She…liked it?

A woman cleared her throat in an obvious attempt at getting their attention. Adelaide reddened as they stepped back from each other and her hand slipped off his arm.

"Having a good conversation, are we?" Minerva said as she walked up to them with Dresden and Gaius. Dresden winked at Regulus. Hopefully Adelaide hadn't noticed.

"Yes, *actually*," Adelaide replied. "*Ahpak, bes bahda dahlen ped, hei neah?*" Regulus recognized the Khast but didn't have any idea what she had said.

Minerva giggled and responded in Khast.

Whatever Minerva had said made Adelaide's cheeks darken. "*Kop reho!*"

That he thought he understood. Best guess? *Shut up.*

Minerva held her pregnant stomach as she laughed again.

Gaius looked at Regulus with sympathy. "They do this sometimes. It's most unfair."

"Maybe you should learn Khast," Dresden said.

"Minerva tried to teach me, but I fear I'm a poor student." Gaius wrapped his arm around Minerva's shoulders, and Regulus envied how comfortable and at ease they looked, with her shoulder tucked between his chest and arm.

"Shall we continue?" Adelaide asked, looking as if she had recovered her composure.

"Right." Regulus nodded. "Nearly there."

CHAPTER 20

ADELAIDE FOCUSED ON MAINTAINING A COMPOSED EXTERIOR as they continued on their way. She left a little extra space between her and Regulus and didn't take his arm again. She still felt a little...dizzy? Winded? For a moment, she'd wondered if he was going to kiss her. If she was honest, she had wished he would, although the thought made her legs feel weak. Adelaide had never been kissed, and the idea of kissing Regulus was both nerve-wracking and tantalizing. Hence, the extra space between them now. Plus, something Minerva had said, even in teasing, troubled her.

Maybe he should talk to Father.

Father was cautious with all his daughters, but with Adelaide most of all. She was the youngest, and more importantly, she was a mage. What if Father—or Mother, who could be even more fiercely protective—didn't think Regulus could be trusted with her secret? Adelaide glanced over. She had a gut feeling she could trust Regulus. *He's a good man. I'm sure of it.* If she wanted to marry him, would Father forbid her?

Oh. A realization hit her with the force of one of her throwing knives, right in her heart. *I'm thinking about marrying him.* A whirlwind of emotions. Excitement. Fear. Confusion. Giddiness.

True, Father would do anything to protect her. But Father loved her, and he trusted her. If Adelaide trusted Regulus, Father would, too. She looked over at Regulus again and caught him looking at her. She blushed and glanced away, smiling to herself.

Might as well admit it. You're falling hard.

"Lady Adelaide!"

Adelaide groaned internally as she recognized the voice. She forced a pleasant smile and turned toward Nolan.

Nolan approached flanked by a couple knights. He had paired an ostentatious aquamarine doublet with a white shirt and navy trousers. A sword hung from a leather belt embroidered with silver thread, as if he feared someone might forget his parents were wealthy. His light brown hair, as usual, was perfect. What a marked contrast to Regulus' loose, open-necked black shirt, plain sword belt, and longer, tousled wavy black hair.

"It is a pleasure to see you, Lady Adelaide." Nolan bowed, predictably snatching up her hand to kiss her fingers. She hated the flamboyant gesture. He bowed toward the rest of the party. "And you as well, Sir Gaius, Lady Minerva. Lord Hargreaves." He sounded terse as he addressed Regulus, but his expression stayed agreeable. "I'm surprised to see you here. I didn't think you competed."

"I haven't had the desire in the past," Regulus said, to Adelaide's surprise. "But I will compete in archery, sword, and joust this time."

"Interesting." Nolan looked at Dresden. "And...tell me your name again?"

"Sir Jakobs." Dresden sounded unamused.

"Right. I don't expect *you'll* be competing? Not allowed, I'd wager."

Shock rushed through her at Nolan's flaunting of Dresden's non-noble blood.

"No," Dresden said, his tone cool. "Only because the officials feared I'd kill some poor noble."

"Mm." Nolan directed his attention back to Adelaide. Sorrow shadowed his face. "My lady, you wound me."

"Pardon?"

He gestured toward her neck. "I had hoped to see my gift around that beautiful neck."

"Oh." Adelaide's fingers drifted to her bare neck. "The necklace was very…um, thoughtful." She floundered. "But—"

"Not your style?" Nolan sighed. "My mother warned me against jewelry, but I wanted something that at least approached your beauty."

How do you politely say, "Thank you, not interested?"

"Perhaps over supper you can tell me more about yourself, and I can send better tokens of my affection in the future."

Supper? Future! Adelaide took a step backward, her words caught in her throat.

"I'm sorry?" Regulus choked out.

Adelaide's palms grew slick. This conversation had careened out of control.

"Good luck with that." Minerva snorted. "Perhaps you should ask Lord Hargreaves what kinds of gifts Adelaide enjoys."

Nolan opened and closed his mouth as he shot a glare Regulus' direction. "I suppose," he said with a pleasant smile, "until I can offer gifts more suited to your tastes, Adelaide, I'll have to win this tournament in your honor."

Adelaide shook her head. "Oh—"

"Has someone else already dedicated their victory to you?" Nolan raised a brow.

"Well, no, but—"

"Good. I wouldn't expect too much from Hargreaves' first tournament, to be blunt."

"I'll enjoy proving you wrong," Regulus said evenly.

Adelaide huffed. Annoying male egos. "Sir Nolan—"

"Please, just Nolan."

"*Sir Carrick*." She took a deep breath. "I think there may have been a misunderstanding."

"Then what is there to misunderstand?" Nolan looked into her eyes. "Every blow with my sword, every hit with my lance. Every win, and my ultimate victory, will be for you. When I am weak, I will look to you and your smiling face will give me strength."

Adelaide raised her brows, jaw agape. *Is he for real?* "Sir Carrick—"

"Nolan," he said, an edge to his voice. She took a deep breath as her irritation grew.

"Sir Carrick," Gaius said. "The lady is trying to let you down gently."

Nolan looked to Gaius, then back at her. "Is this true?"

"I'm sorry. I don't return your feelings."

"Obviously," Dresden muttered.

Nolan glared at Regulus. "Because of him?"

She couldn't contain her irritation any longer. "Because of you! You're insufferable! You're vain and rude and presumptuous!" She clenched her hands into fists as she shoved down the urge to knock him backwards with a magic blast. "Just...go!"

Nolan hung his head. "I apologize profusely, my lady. I meant no offense. My heart ran away with me, and if in my zeal to show you my affection, I appeared vain and presumptuous, I am most ashamed."

His sudden show of humility caught her by surprise. He certainly knew how to speak well when he so desired.

"I would give anything for a chance to redeem myself." Nolan stepped closer. Regulus moved around her, his hand on his sword. She didn't need him to, but she appreciated the protective instinct.

"Lady Belanger asked you to leave," Regulus said, his voice deep and emphatic. Gracious, that was attractive.

Nolan backed up. "As for rude, I blame my sincere desire to protect you from a man I do not believe to be worthy of your trust or your affections." He bowed, then sauntered past, followed by his knights. As he passed Regulus, he said in a voice so low she almost didn't hear him, "I'll see you in the lists, mongrel."

Regulus watched him go, his expression stony.

"I do not like that man," Dresden said. "The villain." He spat.

"Drez!" Regulus snapped.

"That seems harsh," Gaius said. He stood behind Minerva with his arms wrapped around her stomach.

"I've heard things," Dresden said. "Scandalous rumors. About why his engagement was called off."

"Nolan was engaged?" Adelaide asked, the information like a slap to her face. Regulus' expression shuttered at her use of Nolan's first name, and she felt an immediate twinge of guilt.

"It wasn't very public," Dresden explained. "But rumor has it his parents had arranged a marriage for him a couple years back. Some say to Baron Gaveston's daughter, but who knows. He offended the bride's father, who called it off. If that weren't enough to call him a villain, one of the Carricks' servants will swear up and down that Baron Esmil's oldest daughter was forced to join a convent after she was caught…" He cleared his throat. "*With* Nolan Carrick."

Adelaide's face heated as she recalled Nolan's offer to walk her to her room at Carrick castle.

"That's a terrible thing to say based on rumor," Gaius said.

"I've heard something similar." Minerva nodded. "And I know a few young ladies who've admitted to pushing the boundaries of propriety for Nolan Carrick's charm."

Adelaide shrugged. "Hopefully that means he'll easily find someone else to bother with his bravado."

"Or he's run out of other viable options," Dresden said. Adelaide did *not* care for that possibility. She must have looked upset, because Dresden added, "But that seems unlikely. He'll probably have moved on by this time tomorrow."

"Enough about Nolan Carrick." She waved her hand. "He's wasted enough of our time."

Regulus ducked out of his tent and stretched. The sun just peeked above the horizon and the chill air bit through his worn, loose linen shirt and trousers. His bare toes curled into the grass. The clatter of pots, sound of footsteps, rustle of tents, and snatches of quiet conversation drifted through the air. He breathed in deeply as he stretched, and immediately regretted it. The air stank of dust, smoke, horses, and body odor. It smelled like camp and took him back to his days as a mercenary. He had many fond memories of those days, but he wouldn't go back. He didn't miss camping with dozens of sweaty men who hadn't bathed in weeks.

"Good morning, my lord!" Harold beamed as he rounded a tent, arms full of firewood.

"You're particularly cheery today," Regulus noted.

Harold bent down to arrange the logs in the ash from last night's fire. "Never been to a tournament," he said. "It's exciting."

"Never?"

"Never, my lord."

"Huh." Regulus supposed that made sense. Since becoming a lord two years ago, he had avoided tournaments. People were already suspicious of him, with his checkered background and the ease with which he defeated Lady Arrano's champion. Best to keep a low profile and avoid any accidental displays of the supernatural side effects of the sorcerer's mark.

Thinking of the mark made him uncomfortable. Was he endangering Adelaide by courting her? Could he risk marrying her? *Oh, Etiros, do I want to marry her.* He had assumed he would never marry. Too much darkness. Too much shame. But then Adelaide. She gave him hope. She liked his scar. His past and his scar, two things he thought made him undesirable, and she accepted them. But could she accept his mark? Could she love him if she knew the truth? Knew the oath he had made? The evil he served?

Not forever. Until his debt was paid.

If the sorcerer kept his word.

"Are you all right, my lord?" Harold's brow puckered.

"Oh, yes." He smiled. "Just thinking."

"You should do less of that," Dresden said, emerging from the tent opposite Regulus'. "Makes your face all frowny."

"According to you I'm always frowning."

Drez yawned. "Yes, but less so yesterday. I'd like to keep this new trend of smiling Regulus going."

Regulus shook his head and rolled his eyes.

"I agree with Dresden." Regulus nearly jumped out of his skin at the sound of Adelaide's voice. He spun to see her standing with her hands held behind her back on the other side of Harold, who was busy cracking eggs into a pan over the fire. Another woman stood a little behind her to her left, dressed in the simple clothing of a maidservant.

Adelaide wore a dress of deep purplish-red with white, fitted sleeves. The wide collar was embroidered in gold with flowers that matched the color of the dress. A belt of engraved bronze squares rested on her hips. She wore her black hair loose in waves over her shoulders.

Regulus tried to stop staring. "You've made an early start of the day."

She shrugged. "I like mornings. Helps clear the mind."

Adelaide walked around Harold and the fire. Regulus caught her gaze flitting down to his torso. Part of him wished he had put on proper clothes before coming out of his tent, rather than standing there in a thin shirt and frayed trousers. A vainer part of him felt more than a little pleased and wanted her to look. *So long as she can't see the scars through the shirt.*

"I…" Adelaide hesitated, then pulled her hands in front of her. She held a piece of fabric around a foot long and about as wide as his hand that matched the purplish-red of her dress. She blushed as she held it out to him. "I thought…that is, I wondered…" She muttered something in Khast. "Would you wear this?"

Regulus smiled. He hadn't smiled like this in years. His scar pulled on his lips and cheek, the skin so tight it was almost painful. He didn't care. "I would be honored." He reached out, wrapped his fingers around the cloth—and over her fingers.

She smiled back. Lingered for a moment with her fingers against his. She eased her hold on the cloth and pulled her hand away. "I'll watch for you on the field." Adelaide bit her lower lip, turned, and walked away, trailed by her handmaid.

Regulus wished she'd stayed. He was glad she didn't. If she had, he might have kissed her. He watched her until she disappeared between the tents. The soft cloth in his hands still held her warmth. He looked up and saw Dresden smirking.

He pointed at Dresden. "Not. A. Word."

CHAPTER 21

A SQUIRE SQUEEZED PAST REGULUS WITH A MUTTERED "PARDON me." The space around the archery arena buzzed with conversation and hurried footsteps. Regulus moved closer to the low fence surrounding the arena and checked the fabric tied to his upper right arm again. Still there.

He strung his bow and looked for Adelaide. He glimpsed the purple-red of her dress, but then lost her in the crowd. *You're being a fool, Regulus. Focus on the competition.*

"You know," Carrick's cool voice cut through his thoughts, "I may have to review the entry guidelines with the heralds. I'm not sure you carry the necessary lineage to legally compete, Lord Half-Breed."

Carrick stood next to him but looked straight ahead as he adjusted his gloves. He wore armor with engraved edges and lines and points that provided more style than function.

"The law requires proof of nobility on one side only, and proof of legal title." Regulus shoved down his anger. "I am well within my rights."

"Sounds like the law needs adjusted if we're to keep the rabble out."

"Do we have a problem, Sir Carrick?" Regulus turned toward Carrick, reveling in the fact that he towered over him.

Carrick continued looking straight ahead, as unfazed and sure of himself as ever. "Yes, actually. Stay away from Adelaide."

"Excuse me?"

Carrick finally faced him. "I won't tell you again. She's above your station." He shrugged. "A little beneath mine, but that's beside the point. I don't know what she finds so fascinating about your scarred face, peasant blood, and murderer-for-hire past, but sooner or later she'll realize you're not a good match."

Regulus clenched his fist, every muscle taunt. *Save it for the field.* He gritted his teeth. "You should go."

"I'm going. I'm needed in the polearm arena." Carrick's gaze fell to Adelaide's token. "Pity you're competing in archery instead. I suppose I must wait until the sword competition this afternoon to cut that off your arm." He turned and strode away.

Regulus shook his head and tried to focus on archery.

The archery competition went both worse and better than Regulus had expected. He hadn't expected to win, but he had wanted to. He felt Adelaide's token put a little extra pressure on him to do well. To show he deserved to wear it. To not put her to shame.

Adelaide would probably find that ridiculous. He couldn't find her in the chaos of the dispersing crowd, but she hadn't said a word that morning about winning. Still, he wondered if she found his underperformance embarrassing. Not that he did poorly. He placed sixth out of seventeen, which wasn't terrible, all things considered. Although Caleb would be disappointed his lessons hadn't had more of an impact.

Caleb should be competing. Caleb would have won. But that couldn't happen. His knights had come to support him and enjoy the spectacle of the tournament, but not to compete. Caleb's father had been a minor lord, but after his father died and left everything to his three older brothers, Caleb left his old life behind, and he no longer had anything to prove his nobility. Perceval could have competed if he wanted, since he *could* prove his ancestry of nobility.

But, in his own words, he "fought too dirty and had too many hard feelings toward nobles to get in a sparring ring with those prissy pretty boys." Dresden, Jerrick, and Estevan couldn't claim a drop of noble blood. And, unfortunately, lineage mattered at tournaments in Monparthian law, not the knighthood Regulus had bestowed.

Regulus strolled across the massive tournament grounds back toward the tents, Dresden, Caleb, and Perceval beside him.

"Well, I won't say you haven't improved," Caleb said.

Regulus raised an eyebrow. "That sounds like you *want* to say I haven't."

"Oh, no, no!" Caleb held his hands out and shook his head. "I mean you *have*."

"It's the double negatives," Perceval said. "Sounds like you're sayin' opposite of what you said."

Regulus looked at him in confusion.

"What? I went to university, remember?"

"For two and a half weeks." Drez snorted.

"Still longer than any of you, makin' me the most educated member of this band." Perceval inclined his head. "All due respect, Captain."

"And the least genteel." Caleb shook his head with exaggerated sadness.

"I suppose you think you're the most genteel?" Dresden asked.

Caleb bowed with a flourish of his hand. "Obviously."

"I don't know." Regulus scratched his chin. "Drez should get some gentility points for his well-kept beard alone."

Caleb made a sound of protest, his mouth agape. "Now that's just cruel." He rubbed the stubble on his jawline with the back of his fingers. "It's not my fault my beard grows out all scraggly. Besides, the ladies love a little five o'clock shadow."

"Ladies love a full, soft, closely trimmed beard," Dresden said.

"Says the two single men." Perceval harrumphed. "You think I'm clean shaven because I enjoy shaving? Hm? I prefer kisses from my wife, thank you."

"You have a beard like a porcupine, it doesn't count." Dresden stroked his beard.

Regulus shook his head as they arrived at the tents. "All right, enough!"

After lunch, Harold helped Regulus into his armor, and Drez tied Adelaide's token to his arm, tucking the knot under the pauldron to ensure it wouldn't come off. The plain armor emphasized strength and maneuverability over looks. Lots of curves to help blows glance off.

Compared to the bulk of the Black Knight armor, this felt like heavy clothes, so he had to be extra careful to control his strength. Plus, he carried his own sword. A standard broadsword, it was considerably lighter than the massive black sword hidden with the chest of armor in his tent. Although he prayed the sorcerer would not call on him during the tournament, he had no way of knowing when he would next feel his mark burn.

But he couldn't think about that, not now. He intended, for the first time in over two years, to act like his own man. For the tournament, he would forget about the sorcerer's threats looming over him, ignore his recklessness, and be present in the moment and enjoy it. Fight for sport instead of for his life. Love a spectacular woman. Today, he would ignore the darkness. Today, nothing would bring him down. Because today, he wore his heart on his sleeve as literally as possible.

His men accompanied him to the sword-fighting arena. Perceval and Caleb were still bickering about something, while Estevan occasionally interjected, stoking the flames. Harold and Jerrick seemed to be placing bets on whether Perceval would punch Caleb.

"I need to concentrate!" Regulus snapped as they approached the fence surrounding the arena. Waiting competitors and their attendants crowded about. "What in creation are you two fighting about now?"

"Perce thinks he's high and mighty because he got kicked out of university," Caleb said.

"Captain, you think they'll let me and Cal borrow the sword-fighting arena for a minute?" Perceval crossed his arms. The man had about the most intimidating scowl Regulus had ever seen, but Caleb just snickered.

Dresden smacked the back of Perceval's head. "Hey, you're distracting Reg."

"My, my, your men have the decorum of peasant children." Carrick leaned back against the fence, looking at Regulus and his men with clear disdain. "But then, that's presumably what they are. Just like their false lord."

Perceval moved forward. Regulus blocked him with his arm. His blood boiled, but he wouldn't give Carrick the satisfaction of a reaction.

Carrick looked across the arena at the crowds filing into the wood stadium seating. He jutted his chin toward the spectators. "Oh, excellent. Adelaide is here."

Regulus looked where Carrick had indicated as Adelaide took a seat in a box near the center of the arena with the Drummonds.

"She will have an excellent view when you're flat on your back with me standing over you." Carrick smiled viciously.

Keep calm. Regulus took a deep breath and smiled back. "Or perhaps the other way around." He held out his hand. *Never let them see they're getting to you.* "Good luck, Sir Carrick."

Carrick's top lip curled. But then he took Regulus' hand and squeezed harder than necessary as he smiled again. Regulus summoned every ounce of self-control to not just break his hand.

"May the best man win, mercenary." Carrick dropped Regulus' hand and sauntered over to the herald overseeing the event.

"See?" Perceval jabbed his finger in the air. "This. This is why I don't compete. I'd cut that" —he said a few choice words describing Carrick— "head clean off."

"And this is why you're the least genteel," Caleb said.

"Contestants to the field!" the herald called. "All contestants competing in the sword, please enter the arena!"

"I'd recommend not cutting his head off," Dresden said solemnly.

"I'll try to keep that in mind." Regulus kept his tone light and jocular, but he knew Dresden was right. The way Carrick got under his skin... He would have to be careful.

The herald welcomed the contestants and spectators and explained the event. Pairs had been pre-chosen for the first round. Winners would compete in new pairs in the next round, and so on until only two knights remained. One loser picked by Baron Carrick, who sat in a large box centered in the middle of the arena, would compete in the second round to ensure an even number of competitors. There would be five rounds total. Five rounds, five opponents between him and victory.

The herald announced the pairs. Regulus would go eleventh, fighting against Sir Morris MacCombe. Regulus had met Baron MacComb's eldest before. A polite man in his early thirties with a reputation for chivalry and some skill with a sword. The combatants bowed to the spectators and filed out of the arena, except the first two combatants—Lord Thorne, one of Baron MacComb's vassals, and Carrick. Regulus found it suspicious that Carrick dueled first, but it provided a good opportunity to study him, should they end up facing each other. He hoped they would.

Lord Thorne was a short, stocky man with a steely gaze, muscles that protruded from his thick neck, a stubbly gray beard, and long gray hair tied back at the nape of his neck. He had fought in the Trade Wars and had a reputation for smashing in skulls with a war-hammer. It would be interesting to see how he fared with a sword.

The men shook hands then put on their helms. Flaxen horsehair formed a plume on Carrick's. *Let's see if your skill matches your flair, Carrick.* The men drew their swords and circled each other. Regulus leaned on the fence, eyes narrowed.

Thorne attacked with the force of a charging wild boar—all strength and speed, but little finesse. Rather than attempt to block the blow, Carrick sidestepped and parried Thorne's sword from the side. Begrudgingly, Regulus nodded. The force of a blow like that could shatter an arm if taken directly. Despite the force of his swing, Thorne adjusted, attacking from the side before Carrick had a chance to counter. Carrick blocked, moving back to absorb the impact of the blow. Thorne stepped forward, pressing his advantage.

Carrick gave way, backing up here, sidestepping there. Parrying rather than blocking whenever possible. He was letting Thorne wear himself down.

Thorne had a distinct advantage over Carrick in mass and muscle. But Carrick made the smallest movements possible, conserving his energy. Thorne brought a weaker strike from the left, and Regulus had seen enough fights to know Carrick was about to make his move. Carrick stepped into the strike, holding the flat of his blade up to block. With a resounding clang, Thorne's sword pushed Carrick's to the side. Carrick stumbled, and several people gasped. But Regulus noted the careful placement of Carrick's feet as he stumbled, how he adjusted his grip on his sword. A feint. Emboldened, Thorne raised his sword, preparing for a mighty downward swing. Carrick prepared to block the blow. Thorne swung.

Carrick spun to the side and Thorne's sword tore through empty air and slammed into the ground, sending up chunks of dirt.

Carrick moved to the offensive, driving Thorne back. Caught unprepared, Thorne had difficulty getting his stance corrected. He moved backward off-balance, his energy lagging. Carrick, on the other hand, unleashed his speed and strength.

The crowd cheered as Carrick landed repeat blows on Thorne's breastplate. Thorne tried to counter, to turn back to the offensive. Carrick let him, just for a moment, then parried, knocking Thorne's sword aside. He kicked the back of Thorne's knee, and the older man stumbled forward. A blow to his back, and Thorne fell to his knees. Carrick swung, bringing his sword to a stop just before Thorne's neck. Thorne dropped his sword. The crowd applauded and hollered. Carrick would continue to the second round.

CHAPTER 22

ADELAIDE SIGHED AS CARRICK JABBED HIS SWORD INTO THE air, celebrating his victory. Part of her had expected him to be all style and no substance, despite William Carrick's advice not to bet against him. When Lord Thorne appeared to have the upper hand, she felt smug. But once Nolan moved to the offensive, she realized he had always been in control. He had a plan from the beginning, and it worked. Reluctantly, she applauded as he removed his helm. Nolan had his faults, but he *had* apologized. He had not approached her since the afternoon prior. And based on his congenial handshake with Regulus before the contestants entered the field, they must have worked out their differences. It made her dislike him a little less.

Carrick looked directly at her as he bowed. He flashed a charming smile and mouthed something that looked like *"for you."* She clenched her jaw as he turned and swaggered out of the arena. *Never mind.* Some might find his determined pursuit attractive, but she found it annoying. What was his goal, wear her down until she was so tired of saying no, she said yes? How unromantic.

Regulus leaned against the fence, a deep, thoughtful frown on his face. He looked toward her, and Adelaide smiled. His expression softened, and his hand strayed to the strip of fabric fastened to his arm. Minerva poked her side.

"The next competitors have entered the field, in case you missed it while making love eyes at Lord Hargreaves."

Adelaide scowled. "You're ridiculous. What even *are* love eyes?"

187

"The look you were just giving Regulus Hargreaves." Min laughed as Adelaide rolled her eyes.

"How convenient and vague a definition." She looked back at Regulus, but he had turned his attention to the new combatants.

Nobles from as young as seventeen to as old as fifty took their turns in the arena. Most fights ended quickly. Others had her on the edge of her seat as evenly matched opponents went back and forth, gaining and losing the upper-hand at staggering speed. Between each match she looked to Regulus, and he always met her gaze before turning his attention back to the combat.

Finally, Regulus entered the field. Her pulse quickened. Regulus nodded at Adelaide before he turned to his opponent. Regulus was taller Sir Morris MacCombe, but they had similar muscular builds and the same air of resolve as they shook hands. She remembered liking Sir MacCombe at the Carrick's dance, but she hoped Regulus beat him. A loss wouldn't change her feelings, but she wanted Carrick to see Regulus win. And she didn't care to see the disappointed expression Regulus had after he lost the archery contest again.

Regulus pulled on his helm and took up his stance. Feet planted, knees bent. Chin tucked in as he looked through his visor. Adelaide leaned forward and wrapped her fingers around the edge of the wooden bench.

MacCombe shifted to his right, and Regulus did the same, moving his feet in a fluid movement close to the ground. The men circled for a moment, sizing each other up. Both moved at the same time. Their swords met with a ringing clang. Their blades parted as they both carried through their momentum and stepped back. MacCombe swung. Adelaide gripped the bench harder.

Regulus parried, pushing MacCombe's blade aside. As MacCombe adjusted, Regulus attacked, but MacCombe blocked then pushed back. Regulus retreated but kept his guard up and his stance forward. They ranged back and forth, a flurry of attacks, parries, and blocks. Adelaide scarcely blinked.

"Lord Hargreaves is good, isn't he?" Minerva murmured.

"Indeed," Gaius said. "I'd heard he was, but…my word. He's impressive. Did you see how—"

"Shush!" Adelaide released her iron grip on the bench to wave in Gaius' direction.

Minerva giggled. "Are we not allowed to talk about your suitor?"

Adelaide pursed her lips but didn't take her eyes off the duel. "You're distracting me from the sparring."

Gaius chuckled and whispered something to Minerva that made her laugh and hold her belly. Adelaide ignored them, focused on Regulus' every movement.

Regulus moved with ease and controlled awareness. She knew what control looked like. It took control to throw knives quickly with accuracy. A subconscious awareness of your body, of each miniscule movement of your arm from your shoulder to the tips of your fingers. Honed control of the rotation of your shoulder, the straightening of your elbow, even your breathing. Practice until control and awareness became second nature, the movement reflexive, the knives an extension of your hand. That was how Regulus moved. With precision. But there was something else.

He was holding back.

She couldn't pinpoint how she knew. Something about the ease with which he swung his sword. The way he pressed into an attack, but not as far as he could. A forceful parry where he seemed to stop short. It was miniscule. But there was an energy there she knew all too well. A pent-up power that tried to push itself out of every limb. The constrained feeling of keeping her magic caged when it coursed through her and she wanted to let it out, to release the power trapped inside. Something in her gut told her Regulus had strength he wasn't letting out. She just couldn't understand why.

She pushed her confusion away, taking in every strike, every swing. Every crash of metal-on-metal vibrated in her chest. Mac-Combe landed a glancing blow on Regulus' shoulder. Her fingers hurt from clenching the bench, so she grabbed fistfuls of her skirt instead. Regulus fell back, on the defensive. MacCombe swung. Regulus thrust his sword forward. MacCombe quickly countered, batting away Regulus' blade, but now he was off balance. Regulus let the force of MacCombe's counter do most of the work as he swung his sword up and around. MacCombe's sword was too far to his right as Regulus brought his blade around on the side of MacCombe's head.

Regulus didn't pause, landing blow after blow. MacCombe's sword slipped out of his fingers and fell on the dirt as he raised his hands. Regulus pulled back. Adelaide leapt to her feet, cheering with the rest of the crowd. Regulus sheathed his sword and offered his hand to MacCombe. MacCombe accepted the handshake, then retrieved his sword. Regulus turned toward the spectators and removed his helm, bowing toward Baron Carrick. As he straightened, he looked at her and the scarred corner of his mouth turned up in a slight smile. He did not swagger as he walked off the field, as Nolan had, but he held his head up and his shoulders back.

The last four pairs of swordsmen fought, and Baron Carrick called a break while he decided pairs for the next round—and which loser would get a chance at redemption. Adelaide left her sister and the Drummonds and made her way to the waiting competitors.

Regulus grinned as she approached, his silver-gray eyes sparkling. Despite the rivulets of sweat on his skin, making his slicked-down hair stick to his face, he still looked good. Her heart leapt. Behind Regulus, Dresden stood with four other knights.

190

Estevan, the knife-thrower. A muscular knight with a crooked nose and short brown hair. One knight had longer, dark blond hair and a stubbly beard that made quite a contrast with Dresden's thick, short beard. The fourth had dark skin and black, short hair in tight curls. They all looked at her as she curtsied.

Regulus smiled. "Do we need such formality?"

"Do we ever *need* formality?" Adelaide grinned. "Formality is demanded by societal ideas of politeness, not necessity."

Crooked Nose chuckled. "Oh, I like her, Captain."

"Captain?" She hadn't meant to voice her confusion aloud, but she couldn't help it.

Regulus shrugged. "I've told him repeatedly we're not mercenaries anymore. I'm not his captain. But he's stubborn and foolhardy and will never change."

"See?" Stubble said. "Regulus agrees with me. You're an idiot."

"Charming." Dresden rolled his eyes. "I thought you were the genteel one. This is why you don't have a woman."

"I'd contradict you but there's a lady present."

Regulus rubbed the side of his head then gestured to Stubble. "Adelaide, this is Sir Caleb Rathburn."

Rathburn bowed with a flourish of his hand and a toothy grin. "A pleasure to finally meet you, my lady."

"You know Estevan," Regulus said. Estevan bowed. "This is Sir Jerrick Faras." The dark-skinned man bowed with a smile. "And this charming individual," Regulus gestured to Crooked Nose, "is Sir Perceval Williamson."

Williamson gave a stiff half bow but smiled warmly. "Be gentle with the Captain, my lady."

Adelaide cocked an eyebrow. "You're worried I'll hurt him?"

"No. But he's been hurt enough."

Regulus cleared his throat. "Have you been enjoying the tournament so far?"

191

"Oh, yes. I—"

A trumpet sounded, indicating that the competition would recommence. Adelaide adjusted her token on his arm. Not that it needed adjusting. She just needed the excuse to be close to him.

"Good luck," she whispered. She headed back for her seat.

As Adelaide picked her way between spectators, she caught some of them staring. Others glanced her way furtively. She listened closer to the muddled cacophony of voices and latched onto snippets that seemed to be about her or Regulus.

"...matches Belanger's dress."

"Wasn't he a mercenary?"

"...heard her mother's a Khastallander freewoman. Not even noble." Adelaide clenched her jaw.

"...no-good bastard."

"I can't imagine Lord Belanger approves."

"I thought she was courting Nolan Carrick?"

"She's a flirt."

Adelaide ducked her head and made her way to her seat as quickly as she could.

Minerva looked up, but her smile faded. "Is everything all right? You look...upset."

"I'm fine."

The mockery wasn't new. *I don't care. Their opinion doesn't matter.* But it still hurt. However, the fact that some people thought she and Nolan were courting... It both embarrassed her and made her furious. People talked too much. Angry tears threatened to well up, so she shook her head and focused on the competition.

CHAPTER 23

REGULUS SIGHED AS ADELAIDE WOVE AWAY THROUGH THE crowd. A man's voice intruded on his bliss. "Lord Hargreaves?"

He looked over as Sir MacCombe approached. "Yes, Sir MacCombe?"

MacCombe nodded toward Adelaide. "That was Lady Adelaide Belanger, wasn't it?" Regulus nodded. MacCombe looked thoughtful. "That's her token?"

"Yes."

Something dark and dangerous sparked behind MacCombe's eyes. "I was under the impression Nolan Carrick was courting her. There were rumors of a pending engagement."

Dresden snorted, but said nothing.

Regulus tried not to sound too riled. "No."

MacCombe stepped closer, his voice low. "I'm pleased to hear it. I've had the pleasure of speaking with Lady Adelaide. She's a lovely woman. Too good for Nolan Carrick. You fight with honor, Lord Hargreaves of Arrano, and were gracious in victory, so I will offer a word of warning. Nolan Carrick is not lightly trifled with, and there are many who blindly trust the Carrick name. If you have stolen his object of desire, you should watch your back." MacCombe grimaced. "And your love. Especially your love."

Regulus nodded, wanting to ask for clarification but not daring to be rude. "Thank you."

"And one more thing." MacCombe's eyes flashed. "Since you defeated me, I cannot do what I came here to do. If you get the chance—give Nolan Carrick a sound beating. He deserves it more than you know." He walked away.

If Dresden was right about Carrick offending Baron Gaveston and the reason Baron Esmil's daughter joined a convent, that made three baronial families with a grudge against Nolan Carrick. Regulus relished the information. A man made that many enemies, eventually, he'd be ruined.

The herald called the winners and runner-up back onto the field, then announced the eight pairs for the second round. Regulus would go second against Sir Luke Arthur. Arthur had done well in the first round, but he leaned into his right side, making his strikes unbalanced. A small flaw that would be easily exploited.

He had to admit, he was enjoying the tournament. The competition provided more excitement than practicing with his knights. Winning felt more satisfying in a competition, even if he had an unfair advantage. But he held back and tried to keep the playing field as level as he could. He also much preferred this to fighting for the sorcerer.

After watching the first pair of contestants, Regulus reentered the arena. He shook hands with Sir Arthur, a bald man in his early forties built of lean muscle, before putting on his helm. Regulus attacked first, and Arthur parried with expert ease. Regulus half-smiled under his helm. This would be a good duel.

They moved back and forth across the arena, attacking and parrying, thrusting and blocking, swinging and dodging. Regulus kept positioning himself on Arthur's right, causing him to lean more and more onto his dominant side. As Regulus dodged a thrust of Arthur's sword, he moved toward the left and let Arthur continue to attack. The swing from left to right finally came. Regulus stepped back, not blocking or parrying. He had to lean away to avoid the tip of Arthur's blade. Right as Arthur's center of balance shifted a little too far to the right, Regulus swung his sword.

Arthur was too far off center to block the attack, and Regulus' blade slammed into Arthur's back. Arthur stumbled and Regulus landed hits on Arthur's chest and back. As Arthur blocked, Regulus pushed toward Arthur's right. Arthur tripped. Regulus slammed his shoulder into Arthur's left side, and his opponent fell onto his right knee. With a mighty swing of his sword, Regulus knocked Arthur's sword out of his hands. The sword hit the ground a couple feet away. Arthur held up his hands.

The crowd of spectators cheered. The sound filled Regulus to his core. He could imagine a different life, a version of himself that the nobles didn't mistrust or resent. He offered Arthur his hand. Arthur ignored him as he stood and fetched his sword. The rejection tore the illusion away. Regulus sighed, removed his helm, and bowed to the spectators. Adelaide beamed, but her smile seemed dimmed.

Maybe she noticed Sir Arthur's snub. Does she wonder now about giving her token to the son of a servant? Or maybe I'm so convinced this is too good to be true I'm looking for negatives. He smiled and clapped his hand over her token on his arm. She blushed. *I'm overthinking it.* He walked out of the arena.

Carrick won his match, which on the one hand irritated Regulus. He showed no grace in victory, only smug conceit. He entered the arena with the laidback carriage and playful, crowd-winning smile of a man entering a party and left with a kiss for the spectators, a swagger in his step, and a smirk on his face. On the other hand, Regulus now had a one in four chance of facing Carrick in the next round. Never had Regulus so strongly wished to cross steel with a particular person. He forced aside the mental image of knocking Carrick to the ground and focused on the next contestants. He had a one in four chance of dueling Carrick but had equal chances of fighting the other winners. So he studied his potential opponents.

A fifteen-minute recess was called to give the winners time to catch their breath and adjust their armor. Perceval leaned back, his elbows resting on top of the fence.

"Got some decent competition there, Captain." Perceval nodded thoughtfully. "A few of 'em might even make good mercenaries."

Regulus laughed. "Don't let them hear you. Pretty sure you'll offend them."

"Eh, I can take any of 'em." Perceval shrugged. None of them argued. Perce was the best swordsman Regulus knew. He'd even beaten Regulus once.

After the break, the herald announced the last four pairs. Carrick would face Sir Bartley. Regulus would face Lord Barden. Based on their fighting styles, Regulus predicted a win for Carrick. Lord Barden wouldn't be difficult. His aggressive style counted on beating down his opponent so he couldn't strike back. Accordingly, Barden left himself open for counterattack. All Regulus had to do was accept a couple blows rather than blocking them.

Adelaide winced as Lord Barden landed two powerful blows in quick succession on Regulus' chest. Was he even *trying* to block them? Barden swung again, and Adelaide flinched as the blow landed on Regulus' shoulder. Regulus slammed his sword across Barden's abdomen. Barden stumbled back. The crowd gasped. Regulus attacked without pause. Barden tried to block and parry, but his defense was weak. Regulus swung and Barden's sword flew out of his grasp. Adelaide held her breath. Barden raised his hands, yielding the fight. Adelaide applauded, feeling an inordinate amount of pride.

Still, nerves made her twitchy. Nolan had won his match, with a good show of skill, at that. Regulus had a fifty-fifty chance of facing Nolan in the semi-final round. She had confidence Regulus would best Nolan. And yet… She knew Nolan's type. If Regulus lost, Nolan would interpret that as a clear sign of his superiority and Regulus' unworthiness. That was how chivalry worked in romances, wasn't it? Disputes were decided by arms. Suffering defeat while wearing a lady's token dishonored the lady. To the victor go the spoils.

Nonsense. *Love isn't won on the battlefield. A heart is not a trophy.* But Nolan would see a victory in the field as proof Regulus wasn't worthy of her. Before and after each duel, Nolan made eye contact with her. He winked as he bowed. Mouthed *for you* as he held up his sword in celebration. He blew a kiss to the crowd after each victory, but the look in his eyes said the kiss was for her.

I don't want your victories and I don't want your kisses! If Regulus won, perhaps Nolan would be too ashamed to approach her again. *Please win, Regulus.*

The herald announced the round. First up, Regulus and Sir Morrigan, not Nolan. Then Nolan and Lord Thealane. Regulus won his round with ease. He seemed to have found his rhythm.

A nobleman nearby said, "That mercenary is unstoppable." Adelaide found the speaker and watched him out of the corner of her eye. He was pudgy and balding.

"Seems unfair," said a man with a thick silvery blond beard. "Over half these men haven't seen real battle. We've been playing war at tournaments for over twenty-five years. The mercenary, though…"

"True," Balding said. "He's probably killed more men than some of these competitors have sparred with. But can't refuse him entry because he has more experience."

"Probably should have based on his bastardy, though," said a third man she couldn't see around the other two.

Minerva put a hand on hers and whispered, "Ignore them."

"He has a name," she muttered. "A title. He's not *the mercenary*."

"People are selfish and cruel, Ad." Minerva leaned forward, forcing Adelaide to look into her eyes.

"Why can't they get over themselves?" Adelaide gripped her skirt in her hands.

"You know why. The nobles think what is different taints their carefully constructed superiority. Lord Hargreaves is very different. They aren't likely to accept him easily." Minerva pushed Adelaide's hair over her shoulder. "Adelaide, if talk like that is going to bother you, you can't court him."

Adelaide stiffened.

"If you marry him, that won't stop the whispers. It may make them worse." Minerva bit her lip. "We have both heard the things people have said about Mother and Father. I know some nobles are less than thrilled about me and Gaius. If you can't have thick skin, your relationship with Regulus will fall apart." She squeezed Adelaide's hand. "You will have to be certain you love him more than you need acceptance."

Adelaide shifted on the bench. "You don't have to be right all the time, you know."

"That's why I'm here, don't you know." They laughed.

Adelaide looked across the field. Nolan and Lord Thealane had started their match. Regulus watched, his brow furrowed, eyes narrowed. His mouth cocked to the right, making the skin pucker around his scar. As he observed, his arm would twitch or he would duck slightly, or he would move a foot forward or back. As if doing in miniature what he would do if he were one of the combatants. She chuckled to herself. Why was that so...endearing?

She wouldn't say she loved him. Not yet. But like? *Oh, heavens yes*. Find attractive? She recalled Regulus standing in front of his tent in loose linen trousers and a thin linen shirt that hung asymmetrically on his shoulders. Her entire body grew hot. *Double-*

yes. Even with the scar low on the side of his neck she hadn't seen before and the faint scars on his shoulders.

No, she didn't know if she could claim her affection toward Regulus Hargreaves of Arrano as love yet. But she could handle gossip and condescension at least long enough to find out if she loved him.

Cheers pulled her out of her thoughts and back to the field. She tore her gaze away from Regulus. Lord Thealane staggered off the field. Nolan thrust his sword into the air, looking right at her. *For you*, he mouthed. He bowed deeply, winking as he straightened. He sheathed his sword, put his right fist over his heart, and made another bow toward her with a simper. Before leaving the field, he blew the crowd a kiss.

Regulus and Nolan would face each other for the final victory.

Adelaide wiped sweat off her palms on her skirt. *Please, Regulus. For the love of Etiros, please win.*

CHAPTER 24

So, he would fight Carrick after all. Regulus checked Adelaide's token on his arm. He shouldn't be so happy about it. But it would feel good to knock Carrick down. He had hardly kept himself from drawing his sword yesterday, when Carrick kept talking over Adelaide. The egotistical lowlife. But Adelaide had a fire in her and had proven she could and would defend herself. He wouldn't assume she wanted or needed his help. He only stepped in because Carrick started acting aggressive, and he would not abide such behavior.

Anticipation and tension hung in the air as they walked into the arena. A low monotone of whispered conversations buzzed in his ears, too far away and too quiet for him to hear specifics. Did any support him? He saw a couple noblemen shake hands, both with smug expressions. Well, people were betting on him at least. But people bet on horses, hounds, and dice, so that didn't say much. Maybe he had changed some of their minds. Or perhaps some of them would be more open to him. Probably not. He pushed thoughts of the nobles' acceptance away. They had never accepted him. Why would it matter now?

He found Adelaide in the crowd. Maybe it did matter now. What if the other nobles turned her against him? She smiled and winked. *"I don't much care what they think,"* her voice repeated in his mind. The tension in his shoulders dissipated. In the middle of the arena he bowed to the spectators, then turned toward his opponent.

Carrick gave him a haughty smile as they shook hands. "This should be fun, mercenary. Try to last long enough you don't completely embarrass her. I want to win, but I don't want to make her angry. I want her to see which of us is the real man, and which is, well...whatever kind of mongrel you are."

Regulus clenched his jaw until his teeth hurt. He smiled. "You know what, Carrick? You're right."

"What?"

"This *is* going to be fun." With that, Regulus pulled on his helm and drew his sword.

Carrick scoffed and put on his plumed helm. He drew his sword and attacked, moving blade from scabbard to slicing toward Regulus' chest in one fluid movement. Regulus blocked, the impact of their swords meeting jarring his bones. He shoved back on Carrick's blade, pushing it aside. He reversed directions and aimed for Carrick's side.

Carrick recovered and parried with no difficulty. Regulus moved for another attack from above, adjusting his stance as he watched Carrick through the slit in his visor. Carrick inched his left foot back and drew back his right shoulder. Regulus adjusted, stepping to the right and pulling his sword around to swing from the left. Carrick couldn't change course fast enough, and he blocked just as Regulus' sword made contact with Carrick's shoulder. Carrick parried with surprising force, then counter-attacked. Regulus blocked or dodged each blow. He countered with a flurry of combination cuts, thrusts, and swings. Carrick fell back but blocked or parried each attack.

Sweat dripped into Regulus' eyes and trickled down his neck. Every muscle in his body strained with energy. Sunlight glinted off of Carrick's polished armor, making Regulus squint. Carrick blocked another cut, and Regulus grit his teeth. Some part of his brain whispered *you could end this right now. Stop holding back. You could stop his blade with your hand and pull it right out of his grasp.* He licked his dry lips, tasting salty sweat. No. He would win this fight as Regulus Hargreaves, not as the magically enhanced Black Knight.

Move. Keep moving. He stepped into another stance reflexively as Carrick parried and swung for his head. *Look for weaknesses.* He leaned back as Carrick's sword rushed past within a feather's breadth of his visor. He aimed a blow at Carrick's arm. Carrick's grip faltered as Regulus' sword bounced off Carrick's bracer. Regulus pressed his advantage, landing several blows on Carrick's chest and shoulders.

Holding back got harder by the second. His concentration threatened to break as he tired. The rush of the combat seemed like fuel on the fire burning in his veins and muscles, demanding to be unleashed. *Focus! No foolish risks.* Carrick swung for his torso, and Regulus moved to block. At the last moment, Carrick adjusted, lunging around Regulus' side. The edge of his sword sliced into the back of Regulus' knee.

A string of curse words rushed through Regulus' mind as his knee smarted and blood seeped into his trouser leg. He would heal. This fight needed to end before anyone noticed. He spun and swung toward Carrick, who, as he expected, blocked the blow. Regulus pushed their swords to the side and slammed his shoulder into Carrick. Carrick stumbled back and Regulus thrust toward the gap in Carrick's armor under his pauldron. Carrick parried, but Regulus kept moving closer, forcing him to retreat backward.

As they moved across the field, Regulus making attacks for speed, not accuracy, Carrick's stance got weaker and less grounded. Regulus kept an eye on the terrain, and just before Carrick stepped onto an uneven patch of ground, he drew his sword back over his head, leaving himself open. Carrick did what he expected—he swung at Regulus' shoulder. But as Carrick put his foot down and attempted to move forward into his attack, his boot caught. He faltered for the briefest moment as he regained his balance.

With every ounce of control, Regulus brought his sword down. Carrick realized too late he needed to move or block and made an attempt, but Regulus' blade hit the side of Carrick's helm and continued down to his shoulder. Carrick reeled, his grip on his sword slipping. Regulus pulled back his sword and thrust toward Carrick's neck. Carrick parried, but Regulus flicked his blade in a circular binding motion and pulled against Carrick's blade. His grip already weakened, the sword ripped out of Carrick's hands.

Before Regulus raised his sword to Carrick's chest, Carrick dove around him. Regulus turned as Carrick kicked the cut in the back of his knee and Regulus' leg buckled. Pain shot up and down his leg. The cut had started to close, and the impact reopened the wound, making it feel like his flesh was sliced through all over again. He gasped and spun on Carrick, who snatched his sword off the ground. Regulus adjusted his grip on his sword and blocked a hastily thrown attack. Their swords clanged together, and Regulus moved forward, guiding his sword down Carrick's blade. He slammed his head into Carrick's helm.

The impact rang in his ears, made his helm vibrate against his skull. Carrick teetered and lowered his sword. Regulus slammed the pommel of his sword into the side of Carrick's helm. A blow across Carrick's back, and Carrick fell to his knees. Regulus put the tip of his blade against Carrick's neck below his helm. Carrick froze. He let go of his sword and raised his hands.

Regulus swallowed against the dryness in his mouth and throat. His pulse pounded in his ears as he lowered then sheathed his sword and stepped away from Carrick. He offered his hand, but Carrick shoved it away.

"You'll pay for this, Hargreaves." Carrick's voice sounded tinny and muted through his visor. "I'm not done with you." He stomped away without removing his helm.

Regulus turned toward the spectators, his focus shifting from Carrick to the cacophony of applause, cheers...and booing. He removed his helm. Baron Carrick stood, clapping leisurely, but his expression was hard as stone. Regulus' gaze wandered over the crowd. Many stood, some smiling and cheering. Some yelling. He looked to Adelaide. She beamed, her broad smile making her cheeks round and her eyes crinkle as she stood and applauded. Baron Carrick held out a hand and the crowd's excitement dropped off to silence.

"The winner of this year's Etchy Tournament's sword competition," Baron Carrick said, his rich baritone ringing out over the arena, "is Lord Regulus Hargreaves of Arrano."

Most of the crowd cheered, although some jeered. The herald walked onto the field, carrying a miniature model of a knight with gold armor and a silver sword. He presented the little figure to Regulus, who accepted it with a deep bow.

Off the field, his knights greeted him with whoops and slaps on the back and shoulders. His pulse raced. He grinned and couldn't stop. Their exuberance heightened his own soaring emotions. But Regulus locked eyes on the woman moving through the crowd toward him. He shoved his helm and the tiny knight into the hands of one of his men, he wasn't even sure which. He pushed past them, only aware of her.

Adelaide's smile and shining eyes made his breath come faster. He strode toward her, ignoring the congratulations of the men he walked past. He knew what he wanted to do. Grab her by the waist, spin around as he lifted her into the air, and when he put her back down, kiss her. But that would be crazy. They weren't there. Not yet. But as they stopped, a little too close together, ideas of proper and crazy and logical and irrational blurred and then vanished. His chest tightened as he drifted toward her upturned face. His gaze drifted to her lips.

Searing pain prickled his right arm, and he winced. Her smile faded. His heart felt heavy. *Not now. Why now, Etiros? Why at all?* Anger rushed through him, followed by despair.

"Are you all right?" Adelaide placed her fingertips on his breastplate.

"Yes." He forced a smile. "Just the cut on my leg."

Her forehead wrinkled, concern in her eyes. "Is it deep? You should see the tournament physician at once."

"It's fine." He took her hand off his chest and held it. "I've had much worse."

Adelaide glanced at the scar on his cheek then met his eyes. "Still. Better get it stitched." She looked like she wanted to say something else, but she pulled her hand out of his and smiled coyly. "The sooner you get that mended, the more likely you will be able to dance after supper tonight."

She went up on her toes and planted a kiss on his unscarred cheek before he could react. His jaw went slack. He could still feel the soft, warm brush of her lips on his skin after she pulled away.

"See you tonight." She darted away.

"Right," he responded in a breathy whisper. "Yes." *Idiot.* The mark on his arm continued to tingle. A dull pain like a minor burn. He turned and headed for his tent.

"Now *that* looked promising," Dresden said, walking beside him. "So where are you headed in such a hurry?"

"I need to look to my leg." His words sounded blunter and harsher than intended.

"Oh. Right. Yes, good." Dresden dropped his voice to a whisper as they left the crowd behind. "Got to cover that before anyone notices." He nudged Regulus with his elbow. "And then did I hear something about dancing?"

"I don't think I'll be dancing." His throat pulled taut as he spoke in a low, sharp tone. *I'll have other business to attend to.*

"Reg, what's wrong?"

He wanted to scream. To punch something, or someone. To grab the sorcerer by the neck and shove him into a brick wall. He wanted to collapse to his knees and sob. Because he had known better. Now he knew more clearly than ever. His mark had burned right as he stood on the brink of careless joy. At the edge of love. It cut through his euphoria, pulling him back, reminding him what he was.

"Reg, slow down."

He couldn't risk hurting her.

"Is it the mark?"

He couldn't tell her the truth.

"Regulus!" Dresden grabbed his shoulders, forcing him to stop.

He had fallen for a daydream. Tried to live in one of the happily-ever-after romance ballads Caleb sang. But his life wasn't a romance.

"Reg?"

The truth crushed him, like his heart was being squeezed. His lungs compressed. His life wasn't a romance. It was a tragedy. Even if she accepted him, he might hurt her. *Not if you obey,* a selfish voice whispered. *"Such an obedient pet,"* the sorcerer's voice taunted. *"Next time, you won't get to choose."* He pushed Dresden aside.

"Regulus!"

Until he had paid his debt, he had no business loving Adelaide Belanger. Or anyone.

Because he wasn't his own man.

And slaves don't get the girl.

SELINA R. GONZALEZ

CHAPTER 25

AFTER REMOVING HIS ARMOR, REGULUS DOUBLE-CHECKED EACH knot holding the tent flap closed. Dresden sat lounging on a stool in front of the entrance as an extra precaution. Caleb had pulled out his lute and was playing it as loudly as possible. All the surrounding tents were his knights', but Regulus couldn't chance a passerby hearing anything suspicious.

He pulled a chain out from under his armor and over his head. The key hanging on the chain glinted in the lamplight. His hand hovered in front of the lock as he crouched in front of the chest. The mark burned hotter, the pain sharpening as he hesitated. A reminder the sorcerer would not be denied or ignored. He unlocked the chest and pulled out the mirror, then hooked it on a nail he had hammered into the tent post next to his cot for this exact eventuality.

With a deep breath he focused on keeping the anger and bitterness out of his face and voice. He wouldn't risk incurring the sorcerer's wrath in the middle of the tournament campground. "I'm here, my lord."

The mirror shimmered, and the sorcerer appeared. His hood was thrown back, revealing graying brown hair pulled away from his face. Regulus stifled a gasp. He had never seen the sorcerer's eyes before. The whites were bloodshot around coal-black irises rimmed with a thin line of green.

"Good! I—" The sorcerer squinted. "What are you doing? Where are you? This isn't familiar." He moved closer to the mirror, craning his head as if to look around Regulus' tent. "Where are you?"

What good would lying do him? "I'm competing in a tournament."

"A tournament? Interesting. Winning, I'd imagine."

"Yes, my lord," he kept his voice level, "but on my own strength." *I don't owe you anything.*

"Hmph. Ungrateful idiot. But that's not relevant right now." The sorcerer tugged on his beard, his movements frantic. "I've hit a wall. It's infuriating. You get so close to everything you've planned, you think you've thought of everything, that vengeance is finally assured, and just like that…a wall. A wall of my own creating! Isn't that darkly poetic." He glowered at Regulus, as if whatever wall he was talking about was Regulus' fault.

Regulus didn't respond. The sorcerer would get to the point eventually.

"Fix one problem, create another. Just have to do it all over again!" The sorcerer shook his head. "If those thrice-cursed mages weren't already long dead, I'd kill them. Such a hassle. Should have seen it coming, though."

Regulus tried to look uninterested and keep his confusion hidden. *What mages? Should have seen* what *coming?*

"No matter. Always work-arounds. See you, for example." The sorcerer chuckled to himself. "Just time-consuming. And requires *precision*. And it's exhausting."

Regulus clenched his jaw. *Don't ask. Obey. Pay your debt.* If he earned his release, he could court Adelaide. The thought made him much more willing to play the obedient servant.

"I need several very specific things from you," the sorcerer continued. "So pay attention. One thing out of place, and this won't work. And if this doesn't work, I swear by every dark curse I know I will kill you and everyone you care about. Understand?"

Regulus swallowed and nodded. "Yes, my lord." He was grateful the sorcerer didn't know about Adelaide. *Just follow his instructions, and no one will be hurt.*

"Good." The sorcerer crossed his arms. "First, I need a circlet of silver. It must be pure silver, no other metals. Second, I need a bushel of white flowers. Doesn't matter what kind, but they must be white. Third, I need clamshells. Eight large shells should do it. Fourth, and this is where things get difficult, I need the blood of an innocent person. Doesn't have to be a lot, just a few drops. And finally, I need a foot-long piece of a root of a neumenet tree."

"What?" Regulus gaped. "Blood?"

"Of an innocent person, that's important." The sorcerer waved his hand. "Yours won't do."

Regulus winced, guilt pricking his conscience, but moved on to another problem. "What's a neumenet tree?"

The sorcerer groaned. "Don't you know anything?"

Regulus stayed silent.

"Useless. Neumenet trees were considered sacred for thousands of years. They're very rare, and strong vessels of magic energy. People used to try to conceive their children in their shade, hoping to have a baby born with magic abilities. Sometimes worked, too. They have bark like obsidian and leaves that look like shards of glass but feel like feathers."

"And where do I find one?"

"There's one in Holgren Forest."

"But that's a royal forest!"

The sorcerer thrashed his teeth. "And I'm the Prince of Shadow and Ash! That forest belongs to me!"

Regulus recoiled. He had claimed that title the first time Regulus met him. Had bound him to tell any who asked the Black

Knight who he was that he served the Prince of Shadow and Ash. Regulus had assumed the sorcerer was being grandiose. But now he realized—the sorcerer seemed to think himself *actually* royal.

"With all due respect, my lord," Regulus said, trying to sound as humble as possible, "I don't think any sheriffs or forest rangers will care."

"Well," the sorcerer grinned coldly, "then kill them. Better yet, don't get caught."

"Yes, my lord."

"Now, tell me what you're bringing me."

Regulus sighed. "A circlet of pure silver. A bushel of white flowers. Eight clamshells. The…" he swallowed, his mouth dry, "the blood of an innocent person. The root of a neumenet tree." Whatever such specific and odd ingredients were for, he suspected he would regret being a part of it. As if the sorcerer interrupting a wonderful moment wasn't bad enough, that made his mood worse.

"Good. Make your plans. I *must* have everything *before* the next full moon, do you understand?"

Regulus shook his head, trying not to let his irritation with the sorcerer's tone show on his face. "When is the next full moon?"

"You are such an idiot." The sorcerer rolled his eyes. "A useful idiot, luckily for you."

Regulus clenched his teeth.

"Eleven days. You have eleven days. That should be enough time to gather everything. If I don't have all the ingredients on the eleventh day, or if you bring me the wrong ingredients—I will consider your debt unfulfilled. And I will collect in full."

He bit his tongue to stop his panicked protests as a shudder raced down his spine. "And…if I succeed, my lord?"

"Then we'll be much closer to being even." The image shimmered and reverted to a mirror.

Regulus stared at his scarred reflection. Eleven days. The mark had stopped burning. So long as he intended to obey, the mark should leave him alone. He could finish the tournament and still make it on time. He bit his cheek. *"I will collect,"* the sorcerer's voice echoed in his mind. No. He wouldn't be that selfish. He needed to leave Adelaide alone until he was free.

He locked the mirror back in the trunk and opened the flap of his tent. Dresden raised an eyebrow in a silent question. Regulus motioned him inside. Caleb continued to play his lute.

"What did he want?" Dresden sat on the small stool next to Regulus' bed.

"Flowers. Clamshells. A pure silver circlet. The root of a magical tree in a royal forest. Oh, and the blood of an innocent person."

Dresden gawked. "What?"

"I know." Regulus sat down on his cot and put his head in his hands. "He's doing something, working to accomplish some plan. He needs all of that before the next full moon, in eleven days." He dug his fingers into his skull. "If I don't get him the right ingredients on time, he will consider my debt unfulfilled and collect."

"But...that would mean..."

"Yes." Regulus laid back on the cot, his hands clammy and stomach churning. *You'll all be killed.* Acid burned at his throat. "But if I do this, he said we'd be close to being even."

"So the end is in sight."

"But at what cost, Drez?" He sat back up and wiped his forehead with his sleeve. "I have no idea what I'm helping him do! I think...he might have designs on the throne."

"Two years you've done his bidding. He's holed up in that infernal tower. Maybe you're wrong and he's not dangerous."

"Maybe." *I doubt it.* He hung his head. "But I can't refuse him. We know how that ends."

They sat in silence for a couple minutes until Dresden suddenly sat up straighter. "Wait, eleven days?"

"Yes."

Dresden grinned. "Then I propose you go dancing."

"Drez—"

"Come on. It'll cheer you right up. Get you to see some positives."

"I can't." Regulus shook his head. "I was a fool. I can't do this."

"Do what?"

"Court Adelaide!" He yanked his sleeve up, revealing the mark. His face burned with humiliation and guilt. "I'm not the hero in a romance. I let myself forget it, but I received a cruel reminder today."

"You said yourself, you're getting close." The gentleness and pity in Dresden's eyes made Regulus more irritated. "You *will* be free one day. Live like it. You choose who—"

"I am, yes. Right." He shook his head. "What if he orders me to do something I can't? What if…" His throat tightened, and he closed his eyes.

"You won't hurt her."

He met Dresden's eyes. "But what if—"

"You'll do what he wants, and he'll set you free." Dresden spoke slowly, his palms pressed together.

"Free or not, after everything I've done…" Regulus slumped. "I'm not worthy."

"Worthy? Etiros above, Regulus. You're a respected swordsman, a lord who can live comfortably, the best commander I've ever met, and the kindest, most selfless man I know."

Regulus flinched under the praise. "But I—"

"You are on the verge of having everything you never thought you could have. You're a lord with loyal knights. You won a contest of swords, and people cheered. For *you*. They might not all accept you, but some of them are coming around. You've found a chance at love."

Regulus rubbed the mark on his arm, his thumb pressing against the irregular scars. He wanted to believe Dresden. But he was a slave with blood-stained hands. He'd taken lives long before he met the sorcerer, but it wasn't the same. Guilt weighed on his shoulders while frustration mounted. Anger at what the sorcerer had forced him to become. Anger at the guilt that wouldn't die. Anger at Dresden for not understanding his despair.

"You can have a normal life," Drez said. "You can stop hiding in your castle. Stop living behind this wall you've put up around yourself and I've only seen you lower around her. You don't have to live the rest of your life shutting people out. Don't throw that all away."

"I don't shut you out," Regulus said weakly.

"Yes, you do!" Dresden stood and paced away. He turned around and Regulus recoiled from the anger in his friend's eyes. "We know your secret, but you don't let us help. You rarely tell us where you go or what you do. You push us all away! And don't say to protect us. You do it because you're too proud to admit you're afraid." Dresden shook his head. "After two years, I don't know if I can keep having the same conversations with you, Reg. How can I hold you up when you're so determined to drown!"

Regulus' heart twisted as Dresden's frustration stoked his own anger. He yanked his sleeve down. "If that's how you feel, why don't you go? I never asked you to stay!"

"You idiot!" Dresden cursed. "You didn't have to!"

Regulus turned away. "Just leave."

"No." Dresden sat on the ground and folded his arms. "Not until you stop being a fool, believe that you'll get through this, and agree to dance with Adelaide tonight and joust tomorrow. You didn't come all the way here—"

"You don't get it! You don't understand what it's like!" Regulus stood and pointed at the tent door, fury and hopelessness burning under his skin. He hadn't asked for a lecture. "Get out!"

Dresden scowled. "I'm here as your friend. You can't give me orders."

"I can and I am. Leave, or I'll throw you out." Regulus pointed again, more emphatically, but Dresden didn't budge. "Now, Jakobs! Go!"

Dresden turned crimson. "I see." His neck muscles bulged as he swallowed hard and stood. "Anything you want me to do once I leave, *Captain*? Or is it my lord?" He gave a messy, low, mocking bow, his voice bitter. "Command me, master. I live to serve."

Blood rushed to Regulus' face. He dropped his hand to his side. Dresden turned toward the tent entrance.

"Drez, wait—"

"That's a bit familiar for your servant, isn't it, *master*?"

"I didn't—" But Drez walked out of his tent. "...mean it." Shame twisted Regulus' stomach. He groaned and kicked the leg of the cot.

Regulus had never viewed Dresden as inferior, despite their often unequal and complicated relationship. Dresden calling Regulus master had only been to appease Regulus' strict childhood guardian. One of many things Regulus had done over the years to protect his friend. But nothing could erase that Dresden had been little more than a slave for seven years. Nothing negated that there had been times as a captain when Regulus couldn't make an exception, not even for his lieutenant. He shouldn't have snapped. But it was Dresden's own fault for pushing him. And Dresden shouldn't have thrown such a low blow in return.

It took Regulus an hour to cool off and swallow his pride enough to leave his tent, but he couldn't leave things like that. Caleb lounged in front of his own tent, strumming on his lute. Harold and Jerrick were talking while Harold polished a pair of boots. They all went silent and looked up at Regulus.

"He's in his tent." Jerrick looked at Regulus through narrowed eyes. "But enter at your own risk."

Caleb plucked at a string on his lute, pointedly not making eye contact with Regulus. "Haven't seen him that riled in a while."

Thankfully, Dresden hadn't fastened his tent door closed. Regulus ducked inside. Dresden had his double scimitars in both hands, moving through his drills between his cot and a small leather trunk. He spun around just as Regulus entered, and Regulus jumped back. Dresden lowered the blades and bowed his head.

"Yes, my lord?"

"Drez, don't. I told you never to call me that." Regulus chewed on his cheek. "I'm sorry, okay?" *No, it's not okay.* "I crossed a line. I didn't mean anything by it. And I'm sorry."

Dresden's scimitars twitched, but he raised his head.

"You're right. I don't talk to you." Regulus rubbed the back of his neck. "Yes, I'm afraid. Afraid I'll hurt one of you. Afraid you'd lose all respect for me if you knew the things I've done."

"Reg." Drez sighed, hurt in his pinched expression. "Don't you know me better than that? We're brothers. We need each other. Being a lone wolf doesn't make you stronger, just lonely and vulnerable. You used to tell the mercenaries wolves were strongest when they worked together. When did you stop believing that?"

When my presence became a threat. Drez didn't give him time to reply.

"And we're mercenaries. We're not squeamish. Besides, it's not you. It's not who you are. You're doing what you have to; it's not like you enjoy it."

"But I'm still doing it." He stared at the trampled grass beneath his boots.

Dresden shuffled his feet. "If it was me…would you leave?"

Of course not. "I don't know. You've never attacked me in cold blood."

"I've felt like attacking you in hot blood." A hint of mirth crept into Dresden's voice. He placed the weapons on the trunk. "I'm still not abandoning you. Even if I have to tell you a hundred times a day: it's going to be okay, you'll make it through this, you're still worthy, still my brother. And Regulus…it wasn't you. If Harold and I can accept that, why can't you?"

Because it was still my fault. The words stuck in his throat, too raw, too shameful and excruciating to let out of the darkness of his mind. *Because I saw the light in your eyes fading, felt you dying as I squeezed your throat. Because your tear-stained face as you begged me to remember you—when I did, when I knew you, but I couldn't control my own body— still haunts my dreams.*

The cot squeaked as Dresden sat on it. "He hasn't controlled you—"

"He has." Regulus didn't look at Dresden.

"…what?"

Regulus closed his eyes and spoke quietly. "Four times since then. Just not at the castle. A momentary hesitation, a brief refusal, temporary uncertainty. Usually just long enough to remind me he can. And I've been tortured so many times I've lost count." The silence that followed his admission threatened to swallow him alive.

"Etiros above, Regulus. Why?"

Regulus opened his eyes. "He's easily angered. And I'm… stubborn and resentful."

"No. Why haven't you told me?" Hurt reflected in Dresden's eyes.

"Telling you doesn't change it."

"You're a damned fool."

"You're right," he murmured. "That's why I don't deserve Adelaide."

Dresden was silent for a moment. "So? You haven't endangered us; you won't endanger her. Maybe having someone else to protect will help you be smarter. You're better around her, Reg. More hopeful. You should tell her the truth."

"What?" Regulus jerked his head up. "Are you out of your mind?"

"You're so afraid she won't accept you, you're about to push her away. Why not give her that choice? You will lose her by walking away, anyway. Doesn't she deserve a chance to decide for herself if she wants to take the risk? Just like the rest of us did?"

Regulus worked his jaw. Dresden had a point. If Regulus and Adelaide's roles were reversed, wouldn't he want the truth? Wouldn't he want a chance to choose acceptance or not? But if he walked away now…yes, he might lose her. But he wouldn't have to live with the pain of seeing the way she looked at him change. But if she could understand, if she could love him anyway… He longed for her acceptance as much as he longed for freedom.

"Do you even like her, Reg?"

"Excuse me?"

Drez threw his hands in the air. "You're giving up so easily, she must not be that special."

Heat flared in his chest. "Of course she's special!"

"Then tell me why!"

"She's…" Regulus looked away and took a deep breath as he pictured her smile. The thought of her calmed his jittery nerves. "She's smart and capable and confident. She's humorous and kind. She's honest. And…she *sees* me. Not a servant's son, or a mercenary, or a captain. Not someone she owes anything to. More than a walking testament to my father's infidelity. Not an imposter or just a title. Not a slave. I haven't met someone who sees me apart from all of that since we were children. And it took you months to see me as your friend."

As he spoke, he understood. He might never find someone like Adelaide again. And if she could see him now, maybe she could see him in spite of his link to the sorcerer. Drez was right. He wasn't protecting her. He was hiding.

"If you mean all that, how can you walk away?"

"Fine." Regulus nodded. "I'll consider telling her."

"And you'll go to the dance?" Dresden crossed his arms, his gaze sharp, the hard slant of his mouth allowing no argument. "You owe me after that ordering stunt."

Regulus winced. *An opportunity to hold Adelaide in my arms?* He sighed, losing the battle with both himself and Drez. "Yes."

CHAPTER 26

"You know what Mother would say?" Minerva sat on Adelaide's cot. Early evening light still filtered through the heavy green fabric of the tent. A few candles illuminated the interior—her cot on a small wooden frame, Giselle's straw mattress in the corner, and a trunk with a cloak on it. A large rug covered most of the ground.

Adelaide sat on a stool, looking at her reflection in a small mirror hung on the tent wall. She stuck another pin in her hair to hold the ribbon-accented braid in place atop her head. "Probably something cautionary I don't want to hear."

"She'd probably say you can't go getting swept off your feet by any good swordsman."

"I'm not in love with him because he's a good swordsman." She stuck in another pin.

"Ah, but you admit you're in love with him."

"What? I—" She jabbed herself in the head with a pin and winced. "*In love* is a little much. Besides, I thought you were supporting this…whatever it is?"

"Courtship?"

She glared at Minerva. "We're not courting."

"Not officially," Minerva smirked, "but you might as well be. Gracious, after his victory I thought you two were going to kiss. And not the little peck I saw you give him."

"Hmph." Adelaide turned back to the mirror, trying to act nonchalant. There was a moment there…he had been so close. She had felt a fluttering in her stomach. The look in his eyes, intense as a bonfire yet clear as an undisturbed lake on a cool morning. She had *wanted* him to kiss her. To put his hand behind her head and pull her in. For a moment, she had considered kissing him herself. But then that look of pain. That… Sadness in his eyes.

She tried to ignore the nagging impression something was wrong. Maybe she saw in him what she felt in herself. That feeling of lying. Of hiding the truth. When he reminded her of the cut on his leg, she had wanted to heal it. She could have insisted she go with him to the physician's tent, pulled him aside on the way and healed him. Good as new.

As soon as the idea had occurred to her, she decided against it. Not yet. But if she couldn't trust him now, could she ever trust him? Was her hesitance only the echoes of warnings from her parents? Or something more? What should she do when her heart screamed to trust him and her mind urged caution?

Minerva laid a hand on her shoulder. "What are you thinking?"

"About why—or if—I trust Regulus." Adelaide chewed on her lower lip. "I'm too used to *not* trusting. How do I know if I should? Father always says to never let emotions make your decisions. But when your emotions are so involved, how can you tell if you're being rational or not? Am I paranoid not to trust him? Am I foolish *to* trust him?"

Minerva squeezed her shoulder. "These are things you can determine with time, Ad. You don't need to decide if you're marrying him today. Sooner or later, you'll know. Like I knew with Gaius."

"Yes, but you didn't have a secret."

"I knew yours. I still keep that one."

Adelaide paused, her hands poised above her head as she checked the braid. "I'm sorry. It can't be easy."

Minerva shrugged and stroked her growing belly. "Sometimes, I'd like to talk to him. It's not that I don't trust him; I know if I told him he wouldn't tell a soul. But it's not my secret to share."

"But it is mine." Adelaide dropped her hands to her lap. "What if…" She fiddled with the belt of her dress. "What if I tell him, and it's not that he wants to use my power, or he tells someone he shouldn't? What if…"

"What if it scares him?"

Adelaide looked at Minerva. Anxiety gnawed at her stomach.

Minerva chuckled and shook her head. "Based on what I've heard, how he acts, and how he fought today, I'm not sure anything scares that man."

"But what if it's too…strange?"

"Regulus hasn't lived his whole life in Monparth. For all you know, he's met a mage before."

She hadn't considered that.

"All right." Adelaide nodded. "I'll get to know him more. Focus on that, not whether or when to tell him."

"Good." Minerva held out her hand, and Adelaide helped her to her feet. "Ready for supper and dancing?"

Adelaide smiled as her gaze went to Min's belly. "Only if little Adelaide is."

"Oh ho, really?" Minerva laughed. "Gaius' mother is determined it's a boy."

Adelaide laughed and hunched over to talk to Min's stomach. "You're a girl, aren't you? We shall throw knives and climb trees and speak Khast and I'll tell you stories about your mother's childhood shenanigans."

"I think not on that last one." Minerva rolled her eyes as she grinned. "And just because you're the better knife thrower doesn't mean you can steal my job. *If* the little one's a girl, I'll teach her like Mother taught me." Her grin turned mischievous and her eyes glinted. "You can teach future little girl Hargreaves to throw knives."

Adelaide choked on a gasp as her face flushed. "That's it, I'm not speaking to you for the rest of the night, *Tha Lonri*." She took one final glance in the mirror and headed out, Minerva's laughter following her.

Regulus walked into the gate at the end of the jousting arena and looked around, impressed. Benches and tables filled the arena. Lanterns hung from posts positioned around the low walls and in the stands. Candelabras glowed on each table. Commoners crowded stands, taking full advantage of the hospitality of the tournament. They would eat the same food as the nobles, but they weren't allowed to eat with them. Nobles were already finding seats at the tables in the arena. No one told them where to sit in the spirit of the tournament. All hereditary nobles could compete, and thus all were equal at the tournament. Except they weren't.

The nobles sorted themselves. Knighted freemen, like Regulus' knights, sat with the commoners. They could get into the arena if they wanted, no one checked letters of nobility here. A title would suffice. But the legacy nobles made their disdain clear. Even most poor knights felt more comfortable with the other freemen. Within the arena, the wealthier and more famous nobles claimed the seats closest to Baron Carrick's table, positioned below his viewing box in the center of the arena.

Regulus headed for that table. As one of the day's champions, he had been invited to sit with the tournament's host. Baron and Baroness Carrick's high-backed chairs sat in the middle, flanked by two chairs on either side. A page stood to the table's left. A couple other winners were also arriving. Regulus recognized the sturdy man with silver hair as Sir Gerald Malone, champion of the archery competition. He hadn't watched or paid attention to any of the other competitions that day, so he didn't recognize the tall, lithe man with the red hair and beard.

The page directed Sir Malone to the chair on the far right and directed Red to the next seat. He pointed Regulus to the chair on the far left. Regulus leaned on the arm of the empty chair next to him and extended his hand across three seats to Red. "Lord Regulus Hargreaves."

The man shook his hand with a grip like a vise. "I know." He had a deep, commanding voice. "Everyone is talking about you, Lord Hargreaves. I only caught your last fight, but it was impressive."

"And you are?" Regulus felt a little swell of pride, but kept his posture relaxed.

"Lord Frederick Ganlar, son of Duke Ganlar. Long staff champion."

Regulus nearly gasped. As one of three ducal families in Monparth, the Ganlars were practically royalty. Three barons and several lords, including Adelaide's father, owed Duke Ganlar their fealty. What was he doing competing in a tournament held by a lesser noble?

Ganlar laughed. "I know what you're thinking, Lord Hargreaves. I'm here for the same reason as everyone else. Sport, my friend."

"Pardon my confusion, but you came all the way from Nueres Duchy to compete in the long staff?"

"And why not? As you can see, I'm good at it." He held up his hands and lifted one shoulder. "But mostly, I can't compete in Nueres. Men get nervous about fighting their liege's heir. They make mistakes they otherwise wouldn't. Takes all the fun out of it."

"But…why not the sword?" Sir Malone asked the question Regulus hadn't dared.

"Because that's what everyone would expect." Ganlar stroked his big red beard. "I enjoy surprising people. But mostly I enjoy the long staff. It has its own unique cadence. And the added challenge of not being able to rely on any sharp edges."

"Speaking of which, that looked to be a nasty cut Sir Carrick landed on your leg," Sir Malone said. "I'd rather expected you to have a limp."

"Oh." Dread circled Regulus' throat. "It wasn't as bad as it looked. And the physician did a good job."

"Not to be crass," Ganlar said, leaning back in his chair, "but you look like you're not a stranger to pain."

Regulus clenched his fist under the table. "I suppose that's accurate."

"Oh, brilliant." Carrick's voice behind Regulus was cold as ice. "Whose idea was *this* seating arrangement?"

"Mine." Baron Carrick approached the table, his wife at his side. "I'm giving you a second chance to demonstrate honor in defeat. You have one victory and one loss today, but if you continue to act like a child, you will have lost your dignity." His mouth turned down. "So far you're not doing well." Baron and Baroness Carrick took their seats, the Baron sitting beside Lord Ganlar.

Carrick hesitated for a moment, then took the seat between the baroness and Regulus. Regulus ignored him. He sensed Carrick's animosity, and it sparked a reciprocal loathing.

The baron welcomed and thanked the attendees and praised the competitors. Carrick had won the polearm competition. Once the baron gave the word, servants began dispersing food and the cacophony of hundreds of voices in competing conversations filled the arena.

"My mistake," Carrick said, his voice a low whisper, his head angled toward Regulus, "was doing polearm and sword. If I had skipped polearm, I would have had more energy. I would have beaten you."

Regulus bit into a turkey leg. He wanted to ignore Carrick. Pretend he hadn't heard. But what was the saying? Kindness burns like hot coals? Something like that. "You fought admirably, Sir Carrick. Particularly after winning in the polearm. Perhaps you are correct. But regardless, you should not be ashamed of how you fared."

Carrick gripped his flagon so hard his knuckles turned white. "I'm the son of a baron. Shame isn't an emotion I feel. But you will. I promise you."

"Did you say something, Nolan?" The baroness looked at them with a smile, but her eyes were cold beneath her blue wimple. Such an old-fashioned woman.

"Just congratulating Lord Hargreaves on his win, Mother." Carrick's smile looked painfully forced. "And looking forward to tomorrow's joust."

Baroness Carrick sighed. "Perhaps if you had an ounce of humility and a touch more civility, you'd have a wife by now." Her voice reminded Regulus of the time Caleb tightened the strings on his lute too far and one snapped.

Carrick aggressively bit into a piece of roast quail and didn't respond.

Regulus looked over the crowd as he ate, seeking Adelaide. Wherever she was, he couldn't find her among the crowded tables.

"Lord Hargreaves," Baron Carrick's voice cut through his thoughts.

He cleared his throat. "Yes, my lord?" Being so close to the baron felt odd. Regulus hadn't spoken to him in the two years since he'd sworn his fealty and Baron Carrick had confirmed the transference of his title and land.

"I'm curious why I haven't seen you compete before."

The whole table looked at Regulus. The back of his neck itched. "I spent twenty-seven years of my life without a title, unable to compete in tournaments. Once titled, I hadn't changed, only my legal status. I was in no rush to risk my neck seeking glory among those who hadn't yet accepted me when I could finally rest and stop risking my neck for those too rich to risk their own."

The row of faces stared at Regulus in mute shock.

He hadn't intended to be so blunt or accusatory. The words just…spilled out. His mind seemed to relish the chance to lash out instead of suffering judgmental looks and whispered conversations in silence. *Well done, Regulus.*

"Then you're not still a mercenary?" Carrick's haughty tone made Regulus' fingers ache to grip a sword.

"No."

"And why would he be?" Baron Carrick pulled a grape off a bunch on the table in front of him. "Such pursuits are for men cut off, with no inheritance or title."

Carrick shot his father a scalding glance before returning to eating and drinking.

"You think very little of the men who hired you as a mercenary?" Lord Ganlar asked, his expression solemn.

"By and large they seemed to think very little of me," Regulus said, on edge. "When you fight another man's battles and he treats you like a hunting hound, it's difficult to maintain a high regard for that man." He thought of the sorcerer with delusions of royalty. His fingers dug into his leg, and he willed himself to relax.

Ganlar looked thoughtful, if guarded. "I suppose that's fair."

"At least hounds are loyal to their lord. Mercenaries can't even claim that dignity." Carrick sipped from his tankard, the look in his eyes daring Regulus to retaliate.

Regulus kept his tone even. "I never took conflicting contracts, I chose my benefactors carefully, and I refused to work with unscrupulous mercenaries. I only helped innocents, never harmed them. So don't think me without honor because I served no lord. I was loyal to my men, and my men to me." He inclined his head, realizing he should cover his bases. "As Lord of Arrano, I am loyal to Baron Carrick and to the king." *Although I hope they never collect on my fealty.*

"I am pleased to have men with skills such as yours I can count on." Baron Carrick's voice was steady and pleasant, but he didn't look at Regulus. Eventually, the others fell to talking amongst themselves. Regulus ate in silence, and no one asked him any more questions.

After supper, Regulus wove between guests and dodged servants carrying tables and benches, seeking Adelaide. He found her as the musicians started playing. She grinned and his stress evaporated. *Don't get carried away,* he reminded himself.

"May I have this dance?" Regulus bowed and held out his hand.

"I think you've earned it." Adelaide took his hand with a teasing laugh.

Her skin on his sent a thrill up his arm. She wore a scarlet dress with a low square neckline. Swirling gold embroidery covered the bodice and cuffed the sleeves at her elbows. Below her elbows, sheer red fabric hung down to her wrists. A gold pendant set with a small ruby hung from the gold chain around her neck, the gold contrasting well with her soft brown skin. She looked like a dream.

As they danced, everything else seemed to fade. To become less important. More manageable. The awkwardness of supper seemed trivial. Even the mark on his arm seemed inconvenient rather than life-ending. *The sorcerer said I'm getting close.* Adelaide spun, the lantern light reflecting off the red ribbon and gold pins in her black braid. Her arm brushed his, and reckless hope burned anew in his chest. *I can do this. I can love her and earn my freedom.*

They moved through the steps. Closer together, her nearness an ache in his heart. Further apart, her distance suffocating. She spun as the song ended, and Regulus stepped forward. Adelaide bumped into him, her hands resting on his chest. A pleasurable tremor skittered down his spine as his hands found her waist.

His eyes darted down to her lips. The warmth of her body so close to his was intoxicating. He leaned forward. She didn't pull back, but he thought of the sorcerer and hesitated. She deserved to know the truth first. To have a choice. He wanted to kiss her—Etiros above did he want to kiss her—but he wanted her to kiss him with full knowledge of everything he was. She bit her lower lip and his heart raced like a startled deer.

"Come to Arrano for supper," he whispered, breathless. He forced himself to look back at her eyes.

Her gaze dropped momentarily, as if she were disappointed. "When?"

"As soon as you can." Suddenly, he realized she couldn't just come over. Not alone, anyway. "You, your sister. Sir Gaius. I want you to come to my estate for supper."

She cocked her head to the side. "There's the tournament. Then getting back. Five days from now?"

Regulus shook his head, remembering the sorcerer. "I forgot. I have an…engagement. I promised I would help someone and will be away for a few days. In twelve days?"

Adelaide's shoulders slumped. "That's the day before Lord Drummond is hosting Lord Thealane and his family for three days. We won't be able to get away."

"What about in eleven days?" The sorcerer needed his ingredients *before* the full moon, not *on* that day. Regulus could get the ingredients and be back by then.

"All right. I'll check with Gaius and Minerva." She pulled away from him, and he let her go with reluctance. He moved further away from the couples trying to dance around him, some looking at him with pursed lips. Within a couple minutes, Adelaide found him again. She beamed. "We'll be there."

"Six in the evening?"

"Sounds perfect."

Regulus took her hand and danced with her until the musicians stopped playing. They talked and laughed. As the last note faded, he cupped her face in his hands. He swallowed against the lump in his throat. *Not yet.* He wouldn't try to kiss her in front of all these strangers—several of whom cast disapproving frowns their way. No, he wouldn't take advantage of the rush of dancing so close to each other. He still needed to tell her the truth. *Patience.* He brushed a soft kiss against her forehead and stepped away before he lost his resolve.

"I'll see you tomorrow."

Adelaide nodded, a bashful smile on her face. "Tomorrow."

He watched her find her sister and Sir Gaius and disappear among the crowd leaving the arena. He sighed. Deep. Contented. For the first time in years, he knew exactly what to do.

Joust. Win. Take care of the sorcerer's shopping list. Have supper with Adelaide, Gaius, and Minerva. Get Adelaide alone. Tell her everything. And if things went how he hoped, once free, he'd ask her to marry him.

Regulus felt too exhilarated and nervous at once to sleep, so he exited the opposite end of the jousting arena. The waxing moon and glittering stars shone in the cloudless sky. The cool summer night air comfortable after so much dancing.

He wasn't a good dancer, never had been. Adequate, sure. But Adelaide didn't seem to mind. No one had bothered them. Even Carrick hadn't shown his face. And Regulus had been too busy looking at Adelaide to bother noticing anyone else.

Footsteps. A rustling, behind him and to his right. He spun around.

Carrick stepped out from behind a large bush, sword hanging from his belt. "Hello, mercenary." He sneered. "Where are your peasant friends? The Carasian who's always trailing you like a shadow?" Four more men stepped around Carrick, although none of them carried swords.

Regulus reached for his sword. His fingers grasped at empty air. *Feast. Dancing. No swords.* A string of curses went through his mind.

"Missing something?" Carrick drawled. "You look better without the sword. More like what you really are—the son of a servant."

Regulus' hands clenched. "What do you want?"

"I'd like your head." Carrick rested his hand on his sword hilt. "But it would be suspicious if you turned up dead. So, I'm not going to kill you. But I'll settle for your humiliation. Kneel."

"Excuse me?"

"You said you're loyal to my father. Prove it. Kneel."

Regulus worked his jaw and eyed the other men, weighing his options. If he walked away, Carrick could attack from behind. "I do not need to kneel before a spare son with a title beneath my own." Carrick grimaced, and Regulus knew he'd struck a nerve. "But out of deference for your father..." He bowed at the waist. "Have a good evening, my lord."

Carrick glowered. "Break the bastard's arms."

The four men moved forward. Regulus stepped back, trying to decide if he should fight or run. "You would assault a lord?"

Carrick shrugged. "My father and I are not on the best of terms, as you probably noticed. But who will he believe? You? Or me and the sons of some of the most respected knights in Thaera Duchy?"

"All this over a lost contest?" Regulus shook his head, watching the other four men. "Why is it so important to you?"

Carrick's expression darkened. "You think this is about one contest?" He jutted his chin at Regulus. "Take him down."

The other knights lunged forward. Regulus hesitated only a moment. He couldn't risk them discovering his secret. He turned to run.

"Coward!" He ignored Nolan's taunt.

An arrow whistled and Regulus scanned the darkness. An archer stood half-hidden in the shadow of a small tree ten paces ahead of him. He didn't find the arrow fast enough to dodge it. The head bit into his left arm, the shaft sinking deep into his flesh. He gritted his teeth as he changed course away from the archer. The tip of his boot caught on the ground and he tripped. Not enough to make him fall, but enough to slow him. One of the knights threw himself against his back. Regulus fell to the ground.

CHAPTER 27

MINERVA HELD ADELAIDE'S HAND, SQUEEZING IT IN HER excitement as they walked back to their tents. Gaius chuckled and shook his head as Minerva rattled off questions.

"Is he a good dancer? Did you kiss him? He invited just us? How do we dress for that? Did he say anything about courtship? Marriage? Do—"

"Slow down, Min." Adelaide giggled. "One at a time."

"All right, all right. Is he a good dancer?"

"I'll be honest; I've danced with better." She squeezed Minerva's hand. "But that was the most fun I've ever had dancing."

"So?" Minerva elbowed her. "Did he kiss you?"

"Min!"

"Is that a yes?" Minerva winked.

"No." Adelaide bit her lip. "He seemed hesitant. I nearly kissed him myself, but then, I thought…maybe he should know first."

"Know what?" Gaius asked. Her eyes widened in alarm.

"That Father's picky about suitors," Min said. Adelaide relaxed.

"Truth." Gaius laughed. "Curious, though. Hargreaves hasn't invited anyone to Arrano castle since he arrived."

Adelaide shrugged. "I guess you'll see Arrano in eleven days. The third of next month."

"What do we wear?" Minerva rubbed her stomach. "It's not a party, but he is a lord…"

"I'm pretty sure he doesn't care."

"Mm, true, we *are* only invited because he couldn't invite only you."

Adelaide rolled her eyes to hide her embarrassment.

"Did he say anything about courtship or marriage?" Minerva prodded.

"Well, no." She pinched the sheer fabric of one of her sleeves between her fingers. "We were a little preoccupied with dancing. And talking about…everything and nothing. Sword fighting. Daggers. Food. Stories from when we were children."

"Maybe that's something you should talk about before the tournament ends," Minerva said. "Might be a good idea to make sure you're on the same page about where this is going before we go to his estate."

Blood rushed to her face. "Are you doubting his intentions?"

"No, just…" Minerva's expression communicated more than words. Understanding. Sympathy. Love. Protectiveness. "Regulus seems like a good man. I like him. And I won't lie, I like the idea of you living closer." She winked. "But anyone can put on a good act, and I don't want you to get hurt."

"I *can* take care of myself you know."

"I'm not talking about physical pain." Minerva rubbed her thumb on Adelaide's hand as they stopped in front of Adelaide's tent. "I don't want him to break your heart. I want to make sure you're staying grounded."

"Don't worry." Adelaide pulled her hand away and smiled. "I'm using my heart *and* my head."

"All right." Minerva rubbed Adelaide's arm. A comforting gesture she had picked up from Mother. "I'll see you in the morning." She and Gaius headed toward their tent.

Giselle held open the entrance to the tent. "Shall I help you change, my lady?"

Adelaide peered into the dark tent. How could she sleep right now? The rush she had felt when Regulus cupped her face in his hands hadn't quite worn off. She still felt the touch of his lips on her forehead. The strength of his hands on her waist as they danced. Still saw the longing in his eyes. She'd felt pulled to him, like he was magnetic.

No, she couldn't sleep yet. Too much energy still thrummed through her. "Actually," she ducked inside to grab her riding cloak, "let's go for a walk."

As they wandered away from the tents and the accompanying fires and lanterns, Adelaide realized they should have brought a torch. But her eyes adjusted to the moonlight well enough. Giselle followed a short distance behind her, more a consideration of propriety than any kind of safety.

Away from the crowded tents, the noises of the night took over. The whisper of leaves brushing against each other. The chirping of crickets. An occasional croak of a frog or hoot of an owl. Adelaide breathed in the cool air, letting it calm her. Distant shouting jarred her out of her reverie. On instinct, she turned toward the noise. Grunts, shouts, and gasps carried through the night. Pulse rising, she drew her dagger from her boot.

"Wait right here! Understand?"

Giselle nodded, her face pale in the moonlight.

Adelaide hurried toward the sound. The voices came into focus. "...strong!"

"Kick him harder!" A man yelped, others shouted. "Stay down!" Gasps. The sound of flesh hitting flesh.

"Get off me!"

Adelaide's breath came out in a rush. *Regulus?* Magic flared in her veins, a wild inferno of desperate energy under her skin. She ran past a couple trees. Several feet ahead, a group of four men leaned over a man on the ground, hitting and kicking him, while another man looked on. The man on the ground grabbed the shirt of one of the attackers and pushed him away. The assailant stumbled back, and moonlight fell on the downed man's face.

"Regulus!" Adelaide screamed as she ran toward the group.

They all looked up, surprise on their faces, even as one of the men sent his boot into the side of Regulus' head.

Anger rushed through her like fire. "Leave him *alone*!" She swung her dagger, although she wasn't yet close enough to hit any of them. Fire erupted from her hand, traveling down the dagger and throwing an arc of flame toward Regulus' attackers. They yelled and jumped back. Her dagger burned in her hand, and she tossed it aside. She grabbed a throwing knife out of her other boot. "Get back!"

"What was that?" one of the men demanded.

Panic clawed at her insides. "My torch. It went out." She held up her knife as she advanced. "But I still have this knife, and I'll throw it into the head of the next man that harms him!"

The men looked at each other. "Let's go," the onlooker said.

Her hand dropped as she recognized his voice. She looked over, shock replaced by fury. "Nolan?"

Nolan's hard expression was unreadable. "We're done here. I'll leave you with your strong hero." He turned and strode away, followed by the other men. Another man she hadn't noticed walked past her and Regulus, following the others, a bow in his hands. *Fool. You rushed in without checking your surroundings!* Father would be ashamed.

Adelaide dropped to her knees next to Regulus and let the knife slip out of her hand. He pushed himself up.

"Stop! Wait! How badly are you hurt?" She put her hands on his shoulders, forcing him to lie on his back. That's when she noticed the arrow in his left arm.

He grasped her hand with his right hand and sat up. Blood ran down the side of his face. "I'm fine. Honestly."

"You're hurt!"

Regulus lifted his right shoulder but kept his left arm still. "I've been worse."

Her chest heaved as she looked him up and down. Regulus' clothes were torn. Moonlight reflected off the blood on his face and on his arm around the arrow, and he might have additional wounds she couldn't see. "Is anything broken?"

He winced as he shifted. "I don't think so." He still held her hand in his. "What are you doing out here?"

"I was going for a walk." She pulled her right hand free and reached for his head. He gasped and jerked away when she touched his hairline. She clenched her jaw. "What happened?"

"It doesn't matter."

"You're hurt! And Nolan…it matters!"

"I'll be fine." He rubbed a circle on her hand with his thumb. "Thank you."

"We have to tell Baron Carrick."

"Adelaide, no."

"What?" She looked into his eyes. "What do you mean, no?"

"It's not worth it. I'm fine. Dresden has stitched me up plenty of times. He'll make short work of my arm. Okay?"

She looked at the arrow embedded in his arm. How he was acting so unbothered, she didn't know. She was about to ask if she should go find Dresden when he spoke.

"Adelaide." Her pulse quickened. Her mind screamed an alarm at his odd tone. "I didn't see a torch."

Her breathing turned shaky. Blood drained from her face. Her hands felt clammy, so she pulled her hand free of his. "I…tossed it aside when it went out." She looked toward where she had thrown her dagger. Why was she lying? Because she wasn't used to telling the truth. Because her parents had been so afraid of the truth. *I want to trust him. I should tell him…*

Regulus gently pulled on her chin, turning her face back toward him. "I've seen something like that before. In Vanelt. A mage gifted in manipulating fire working for a circus." There was no accusation in his voice. Just an observation. Only kindness, and a touch of sadness, showed in his eyes. The warmth in his tone calmed some of her panic.

"I…" She licked her lips, unsure how to proceed.

"It's okay." He cupped the side of her face in his large hand. "I won't tell anyone. And you don't have to talk about it. I shouldn't have said anything."

"My parents…" She swallowed. "They worry it's dangerous. After…"

"After The Shadow."

She nodded, her breathing normalizing. "You don't…" She put her hand over his on her cheek. "You aren't afraid? Or angry I didn't tell you?"

"What? No!" Regulus scooted closer and grimaced. "You just saved me. How could I be afraid of you? And I can't imagine what it's like to be, possibly, the only mage in all Monparth. You must feel so alone." His voice held sympathy. Like he knew the burden of carrying a secret.

"I wanted to tell you," Adelaide whispered, "but I'm so used to hiding. My parents don't want me to use my power at all. They're afraid." Her words rushed out, fed by relief at no longer hiding and the need to explain herself. "Afraid The Shadow will find me if I use my magic. Or that people might try to kill me before I could hurt them. Or that others would try to use me."

He nodded. "I can see the wisdom in hiding a truth that dangerous."

"I'm sorry—"

"No, don't apologize." He rubbed his thumb over her cheekbone. "Wait." He looked around. "Are you out here all alone?"

She gestured vaguely behind her. "I left my maid back there when I heard shouting."

"You heard shouting, so you ran toward it?"

"It sounded like someone needed help."

Regulus chuckled. "Brave like a tigress indeed."

She bit her lip. "Do you think Nolan or any of his friends noticed?"

"None of them seem particularly bright. I'm sure you're fine." He smiled. "But you might want to try not conjuring fire if you want to keep being a mage a secret."

"I didn't do it on purpose!" Adelaide groaned. "It's…sometimes difficult to control. Although I'm getting better." *Which means I can help.* She straightened and scanned the shadows. "Hello? Anyone there?"

Regulus lowered his hand from her cheek. "What—"

"Shh." She listened and watched the darkness. "Just checking. All right. I don't think anyone is around."

"Why—"

Adelaide held out her hand and summoned a ball of azure-tinged light. It hung in the air, illuminating Regulus' wounds. "I can't believe Nolan would attack you." Literally. Her mind refused to believe what she had seen. As if there had to be another explanation. She clenched her teeth as she inspected the arrow buried in his upper arm. "Why would he do this?"

Regulus gazed at the orb, lips parted. "To send a message. To humiliate me. To prevent me from competing tomorrow. Take your pick."

She gently parted his hair and found the cut on his head. It wasn't as bad as expected. "You'll compete tomorrow," she declared. "And you'll knock Nolan Carrick off his horse." She held her hand over the cut. Warmth spread across her glowing palm as the blue light made the blood look purplish.

"What are you… Oh." He relaxed, and she focused on the cut until it closed.

"That felt like…" Regulus blinked a few times. "Comforting. It eased the pain and then… The pain just left. I felt nothing." He touched his head. "There's not even a scar?" His voice held wonder.

"I can do more." Adelaide blushed. "Or I'm trying, anyway. I'm teaching myself."

"I thought you said your parents didn't want you using your powers?"

"They don't know." She wrapped her hand around the protruding shaft of the arrow. "I'm sorry." She met his eyes. "This will hurt, but only for a second."

He nodded. "Nothing I haven't felt before."

Adelaide ripped the arrow out of Regulus' arm. He groaned through clenched teeth as blood poured from the gaping hole. His muscles bulged against the sleeve. She held her hand over the wound, energy coursing through her arm and out of her hand as light shimmered from her palm. Regulus relaxed. The wound pulled together and closed. She lowered her hand and let the sphere of light go out before anyone could wander by.

"Is there pain anywhere else?"

He shook his head. "They weren't able to do much before you scared them off."

"Are you sure?" It felt good to use her powers. To help someone, like she had wanted to do for so long. *And nothing terrible has happened.*

"I'm sure." His gaze held hers, his gray irises silvery in the moonlight.

She smiled sheepishly. "You don't mind?"

"Mind? I think it's wonderful. You're wonderful." He brushed a curl of hair behind her ear. "Mage or not."

Her heart danced. *Kiss me, damn you.*

"Thank you." Regulus' voice lowered, becoming husky. He leaned forward. "You're spectacular. Breathtaking. Adelaide... I..." He trailed off as his fingers tangled in her hair.

Adelaide couldn't stand the tension anymore. She closed the space between them and kissed him. As her mouth met his, her breath seemed stolen away. Her eyes closed; her mind emptied. She started to pull away, afraid she'd been too forward, or done it wrong. But Regulus grabbed her waist and kissed her. She sank into him, breathed him in as she wrapped her arms around his neck. A spark of reckless joy ignited in her chest and she trembled. He gripped her waist firmer, pulled her closer against his muscled chest. Slowly, his mouth left hers, his quick breaths hot on her lips. She opened her eyes.

It took her a couple tries to speak. "I should go. Before Giselle panics." *And before I forget which way is back.* She stood.

"Wait." He grabbed her hand and gently pulled her back down. Her breathing hitched as he leaned forward. Regulus kissed her again, and Adelaide felt weightless and invincible all at once. He pulled away too soon, and she sighed. He chuckled.

Adelaide's eyes flew open. "What?"

"It's just..." He ran his thumb over the back of her hand. "You've bested me. You've won my heart." He looked into her eyes with gentle longing, bordering on adoration. Like she was the only thing that mattered, the only person he ever wanted to look at. It was so close to the way Father looked at Mother, Adelaide's throat caught.

She touched his face, her fingers caressing his scar. She didn't need to think anymore. Her heart had taken over. She kissed his lips, then his scar. His hand released hers and pressed against her lower back as he kissed her, pulling her close while his other hand buried in her hair.

"Adelaide? Oh, thank Et—*Hargreaves!*"

She jumped at Gaius' uncharacteristically enraged voice and broke away from Regulus' kiss. Regulus' hands tightened on her as his eyes snapped open, alert and battle-ready.

Adelaide looked back and saw Gaius and two of his knights running toward them, swords drawn. Shuddering light from a torch one of the knights carried spilled over her and Regulus as the men slowed. Regulus released her.

"Gaius?" She flushed as Gaius grabbed her arm and pulled her to her feet.

"Are you hurt?" He held her hand up in the torchlight. "You're bleeding!"

"No, I'm fine—"

Gaius turned and pointed his sword at Regulus, still holding her arm. "I might just run you through if you don't have a good explain, Lord—wait, are *you* bleeding, too?"

"Gaius!" She yanked her arm free. "I'm fine, it's Regulus' blood!"

Regulus touched the blood on the side of his face. "It's only a scratch."

"And your arm, too." Gaius lowered his sword, the anger on his face softening. "What happened?"

"Nolan Carrick and his friends attacked him." Adelaide's anger returned full force.

"It was just some ruffians. Probably had too much to drink," Regulus said, holding up a hand. "I didn't see any of their faces. And I'm fine. A couple minor scratches."

She clenched her jaw. Nolan shouldn't get away with it simply because his father was a baron. Anger stirred her magic, but she forced it down.

"I see." Gaius sheathed his sword and rounded on Adelaide. "So you're not hurt?" He looked her up and down.

"I'm fine, Gaius."

"Actually," Regulus stood, "she saved me. Threw a torch at the miscreants and threatened to put a throwing knife through their skulls. Speaking of," he bent down and picked up her dropped throwing knife, the light from the torch glinting on the blade. "This is yours."

"What are you doing here?" Adelaide asked Gaius as she returned the knife to her boot.

"Giselle came and got me. She said you went running off toward what sounded like shouting and ordered her to stay behind, but she was worried for your safety. Min's in a panic." He looked at Regulus, lips pursed. "And then when we arrived there was only you two, alone, in the dark, on the ground, a bit...tangled..." Adelaide's face heated.

Regulus inclined his head. "I understand your concern. But I assure you, I would never hurt Adelaide. Or intentionally impugn her honor."

"*And* I can take care of myself, Gaius."

"Clearly. But even champions can be taken by surprise." He gestured to Regulus. "You're Minerva's sister, so you're my sister, too. That is both a privilege and a duty, and one that I take as seriously as protecting my wife."

He was right, and just being kind. Even if his protectiveness grated on her nerves. "Thank you." Adelaide smiled. "Minerva is lucky to have you."

Gaius grinned. "I assure you it's the other way around, but I try." His smile vanished. "As for all...this. I think it would be best if all parties returned to their own tents immediately."

"Yes, of course." She looked at Regulus. "I'll find you before the joust tomorrow?"

"I'll be looking for you."

Adelaide walked over to the knight with the torch. "Could I borrow that? I dropped something." He handed her the torch, and she scanned the ground for her dagger. After a moment, she found it. It looked normal and was cool in her hand. She slid it into her boot and handed back the torch. "Shall we?"

CHAPTER 28

BLOOD TURNED THE WATER IN THE BOWL PINK AS REGULUS wrung out the cloth. He turned back toward Dresden.

"I mean, I thought about telling her." Regulus scrubbed at the blood on his ear, looking at his reflection in the small square mirror propped against the side of the tent, its bottom edge resting on his cot. "But then she kissed me..." He sighed, remembering the taste of her lips, the feel of her body pressed against his. Nothing in his life had ever felt as *right* as holding Adelaide, kissing her. "It didn't seem like the right time."

"How is that not the right time?" Dresden threw out his hands in annoyance. "You were sharing secrets!"

"And what was I supposed to say?" Regulus plunged the rag back into the bowl of water. "'Oh, you're a mage? I owe a life-debt to a sorcerer. You know, the corrupted, evil version of you? He completely owns me and runs my life and people I care about will die if I don't do his bidding.' In what world is that a good response to being healed or kissed by a beautiful woman?"

"That's...okay, that's a valid point. But this could be good. You said it yourself. The sorcerer is a corrupted mage. Maybe a mage can undo what a sorcerer did."

Regulus rubbed the wet rag through his hair. "I wondered the same thing, that's the only reason I told you. I promised her I wouldn't tell anyone she's a mage." He smiled wryly. "But I know you can keep a secret."

"I suppose I am something of an expert." Dresden stroked his beard.

"But not even the others. No one."

"I get it. But…you don't look like you took a beating. Won't Carrick notice?"

Regulus tossed the cloth back into the bowl. "I'll be wearing armor. It was dark, so not as if he could have seen my injuries to even know what to look for." He pulled off his shirt and threw it on the ground. "Well, that's a perfectly good shirt ruined."

Dresden crossed his arms and leaned back on the stool, using a tent pole as a backrest. "Don't go too easy on Carrick tomorrow. The world would probably be better off if his neck snapped when he gets knocked off his horse."

"I'm not a murderer." He wiped dried blood off his arm. "Besides, we might not even face each other."

"If he's as good with a lance as he is with a polearm and a sword, you probably will."

"I don't think it's about the tournament for him." Regulus pulled on a linen undershirt. "It's about Adelaide. He thinks he can win her over if he defeats me. He's fixated. Maybe I should let him win. If he wins and realizes Adelaide *still* doesn't want him, maybe he'll find a new obsession."

Dresden frowned. "Didn't you say she *told* you to beat him? To 'throw him off his horse?'"

"She was angry."

"And you're not?"

"Of course I'm angry!" Regulus sat on his cot. "But it drew Adelaide and I closer together, so it worked out. Carrick is just a spoiled noble brat. I've dealt with his ilk all my life."

"Sure, but the last time someone tried to murder you, we became mercenaries."

"That was different. And he didn't try to murder me." Regulus kicked off his boots. "I probably should let him win. But you know as well as I do, I can't. It's not who I am."

"Thank Etiros." Dresden stood and stretched. "I was worried falling in love had addled your brain." He exited the tent.

Regulus laid back. Yes, he had a growing hatred for Carrick. But right now, all he could think about was Adelaide. How beautiful and brave and kind she was. Her kiss. Why dwell on hate when he had so much to love?

CHAPTER 29

"Pardon me." Adelaide darted between a page leading an enormous gray destrier and a knight decked in full heavy jousting armor. Dresden waved to her across the chaos of knights, attendants, and horses. A squire ran past with a panicked expression, his shouted "sorry, my lady!" muffled in the rattle of armor and stomp of hooves. A white horse lowered its head, and she spotted the back of Regulus' head, his black locks curling near his neck. She dodged the end of a lance as a page walked by.

Regulus turned as she approached, his face wrinkling into a wide smile. "Good morning, Adelaide."

"Good morning." She held out a strip of dark green cloth that matched her sleeveless dress. The sleeveless style wasn't fashionable, but her skin welcomed the warm sunlight and the cooling gentle breeze. Honestly, as pale as some of these Monparthian women were, they could stand to ditch sleeves on occasion.

Regulus took the cloth, letting his fingers slip over her hand and down to the fabric. "You look beautiful."

Adelaide took in his armor, bulkier and thicker than yesterday's sword-fighting armor. "You look handsome and heroic."

His face contorted in a grimace but returned to a pleased smile before she could even blink. "I'll look for you in the stands."

"You better. Try not to break anything other than your lance."

"Here I thought the lady visited her knight before a joust to wish him luck."

"Please." She smirked. "I have a feeling you don't need luck."

"A little extra luck never hurt anyone," he said with a shrug, his tone teasing.

Her heart fluttered. "All right." She reached up and grabbed the back of Regulus' neck, pulling his head down to hers. Her fingers wove through his hair as they kissed. She stepped back, her heart beating fast, her emotions a whirlwind of light and song and beautiful, perfect things. Her fingers slipped off his neck. He opened his eyes, a dazed look on his face. She bit back a chuckle. "Good luck."

"I think you broke him." Dresden held a fist over his mouth. From the twinkling in his eyes, he appeared to be trying not to laugh.

Regulus blinked. "Don't you have something better to do?"

"The only thing I have to do is tell you to get to the lists before you're late."

"I thought that was my job." A thin young man walked closer. He had a mess of dark blond hair and a short, patchy beard. He held a helm in one hand and clutched the reins of one of the tallest destriers Adelaide had ever seen in the other. The muscles across the black stallion's broad chest rippled as he stomped his foreleg.

Adelaide gasped in admiration. "Is this your horse?"

"This is Sieger." Regulus moved to the horse's shoulder and patted its thick neck. He pointed to the youth. "And that's my squire, Harold."

Adelaide held her palm out to Sieger. "He's gorgeous!" Sieger rubbed her hand with his soft muzzle.

"Bad news, Reg," Dresden said. "Your horse has stolen your lady. You're only handsome, but he's gorgeous."

She shook her head at Dresden, then looked back at the horse. Sieger's wavy black forelock tickled the back of her hand as she rubbed between his eyes.

"He likes you," Regulus said. "He's picky about who he lets touch his face."

"I'd best let you get to the arena." She scratched under Sieger's chin. "Take care of him, Sieger." The horse whinnied, as if agreeing.

Regulus tensed. His hand moved to his belt, but he wasn't wearing a sword for the joust. Adelaide followed his icy gaze as she turned around. Nolan stared at Regulus with obvious rage and a little confusion.

"Competing, Hargreaves?"

Her stomach twisted at the venom in his words.

"Why wouldn't I be?" Regulus said flatly.

Nolan shrugged, his armor creaking. A vein in his temple pulsed. "Sure you're in good enough shape to hold your own with a lance?"

"I'll manage fine."

"Hm." Nolan shifted his gaze from Regulus to Adelaide. His eyes narrowed, and he tilted his head to the side, considering her. "You look...enchanting, my lady."

A feeling like a ball of hot lead settled behind her sternum. *He knows. Oh, Etiros, he knows.* She swallowed against the tightness in her throat.

Nolan eyed her token in Regulus' hand. "Hopefully you don't regret that." He offered a curt bow and continued on, followed by a squire leading a large white horse with a braided mane and tail.

"Hey." Regulus put a hand on her shoulder. "Ignore him."

She forced a smile and laughed nervously. "Yes. I'll see you soon." She rushed away, weaving between knights and mounts and servants.

Minerva frowned as Adelaide approached. "What happened? You look frightened."

Adelaide gulped. Her fear was that obvious? "Nothing. Everything's fine."

"You don't sound fine." Gaius shook his head. "Shouldn't have let you go alone."

"Nothing happened. I just…" What could she say? Gaius didn't know her secret. And there were so many people around.

Gaius' expression softened. "He'll be fine. He seemed all right last night, and he's strong. If he has anywhere near the skill on a horse that he demonstrated yesterday on foot, I'm sure he's in no danger."

"Thank you, Gaius."

As they walked toward the stands, she pulled Minerva back. With their arms linked, she leaned in close. "I need to tell you something about last night."

Minerva glanced at her but said nothing.

"I messed up. It was an accident. I saw Regulus on the ground, getting pummeled. I didn't mean to. It just happened." She glanced around, making sure no one appeared to be trying to overhear her whispered conversation.

"What happened, Adelaide?" Minerva's hushed words came out in a rush.

"Fire. I threw fire at them. I said I had a torch that went out," Adelaide added in response to Minerva's horrified squeak. "But, I think they bought it. Most of them."

"Adelaide…"

"Regulus knows." Adelaide lowered her head, keeping her voice as quiet as possible. The sounds of the chattering crowd also headed to the joust helped hide their conversation. "You were right. He'd seen magic before. He didn't care, and he promised not to tell. And I trust him."

"Then why do you look so worried?"

"Nolan." Her lower lip trembled. "I saw him just now. The look he gave me…something he said… I think he knows." Her breath came out shaky.

"Are you certain?" Minerva clutched Adelaide's arm, her fingers digging into her skin.

"He's at least suspicious. Curious." She adjusted her arm, and Minerva's grip lessened. "What do I do, Min?"

Her sister shook her head. "I don't know. I'm not sure there is anything you *can* do, other than be cautious and alert. This is why Mother and Father didn't want you using your abilities."

"It's not as if something like this hasn't happened before," Adelaide reminded her. "It's part of why I wanted to learn. To control it."

"That's working splendidly."

Adelaide looked at the ground.

"I'm sorry. That was cruel. It's going to be all right. Worrying won't fix it. So let's enjoy the joust, and figure out what to do if, and only if, this becomes a problem."

"All right." She nodded as the tightness in her chest eased. "Good."

They found some seats close to Baron Carrick's box. All the signs of the feast from last night were gone, replaced by a tilt, the wooden fence running down the middle of the length of the rectangular arena. Once nearly everyone was seated, a herald sounded a trumpet, and the competitors rode into the lists. People applauded, loud cheers going up now and then as favorites rode past. The competitors, twenty-six in all, rode once around the arena. They sported a variety of decorative pieces, from plumes on helms to full body caparisons on horses. Some knights, such as Regulus, had little to no decoration, and wore simple armor. While all the horses wore criniere armor pieces over their chests, they had a wide range of barding, from full armor to only the criniere.

Regulus received a few cheers from people who had been impressed with his performance in the sword competition. He nodded at Adelaide as he passed, a crooked smile beneath his raised visor. She heard the name "Belanger" from someone seated lower down in the stands and strained to hear, even though her gut told her she shouldn't.

"Well," a man said, "he traveled all over as a mercenary. Probably developed a taste for foreign women."

"Not to be crude," a woman said, "but it seems fitting, doesn't it? They're both mongrels of sorts."

A loud cheer as another jouster rode past drowned out the conversation. Other conversations filled her ears, and she couldn't hear any more. Adelaide's eyes stung. She gritted her teeth. But the woman was right, in a way.

They *were* both mongrels of sorts, although she hated that derisive term. Both looked down on because of their parentage. Maybe it was fitting, but not in the judgmental way the snobby noblewoman thought. Perhaps that was why they were so comfortable. Why they understood each other so well.

She watched Regulus ride out of the arena, a pleasant warmth settling in her chest. Let them talk. Their talk had never determined her worth, and it wouldn't define her now. Talk didn't determine Regulus' worth, either. And if they couldn't see him for the good man he was—a man who wouldn't press charges against his attackers, a man who accepted her secret without question, fear, or selfishness, a lord who treated his knights as equals—their loss.

The first competitors took their lances, and Adelaide got caught up in the excitement of the joust. Baron Carrick had opted to choose combatants at random, rather than using a tree of shields. Apparently last year the right to choose your own opponent had been abused to further personal feuds, and Carrick wanted to keep things civil.

To her right, a knight with a small metal eagle with spread wings on his helm rode a dappled gray destrier with hooves the size of supper plates. On the other side of the arena, a knight rode a blue roan with a spiked chanfron over its face. Hooves pounded the ground as they charged, sending up little clouds of dust. Lances shattered with a resounding crack. The first pass ended in a tie, with both men landing solid hits on the other's ecranche, the small shield affixed to the left shoulder. Both lances broke. Three points out of a possible four—one for broken lance, two for hitting the ecranche. They had two more passes to secure victory in the round. Unless, of course, one unhorsed his opponent in the second pass.

Adelaide shifted forward in her seat as the knights re-queued. The horses nickered and pawed at the ground, waiting for the squires to release them to charge again. The knights picked up their lances and the squires dropped the reins. A roar went up from the crowd as the horses surged forward, power in the thunder of their hoof falls. The knight on the blue roan struggled to couch his lance, and the tip bounced off his opponent's breastplate. Eagle knight's lance crashed into the other knight's solid visor. The lance exploded from the impact, sending shards flying high into the air. Adelaide gasped, as did most of the rest of the crowd, as the second knight's head whipped back. His left hand grabbed desperately at the pommel of his saddle as he leaned backward until his back hovered over the blue roan's flanks. But he kept his seat.

One point for the knight on the blue roan. Four for eagle-helm knight. Adelaide enjoyed the joust for the tension, the uncertainty of it all. The eagle knight's chances looked good. He just needed to get another good hit. But if their luck reversed in the third tilt and they tied, they would have to take an extra pass. If the blue roan knight could unhorse eagle knight, he would win. She tapped her hands on her lap in anticipation.

The knights charged forward again. Their horses leaned away from each other as they met in the center of the arena. The snap of breaking lances echoed as pieces of wood scattered. Blue roan knight had managed a clean hit on eagle knight's chest but had missed the ecranche. Eagle knight hit the ecranche and won by four points.

Adelaide applauded. The knights exited the arena and the next competitors entered while servants cleared wood shards from the ground. The matches flew by, not least because of how easy it was to get caught up in the crowd's fervor. Nolan won his match. She didn't applaud him. He didn't acknowledge her.

At last, Regulus entered the lists. Green fabric fluttered around his right bicep, tied around his armor. He smiled at her before closing his visor over his face. Only two thin slits indicated where his eyes were under his helm. His opponent, a knight who looked more mountain than man, rode a brown destrier as large as Sieger. *How in creation is anyone supposed to unhorse him!* A caparison of red chevrons on a field of dark blue covered the horse to its knees. She recognized the heraldry. *Must be Sir Edgar Druadan.*

Her heart pounded as Regulus and Sir Druadan charged each other. As hooves threw up clots of dirt and horse nostrils flared, they leveled their lances. Adelaide leaned forward, clenching her fists. The impact of their lances on each other's ecranches and the simultaneous burst of lances into tinder sounded like a clap of thunder. Both men swayed in their seats, but kept their balance. The crowd roared in delight. Adelaide released a shaky breath.

They rode to the end of the arena and wheeled around. Pages handed them fresh lances. Minerva reached over and squeezed her fist.

"Relax!"

"I remember you being similarly tense last time Gaius tilted," she scolded.

Minerva laughed. "All right, that's true."

Her gaze remained trained on Regulus as the horses leapt forward. The pounding of their hooves seemed to vibrate in her chest. Both men's heads snapped backward as lances met helms. Her eyes widened and her nails bit into her palms. Splintered wood

rained onto the ground. Regulus swayed but made it to the end of
the arena. Harold turned Sieger around. Regulus shook his head and
adjusted his helm before taking a new lance. She looked to the
opposite end of the lists. Druadan had also maintained his seat.
They were tied.

Her jaw hurt from clenching her teeth. She released a long
exhale and tried to shake some of the tension from her shoulders.
Both men raised their lances, signaling they were ready. Their
squires released the reins. The horses charged. Adelaide pressed her
palms together and raised her hands to her mouth, her thumbs
tucked under her chin. Hooves thudded. The crowd cheered.

Druadan's lance pummeled into Regulus' visor, pushing his
head back as the lance snapped in half. Regulus' lance slammed into
the left side of Druadan's chest, just shy of his ecranche. The lance
bowed. Regulus leaned forward, even as his head whipped backward. Adelaide gasped.

Druadan leaned back in his saddle. The broken lance slipped
from his grasp, clattering to the ground. Regulus' lance burst,
sending out shards like dozens of forcefully thrown wooden knives.
Druadan flailed as he twisted backward and sideways over his
horse's flank. He hit the ground with a clang. Regulus had won.

Adelaide leapt to her feet, applauding as a cacophony of cheers,
gasps, and boos erupted from the crowd. Regulus leaned forward
on Sieger, his head swaying from side to side. She froze. *Oh, Etiros,
please. Let him be all right.*

Harold seized the reins and stopped Sieger. Adelaide looked
over the heads of other standing spectators, watching with bated
breath. Regulus removed his helm and looked back over his
shoulder. He caught her gaze and smiled. Relief rushed over her as
she smiled back.

CHAPTER 30

REGULUS STRETCHED HIS NECK. THE PAIN WAS FADING, BUT that was cutting it close. Sure, he had seen knights take similar blows and walk away. But not exactly fine; a hit like that often sent knights home. Hopefully, everyone was too caught up with his opponent's unhorsing to notice him take a blow that could have snapped his neck in half. In fact, he suspected something *had* cracked. The sorcerer's dark magic was at work, making his neck tingle and ache.

Once free, he would have to relearn how to fight without the ability to take risks he knew might kill him. Learn how to fight to live again, instead of accepting he couldn't die.

One thing he knew, he wouldn't miss how it felt. The pinching, the burning, the prickling. So different from Adelaide's healing. That had been soothing. Cool and warm all at once. Numbing and mending without pain and leaving no scars. If it wasn't already clear that the sorcerer's healing came from a place of corrupted magic, Adelaide's magic proved it.

As Regulus stretched and waited for his next joust, his thoughts wandered. What a pair they made. Adelaide also carried a weighty secret that she lived in fear of someone discovering. But her secret, while dangerous, at least was not *bad*. Not like his. He worried that the pure magic in her would sense the corrupt magic in him. But if she hadn't detected it yet, she couldn't, right?

He had to tell her the truth.

He rubbed Sieger's neck as he checked him over, looking for any cuts or protruding bits of lance. The simple criniere protected

Sieger's shoulders and chest, the areas most susceptible to damage from broken lances. He had a couple small nicks on his lower legs, but nothing concerning.

The roar of the crowd provided a buzzing backdrop to his thoughts. He had to tell her, but the thought of losing her made his heart physically ache. Was that ridiculous? He hadn't even known Adelaide long, yet... He felt like he had known her forever. Or like he had been waiting forever to know her.

Dresden sauntered over and stood on the opposite side of Sieger. He leaned across the saddle. "It should please you to know that Adelaide looked absolutely terrified for you."

Regulus' brow furrowed. "Why would that please me? I don't want her terrified."

"When you're jousting? Yes, you do, numbskull." Drez rolled his eyes. "She's scared you'll get hurt. It means she cares about you and what happens to you. The more terrified, the more she cares."

"I, on the other hand," said a smug voice behind him that he quickly recognized as Carrick's, "sincerely hope you fall and break your neck."

Regulus turned as Carrick's page led his horse past, but Carrick paused.

"I'd rather hoped your neck would snap with that last hit, but I guess it wasn't as hard a hit as I wanted it to be."

"What exactly is your problem?" Dresden rounded Sieger's flank.

Carrick looked down his nose at Dresden. "Your master and I are talking, Carasian."

Regulus put himself between Drez and Carrick before Drez did anything stupid. "I hold no malice for you, Sir Carrick. I see no reason for this continued hostility."

"*You* hold no malice for *me*?" Carrick laughed. "Ah, but I have more than enough for *you*. You've taken something I want, something I need. I won't rest until she's mine."

Regulus' hand curled into a fist. His jaw tensed. "Adelaide is not *something* to be taken or owned. She's a person who makes her own choices."

"Then she's made a profoundly stupid choice." Carrick stepped closer. "She should be honored I want her. Flattered that someone of my quality would desire her, common Khastallander mother and all. And yet she settles for a nobody." He sneered. "An illegitimate mutt turned mercenary who doesn't deserve the title he shouldn't even have."

Regulus exhaled. If he could keep his temper when taunted by the sorcerer, he could do so when facing Carrick. Several nearby lords, knights and squires watched them out of the corner of their eyes. Not one said anything. Suddenly, Regulus latched onto something Carrick had said. "What do you mean, you *need* her?"

"Doesn't matter. I just want you to know the stakes. I have no intention of playing fair. If I were you, I'd bow out before anyone gets hurt."

Regulus stepped forward, capitalizing on his height to look as menacing as possible. "Are you threatening Adelaide?"

"Don't worry, I won't hurt *her*." He glanced at Dresden, then looked back at Regulus and sneered. "I'm saying you should consider what you're willing to lose to keep her." He walked after his horse toward the arena.

"Did…did he just threaten me?" Dresden sputtered.

"I think it was a pretty generalized threat against me and anyone in my circle," Regulus said grimly. "He's insane." All the same, he sent up a quick prayer to Etiros that Carrick wouldn't act on his threats.

Drez gestured at the men in the area and muttered, "And no one cares."

Regulus unseated his next opponent in the first pass, which the crowd greeted with exuberant cheers and some disgruntled boos. The next joust he won by five points. Then he faced Carrick.

His anger flared as he stared at Carrick down the list. Carrick gave him a smug smile before closing his visor. *"I'd bow out before anyone gets hurt."* *Should have heeded your own advice, Carrick.* Sieger shifted beneath him, eager to charge. Regulus adjusted his grip on his lance and raised it above his head. Carrick did the same. Harold released the reins.

Wind whistled in the gaps in his armor. Sieger's chest heaved as he raced down the list. Regulus brought the lance down, couching it in the crook of his arm. He aimed for Carrick's heart. The lance slammed into Carrick's chest, sending a shudder down his arm. Carrick's lance hit Regulus' helm but bounced off. Regulus' lance bent and shattered, making the bones in his arm vibrate. Carrick flipped backward off his horse.

Under his helm, Regulus smiled.

He reached the end of the arena and wheeled around. Pages rushed to help Carrick to his feet, but he pushed them away and strode off the field—albeit with a slight limp. Regulus pulled off his helm and looked at Adelaide. Her wide smile accentuated her round cheeks. He would do anything for that dazzling smile. She nodded at him while she applauded. He looked at Carrick, exiting the gate at the end of the arena. Carrick looked back and held up a fist.

The message was clear. This meant war. Carrick's feud was only getting started. Regulus' spirits fell. What had he done?

Regulus' last couple matches were close—he won by only one point in the semi-final, and was losing the final joust by three points until he unhorsed his opponent. But he won. He had to admit, he enjoyed the cheers. Between the thrill of the joust and the applause and Adelaide's smiles meant for him alone, he felt like he could fly.

The exhilaration of winning buried even worries about Carrick's plans for revenge.

He rode Sieger to the middle of the arena and dismounted in front of Baron Carrick's box. Servants carried in a narrow, tall wooden podium and a set of steep wooden steps. They placed the podium in front of Carrick's box with the stairs behind it. Once atop the podium, Regulus removed his helm to cheering from the spectators.

Baron Carrick moved to the barrier at the end of his box, standing a couple arm's lengths away. He raised his hands. The noise of the crowd hushed.

"Lord Regulus Hargreaves of Arrano," the baron said, his voice ringing out over the arena. "Today you have demonstrated your horsemanship, your skill with a lance, and your prowess on the battlefield." Cheers. A smile tugged at the corner of Regulus' mouth, but he focused on looking dignified.

"You have thrilled and entertained with your expertise and strength and impressed with your precision," the Baron continued. "You have earned our respect and admiration and honored the lady whose token you wear."

Regulus' gaze darted toward Adelaide, a small smile breaking his serious deference.

"You have tilted and emerged victorious. It is my honor as host of the Etchy Tournament to name you champion of the joust!" Baron Carrick applauded and the crowd joined in. As the cheering quieted, the Baron turned. A servant handed him a bulging leather pouch and a dagger with a handle inlaid with swirling ivory and sheath inset with small circles of mother-of-pearl. "In recognition of your triumph, I award you the prizes of the joust."

The Baron held out the pouch of coins and dagger. Regulus tucked his helm under his arm and retrieved the prizes of coins with a bow.

"Ladies and gentlemen," the Baron gestured for him to turn around, and Regulus turned and faced the other side of the arena. "I present to you your jousting champion, Lord Regulus Hargreaves of Arrano!"

Regulus bowed as the crowd hollered and whistled and applauded. Large groups stood, honoring the champion of the joust. Honoring *him*. Some ladies waved handkerchiefs and scarves at him. A few even blew him a kiss. His face heated, and he looked to Adelaide. She was looking right at him and grinning, apparently not noticing the other ladies. He breathed a sigh of relief, even as part of him enjoyed the unusual attention. Harold had walked into the arena during the prize ceremony and held Sieger's reins. Regulus handed him the pouch of coins and dagger. He took the reins and remounted. Sounds of praise followed him out of the arena.

After changing out of his armor and a quick, cold bath, he set out to find Adelaide. He held the prize dagger in his hand. He had to ask a few servants and a couple knights for directions, but soon enough he found the Drummond's and Adelaide's tents. Adelaide sat on a stool in front of her tent, combing her glossy dark hair. Regulus held his hands and the dagger behind him as he approached. She spotted him and smiled.

"Congratulations, champion of the joust." Adelaide stood and set the comb down on the stool. "What brings you to our humble tents?"

He laughed. "I heard a rumor there's a beautiful lady here who fancies me. You wouldn't happen to know anything about that, would you?"

Adelaide feigned shock. "That's a scandalous rumor. You should be ashamed."

"If loving her should make me ashamed, then I am the most ashamed man in Monparth."

She snorted and shook her head.

"Okay, that sounded better in my head," he admitted. "But I do have a reason for being here, other than seeing your smile again."

She blushed. "Oh?"

"Three things, actually." He brought his hands in front and presented the dagger on his palms. "I haven't been able to think of anything other than giving you this since Baron Carrick handed it to me. It is beautiful yet strong. Elegant yet dangerous. Like you."

"Regulus…" Adelaide ran her fingertips over the sheathed dagger. "But this is yours."

"And I want you to have it. I can't think of a better owner."

Her fingers brushed his palm as she picked the dagger up. She pulled the dagger out of the sheath and admired the blade, assessed its weight and tested its balance. Rubbed her thumb crossway over the edge to check its sharpness. He grinned as she evaluated the dagger in much the same way knights considered a new sword.

"Are you certain?" She slipped the dagger back into the sheath. "This is exquisite. The craftsmanship is superb."

"An exquisite dagger for an exquisite woman. I can't think of a better gift to start our courtship."

Adelaide's gaze snapped up to his eyes. "Our…" Her lips parted in what looked to be pleasant surprise.

He took her hand, his heart stuttering with nerves far worse than those before a battle. "I was hoping you would be favorable to me asking your father for his permission to court you? I won't be able to yet. My business for my friend will take me in the opposite direction, and I'd rather ask him in person than by letter."

"Yes," she murmured. Then louder, "Yes!"

"Smart decision to ask in person," Minerva said from the side. "Father turned down several potential suitors for his daughters over the years because he said asking by messenger demonstrated either laziness and lack of resolve or cowardice. Caused quite a fight with our half-sister Dulcina on one occasion."

Goosebumps prickled his arms, and he looked to Adelaide. "Is your father likely to turn me down?" *He could do better for his daughter than a bastard.*

"Father can be...protective." Adelaide sighed. "But if you ask him bearing letters from myself and Minerva, that should help."

"I'll write a letter of recommendation, if that will help," Gaius said, walking around a tent and putting his arms around his wife. His eyes narrowed. "Assuming there's no more nonsense like last night."

"No, of course." Regulus nodded, a lump in his throat. "Definitely. Thank you."

"You said there were three things," Adelaide reminded him.

"Right." He cleared his throat. "Baron Carrick said the lady whose token I wore during the joust may dine with me at his table tonight. Would you do me the honor of accompanying me to tonight's feast?"

"I would love to!" She looked at Gaius and Minerva. "If...that's all right."

Minerva rolled her eyes. "As if anyone could stop you, anyway."

Supper passed pleasantly. Carrick sat with his parents, but he sat on the opposite side and didn't address Regulus or Adelaide the entire meal. After supper, he occasionally caught sight of Carrick laughing with other knights or dancing and flirting with various ladies.

He and Adelaide danced and laughed and talked. She told him about her mother taking her away to a cottage in the woods from age four to seven, until she no longer caused fires or made her hands emit light by accident. All to keep her abilities secret. How it took years for her and Minerva to get close after that, and how her half-siblings treated her with suspicion or indifference. They talked around her magic, never using the word and keeping their voices low.

He talked a little about his childhood. How he lived at Arrano with his mother, calling Lord Arrano Father despite Lady Arrano's protestations—until the birth of a legitimate son when Regulus was six. Then his father sent him away to live with a distant cousin halfway across Monparth. He mentioned training as a knight but never being treated as an equal. But instead of recounting sob stories about his cousin's cruelty, he focused on humorous tales, such as the time Drez got boxed on the ears by a cook at fourteen after he tried to flirt his way into stealing food.

Adelaide laughed. "So the noble household Dresden joined, that was your cousin's? Was he already there when you arrived, or did you meet him later?"

Regulus glanced away. He didn't want to lie to her, but Drez was sensitive about that. "You can't tell him I told you."

She chuckled, her confusion evident. "All right…"

"And don't think worse of him." He hesitated. "Or me."

Her forehead wrinkled.

"When I was eleven," he said quietly, thankful for the music and party conversation to cover his voice, "my father decided I needed a servant. He sent money to his cousin, who found Dresden's family. They needed the money."

"He…" Adelaide tripped, and they stopped dancing. "He was your servant?"

"I held his indenture for seven years. I should have released him sooner." Regulus forced himself to meet her eyes. "He was my only friend. I asked him to become a mercenary with me, and he did. And when I became a lord, I knighted him. He's my brother, not that I deserve him."

As Adelaide stared, he tried to interpret her expression. It wasn't judgement or distaste, she looked…pleased. She dropped his hands and embraced him, laying her head against his shoulder. He wrapped his arms around her, despite the glares from couples trying to dance around them, and kissed the top of her head.

The night ended too soon. But before everyone headed back to their tents, Adelaide kissed him again. Her kiss both set all his senses on edge and dulled them at once. The crowd around them faded like dying embers while his all-encompassing awareness of her lit his heart on fire. But then her sister was there, and he had to say goodbye. His chest ached as he watched her leave.

His knights walked back with him. After Carrick's attack, they had no intention of letting him wander unprotected. Perceval carried a torch, illuminating their way as clouds obscured the moon. The men laughed and discussed the ladies they had danced with and the amounts of mead they had drank. Their jocular mood vanished as they arrived at the tents to find chaos. One tent had collapsed, as if something had fallen on it. No fire or torches burned as they should. Scattered ashes and scuff marks in the dirt indicated a scuffle.

"Harold?" No response. Regulus' pulse quickened. "Harold!"

"Over here." Coughing. "My...lord."

Regulus snatched the torch from Perceval and darted toward Harold's muffled voice coming from the other side of a tent. The others followed, murmuring their surprise and concern.

Harold sat on the ground next to Sieger, who was lying on his side, his nostrils flaring and chest heaving with labored breathing.

"Sieger?"

"I...I tried to stop them, my lord." Harold looked up. Dust covered his face, except where streams of tears had washed the dirt away. Dried blood covered his mouth and chin, and his nose had a new crooked bump. A green and purple bruise blossomed around his right eye. "There were too many." Harold coughed and winced, putting a hand to his chest. "Four of them. Their faces were covered. I'm sorry…" He choked back a sob.

Regulus fell to his knees and laid a hand on Harold's shoulder, his gut twisting. "Harold…" He looked over his squire, noting his disheveled clothing and the blood covering his hands. Rage burned under his skin. "How badly are you hurt?"

"Mostly bruised." Harold coughed and groaned. "Maybe a cracked rib." He looked at Sieger, his lower lip trembling. "The blood is…it's Sieger's."

Regulus' breath caught. He moved around Harold and held out the torch. Sieger whinnied painfully and raised his head. The torchlight reflected in his eye, open so wide white showed around the edges. Regulus' gaze fixed on Sieger's legs. They had sliced his legs.

The low-life cowards had beaten his squire and cut his horse's legs.

Rage burned down his throat and lit an inferno in his chest. Blood-soaked cloths wrapped around the lower part of all four of Sieger's legs. Regulus clenched his jaw. The torch in his hand snapped in half as he squeezed it. Without a word, he strode away.

"Regulus." Dresden ran after him. "Regulus!" Dresden grabbed his arm. "Where are you going? You can't attack the son of a baron without proof."

"I'm not," he said through gritted teeth. "Tell the men to tidy up the camp and get a fire going. Get Harold to a cot. And put a tent over Sieger. I'll be back soon."

Dresden stopped as Regulus broke into a jog. "Where are you going?"

"To get Adelaide."

CHAPTER 31

"ADELAIDE!" THE PANIC IN REGULUS' VOICE CHILLED ADELAIDE to her core.

She pushed Giselle aside and ran out of her tent, not caring that Giselle had eased the lacing on the back of her dress and that it sagged a little around her shoulders.

Light from a nearby torch reflected in Regulus' wide eyes. His scar pulled at his skin, wrinkling against his grimace. "I need your help," he panted. "Please."

"What's going on?" Gaius walked out of his tent, followed by Minerva. "Lord Hargreaves?"

"Please," Regulus begged. "I need your...I need your help."

"Help for *what?*" Gaius demanded.

"Regulus, what's wrong?" Adelaide placed a hand on Regulus' forearm and his shoulders sank further.

His throat bobbed as he swallowed. His chest heaved. "Harold and Sieger. They've been attacked. They're hurt."

"What?" she gasped.

"Harold says he's all right, but...I...he—I'm not sure he is." Regulus hung his head. "And Sieger..." His voice broke. "I—I might have to... Please." He took a shaky breath as his shoulders quivered, and her heart cracked. "I... I understand if you can't help. But...I had to ask." He met her eyes. "I'm sorry. I had to ask."

Fear slid like ice down her spine. *Someone could find out.* But he looked so broken. *Nolan might already know, anyway...*

"This is my fault," he whispered, looking away.

"Nolan," she guessed, anger melting away her fear.

Regulus shook his head. "He was mingling with other nobles all night. But he has to be behind it."

If Nolan was behind the attack, and if Nolan suspected her magic, healing Regulus' horse would confirm her power. But if Nolan was behind the attack, it was likely because he hated she had chosen Regulus. It wasn't Regulus' fault, or hers. But she understood his guilt.

Regulus lifted his head, hope dying in his pain-filled eyes. "It was selfish to ask. I'm sorry." He turned to leave, but she slipped her hand down to grip his shaking hand. Her gut wrenched.

"Take me to them."

He paused and gave her a relieved smile. "Thank you." He started forward, but Minerva stepped into his path.

"Adelaide—"

"I can help." She met her sister's glare with determination. "Mother always encouraged kindness. If I can help, I will."

"Adelaide," Minerva repeated, her tone harsh. "You—"

"This is my decision, Minerva. Mine." Adelaide led Regulus around Minerva, their hands still clasped.

"What is going *on*?" Gaius' voice crept toward a shout.

Adelaide looked back at him. "You might as well know. Come on." She looked to Regulus, and he led the way, his footsteps rushed. Gaius followed.

After several minutes of hurried walking, Regulus slowed. They rounded a tent and Dresden looked up from a fire in surprise. "She came?"

Adelaide raised a brow at Regulus. He turned red. "Dresden has kept more secrets for me than I can count. I know I promised—"

"It's all right." She understood. She never could keep things from Minerva for long.

"Where's Harold?" Regulus asked.

Dresden pointed at one of the tents, and Regulus led her inside. Estevan and the blond knight—Caleb, if she remembered correctly—stood as they entered. Caleb held a soiled, wet cloth in his hand. Harold laid on a cot in the middle of the tent.

"I gave him my bed," Estevan said. He looked at her. "Why's—"

"Wait outside," Regulus said. Caleb and Estevan glanced at each other uncertainly but left the tent.

Gaius crossed his arms. "I'm not waiting outside."

"That's fine." Adelaide knelt next to the cot. Harold's eye was bruised, his nose broken. His breath came short and sharp, his face pinched. Her hands felt clammy. What if she *couldn't* help him?

Regulus knelt on the other side of the cot, his eyebrows knit. "Can you help?"

Harold watched Adelaide with wide, confused eyes. She wet her lips. "I'll try. Where does it hurt most, Harold?"

"My—" Harold groaned. "Ribs." He placed a trembling hand over the left side of his rib cage. "It's a dull pain, but sometimes, it," he winced, "it feels like I'm being stabbed."

She pushed his shirt up. Blue bruises covered his left side. Regulus cursed under his breath.

"Are you a physician?" Harold sounded bewildered.

"No." Gingerly, Adelaide prodded Harold's ribs. He grimaced. Her fingertips brushed a sharp edge. Harold yelped, and she drew her hand back and bit her lip. Self-doubt chilled her. Regulus grabbed Harold's hand and put his other hand on Harold's shoulder, steadying him.

"Sorry. I needed to know where to focus." She looked to Regulus. "I've never healed a bone before."

Regulus nodded, a vein on his temple standing out. "I understand."

She held her palm over Harold's broken ribs. *Help me, Etiros.*

Gaius moved closer. "What is—" Her palm shone. "—going…" Gaius's words died on his lips.

Warmth spread across her hand. Harold sighed and his breathing normalized. Energy drained from her, like a cloth soaking up water. Somehow, she could sense the bone. As if she could feel it moving and coming back together. The bruising faded. She lowered her hand as it stopped glowing. She pressed on his ribs, and relaxed when they felt whole and Harold didn't cry out. She'd done it. Pride and joy surged along with gratitude to Etiros for her gift. She pulled her hand away.

"You can sit up now."

Harold sat up and pulled his shirt down. "How did you *do* that?"

"You're…you're…" Gaius sputtered.

"A mage, yes." She tilted her head, studying Harold's face. "Close your eyes."

He did, and she placed her palm over his nose. She heard the bone snap into place as his nose straightened. Harold jumped, but didn't whimper or open his eyes. The bruise over his eye turned yellow then disappeared, and she dropped her hand. "You can open them now."

Harold opened his eyes and touched his nose. "Thank you, my lady. I…I can never repay you."

"A good start is keeping her secret," Regulus said. Harold nodded.

Adelaide stood. "Sieger?"

Regulus clapped Harold on the shoulder and met his eyes. Something unspoken passed between them, and Regulus wrapped one arm around the squire's shoulders in a quick embrace. Regulus' eyes glistened as he stood. "Sieger's this way."

"Um," Gaius said. "I have questions—"

She nodded. "Later."

Regulus led her outside, and Gaius followed. The knights, standing around the fire, watched them duck inside another tent with curious expressions. The sharp scent of sweat and blood mixed with dirt stung Adelaide's nostrils. A lantern hung from the tent poles. The tent was otherwise empty, except for Sieger.

Sieger laid on his side, foam around his mouth as he panted. Blood seeped through the bandages around his lower legs and into the ground. He tried to get up as Regulus entered. The stallion released a neigh that sounded like a scream and flopped back onto his side. Regulus paled to the same whiteness as his scar.

"Oh, Sieger." Adelaide sat on the ground as her throat constricted. "He's lost a lot of blood," she murmured.

"I know." She barely heard Regulus' response.

"I think I can heal the cuts, but I don't know if that will be enough." She didn't look up as he sat next to her.

"I won't blame you if…" He trailed off, and from the tension in his voice, she knew he couldn't bring himself to say it.

She unwrapped a bandage and gasped. The cut exposed bone. She closed her eyes and reached for Regulus with her left hand. He took her hand. She held her right hand over the uncovered wound. The flesh pulled, moving back together, covering the blood and bone. Even after she sensed that the wound was closed, she kept going, praying it would help counteract the blood loss. She did the same for the other three cuts. When she had finished, she felt drained, as tired as if she had run a great distance. She leaned back into Regulus' shoulder. A wave of dizziness made her sway.

Regulus wrapped an arm around her. "Hey, easy. Are you okay?"

"Just tired." She wiped sweat from her brow. "I've never used that much magic before."

Sieger raised his head. He pulled his legs under himself and nuzzled Regulus' head, playing with his hair with his lips. Regulus laughed. Sieger lowered his head, lying on his stomach with his legs tucked under him.

"He must be tired from the stress and loss of blood," Adelaide mused.

"But he seems better." Regulus sounded considerably calmer. "I feel like he's going to be okay."

"I hope you're right."

They sat there for a moment in silence, the fingers of her left hand entwined with his and his arm wrapped around her shoulders. She liked it. The press of his muscular body, the gentle movement of his chest, the way he held her shoulders like he couldn't bear to let her go. She laid her head on his shoulder.

Gaius cleared his throat and Adelaide blushed. He still stood behind them. She'd forgotten he was there. "Can I ask my questions *now?*"

CHAPTER 32

GAIUS ASKED A STRING OF QUESTIONS ABOUT WHEN, HOW, what she could do, and who knew. Adelaide answered every question, even though she looked exhausted. Regulus didn't mind all the questions, though. He would have sat there all night with her tucked against him, their fingers laced together. But her eyelids drooped, and weariness tugged at him. Once Gaius was satisfied, Regulus helped her to her feet.

"I can't thank you enough." Regulus placed his hand on the side of Adelaide's neck and caressed her jawline with his thumb. "I am forever in your debt. And I promise, my men won't tell anyone. I trust all of them."

She leaned into his hand, her skin warm on his palm. "I'm glad to finally help. I hate hiding." She looked down. "But I'm also not sure I'm ready for everyone to know. So I appreciate the promise."

"You have a beautiful heart," he murmured.

"What are we going to do about Carrick?" She looked up, anger burning in her tired eyes. "He can't get away with this. I don't care if he was at the feast all evening. He *had* to have sent the men who did this."

"I can't prove that. And as relieved and thrilled as I am that you were able to heal them...there's no evidence an attack happened at all."

She worked her jaw. "And what if he tries again?"

"My men are exceptional fighters. And in the morning, we're heading back to my castle. He won't be able to do something like this again." *Let him try. I'll kill him.*

"It's not right."

"I know." He pulled her into an embrace.

Adelaide wrapped her arms around him and leaned her cheek on his shoulder. It amazed and bewildered him how comfortable they felt together. "What did you mean when you said it was your fault?"

"What? Oh." He took a deep breath. "Something Carrick said. A vague threat I didn't heed." He glanced at Gaius, who stood near the tent entrance, looking anywhere but at them. "I should have let him win the joust."

Gaius shook his head. "No. There's something else at play here. Something far more personal than a lost joust. And I suspect you know what it is."

Regulus clenched his jaw. He wouldn't say it. Not in front of Adelaide. He wouldn't put that pressure on her. He met Gaius' eyes, then looked down at Adelaide's head resting on his shoulder. Gaius squinted. His jaw slackened as he understood. He opened his mouth to say something, but Regulus shook his head.

He pulled away from Adelaide, even though he hated to do so. "You should return to your tent. You look exhausted."

"Can I see you in the morning?"

"I'm afraid not." His shoulders fell, thinking about all he had to do. About the truth he hid from her. It made him nauseous after what she had done for him. But he could hardly tell her in front of Gaius. "We'll be leaving before daybreak. And you need to rest. But I'll see you for supper on the third." He kissed her forehead. *And I'll tell you everything.*

Everything.

CHAPTER 33

ADELAIDE FELL ASLEEP AS SOON AS SHE PULLED ON HER BLANKET. She hadn't slept so soundly in ages. But when Giselle woke her, she felt refreshed. The festival grounds echoed with the sounds of tents being collapsed, horses and carriages prepared, and the chatter of everyone from nobles to servants. While servants loaded their belongings onto palfreys and mules, she took Zephyr and found a small grove of trees a short ride away. A quiet place where she could feed him oats and a few sugar cubes in peace and not worry about being in the way.

After a short while, hoof beats approached. She turned to look, expecting Sir Gaius or one of the Drummonds' servants. Zephyr's lips tickled her outstretched palm, and she smiled. But then she saw the intruder's face. Her smile vanished as she clenched her jaw. "You're not welcome here, Sir Carrick."

Nolan chuckled, as if she were teasing. He dismounted and sauntered closer as her whole body tensed. "That's hardly polite of you."

"I know what you did," she said, her voice low and accusing.

"And what's that?" His playful tone and crooked smile taunted her as he moved closer.

"Regulus' squire and horse were attacked last night. I know you're behind it." She raised her chin. "So you are not. Welcome. Here."

"Interesting." Nolan stepped closer and rubbed Zephyr's neck, looking at the gelding in admiration. Her heart pounded against her ribs. "Because I know something, too." He met her eyes. "*I know what you are.*"

She stopped breathing. Icy tendrils wormed through her chest. "What are you talking about?" She had meant to speak with confidence, but her words came out breathy.

"I wasn't certain what I saw when you showed up and played the knight to Half-Breed's damsel. An amusing moment, that. But then the mercenary didn't sustain injuries. I heard you visited the mongrel's camp last night. And this morning, he apparently rode his horse away before dawn, despite whispers the horse was maimed. I also heard a rumor someone broke his squire's nose, but he looked fine. The look on your face confirms my theory."

The last sugar cube in her hand slipped from her fingers and fell to the ground. She felt light-headed. Goosebumps pricked her arms.

Nolan laughed and looked back at Zephyr, still stroking her horse's neck. "Don't worry. I won't tell." He shrugged. "Not yet, anyway."

"What do you want?" Her voice sounded hoarse.

"I would have thought it was obvious, my dear." He gave her a wicked grin and stepped toward her, his hand falling from Zephyr's neck. "I want *you.*"

Indignation crackled under her skin. She clenched her fists. "You're out of your mind."

"No. I just know what I want. And I get what I want. Marry me, Adelaide."

She fixed him with a death glare. "What in creation makes you think I would ever marry *you*? After everything you've done?"

"Oh, I realized a while ago I wasn't going to win you over by charm alone." He gave a dismissive frown. "I'm not used to that, to be honest. I thought to scare you away from Hargreaves, but that failed too. When I left you with him after the attack, I hoped you'd see him as weak and move on, but no. I thought I would threaten the mercenary into leaving you. But that seems to have failed as well."

"So what?" Her thoughts turned to the weapons stowed in her boots. "You're here to threaten me now?"

"Not threaten yet, no. Blackmail. I know your secret, Adelaide."

Nervousness made her shiver, but she squared her shoulders. "Fine. Tell who you will. I'm done hiding who I am."

One side of Nolan's mouth curved up in a condescending smile. "You say that, but I don't see you broadcasting your," he lowered his voice conspiratorially, "abilities." He crossed his arms. "I can't say I blame you. If everyone like me had been brutally hunted down and murdered, I also would want to keep my identity secret."

She narrowed her eyes. "Listen closely. I would rather the entire *world* knew my secret than *ever* marry you. Why are you so desperate, anyway? If ladies usually find you so charming, why am I so important? What makes you want to marry *me* so badly?"

Irritation clouded his eyes, but then his usual careless smile returned. "I know your secret; you might as well know mine. I'm out of viable marriage options. Either my brothers already married into the best families, the families of my station don't have eligible daughters of a decent age, or…" He shrugged. "I've burned one too many bridges, it seems. My *gracious* parents," he spat the words, "have threatened to disinherit me. They gave me a deadline, and if I don't marry, they'll disown me and throw me out of Carrick Barony with no inheritance. I'm down to a month."

"How tragic for you." *Serves you right.* "Go bother another young lady."

"Ah, but why would I do that? I had resigned myself to marrying some moderately attractive woman who would have a smaller dowry than a nobleman of my standing deserves—"

Adelaide snorted. "What a shining example of chivalry you are."

He ignored her and continued. "And then I met you. The daughter of the renowned, wealthy war hero Lord Alfred Belanger. You would come with respectability, in spite of your mother. Prestige. And, I'm certain, a generous dowry." His smile took on a wolfish, hungry quality. "And to top it all off, you're beautiful. Even with your Khastallander complexion."

"Is this supposed to improve my opinion of you? Because it's having the opposite effect."

"No." Nolan's voice became low, menacing. "It's so you understand what is at stake. My entire life hinges on marrying. And you're the best option, sweetheart. At this point, likely my only option. And the only thing that stands between me and the lifestyle I want, I *deserve*, is that thrice-accursed mercenary."

"And me." She folded her arms. "I won't be bullied any more than Regulus."

"You don't want to go to war with me, love." He stepped forward and she stepped back, pulling her dagger out of her boot with practiced speed. She had picked too secluded of a spot. No one could see his aggressive behavior.

"Take another step and I'll cut your heart out."

Nolan looked at the dagger in her hand, the one Regulus had given her. He grunted. "Very well, my lady." He turned toward his horse. Some of the tension drained from her body and she lowered her dagger.

Nolan spun around and lunged forward. She cursed herself for lowering her guard as she stepped back and slashed at his face. He dodged, but the tip of her dagger still nicked his cheek. Blood beaded from the cut and Nolan hissed and grabbed her wrist with both hands. She reached for his face with her free hand, but he wrenched her hand down, twisting her wrist. Adelaide yelled and dropped the dagger. He caught her other hand right before her fingernails scratched his eye.

"That. Stung."

"You dare assault a lady?"

He released her and Adelaide stepped back. Tears stung her eyes. She cradled her throbbing wrist with her other hand.

"Just showing you I'm not to be trifled with." Nolan nodded at her wrist. "I'd apologize, but I imagine it'll be whole in no time." He bent down and picked up the dagger. "This is nice." He stuck it in his belt.

"Give that back!" She reached for him and whimpered as the movement sent a stab of pain through her wrist.

He wiped blood off his cheek, but lines of blood continued to flow from the shallow cut. "So demanding."

There was still no one in sight. She raised her left hand as a ball of fire grew in front of it.

He clicked his tongue and shook his head. "I wouldn't do that. Do you think no one knows I'm here? You kill me and you'll be hanged for murder."

"Maybe I don't kill you," she bit out. He could be lying. But she wasn't confident enough to risk being accused of murder. And if his body was found scorched to death, she would have a lot of explaining to do.

All humor fled Nolan's face. "*Now* I'm threatening you. All I have to do is say a word, and I have men who can discretely sabotage your sister's carriage. I can't imagine a carriage wreck being healthy for her or the baby."

Adelaide gasped. *Etiros, no.* She wanted to believe he wouldn't. But after Harold and Sieger… Nolan looked at her with cold, indifferent resolve. She dropped her hand to her side, the flames extinguished.

"Good girl."

"You still can't take that," she said, but her voice held no confidence. "Your father gave it to Regulus."

"Who gave it to you, and you kindly gave it to me."

Adelaide felt helpless. She had never felt helpless. Her mother hadn't raised her to be helpless. *Etiros, what do I do?* She could roast Nolan alive, or throw a knife at his back as he walked away, even though she was far less accurate with her left hand.

But she couldn't. She couldn't put her family at risk. And she didn't want to hang for murder—or even really want to kill again. He tapped his foot on the ground, waiting.

"Please." Adelaide lowered her head, staring at the ground. Her wrist ached and her eyes watered. Her heart felt made of lead. "Please."

"All right." She looked up, surprised. "I'll give it back." He leered. "For a kiss."

"Troll take you!"

Nolan shrugged. "Have it your way." He turned and walked away, Regulus'—her—dagger still in his belt. He mounted his horse. "See you soon, love. And if I were you," he smiled cruelly, "I'd think very carefully about how you will answer next time I ask for your hand."

After Nolan left, Adelaide healed her wrist. Tears of despair stung her eyes as she sent anguished, rage-filled prayers to Etiros. She waited until she had stopped crying to ride back to camp. She couldn't tell Minerva. Minerva would tell Gaius; Gaius would challenge Nolan. Adelaide had seen them both fight. Nolan would win.

Minerva would be a widow with a baby due in three months.

No. She wouldn't put Minerva and Gaius in the middle of this. She wouldn't risk their safety and their lives. A month didn't give her much time, but at least Nolan wasn't trying to force her into marrying him next week. She would tell Regulus after their supper. They would come up with a plan together. She combed her fingers through Zephyr's mane.

Maybe Regulus would ask her to marry him. She couldn't marry Nolan if she was betrothed to Regulus.

Right?

CHAPTER 34

REGULUS DUG THROUGH HIS CLOSET, TOSSING ASIDE SHIRTS AND trousers and boots. Where had he put it? He glimpsed a corner of the small wooden box and seized it. The silver inlay of an *A* on the lid gleamed in the sunlight streaming through his window. The oak box was about the same size as both his hands, and heavy. He undid the latch and opened the box.

Inside, a large silver medallion stamped with a rose over crossed swords rested on red satin. The Arrano crest. The pure silver medallion had been left to Regulus, along with everything else, when his half-brother died and his father's title transferred to him. Lady Arrano had thrown it at his head after he defeated her champion.

Regulus had tried to give it back to her. She could have sold it. But she resented his kindness. So it sat in its box, buried deep in his closet. Now his blacksmith would fashion it into a circlet for the thrice-accursed sorcerer. He snapped the lid closed.

One ingredient out of five.

He had already instructed his bewildered steward to find and purchase fifteen clams. They didn't even have to be in good condition, he only needed their shells. But he decided to play it safe and get more than necessary. Just in case. Steward Preston didn't question the uncharacteristic request.

Regulus had talked to Jerrick and to Perceval's wife Leonora about flowers. They both did some recreational gardening and knew a good amount about plants. Between the two of them, they assured him they could secure a bushel of assorted white flowers.

That left the neumenet root and the blood of an innocent. Regulus dropped off the medallion with his blacksmith before heading out. Holgren Forest was over a day's ride away. It had already taken a day and a half to get back to his estate. He had spent the prior afternoon and evening making arrangements. Best not to delay.

Sieger had made a full recovery. Even after the long trek back to Arrano, his stallion was eager to leave again. As Regulus had decided he wanted to draw as little attention to himself as possible, he left the Black Knight armor behind. Dresden accompanied him. Regulus had tried to talk him out of coming, but between the risk of getting caught entering a royal forest without a permit, concerns about a chance encounter with Carrick, and anger over hiding how bad things had been with the sorcerer, Dresden would not be dissuaded. Regulus decided to be thankful no one else tried to tag along.

Dresden's concerns proved unfounded. They arrived at Holgren Forest the following morning without incident but searched all day without finding the neumenet tree. Holgren Forest was large, so they had a discouraging amount of ground to cover. When darkness fell, they were deep in the forest. They had no choice but to make camp and hope no forest rangers, or worse, a royal sheriff, happened upon them.

They spent the next day searching. Every snap of a branch or sudden rustling put Regulus on edge. Several deer startled him, and Dresden teased him relentlessly about being more skittish than a doe. Despair crept in as the shadows deepened in the forest.

"Reg." Dresden pointed. "Did you see that?"

"What?" He turned Sieger, scanning the branches where Dresden pointed. Then he saw it. A flash of light. Like sunlight on water, but high in the trees.

Like sunlight on glass.

Bark like obsidian and leaves like shards of glass but soft as feathers.

They rode toward the flashes of light. They rounded a large willow and Regulus held up his hand to shade his eyes, squinting.

Some twenty paces ahead stood a tree several stories tall. Wide branches spread out, stretching over a meadow and nearby trees. He couldn't look directly at the branches. Sunlight reflected off tens of thousands of silvery-white leaves, illuminating the surrounding forest. No trees stood within ten paces of its massive, shiny black trunk. Light bounced off leaves and gave the obsidian bark a dull glow. After a moment of gawking, he rode forward. Dresden followed.

The closer they got to the tree, the more leaves from the neumenet tree covered the ground. As long as his hand and no wider than two finger's breadth and opaque, they looked like shards of glass after a heavy frost. He dismounted and retrieved a spade from his saddlebag. The leaves made a quiet rustling beneath his feet as he walked closer to the trunk. Like walking on straw. Curious, he knelt down. He touched one, half expecting it to cut him. Instead, it gave way beneath his fingers. He picked the leaf up. It was solid, yet light and soft to the touch. He dropped it, and it drifted to the ground.

He had the strangest sensation. Like the earth and forest around him were extra alive. The bizarre whisper of a breeze in the leaves of the neumenet tree above him sounded at once welcoming and foreboding. As if the tree itself invited him to rest in its shade, but with an undercurrent of doubt and warning. He shook his head and scanned the ground. Paranoia.

He saw a hint of black root breaking the surface of the ground and knelt next to it. Dresden joined him, also bearing a spade. Together, they dug around the root until a little over a foot was exposed. Regulus' hunting knife made a high-pitched rasp as he sawed through the black wood. Dresden started on the other end, and the sound made Regulus' ears ache.

Unlike the trunk, the root had no shine. But it was hard, sweat-inducing work. Every so often, a low, rumbling creak sounded from the trunk. Almost a groan. As if the tree felt pain. *Ridiculous. Trees don't feel pain. Right?* He wiped away some sweat from his forehead before it dripped into his eyes. *This is wrong.* He felt in his soul there was something special, sacred even, about this place. About this tree.

But his freedom depended on getting this root.

His future. His ability to marry Adelaide.

Etiros, forgive me. I know I ask often. But forgive me.

Finally, he cut through the root. He could have sworn the tree shuddered. Glittering leaves drifted to the ground all around. He shifted and took over for Dresden, who sat back, panting. It took another couple minutes to cut through again. He picked up the root and strapped it to his saddlebags. A woody groaning followed them away from the tree. Regulus' heart and conscience felt heavy.

They made it back to Arrano without being stopped, but Regulus didn't relax until they arrived. They had been gone nearly five days. Eight days had passed since the sorcerer contacted him. Adelaide would arrive for supper in three days. It would take two to get to the sorcerer's tower and back.

To his relief, everything else was ready. The circlet complete. Fifteen whole clamshells were in a bag, cleaned and ready. A guest bedroom was crowded with white flowers in vases, bowls, and jars. He only needed one more thing. One more thing to ask Etiros to forgive him for.

He knocked on Harold's door. The small tin vial and knife in his hands seemed heavy as a boulder. Harold opened the door and smiled.

"What can I…" Harold's brows knit. "What's wrong, my lord?"

Regulus exhaled and his shoulders dipped down. He hated himself for doing this. His hands grew slick. His head ached.

Harold looked down at the vial and dagger in Regulus' hands. "My lord?" The confusion and anxiety in his voice made Regulus' stomach turn.

He looked away from Harold's face, unable to meet his eyes as he held out the knife and vial. "I…" He swallowed. "I have to ask something of you."

"I don't understand."

"I need…" Another gulp. "The sorcerer needs your blood. The blood of an innocent person. You have a good heart, a kind soul, and have never killed." He tasted bile at the back of his throat. "He said he only needs a few drops. I'm not asking as your lord." He forced himself to look at his squire. "I'm asking as your friend. I won't force you—"

"This will help free you?"

"I hope so."

Harold nodded, then took the dagger. "My life is yours, my lord. I can spare a few drops of blood. That's a small favor." He made a small cut on the side of his hand. He held the blade against the wound and blood pooled on it.

Feeling wretched, Regulus pulled the stopper out of the vial. Harold placed the tip of the dagger in the top, and a small rivulet of blood dripped in. Regulus replaced the stopper. Harold handed back the dagger and held his other hand over the cut.

"Thank you," Regulus said quietly. "You're a good man."

Harold shrugged. "I have a good example to follow."

Regulus trudged up the stairs, the vial of Harold's blood clutched in his hand. *I don't deserve your admiration.*

Regulus didn't wear the Black Knight armor on the way to the sorcerer's tower, either. Let him be angry. Regulus needed speed, not theatrics. His saddlebags bulged. One end of the black neumenet root stuck out from under the flap. Leaves from the flowers poked out everywhere. If anyone stopped him, they would have plenty of questions.

He kept off the main roads, cutting across fields and through woods to take the most direct route. Stars appeared as he reached the dead forest surrounding the sorcerer's tower. Moonlight made the barren white trees look ghostly. He dismounted and knocked on the door. After a couple minutes, a deadbolt clanged on the other side of the door. The door opened, and the sorcerer stepped onto the threshold. Firelight flickered inside the tower. Even standing a step below him, Regulus stood taller than him. But the dark power emanating from the sorcerer made Regulus feel weak.

"Ah. You're early." The shadow cast by the sorcerer's black hood hid his expression. The black stones set in his red and black belt seemed to absorb all light, while the silver hairs in his brown beard glowed white in the moonlight. "Come on. Bring it all in." He turned and went back inside, his tunics and robe rustling.

The sorcerer had never invited Regulus inside. He recovered from his momentary shock and removed the bulging saddlebags, then followed the sorcerer.

The ground floor consisted of one large circular room. A modest fire burned in a huge stone fireplace across from the door. An ornamental rug covered the entire floor beneath a leather armchair. Two floor-to-ceiling bookshelves stood on either side of the fireplace, filled with leather-bound tomes and stark white human skulls. The sorcerer headed up a spiral staircase to the right of the door.

"Close the door," he called as he disappeared around a curve. Regulus nudged the door closed with his boot and followed.

They passed two more open circular rooms as the staircase spiraled around the outside of the tower. Regulus peeked through the open doorways as they passed. One had several desks, some covered with open books, others with large pieces of parchment. Another fire crackled in the fireplace behind a desk covered in rocks and gemstones of various sizes and colors. The next room contained a massive four-poster bed, a small writing desk, and a closet. Were any clothes in the closet? He'd never seen the sorcerer wear anything other than the layered black and red tunics and robes he wore now. None of the rooms had windows.

The staircase opened into the final room at the top of the tower. A long table with a workbench sat in the middle of the room. Four gold rods were laid end-to-end on the table. He recognized the one that widened at the top as the first thing the sorcerer had made him retrieve. The sight of it gave him flashbacks to the first time he had discovered he couldn't die. A minotaur had impaled him on a spear. Right through his chest. He recognized two of the other three pieces as well with a sickening twist of his stomach. He'd killed a monk who wouldn't get out of way for one of them. Not on purpose. He'd tossed him aside, still adjusting to his new strength, and the man's head had cracked open on the stone wall of the monastery. The man's vacant eyes still haunted him.

Positioned just above the rods lay the strange hollow gold egg he had taken from the dragon's lair. As he looked at the five pieces positioned in a line, he realized they belonged together. They formed a staff. But the sorcerer hadn't forged them back together.

Regulus looked around as the sorcerer motioned him inside. A bronze mirror identical to the one locked in his chest hung on the wall near the fireplace. Light flickered from the fire and from numerous candelabras on the walls around the room. Smaller desks were placed around the edges of the room, covered in various flora in glass jars. A large, shallow bronze bowl sat on one of the tables. The sorcerer pushed aside some books piled on another table.

"Unpack it all here so I can examine it," the sorcerer commanded.

Regulus complied. The flowers came out first and the sorcerer grunted approval. The sorcerer snatched up the neumenet root, inspecting it and muttering to himself while Regulus emptied the bag of shells onto the table. Apparently satisfied, the sorcerer set the root next to the flowers. He checked the shells while Regulus set the silver circlet on the table.

"Hm." The sorcerer picked up the circlet. His hands glowed with green light and the circlet made a quiet thrumming sound. "Pure. Good." He put the circlet down and Regulus exhaled in relief. "And the blood?"

Regulus handed him the vial. "From my squire. A good young man who has never taken a life. An innocent if I ever met one."

"Excellent." The sorcerer removed the stopper and peered inside. "Should be enough."

"Will that be all, my lord?" Regulus stepped back from the table.

"For now." The sorcerer replaced the stopper and set it next to the other ingredients.

Regulus clutched the saddlebag. Nothing but dried venison, a bit of rope, and a spare dagger left in it now. "And...my debt?"

"You annoy me with your constant nagging." The sorcerer pursed his lips. "I'd think you would be more grateful. I made you the strongest, fastest man in Monparth, possibly in the world. And immortal. Yet you can't wait to give it up."

I want to be free. "You mentioned this," he indicated the ingredients, "would get me close."

"Fine." The sorcerer waved his hand. "One or two more tasks, and your debt will be paid in full. I'm close now." He looked away, and Regulus followed his gaze to the separated staff on the table in the center of the room. "So close I can taste it. This time, I won't fail."

The sorcerer looked back to Regulus. "I'll be needing you soon. You must be prepared to act quickly when the time comes. Now go." He waved his hands like he was shooing away a small child. "Your presence irritates me."

Then why trick me into being your slave in the first place! But Regulus turned and left.

CHAPTER 35

THE PRINCE OF SHADOW AND ASH SPENT THE NEXT TWO DAYS preparing for the full moon. Thanks to that gratingly honorable mercenary-turned-lord, he could take his time. Make sure everything was exact. The roots and shells ground into powder. The flower petals plucked and dried. It was time consuming, but life had taught him patience and the value of doing things properly. He rubbed his scarred shoulder. It would be different this time. If he could find what he needed. Ironically, the same thing that had stopped him last time.

The full moon rose into a clear sky. He moved a table into the moonlight spilling through his window and placed the wide, shallow bronze bowl on top and filled it with water. He mixed in the ground root. Once the water was black, he used his sorcery to heat the black water to boiling. Next, he stirred in two handfuls of powdered shells. After the shells had dissolved, he forced the water to cool, making the bowl glow a dim green, then covered the surface of the water with the dried petals. He enchanted the silver circlet so it would float and positioned it in the center of the bowl. All part of activating the magic inherent in the items, or imbuing them with his own magic.

Last, he opened the vial. The enchantment he had placed on it as soon as Hargreaves had given it to him kept the blood as fresh as possible. He tilted the vial and three drops of blood dripped into the center of the bowl, staining the petals red. He held his hands over the bowl. Emerald light radiated from his palms. Steam and smoke rose from the bowl. The petals inside the silver circlet melted and silver bled into the water. He mentally reached out, drawing more energy to replenish his magic from the forest outside as green light swirled around him. He had to reach farther and farther each time he needed extra power.

The water inside the circlet shimmered silver with a greenish tint, then became clear as glass. An image shifted into focus and the sorcerer dropped his hands to his side and scrutinized the image.

An infant. He snorted in disgust. Useless. He waved over the bowl, and the image shifted. A scrawny young man stumbled out of a tavern, obviously drunk. As if this pathetic creature could possibly have enough control to do what he needed. Would not even be worth the effort to have him killed. He waved his hand again. A young girl no older than four with tight blond curls bounced on a middle-aged man's knee.

"Curse my thoroughness!" The prince waved his hand again, rage boiling his blood.

A young woman. Probably noble, based on her fine clothing. Certainly wealthy. Her skin was dark for a Monparthian. Maybe Carasian or Khastallander. But she had to be in Monparth, since he had only searched within the kingdom. She smiled and laughed between sips of wine, looking confident and at ease. He held his hand over the water and pulled up, forcing the image to move in on her face. Bright, intelligent brown eyes. He pushed back down toward the water, and the image pulled back, showing more of her surroundings. A smile curled his lips. He stroked his beard and leaned back from the bowl.

"Interesting."

CHAPTER 36

"HOW DO I LOOK?" REGULUS RAN HIS FINGERS THROUGH HIS HAIR.

Dresden rolled his eyes. "Like you always do."

"This is a bad idea." Regulus paced back and forth in the foyer, the clack of his boots echoing in the vaulted ceiling. Magnus padded along after him, tongue hanging out of his mouth and tail wagging. Two curving staircases rose on either side of the room, meeting at the top and leading into the great hall. The only decorations were a couple suits of armor on either side of the door centered between the two staircases that led to the wine cellar. He had never cared for ostentation, so when he moved in, he had cleared away the over-sized vases and faded blue carpets that reminded him too much of his father's wife. Besides, he had never had guests before.

"What if I can't get her alone to explain? What if she doesn't understand?"

Dresden leaned against one of the stone bannisters. "Relax."

"What if supper is awkward?" Regulus stopped short and Magnus pushed his head under his hand. He scratched behind the big dog's floppy ears. "I think Sir Gaius has mixed opinions of me. What if I do something he dislikes? Or worse, I do something that offends Lady Minerva?"

"You're offending me with your incessant worrying."

The doors to the foyer swung inward and Regulus turned. Magnus stepped in front of him with a low growl. Steward Preston led Adelaide, Gaius, and Minerva into the castle. His anxiety melted away as she smiled. "They're friends, Magnus."

Magnus looked back at him, his tongue hanging out of what looked like a grin.

Adelaide knelt in front of Magnus. "Hello, Magnus." He panted as she scratched beneath his chin. "Aren't you a handsome big boy. Regulus told me all about you." Magnus licked her bare forearm—she wore a sleeveless dress today. She laughed.

"First your horse, now your dog," Dresden said. "Maybe she wants to steal your animals, not your heart."

Adelaide stood and crossed her arms, but he caught the slight blush in her cheeks. She cocked an eyebrow. "Really, Dresden," her tone was teasing. "If you put as much effort into your manners as you did into maintaining your beard, you'd have a wife by now."

"All right, all right." Dresden laughed. "The lady knows how to spar. I humbly fold."

Regulus held out his arm. "Shall we head in?"

Adelaide took his arm and they entered the hall. Magnus pushed between them, rubbing against their legs. He looked from one to the other, whimpering for attention. They moved to their seats as the rest of his knights arrived to join them for supper. Perceval's wife Sarah and Jerrick's wife Leonora joined as well. Adelaide sat in the chair to the right of the head of the table, Gaius in the chair to the left. Regulus pushed in her seat and sat down. Magnus laid between his and Adelaide's feet.

Contrary to his fears, supper progressed wonderfully. Gaius seemed relaxed and Minerva was as sassy as she was sweet. Adelaide's laugh made his heart soar. The warm chatter that echoed down the long table filled his soul. This was all he ever wanted. To be surrounded by people he cared about and who cared for him in return. To see the joy on their faces.

Halfway through supper, Estevan regaled them with a story about the time Perceval stepped in a hunter's snare and refused help for an entire hour while he kept trying to cut himself down, all while hanging upside down. Regulus reached for his goblet, watching Adelaide's eyes sparkle with mirth. Searing pain sliced up his arm. His hand jerked, and he knocked over his goblet with a clatter. Wine spilled over the table. He clenched his teeth against the stabbing, burning sensation covering his right forearm. The mark had never hurt like this when the sorcerer summoned him before.

Estevan stopped mid-sentence. All eyes turned toward him.

"Regulus? What's wrong?" Alarm rang in Adelaide's tone.

"Nothing." Another stab of pain. He gripped the edge of the table. "An old injury acting up. Excuse me for a moment." He left the table, their stares clinging to him.

Magnus followed, but he shook his head. "You stay here, boy." Magnus cocked his head, and Regulus pointed back toward the table. The dog padded back and laid down at Adelaide's feet. It pleased him Magnus liked her, but the searing pain commanded his attention.

Dresden cleared his throat. "You haven't gotten to the best part yet, man! Keep going."

Good old Drez.

The pain kept increasing, spreading from his arm to his shoulder to his chest. Regulus raced up the stairs, stumbling as his ribs ached. He threw open his door and slammed it behind him. He fumbled with the key, his hand shaking from the pain that wasn't abating despite his obedience. It seemed to take forever to lock the door. *I'm coming!* He cursed.

He struggled again with the lock on the chest. What in creation was the sorcerer's problem? He yanked out the mirror and the pain eased. "I'm here." He hung the mirror on the wall and stepped back.

The mirror shimmered and the sorcerer appeared, an ecstatic grin on his face. The pain vanished.

"Yes, my lord?" Regulus said, not hiding the irritation in his voice. "What's with the…urgency? What if I had been out?"

"I knew you weren't," he said, as if this were obvious. "I've found what I'm looking for."

Regulus sighed. "Which is?"

"You see," the sorcerer bobbed up and down, as if rocking back and forth onto his toes, "some twenty or so years ago, I lose count, I tracked down and killed—or rather, had killed, mostly—every mage in Monparth. Every sniveling idiot with pure magic in their veins."

"You…" Regulus' jaw dropped. *Of course. Idiot.* Of course the self-proclaimed Prince of Shadow and Ash *was* The Shadow that had caused the extinction of mages in Monparth. His thoughts turned to Adelaide downstairs. *Almost extinction.* Panic surged, but he snapped his jaw closed.

"Yes, that was me. Who else could have that much power?" The sorcerer paused, but Regulus didn't know how to respond, so the sorcerer continued. "The trouble is, the final relic I need is hidden behind an enchanted wall. It's like a gigantic lock. And only a *mage*," he snarled, "can open it. It repels sorcery."

"So you used those ingredients to find mages again," Regulus guessed, his spirit sinking.

"What do you know. You're not a complete idiot."

Regulus tried to keep his voice from shaking. To look indifferent and uninterested. "Did you find any, my lord?"

"Oh, yes." A sickening grin spread over the sorcerer's face. "Would you believe a mage is downstairs, in your home, this very moment?"

No. No, no, no. "Downstairs?" The word came out choked. *Etiros, please, no!*

"Yes, pretty young woman." The mirror turned watery and shifted to an image of Adelaide in Arrano's hall. She rested her chin on her palm, her elbow propped on the table as she spoke. The image shifted back to the sorcerer.

Regulus swallowed back the bile rising in his throat. "You… you're certain?"

The sorcerer's smile turned into a frown. "I don't make mistakes! She's a mage as certainly as I'm a sorcerer. Hopefully she has the power to do what I need. What's her name, anyway?"

Regulus grit his teeth. His hands balled into fists.

"I asked you a question, boy."

Pain burned his arm, and he grunted.

"Her name?"

He stared at the ground, clutching his forearm. "Adelaide Belanger." The pain subsided.

"You told the truth. Very good. At least bringing her to me should be easy. You know right where to find her."

Regulus hung his head. "Please. Don't kill her."

"I won't kill her, weren't you listening? I just need her magic."

And after you've used her magic? He swallowed hard. "Surely there is someone else—"

Agony exploded up his arm. He clutched his chest and doubled over as the pain spread from his sternum. A moan stuck in his throat.

"I. Want. Her. As soon as possible."

Shouts sounded from the hallway. Cries of "Lord Hargreaves!" echoed up the stairs.

Confused and gasping for breath, Regulus looked toward the door. He panted out, "My lord, I should go check—" before he fell to his knees as the pain redoubled, spreading over his entire body.

"You will bring her to me."

Regulus' eyes watered as his breathing grew more labored. The shouts continued, muffled and unintelligible.

"I…can't…" He swallowed back a scream as it felt like fire filled his veins. His vision blacked out, and he curled into a ball on the floor.

"You're my slave. You do what I tell you."

His heart felt like it would burst. Dying. He was dying. *Etiros...save me.*

"Do this, and your debt will be paid."

The pain ceased. Regulus took several deep breaths to steady himself. The darkness shrouding his vision receded. He stood, his knees shaking.

"I expect to see you tomorrow with Belanger. I don't want to harm her. But you must bring her." The sorcerer's voice became dark and menacing. "If I have to force you, every pain I have inflicted on you will seem as nothing compared to the pain *you* will inflict on everyone you care about, including the girl. And then you will die in more pain than you can imagine."

Regulus looked up. The mirror was blank—just a bronze mirror. He stuffed it in the trunk as someone pounded on his door. The muffled shouting from downstairs continued.

"My lord!" Harold sounded panicked. "I am sorry, but you *must* come downstairs."

Regulus opened the door. "What is it? What's going on?"

"We couldn't stop them," Harold panted. "The sheriff has a warrant—"

"Sheriff?" Regulus cursed. They had been spotted in Holgren. Someone must have recognized him or his description. Regulus grabbed his sheathed sword from next to his door and pushed past Harold, fastening the belt around his hips as he hurried down the stairs. If he was going to be accused of hunting in the royal forest— a theft against the crown—he needed to look like a lord.

Because a lord might get away with a heavy fine. But a commoner could be hanged. If they tried to hang him, he would live. He would be exposed for the monster he was.

CHAPTER 37

ADELAIDE WATCHED REGULUS GO WITH AN UNSETTLED FEELING in her gut. He was hiding something. Dresden urged Estevan to continue his story. She would have to ask Regulus for the truth later—when she told him about Nolan's threats.

Regulus' abrupt exit distracted her from the end of Estevan's story. Something about Perceval injuring himself trying to escape from a hunter's trap. The other knights laughed like this was the funniest thing in the world. Their laughter was infectious, even though Adelaide scarcely understood the cause.

"That's why he's the blockhead and I'm the smart one," Caleb said, his tone serious but mirth in the wrinkles around his eyes.

Perceval pointed at him. "No, you're the one askin' for a beating."

Caleb gasped and put a hand over his heart. "To say such things in front of ladies! Including your own wife!"

Leonora giggled. The curvy brunette wrapped her hands around Perceval's muscular upper arm and leaned against her husband's shoulder. "He has a point, Cal. You'll push him too far one day." She winked.

Adelaide laughed and propped her elbow on the table, resting her chin in her hand. "What is it between you two?"

"Ah, see that's all on account of—"

"Caleb Rathburn you shut your obnoxious mouth!" Perceval threw a bread crust at Caleb's head, which he ducked.

"Don't interrupt me when I'm talking to a lady." Caleb clicked his tongue. "What *would* your instructors at university say?"

Adelaide looked at Perceval than back at Caleb. "Perceval went to university?"

"Perceval got kicked *out* of university," Caleb said.

"I quit!" Perceval snatched up his goblet.

Dresden leaned toward her. "This is a common argument," he whispered.

"Why were you kicked out or...quit? Whichever it was," Gaius said as he cut into the roast quail on his plate.

"Well, see—" A loud banging from the foyer interrupted Caleb.

Dresden frowned. "That's odd." He rose from his seat and headed out of the hall. "Pardon me a moment."

"You cannot barge—" Adelaide recognized the voice of the steward who had greeted them in the courtyard.

"I am the Sheriff of Relton, and I serve the king!" another man's voice interrupted. "These men are my deputies. The others are here in case of trouble."

"Trouble? What business has a sheriff here?" Dresden's voice. "Why—Carrick."

A tremor ran down Adelaide's spine. Surely Nolan wasn't here? Now?

"*Sir* Carrick. I'm here as a witness, as are my knights."

Her stomach churned, her appetite gone.

"I am here to arrest Regulus Hargreaves for treason," the sheriff said. Her head spun.

"Treason?" Dresden's voice echoed as he shouted. "You're out of your mind!"

"Where is your master, Carasian?" Nolan asked. She could hear the sneer in his voice.

"My *lord* is not. Present."

"Check the hall," the sheriff ordered. A moment later three men she didn't recognize strode into the hall, followed by a red-faced Dresden.

"This is an outrage!" Dresden shouted. "Lord Hargreaves isn't even home! And you have no proof! How can you possibly—"

"He was heard conspiring to kill the king," the sheriff said as he walked into the hall. He was of average height, with a drawn countenance and a balding head.

"That's ridiculous," Adelaide blurted.

The sheriff looked down his nose at her. "You are hosting guests without your lord present?" He eyed the empty chair at the head of the table. "Or perhaps you mean the treasonous coward has already fled." He raised his voice. "Hargreaves, show yourself!"

Three more men walked in. Nolan and two other knights. He stopped in his tracks and stared. "Adelaide? What are you doing here?"

She stood, glaring. "*I* was invited! What are *you* doing here?"

Nolan shrugged. "I'm here to positively identify the man whom my knights and I heard discussing plans to murder the king."

All of Regulus' knights stood, shouting over each other, protesting Regulus' innocence and accusing Nolan and his knights of lying. Magnus stood, too. He stalked around the table and growled at the intruders. Gaius stood and turned toward the men.

"Gentlemen," he said, his voice calm and level, "perhaps there has been a misunderstanding. I hardly think Regulus Hargreaves capable of plotting treason. What reason could he possibly have?" Regulus' knights shouted their assent.

"The courts will determine the truth!" the sheriff bellowed.

"There's no proof!" Adelaide shot back. "Just his word against theirs!" She pointed at Nolan. "Nolan Carrick has a personal feud with Lord Hargreaves. He is lying!"

Regulus' knights talked over each other again, confirming what she said and calling Nolan all kinds of unsavory names. Nolan and his knights put their hands on their swords, as did the deputies. Perceval was the only one of Regulus' knights wearing a sword, and he put his hand on his sword as well, pushing his wife toward the door at the far end of the hall with the other. Leonora grabbed Sarah's hand, and they left the hall. Estevan pulled a strange dagger from the back of his belt. It was long, curved and sharp along one edge, with no handle. Opposite from the sharpened edge was a grip with four holes. Estevan put his fingers through and held the grip in his fist. Jerrick and Caleb grabbed carving knives off the table. Dresden eyed a sword hanging on the wall on the other side of the intruders.

Gaius held out his hands. His face was pale as he moved to shield Minerva. "Now, gentlemen. Let's not be hasty." Magnus barked between low, rumbling growls.

"Magnus!"

Adelaide spun toward Regulus' voice. Magnus ran to Regulus in the stairway but continued to snarl. Regulus now wore a sword. He stroked Magnus' head. "Upstairs." The dog whined, but obeyed, and Regulus shut the door behind him. "I demand to know what is going on!"

"That's him." Nolan pointed at Regulus.

"Regulus Hargreaves," the sheriff said, "you are under arrest for conspiracy to commit treason against the crown."

Regulus looked confused, then angry. "Carrick." He said it like a curse word. "You dare come into my home and spread lies?"

"My men and I overheard you talking to some other men," Nolan said, motioning to the knights on either side of him, "plotting to murder the king."

Perceval drew his sword. Nolan, his knights, and the bailiffs did the same. Regulus followed suit.

"In here!" Nolan called.

A dozen more men poured into the hall, all wearing swords. Adelaide's lips parted in shock. Gaius grabbed Minerva and pulled her away, toward the far end of the hall.

"Adelaide!" Minerva called, her voice desperate.

"Go," she said. Gaius hurried Minerva out of the hall.

Nolan nodded at Adelaide. "You should go, too."

"I'm not leaving until you take back your accusations."

"Hargreaves will stand trial. The courts will determine if the accusations are true," the sheriff repeated.

"And who will the courts believe?" Regulus shouted. He strode away from the closed stairwell door until he stood near her at the head of the table. "How am I to prove what I did or did not say? When was this supposed to be? I've been away on business. Does that even matter to you? To the courts? Or only the word of a baron's son? I'll take my chances with my sword, thank you." He spun the sword around like it weighed no more than a stick.

Nolan rolled his eyes. "An honest lord would come willingly, Half-Breed." Adelaide could have punched his perfect face.

"As an agent of the crown, I am authorized to use any force necessary to take you into custody so you can stand trial." The sheriff ignored Regulus' questions. Doubtless because he knew that the judge would favor the testimony of a baron's son over the word of a lesser lord and former mercenary. The sheriff nodded to the three bailiffs, and they moved toward Regulus. "If you resist, you will be killed."

"So my choices are death or death?" Regulus said, his voice hot with rage. He leaned toward her and whispered, "You need to leave. Now. I'm sorry."

"If you are innocent, you have nothing to fear." Nolan sneered.

Sure, right. Adelaide stepped in front of Regulus. "This is nonsense!"

Nolan scowled. "Get her out of here."

Four more men stepped toward her and Regulus. Her first instinct was to pull her dagger from her boot, but what good would that do? There were close to twenty men in the hall, including Nolan and the sheriff. Regulus gently grabbed her arm and moved her aside.

"No one touches her." Regulus looked at Nolan. "You have a problem with me? Fine. Be a man and challenge me to a duel."

Panic rose in Adelaide's chest. *Etiros, how do we stop Nolan?*

"Mm, no."

"Then I challenge you!" Regulus pointed his sword at Nolan.

"Ha." Nolan shook his head. "I don't have to accept a challenge from a man accused of treason."

"You think these men are enough to take me and my men?" A menacing smile spread over Regulus' face and for the first time, Adelaide understood the mercenary that was all some people saw when they looked at him.

"Confident, aren't we?" Nolan shrugged. "I'd wager they could, but if they can't, there's another ten in the foyer and fifteen more on standby in the courtyard. You can't escape."

"I don't run," Regulus said in a low voice. He raised his sword and adjusted his footing.

Adelaide clenched her fists. *No, no. This can't be happening!*

"If you fight back, what happens?" Nolan asked with a wicked smile. He pointed to Regulus' men. Perceval still held his drawn sword, his eyes fixed on Regulus like he was waiting for a signal to attack. Caleb and Jerrick held the carving knives at the ready, their eyes roving over the men in the hall. Estevan paced back and forth, a cat ready to pounce. Dresden's fingers twitched, his gaze fixed on the knight nearest him. "If they fight with you, they'll die with you."

"That's what we do," Perceval said, his tone icy cold. "I know loyalty must be a difficult concept for a snake like you."

"You want to be the first to die?" Nolan's lip curled up in a sneer.

Perceval took a step toward Nolan, and Nolan's knights moved to intercept him. Adelaide felt rooted to the floor, her voice trapped in her throat.

"Stand down, men," Regulus said, his voice heavy. Perceval froze, as did the knights. They all looked at Regulus.

Adelaide's breath caught. Regulus' sword clattered to the stone floor, and the sound made her jump as it reverberated through the hall. Regulus raised his hands.

"I surrender."

Adelaide froze. The men who had been moving toward her jumped forward and surrounded Regulus. Two of them grabbed Regulus' arms. Perceval and the others stared at Regulus, their disbelief clear.

"I said, stand down," Regulus repeated as the knights pinned his arms behind his back and pushed him toward the doors. Perceval sheathed his sword, his face red.

"What? No!" Adelaide grabbed at one of the men and tried to pull him off Regulus. "Let him go!" Another man pushed her away as they hurried Regulus out of the hall. Her boot caught on the hem of her skirt, and she started to fall.

Hands grasped her arms and steadied her. Nolan smiled, a picture of carefree calm. "Easy there."

She pulled away. Regulus had already disappeared through the doorway out of the hall, trailed by his fuming men. "What is wrong with you! What are you *doing*?"

"I would have thought it was obvious. Getting rid of an obstacle." He looked at her patronizingly. "I warned you. You don't want to go to war with me."

"Treason? They'll *hang* him!"

"I certainly hope so."

"You…" That's when she saw the dagger in his belt. Regulus' dagger. Her dagger. He must have caught her gaze, because he rested his hand on the hilt and smirked.

Maybe she should just kill him. Then there would be no witnesses to Regulus' supposed crime. Just several witnesses for her, murdering a baron's son in front of a sheriff.

"You can put a stop to this, you know." Nolan stepped closer. "Say you'll marry me, and I promise, the bastard will live. I'll leave him and his alone."

The breath seemed sucked from her lungs. She couldn't even push her *never* past her stuck tongue. She looked toward the door. Regulus' men stood on the other side, at the top of the stairs leading down in the foyer, their backs to her. The sheriff stood in the hall, watching her and Nolan with disinterest.

"I guess he dies, then."

She looked back as Nolan crossed his arms and stared into her eyes. Waiting for her to break.

"You know, others were with him, when he was plotting treason." He looked at his fingernails. "One of whom, now that I saw him here, looked suspiciously like your brother-in-law."

Adelaide covered her mouth with her fist and gasped. Her gut clenched. *Etiros, please.* Her face burned. So did her hands, and she clenched her fists tighter to keep her magic under control. "You're a monster."

"I'm just a man willing to do whatever it takes to get what I want." The icy look in his eyes made her shiver.

"You think I could ever love you?"

"Eventually, yes, I think you will." He shrugged. "But I don't need you to love me. I need you to marry me and act happy about it."

No. This was all wrong. This wasn't supposed to happen. She had to…had to… Her shoulders drooped. She had to protect her family. And she couldn't let Regulus die because of her. "Fine," she whispered.

Nolan stepped so close her skirt brushed his boots. "What was that?"

"I'll marry you." The words tasted like vinegar. "So long as they *all* live. You can't let them hurt or kill Regulus."

Nolan grinned. "Sheriff!" He stepped around her. "I've just realized—we've got the wrong man. Turns out he's innocent." Nolan held up a hand, as if saying *oh well.*

"You want him arrested, or don't you?" the sheriff huffed.

Nolan took Adelaide's hand and strode toward the sheriff, pulling her along. "Not anymore." He lowered his voice. "Don't worry, you'll still get paid."

Adelaide's mouth hung open, but both men ignored her as they walked out into the foyer full of armed men, with Regulus in the center. Gaius and Minerva stood off to the side. Minerva's eyes were wide in her ashen face. Gaius's forehead wrinkled and his lips pinched, eyes narrowed. Nolan, Adelaide, and the sheriff passed Dresden and the others at the top of the staircase as they walked down toward Regulus. The sheriff approached Regulus, and Nolan followed with Adelaide in tow.

"You say this *isn't* the man?" the sheriff asked Nolan.

Regulus looked at the sheriff in surprise, then at Nolan. His eyes flashed when his gaze landed on her hand in Nolan's.

"I realized it when I was talking to Adelaide," Nolan said flippantly. "The man looked almost exactly like Hargreaves, but now that I look at him, he's far too tall. The man I overheard was about Adelaide's height, so it couldn't be Hargreaves."

Regulus stared at Nolan like he was seeing a specter.

"It seems you are innocent after all," the sheriff said to Regulus. "Forgive us the intrusion." He bowed stiffly. "Release him." The men holding Regulus stepped back and his arms fell to his sides.

"A simple mistake, I'm afraid," Nolan said with a wave of his free hand. "My apologies. However, threatening to attack bailiffs, agents of the law, and all this fighting to the death bravado..." He clicked his tongue and put his arm around Adelaide's waist and pulled her against his side. She wanted to recoil from his touch, but she bit her tongue and forced herself to stand still. "I don't want my betrothed around such violent men."

"Your..." Hurt and confusion flickered over Regulus' face before the fire in his eyes returned even brighter. "What happened?"

"Didn't she tell you, Hargreaves?" Nolan gloated. "We're engaged to be married." He pulled the dagger from his belt and held it out on his palm. "She gave me this as a token of her affection and a symbol of our betrothal."

Regulus' face pinched as he looked at the dagger. The dagger he had given her. She clenched her jaw, her stomach roiling. He looked at her. "No," Regulus said. Then again, his voice stronger. "No."

"I'm sorry, Regulus." Her voice sounded strained, and she swallowed. What lie to tell to get him to stand down? If Nolan had paid off the sheriff, he would only have to say the word and these men would run Regulus through on the spot and claim he had resisted arrest. "This isn't how I wanted to tell you."

"You...but..." Regulus reached toward her. Nolan pulled her back and pointed the dagger at Regulus. Several men around them drew their swords. Regulus held up his hands and stepped back as Nolan returned the dagger to his belt.

"What is this?" Minerva's voice. Adelaide looked over her shoulder as Minerva and Gaius wove between armed men toward them. "You two are not betrothed!"

"Well, we have to speak to your father to make it official, but she has accepted my proposal." Nolan squeezed her waist. "Isn't that right, love?" He sounded so cavalier.

"Yes." She couldn't meet Minerva's eyes.

Gaius's cheeks reddened. "You're lying."

No, Gaius. Please don't.

"If I know anything about my sister," Minerva spoke with the sharpness of the daggers they had trained with, "I know she wants nothing to do with you." She looked at Adelaide. "Did he hurt you?"

"No." Adelaide forced herself to look at Minerva, begging her with her eyes to stop. To accept it. "I…" Her tongue stuck in her mouth. She thought of Regulus, being forced to his knees in front of an executioner. Of Gaius beside him. With all sincerity, but not about Nolan, she said, "I love him." *I love him.* The realization cracked through her heart. *I love Regulus more than I hate Nolan.*

"Horse manure," Dresden spat as he walked down the stairs. "What did he do?"

"You think I, a man of chivalry, would harm or threaten a lady?" Nolan sounded hurt and disappointed. He turned and brushed her hair behind her ear. "How could I hurt you, love?" His voice was soft, his eyes tender. He played the part maddeningly well, but his false gentleness filled her with disgust.

"She looks uncomfortable," Gaius ventured.

Nolan frowned at Gaius. "I had expected joy for our announcement; not to be attacked like this." His fingers dug into Adelaide's side, pinching her.

"I was wrong about Nolan." She forced a smile and laid a hand on his chest. "I was confused about my feelings." It felt like swallowing sawdust. "He's a…worthy man."

"Like hell." Regulus pointed at Nolan. "After what he did—"

"Regulus," Adelaide said. This was not going well. *What did Nolan think would happen?* "Lord Hargreaves." Regulus blinked like she had slapped him. "You have to let me go. Please. It's for the best."

"Best for who?" Gaius demanded.

"Adelaide, obviously." Nolan gestured around the foyer. "Look around. This place looks like a mausoleum. Tight on funds, Hargreaves? Based on the state of this place, I'm shocked you could afford the tournament entry fee. What can you offer the daughter of Lord Alfred Belanger? Or were you hoping to seduce your way into a dowry? You have nothing a woman of Lady Belanger's pedigree desires or needs."

Regulus opened and closed his mouth like he was trying to formulate a response but couldn't. He looked to Adelaide, his eyes full of doubt and questions. Adelaide's heart twisted. *No, Regulus. Don't believe that.* She couldn't help but note the bitter irony of Nolan accusing Regulus of using her for riches.

"But..." Regulus' throat bobbed. "He... Harold and—"

"Nolan wasn't behind the attack." Adelaide stared at the floor.

"I was appalled when I heard," Nolan said. "Attacking a boy and a defenseless animal? That's unforgivable. I hope you find out who did it."

Regulus stepped forward and drew back his fist. Several knights drew their swords and pointed them at Regulus. Adelaide sucked in a breath and held it as a knight placed the edge of his blade across Regulus' neck.

Nolan chuckled darkly. "I wouldn't try anything, mercenary."

Regulus' shoulders heaved, but he lowered his fist. A vein in his temple pulsed as he stepped back. Adelaide's chest shuddered as she released her breath.

Nolan brushed his lips against Adelaide's cheek and she barely suppressed a grimace. "Frankly, we don't owe any of you an explanation." He looked at Regulus. "We shouldn't linger in the house of murderers. Don't you agree, love?" His thumb pressed into her side.

"Agreed," she licked her lips, "my love."

Regulus took a tiny step back, his lips parted, eyes pinched, posture sagging as if he could scarcely stay standing. She looked away from his anguish. *Better heartbroken than dead.*

Nolan guided her toward the front entrance. "Don't bother following us, mercenary."

Night had fallen. The full moon cast long shadows across the courtyard and highlighted the group of armed men bearing torches standing at the ready.

"You there," Nolan called to a servant walking through the courtyard, "Lady Belanger and Sir and Lady Drummond require their horses at once." The man nodded, then changed course.

Several saddled horses stood grazing in the courtyard. The sheriff and bailiffs headed to their horses and mounted. Nolan left her side and retrieved a bulging pouch from a brown riding horse's saddlebag and handed it to the sheriff. Nausea grew in the pit of Adelaide's stomach. She moved next to Minerva and Gaius.

"What happened?" Minerva whispered. "Did he threaten you?"

Nolan turned away from the sheriff and looked at Adelaide. She shook her head. The sheriff and the bailiffs rode out of the courtyard, and all but the two knights who had entered the hall with Nolan left with them.

Nolan sauntered over, confident, cocky, and at-ease as always. Hatred burned her skin and coiled in her chest, making her fingers itch for a blade and magic tingle along her skin. Servants led Zephyr and the horses drawing Minerva and Gaius' carriage into the courtyard as Nolan stopped in front of her.

"I imagine this has been a frightening and exhausting evening." Nolan brushed her hair over her shoulder. "It's best you get home as soon as possible." He looked to Gaius. "My knights and I will gladly accompany you, for safety and peace of mind." He ran his hand down her bare arm and clasped her hand.

Adelaide stared at the backs of the men leaving the courtyard. He had no intention of affording her an opportunity to tell Gaius and Minerva the truth. Her heart sank.

"Oh." Gaius cleared his throat, sounding ill at ease. "That's not necessary."

"Please, I insist," Nolan said.

"Are you going to have a sword held to my throat if I refuse?" Gaius snapped. Adelaide tensed, squeezing Nolan's hand in her panic.

"Why would you refuse?" Nolan sneered. "Don't you want me along, Adelaide?"

She forced as much pleasantness into her voice as she could. "Of course I would like my betrothed to accompany us."

As they rode away, she cast one last look back at Arrano castle. *I'm sorry, Regulus.*

CHAPTER 38

REGULUS STARED AT THE CLOSED FRONT DOOR. ALL HIS anger—at the sorcerer, at magic, at Carrick, at the sheriff—had melted away, leaving him hollow and numb. What had just happened?

"Did you see anything?" he demanded of Dresden. "Did he hurt her?"

"I was too focused on you." Dresden's look of pity grated on his nerves. "But she looked unharmed."

Nolan must have threatened her. There was no way she *wanted* to marry that villain. She couldn't.

Regulus stepped toward the door, his heart fracturing while Adelaide calling Nolan *my love* replayed in his mind. "Something's going on."

Dresden blocked his path. "They have a small army. Carrick will have you killed if you try to stop them from leaving."

Regulus groaned and turned away. But then…there might be one blessing here. He had asked Etiros for aid, and now he had a valid barrier to bringing Adelaide to the sorcerer. Carrick would see to it he never went near her again. As much as it hurt, Regulus could let her marry that rogue if it kept her safe from the sorcerer. He ran back to his room, ignoring his men's shouted questions. Once he had locked the door to his room, he pulled the mirror back out. He had never tried this, but why shouldn't it work?

"I need to talk to you."

Nothing.

"It's about the mage."

After a moment, the mirror shimmered, and the sorcerer appeared. "What? What is it?"

"I can't bring you Adelaide Belanger. She is beyond my reach."

"Likely story."

"She's engaged to a personal enemy of mine." He closed his eyes for a moment, the words bitter. He worked his jaw, forced himself to continue. To see the blessing in this waking nightmare. "He's taken her, and he won't let me near her. Who else is there?"

"There is no one else!" the sorcerer shrieked. He took a deep breath, then spoke calmly. "She's in no danger from me. I need her to open a door. That's all."

"But there is no way for me—" He gasped as his mark burned. He wanted to claw it off, but he knew that didn't work, so he gritted his teeth against the pain.

"You've killed a dragon! You can handle some nobleman!" The pain in his arm subsided. "It's simple. Once she helps me, I'll remove the mark and let you both go. I'll be gracious and give you two days to bring her to me. But if in two days I don't have her, you will carve your friend's heart from his chest. And I'll kill the mage when I'm done with her." The sorcerer disappeared.

Regulus stared at his reflection, his mind blank. Someone knocked on his door. More by habit than by conscious decision, he crossed to the door and opened it. Dresden walked in, followed by Magnus.

Regulus moved back, his footsteps heavy. "He wants Adelaide."

"Carrick? Obviously."

"The sorcerer." Regulus sank onto his bed, exhausted. Magnus jumped up and laid his head on his lap. He couldn't even muster the energy to stroke Magnus' head.

"What? Why?"

"He needs her magic. He says he doesn't want to hurt her." Regulus stared at the cold fireplace. "Bringing her will repay my debt. And if I don't…" His gaze darted to Dresden as he shuddered. "You're all in danger."

"Then what's the problem? You know what you have to do, so let's make a plan."

"I can't!"

"Because of Carrick?"

"Because I love her!" Traitorous tears ran hot down Regulus' cheeks. He wiped them away and looked down at Magnus' large furry head in his lap. "What if the sorcerer takes her captive? What if he makes *her* his slave? Or—"

"What if you don't do it?" Dresden asked roughly. He stood across from Regulus with a forbidding expression, his arms crossed. "Best-case scenario, he sends someone else. Someone who might hurt her. Worst case—you kill us all, kill the Drummonds' guards to get her, and take her while not yourself and covered in the blood of her family and friends. You don't have a choice, Reg."

He opened and closed his mouth several times, trying to think of a response. He had considered having Dresden chain him in the cellar, where the sorcerer couldn't make him hurt anyone. But that was assuming the sorcerer couldn't use sorcery to lose his bonds. And didn't account for the sorcerer sending someone else. He had killed every mage in Monparth without Regulus, he could capture one inexperienced mage without him.

"There is the chance Adelaide can heal it," Dresden said.

"And if she can't?"

"Then nothing has changed." They looked at each other for a long moment.

"There is another option," Regulus said slowly. "It wouldn't kill me."

Drez paled. "No. He said he won't hurt or kill her, and then you'll be free. You're so *close*, and it might not even work."

The thought turned his stomach, but it was better than hurting Adelaide. "But it—"

"Damn it, Regulus!" Dresden punched the back of the armchair. "I'm not cutting your arm off! I'm not letting you do it, either! We discussed this! The mark came back when you cut it out; what if it just moves? You'll have accomplished *nothing* but losing your arm. She'll be okay. He'll keep his word, just like he has so far. You'll both be fine, you'll be free, and you'll be glad to have both arms."

Regulus opened his mouth, but Dresden pointed at him, his hand shaking.

"You promised me. You *promised*."

Regulus nodded. Relief and guilt warred within him. Relief at solid reasons for not cutting off his arm, or worse. Guilt that he wasn't strong enough to do whatever it took to protect Adelaide. Guilt that he had nearly broken his promise to Dresden to endure and not hurt himself again.

"All right. I'll start figuring out how to…" He hung his head. "How to kidnap her."

CHAPTER 39

ADELAIDE POSITIONED HERSELF CLOSE BY THE SIDE OF Minerva and Gaius' carriage, but it didn't take long for Nolan to move from behind the carriage and ride up next to her. He snatched the reins from her and pulled them over Zephyr's head and out of her reach.

"Hey—"

"We need to talk, love." He kicked his horse forward, leading Zephyr after him, much to Adelaide's displeasure. Once they were well ahead of the carriage, he let the horses slow.

"What?" She threw all her rage behind the word.

Nolan glanced over, the moonlight casting shadows over his disapproving frown. "Now, now, let's try to be civil—"

"Civil!" She grabbed for the reins, but he moved them out of her reach, causing Zephyr to drift closer to his horse. She leaned back and crossed her arms as Nolan tied her reins to the pommel of his saddle. "Civil would be giving me my reins back. And civil isn't blackmailing and threatening me into marrying you. Civil isn't bringing false accusations against an innocent man—"

Nolan's snort cut her off. "Innocent? He's a mercenary and a bastard who drove his father's wife out of her home. Even if he didn't plot treason, *innocent* is a stretch."

"She left because she wanted to. He's not a mercenary anymore, and you can't be guilty for your blood or the circumstances of your birth."

"Once a mercenary, always a mercenary." He shook his head. "But I don't want to talk about the mongrel. I want to talk about you. About us."

Adelaide ground her teeth. If she found a way around Nolan's threats, there would be no *us*. Instead, she latched onto her irritation at his constant and unfair commenting on Regulus' birth. "Oh, so you want to talk about the *other* mongrel?"

"What?" He twisted toward her. "Oh. The half-Khastallander thing? It doesn't bother me. You are your father's daughter, that's what matters."

"*Meim apaneh mahn keh bateh hohm*," she snapped, then translated for him. "I'm my mother's daughter. I'm Khastallander, too."

"Well, obviously." He gestured at her. "But you're still attractive, regardless."

Her face heated. "Regardless? Thank you, that's so flattering."

Nolan reined in his horse and they stopped. "I'm trying to compliment you." His warm, husky voice didn't match the way his brows pulled together in annoyance. He leaned toward her and placed his hand on her hip as he moved in for a kiss. *Not likely.* Adelaide kicked Zephyr's sides, and the horse bolted forward, as did Nolan's horse.

"Charming," Nolan said once he'd recovered from the unexpected movement. "You'll have to kiss me eventually, you know."

Heat spread to her scalp. "Insulting my appearance and heritage is a good way to make me want to avoid that."

"I didn't..." He sighed heavily. "Look, I'm sorry, all right? I didn't mean to offend you. That's the last thing I want. You're beautiful, end of story."

She glanced at him out of the corner of her eye. "Anything else you would like to apologize for while you're at it?"

"Mmm, no?"

"You *hurt* me," Adelaide hissed, trying not to let her voice carry back to the carriage. "You threatened my family. And you tried to get Regulus killed!"

"I was making a point." He spoke airily, as if none of this mattered. "You healed, as I knew you would. I don't want to hurt your family, and since you've agreed to marry me, that shouldn't be a problem. As for Hargreaves, I'm sorry you were there. I'm sorry if I frightened you. And frankly, I'm sorry I let him go."

Adelaide opened and closed her mouth, at a loss for words. She wove her fingers into Zephyr's mane to keep her anger—and her magic—at bay. She stared straight ahead, unwilling to so much as look at Nolan. "You didn't frighten me, you infuriated me. And, just to make it clear, the last thing I want is to kiss someone who threatened the life of the man I *actually* love."

In a blink, his hand circled her wrist and squeezed. She tried to pull away, but he dug his fingers into the underside of her wrist. "Listen closely." His voice was low and threatening. "You're betrothed to *me*. You are going to forget about Hargreaves, or I'm going to forget about sparing his life."

"You're hurting me."

"Good." He pushed her arm back toward her and released his painful grip. "Now you know how I feel when you talk about *him*. So we're even."

She massaged her wrist. *If Father finds out how he treats me, he'll cut Nolan's head clean off. If Nolan doesn't orchestrate an accident or something first.*

Nolan rubbed his forehead. "I'm sorry. That was uncalled for. I don't want to have to hurt you. I love you. Just...accept me. Don't fight me. And I'll be kind in return."

Right. Because love looked like veiled threats? *Love isn't meeting a sharp tongue with a hard fist. It's not earning kindness. That's control and fear, not love.* But she couldn't risk his threats shifting from her to Minerva and Gaius, so she kept silent.

"I don't lose," Nolan said, his voice low. "I'm a spare son. I'm used to fighting for what I want, even if it takes time. I had to work harder, be stronger, smarter, more charming, just…more, to get the same recognition as my brothers. If I'm not given respect, I take it. Fighting me won't end well."

Adelaide slumped in her saddle. Best to appear compliant until she figured something else out. She stayed quiet the rest of the ride back to the Drummond estate. When Nolan tried to discuss wedding dates, how long it would take her to make a dress, or where they would live, she responded with single-syllable words.

Nolan insisted on helping her dismount in the courtyard. He had returned her reins shortly before they arrived, so nothing looked amiss when Gaius and Minerva stepped out of their carriage. They watched as Nolan took her hand and guided her to the ground, but Minerva looked halfway between confused and concerned. Nolan took Adelaide's arm and led her to the door, giving her no opportunity to speak to her sister.

Lady Drummond opened the door just before they reached the entryway. "So, was Arrano—Sir Carrick!" Her eyebrows shot up, and she curtsied. "Why…it is a pleasure to see you. What brings you to our home?" Her gaze fell on Adelaide's arm hooked through Nolan's, and a smile cracked her face. Adelaide wanted to pull her arm free but didn't dare. She needed to play the part if she didn't want to raise Nolan's ire.

"Lady Drummond." Nolan simpered. "There was a bit of confusion and a case of mistaken identity. My men and I thought we overheard Lord Hargreaves plotting against the king and accompanied the sheriff to arrest him for treason."

Lady Drummond gasped. "Wouldn't surprise me in the least. I hope the scoundrel didn't give you trouble!" She looked past them at Gaius and Minerva, worry creasing her forehead. Adelaide winced at *scoundrel*. Lady Drummond would believe Nolan, after all her conspiring to get them together.

"Fortunately, we realized it was a mistake," Nolan said, "and Hargreaves was not the man we overheard." Adelaide clenched her jaw tighter. "Unfortunately, I didn't realize that until after Hargreaves tried to fight fifty men and did a great deal of yelling." Nolan patted Adelaide's arm in a sickening gesture of comfort. "The whole ordeal was understandably upsetting to the ladies, so instead of heading straight home, I accompanied my betrothed. To help put her at ease."

Lady Drummond clasped her hands together and giggled. Adelaide's stomach turned. "Betrothed? Oh, Adelaide, that's wonderful! Congratulations!" Lady Drummond covered her heart with her hand. "I'm so glad you realized what a catch Sir Carrick is before things went any further with that strange Hargreaves. I honestly don't know what you saw in him, with his past and the…" She traced her finger over her cheek where Regulus had his scar.

Adelaide's shoulders shook as she exhaled and tried to keep calm. Nolan seemed to be waiting for her to say something, and when she didn't, he cleared his throat.

"Yes, well. I made the offer at the tournament, but she wanted to think about it. When she saw the violent and foolhardy way Hargreaves reacted to being lawfully placed under arrest, she made her choice." He smiled. "Right, love?"

"Right." She forced a smile.

"Well, come in, come in!" Lady Drummond stepped out of the doorway and Nolan led Adelaide inside. "I hope you will stay the night, Sir Carrick. And join us for breakfast in the morning?"

Oh, no.

Nolan smiled. "Thank you, Lady Drummond, that would be perfect." His gentle squeeze on her arm told her he had been counting on that invitation.

Minerva entered after them, followed by Gaius. She regarded Nolan with narrowed eyes. "Ad, I don't recall you mentioning Sir Carrick proposing. Surely you would have told me."

Nolan's fingers dug into her arm. She swallowed and gave a noncommittal shrug. "I didn't want someone else's opinion to cloud my judgment. I needed time alone with my thoughts." She met Min's eyes and hoped she saw the apology written there—and the plea that she not continue this line of questioning.

"It is odd." Gaius' hand tapped his leg as he pushed the door closed. "With all due respect, before the tournament, Adelaide was clear she wasn't interested."

"And I changed her mind." Nolan slipped his arm out of hers, looped it around her waist and drew her against his side. She desperately wanted to push him away. "I helped her understand what a smart match we make." He ran his fingers down her cheek, making her skin crawl, and turned her face toward him. "We had our misunderstandings, but we're on the same page now, aren't we, love?"

"Yes," she whispered, stiff as a frozen tree. "Dear."

She realized what he was doing just before his lips met hers. Her hands curled into fists. It was a quick peck, a brief brush of his lips that didn't even give her enough time to pull away, but enough to make her feel used and her skin itch.

Lady Drummond tittered. "Oh, look at you blush!"

It doesn't mean what you think it does. "I'm quite tired after this...ordeal." Adelaide slipped out of Nolan's arm and headed for the stairs. "Goodnight."

"That was...brusque," Gaius said as she turned up the stairs.

"Ad, wait." Minerva hurried after her. Adelaide paused and turned back. Nolan looked at her with warning in his eyes. For one terrifying moment as Minerva passed Nolan, Adelaide's heart seemed to stop. *Don't you touch her.* But Minerva passed Nolan without a problem and was by her side as they headed up the stairs.

Minerva waited until they were close to Adelaide's room before she spoke. "What's going on? You love Regulus, don't deny it. And I saw your fists when he kissed you. What happened?"

Adelaide looked over her shoulder. They were alone in the hallway. Nolan wouldn't overhear. All the same, she didn't answer. Instead, she grabbed Min's hand and hurried into her room. Once inside, she locked the door, then sat on her bed. Minerva sat next to her.

"If I tell you, you have to promise not to tell another soul. Not Gaius, not Mother or Father. No one."

Minerva's frown deepened. "Adelaide, what—"

"Promise me."

"How can I promise that when I don't know what's going on?"

Adelaide's shoulders slumped. "Just promise, Min. Please. Or I won't tell you."

"Fine." Minerva didn't sound happy, or convincing. But Adelaide couldn't keep this in any longer.

"He didn't exactly ask me at the tournament. After I helped Regulus…" Adelaide buried her face in her hands. "Nolan figured it out. He threatened to reveal my secret if I didn't marry him and told me to think about that. And tonight…his plan was to kill Regulus to remove him as—as a rival." She drew in a ragged breath.

"He said he would drop the charges against Regulus if I agreed to marry him. If I don't marry him, he'll have Regulus killed." Adelaide lifted her eyes to Minerva's horrified expression. "You can't tell anyone! He'll hurt…everyone. If he duels Gaius, he'll win. He threatened to hurt you, to orchestrate a carriage accident. He threatened to have Gaius arrested, too."

Minerva's hands covered the lower half of her face.

"You can't tell anyone. Not until I figure out a way to make sure he can't make good on any of his threats."

Minerva stood, her arms wrapped over her pregnant stomach. "I...Adelaide. This is insane. How are you supposed to keep him from making good on his word? We can't wait until you're married to him!"

"Keep your voice down." She held her hands up and glanced toward the door. It would be crazy for Nolan to be on this floor. Lady Drummond wouldn't stand for the impropriety. But Nolan was a snake. "I couldn't let him take Regulus. He wouldn't have lasted the night. And I couldn't let him arrest Gaius."

Minerva chewed on her thumbnail. "We have to tell Father."

"And then what? Gaius gets attacked like Regulus' squire, Harold? Something happens to you? I couldn't live with myself, Min."

"And I can't live with you married to someone capable of doing any of that!" Minerva sat back down and placed a hand on her arm. "Gaius is already suspicious that Nolan threatened you or something. He..." She hesitated. "Hasn't hurt you?"

Adelaide shrugged. "Not really." *Nothing permanent. For me.* She patted Minerva's shoulder. "Get some sleep. And tell Gaius everything is fine. Tell him I want this." She tried to smile, but her lip quivered. "Act like everything is fine at breakfast."

"I don't like it." Minerva embraced her tightly and the tears Adelaide didn't realize she'd been holding back threatened to spill. "I'll play along for now. But I'm not letting you marry a man you hate."

"He's handsome, at least." Her attempt to lighten the mood didn't help the sickened feeling in her gut. "I mean; it could be worse." A tremor ran through her body and Minerva hugged her tighter. "I'll be all right."

Nolan and his knights joined them for breakfast. Adelaide suffered through Nolan talking about how enamored he was with her and Lord and Lady Drummond's warm congratulations. Minerva watched with fire in her eyes as Nolan's hand traced up and down Adelaide's rigid back and tangled in her hair. Adelaide spoke little. Gaius didn't make eye contact with her or Nolan.

After breakfast, Adelaide headed to the stables. She needed some time alone to clear her head. She didn't even ask for help, but prepared Zephyr herself. The stable gate creaked.

"Don't you have servants for that?" Nolan strolled in, looking as debonair as ever.

She stiffened. "What do you want?"

"Just checking on my lovely bride-to-be." He flashed a toothy smile that made him look beastly. "Making sure you're not having any...foolish ideas. I'd hate for anyone to get hurt."

She pulled the bridle over Zephyr's head. "Murderer."

"My dear, I would never."

"Right, you'd have someone else do it for you." Anger made her hands shake as she struggled to buckle the bridle in place.

"Maybe I'll hire one of Hargreaves' so-called knights." He leaned back against the stall on the other side of Zephyr. "They kill for money, don't they? I wonder if they'd off their master for the right price."

Adelaide stilled. "We agreed. I'll only do this if he's not harmed."

"Mm, fine. But honestly, I'd be doing the world a favor."

"You're a fiend." Her face burned as she double-checked the cinching on the saddle.

"No, I'm your betrothed." He leaned across Zephyr's saddle, his face inches from hers as she straightened. "So how about a kiss?"

"Get your face out of mine or I'll cut it."

Nolan slapped her, and she blinked, stumbling back from Zephyr's side. She covered her stinging cheek with her hand. He moved around Zephyr, gaze fixed on her. "You're awfully rude for someone who has lives depending on her good behavior. Including your own. I know your secret, remember?"

"And I told you I don't care who knows, remember?" Her cheek still stung, but she set her jaw and lowered her hand. She wouldn't give him the satisfaction of seeing her pain. "I'll marry you to keep you from having Regulus or anyone else killed. But I won't fawn over you."

"What I'm hearing is you're only agreeing to marry me so long as you can't think of another way to keep me from having the mercenary's head chopped off."

Danger echoed in Nolan's words, so Adelaide didn't answer. But the look on her face must have confirmed his suspicion, because his lips curled into a scowl. He stalked toward her and she backed into the wall, her palms flush against the rough wood. He darted forward and grabbed her face. His body pressed into hers, and the frantic beat of her heart reverberated into his chest.

Nolan leaned forward, his mouth by her ear. Adelaide shook as his fingernails dug into her cheek. "I don't know what you see in that scarred mongrel that you don't see in me. But you're pushing your luck, *sweetheart.*" He released her face and leaned back. His gaze fixed on her lips. "Why fight me? I've been told I'm an excellent kisser."

Fury and revulsion drove back her fear. She put her hands on his chest. A blast of blue light pulsed from her palms and sent him flying backward. Zephyr whinnied as Nolan shot behind the horse, hit the opposite wall of the stable, and fell to the ground. He sat in the straw and dirt and glared up at her. She could kill him now. Throw a magical spear through his heart. And probably hang for his murder.

"I'm going for a ride, *sweetheart.*" She drew herself up to her full height and raised her chin. "I'll be back when I'm back. Please, follow me. If you do, I'll put a knife through your throat and claim you surprised me, and I thought you were a bandit. I'll shed many tears."

Nolan bared his teeth in a silent snarl. "You'll be back in an hour or I'll take Gaius and my men and come looking for you. You won't kill me in front of witnesses."

"Fine." Adelaide led Zephyr out of the stables. She didn't know where she was going. She didn't care. But as the events of last night ran over and over again through her mind, she found herself on the road leading to Arrano. Let Nolan go looking for her. She urged Zephyr into a trot. She had some explaining to do.

CHAPTER 40

REGULUS SAT IN THE HALL LONG AFTER A SERVANT CLEARED away his breakfast. The silence in the room pressed around him. Sunlight from the windows set high in the hall walls streamed across the table. He scratched Magnus' head and stared at nothing. He had tossed and turned most of the night, trying to think of a way to protect both Adelaide and his men. Every idea had holes. Dresden was right. Obeying was the best option.

The question was how to get her. The simplest way would be to take her unseen, but he didn't have time to stalk the Drummonds' estate until she wandered away on her own. He could go as the Black Knight and demand her. There would be a fight, people would get hurt. Or he could hope Carrick wasn't around, ask her to walk with him—

The door to the foyer groaned open and his steward walked in. "My lord." He bowed. "Lady Belanger is here to see you."

"What?" Regulus stood, knocking his knees on the table. "Just Lady Belanger?"

Adelaide walked in, wearing a long-sleeved gray riding dress with an asymmetrical skirt that ended above her knees in the front, revealing black fitted trousers and boots.

"Just me." She smiled, but it was weak and forced. The steward left, closing the door behind him. Magnus bounded over to Adelaide, and she rubbed his head.

"Adelaide." Regulus rushed to her, reached for her—but stopped shy of grabbing her shoulders. The momentary joy of seeing her fled behind his confusion over last night and his heartache at what he had to do. His hands fell to his sides. "Why are you here?"

"I…" She looked defeated. "I wanted to explain. No, I *need* to explain. I don't want you to think…"

"I knew it." He tensed as his pulse pounded. "Carrick threatened you."

"He threatened you. And your knights. And Gaius and Minerva." Adelaide placed her hand on his chest. "I couldn't let you or anyone else die. The whole arrest—he was trying to get you killed! He told the sheriff he was mistaken after—"

"After you promised to marry him," he finished. He'd suspected as much. It didn't make him any less angry.

"He's a coward without honor." Her hand balled into a fist against his chest. "You can't challenge him. He'll have you killed or arrested before he would fight you. You can't tell anyone. I'm only telling you because you deserve to know. I can't stand by while he hurts or kills people I love." She looked into his eyes, and he saw her anguish. "Please. I can't let him—"

"Shhh." Regulus grabbed her shoulders and pulled her to his chest. As he held her, a thousand emotions battled within him. Relief that Adelaide didn't want to marry Carrick. Anger that Carrick was forcing her into a marriage she didn't want. Fury that she didn't want him to fight for her, even if he understood the reasoning. Resentment that she was right. Carrick would never duel him. Happiness that she cared enough that she didn't want him to die. Sympathy, because he understood doing things you hated to protect the people you loved.

But mostly panic and sorrow. Because she was here. Alone. Already the mark burned as he ignored his opportunity.

"Adelaide…" He stepped away, his guilt drowning him. "I need to tell you something. We should sit." Regulus returned to his seat and Magnus loped after him. After a moment, Adelaide sat in the seat to his left. He hesitated. He had never told anyone this story. Before Adelaide, anyone who mattered already knew. They had been there.

"Regulus?"

"This isn't how I wanted to tell you. This isn't the circumstances I wanted. But you deserve the truth." He looked at her, shame heavy on his soul. "You've been honest with me, and I've lied in return. Pretended I'm not what I am."

"I don't understand." He winced at the undertone of alarm in her voice.

He traced a knot in the tabletop with his finger. "A little over two years ago, I was leading a small company of fifteen mercenaries. We were near the Tumen Forest for a contract dealing with a couple territorial gryphons. We came across this boy." He took a breath to steady himself, the memory still fresh. "He begged us for help. Said his village was being attacked by goblins. He was destitute. Not even shoes on his feet. There would be no money in helping. But I couldn't turn my back on him. So we followed."

She watched him, clearly trying to understand why he was telling her this now.

"He didn't lead us to a village; it was just a forester's hut. He ran in, and I followed. His parents were bound and gagged inside. The boy went to help them, and I turned around as this…flash of green light nearly blinded me."

"Green light…" Adelaide looked down at her hands and her eyes widened. "A sorcerer?"

"Yes." He swallowed. "I couldn't tell at first. There was a man in dark robes throwing fire and sharp projectiles that glowed green. My men were falling. Dying. I rushed him with my sword, but…" He looked at his palm, remembering. "The hilt burned in my hand and I dropped it. The sorcerer held enchanted ropes, binding my men who were still standing. They couldn't fight or get free. The ropes curled around their throats. I went for the man with my bare hands."

His hand trembled. Adelaide covered it with hers. Steadied him. He took a deep breath and continued.

"A blast of light knocked me back. I looked up to see my men choking to death. Dresden. Perceval." Regulus dug his fingernails into the wood. "Estevan. Jerrick. Caleb. Even Harold, a baggage boy who barely knew how to hold a sword. So many were already dead—" His voice broke, and it took him a moment to continue. "The sorcerer gave me a choice. Watch the rest of my men die and the forester and his wife and son burn alive—or swear to serve him."

Her mouth hung open, but she didn't speak.

"I didn't think, I just agreed." His breath escaped in a shaky exhale. "He made me take an oath. I would serve him until I had repaid the life-debt for every person he didn't kill that day. I've done his will ever since. He has me retrieve things. Magical plants. Ancient relics. I've stolen for him... Killed for him."

Her hand slipped off his. Silence pressed against him. His chest burned. He couldn't bring himself to look at her, to see the horror and disgust. He hid his face in his hands. *I knew she wouldn't want me if she knew the truth.*

To his surprise, her fingers clasped his hands. She pulled them away from his face.

"You did what you had to in order to save the people you love." He met her eyes and saw kindness, understanding, and sorrow. "That sounds familiar."

If it wasn't for what he had to say next, her understanding and acceptance would have soothed him. Comforted him. Healed him. Instead, it destroyed him.

"There's more." Regulus freed his hands from Adelaide's grasp. "The sorcerer wants something different this time." He closed his eyes. "A mage." He wouldn't take the coward's path. He looked at Adelaide. Her kind, beautiful deep brown eyes narrowed. "He wants you."

CHAPTER 41

"WHAT?" IT SOUNDED MORE LIKE A GASP THAN AN ACTUAL word. Adelaide's pulse quickened, and she pulled her hands back as the betrayal seared straight through her. Her magic awakened in response, warming her palms. "You told a sorcerer about me? I trusted—"

"No!" Regulus held up his hands, his face pale as he shook his head. "I swear I didn't tell him, not a word. He did something to find mages, and he found you. He needs a mage to open some kind of door."

At least he had kept his promise to guard her secret. And it didn't even matter. But now...would he hand her over to this sorcerer? "You're not...you won't...you can't want to—"

"I don't want to," Regulus said, agony in his words. "But I have to."

"You can refuse!" Fear and anger gave an edge to her voice. She tried to rein it in, but her hysteria rose. "You don't have to—"

"No." She jumped at Dresden's voice and looked toward the dark stairway in the corner. Dresden emerged from the shadows and strode over, his eyes furious. "You didn't tell her everything. Show her."

Regulus' gaze dropped.

"Show her!" Dresden grabbed Regulus' right arm and pushed up his sleeve. "Tell her the full truth!"

Rough scars marred the underside of Regulus' forearm. Against the scars, a black mark stood in sharp contrast—two hollow diamonds laid end-to-end with another half diamond open towards his wrist.

She eyed the tattoo, confused. "What is it?"

"It appeared when I took the oath," Regulus said quietly as Dresden dropped his arm. "It's a link, from the sorcerer to me. So he can control me."

Her mind struggled to keep up. "How?"

"Like this." Dresden reached across the table and grabbed her hand. He yanked it over to Regulus' arm and forced her palm against the mark. She yelped as heat burned her skin. She tried to pull away, but Dresden held her hand in place a moment longer before releasing her. Her hand still burned.

"He tortures Regulus," Dresden said, venom in his voice. "Because he's not obeying. He knows what his orders are, and he's not fulfilling them. Somehow, the sorcerer knows, and uses the mark to punish him into compliance."

"You're in pain?" Guilt and pity replaced the betrayal, even as fear put a vise around her chest.

"It's not bad right now." Regulus pulled his sleeve down, hiding the mark.

"The sorcerer can manipulate it, make the pain spread." Dresden sat in the chair to Regulus' right. "Cause him to writhe on the floor, screaming in pain. But maybe there's something you can do."

"You think I…" Adelaide gulped.

"Maybe you can remove it," Regulus whispered, but his voice rose with intensity. "Corrupted magic put it there, maybe pure magic can remove it."

"I…" She hesitated, full of self-doubt. Could trying make things any worse? And if she succeeded, Regulus wouldn't be in pain. And he wouldn't have to bring her to this sorcerer. Yesterday, she would have said he would never betray her. But today, faced with sorcery she didn't understand and knowing he would be tortured if he didn't... She couldn't rely on his strength of will to resist a force like that. "I can try."

Regulus rolled his sleeve back and held his arm forward. Nervous, she reached out, summoning her power. Her palm warmed and glowed with soft blue light as she stretched her hand out over the mark. The light grew in intensity, bathing his skin. Some of the scars around and under the mark faded, but the mark seemed just as dark and defined. She summoned more power, trying to will the mark off his arm.

Regulus screamed. Adelaide yanked her hand back, terror stealing her breath. He pulled away from her, clutching his arm to his chest and knocking over his chair with a clatter as his screams pierced her ears. Magnus jumped to his feet with a growl. The dog barked at her then whined at Regulus. Regulus continued to scream and fell to his knees, his eyes rolling up into his head. Her light died as she clenched her fist, her heart pounding. *What did I do? What do I do?*

She pushed away her chair as she stood, trembling. "Regulus!" She reached toward him and Magnus snarled. Dresden grabbed the huge dog.

Magnus snapped at him, but Dresden said in a firm voice, "Magnus, upstairs. Obey!" The dog tucked its tail and whined. "Magnus, go upstairs," Dresden commanded over Regulus' howls. The dog headed up the stairs, and Dresden closed the stairwell door behind him. He went to Regulus and grabbed his shoulders. "Regulus!"

Regulus stopped screaming, and Adelaide leaned against the table, relieved. His arm fell to his side. He looked at her, his expression unreadable. Dresden released Regulus' shoulders and took a step back, caution radiating from him. "Reg?"

"Oh, dear me." Regulus shook his head and stood. "Tried to remove our bond again, did you, Hargreaves?" He clicked his tongue. "Naughty boy. And you." He looked Adelaide dead in the eyes, his gaze filled with loathing that hurt far worse than when she thought he'd shared her secret. "Stupid little she-mage. That. *Hurt.* I don't appreciate it. You're giving me second thoughts about the whole not-harming-you thing."

She recoiled, bumping into a chair. Did Regulus just…talk to himself? Stupid she-mage? Nothing he said made sense. "Regulus?"

"No." Dresden placed himself between her and Regulus. "It's the sorcerer." His voice wavered, and the hand he held out to shield her shook.

"He can do that?" Her tongue stuck, threatening to choke her.

"That's Prince of Shadow and Ash to you." Regulus glanced at Dresden with distaste. "Yes, I can do that. Not for long. But long enough to make him kill one or both of you. The bearded one and that squire barely escaped last time." He smiled, cruelty in his usually kind eyes.

"Run!" Dresden looked over his shoulder. "Just avoid him long enough—"

Regulus bolted forward with unbelievable speed and grabbed Dresden by the neck. Dresden clawed at his hands as Regulus lifted him into the air. Like he was tossing aside a dirty shirt, Regulus threw Dresden. Dresden flew several feet and landed with a horrible thud and a sickening crack as his head hit stone. Adelaide's heart lodged in her throat. Dresden moaned, and she gasped. *He's alive.* But now Regulus' icy gaze fixed on her.

She drew her dagger from her boot as she stumbled away, tripping over a chair. *This can't be happening. This* can't *be happening.* That wasn't Regulus. But it was. Did she dare use her dagger against him?

"I need your pure magic, girl." Regulus advanced toward her. "There's at least a couple others, but they'd hardly be useful. Drunks and children. So, you see, Hargreaves has a choice."

It was surreal to see Regulus with cruelty in his eyes. To hear him talk about himself as someone else. Her heel caught on an uneven bit of stone, and she fell backward.

"He can bring you to me, you help me, everybody lives and is happy. Or he can kill you." Regulus lunged.

She half-heartedly stabbed toward his right shoulder, but he grabbed the blade with his left hand. Blood seeped between his fingers.

"You can't kill him to save yourself," Regulus' voice said. "His life is tied to mine. So long as I live, he lives." Regulus' right hand closed around her neck.

His large hand encircled her throat and squeezed, his skin hot against her throat. She released the dagger and pulled at his fingers, coughing and choking. He pulled her to her knees. Her throat and lungs burned from the effort to breathe. Her thoughts turned fuzzy. He dropped her dagger, and it clattered to the ground.

"Please," she croaked, "stop..."

The edges of her sight turned black. Bright spots swam in her vision as Regulus' sneering face went in and out of focus. She scratched at his hand but felt herself weakening. *Etiros, he's going to kill me! I'm. Going. To. Die.*

He released her and stepped back. She fell on her hands and knees, gasping for air and coughing. Her throat felt raw, like she had been screaming. Her neck ached and throbbed. She looked up in fear as she struggled to catch her breath. But Regulus had withdrawn a couple feet and collapsed to his knees on the ground. He rested his arms on his legs, palms up, his left hand dripping blood, and stared at the floor.

Dresden, one hand clutching his head, staggered over. He hesitantly put a hand on Regulus' shoulder. Regulus flinched, but otherwise didn't move.

Adelaide healed her neck and dropped her hands to the cool stone. As her breathing evened out, she eyed Regulus, trying to determine if he had regained control. His cheeks glistened in the sunlight, and she realized he was crying.

She moved closer, swallowing back her fear. That wasn't him. Regulus wouldn't hurt her. Not as himself. Slowly, she reached for him. "Regulus…"

He drew back from her touch. "Don't," he whispered. "Don't come close."

She looked at her hand and pulled it back. "Oh. Right. I'm sorry. I didn't mean to—"

"What?" Regulus looked up, his brow furrowed above watery eyes. "Why are you apologizing?"

She swallowed, her mouth still dry. "For hurting you."

Bewilderment showed in his expression. "You…think I blame you?" He laughed, but it was a bitter, angry sound. "You tried to help. Then I…" He choked and looked away. "I hurt *you*. I'm sorry. I feared something like this would happen." He hung his head, his chin resting on his chest. "I should have stayed far away from you. I should have ended this before it began."

She wrapped her arms around her torso as his words slashed into her heart. Her gaze dropped to the stone floor. "You wish we didn't know each other?"

"Maybe the sorcerer would have picked someone else if you hadn't been with me when he searched for a mage. Now you're part of my mess. Now you're in danger." His voice seemed small in the vast hall.

She moved closer to him. Blood pooled on his left hand. If she attempted to heal it, would her magic clash with the sorcery within him again? It hadn't last time she healed him. But the fury in his eyes as he had strangled her made her hesitate. *Coward.*

"I've tried everything to break the bond." Regulus clenched his fists. The muscles in his neck bulged with tension. Understanding of the scars on his arm dragged her heart down to her gut. "I can't even die." The whispered words hung in the air between them.

Dresden paced back and forth behind Regulus' bent form, his hands clasped behind his back. "You have to help him. The sorcerer said if Regulus brings you to him, his debt will be repaid. He will be free."

Regulus shook his head. "He could be lying."

"Here." Adelaide took his left hand, pulled back the fingers. "Let me…" Blood still covered his hand, but she didn't see a cut. "You…healed."

"Hm?" He looked down. "Oh. Yes."

"I thought sorcery couldn't heal."

"Not the way pure magic does," Regulus said. "This is evil. Corrupted. It hurts as it heals…and sometimes after. It leaves scars. And it doesn't heal minor injuries. Just ones that affect my ability to be a useful slave. I could have bled out. My bond to the sorcerer won't allow that. So it healed." His tone was flat, emotionless.

"Reg." Dresden sat at the table. "You can't avoid this."

"I know," Regulus murmured. He looked at Adelaide, sorrow and apology in his eyes. "I can't let him… *I* can't kill you. Or Dresden. Or Harold. Innocent people, people I care about, will die at my hand." His gaze fell to her throat, his face twisting with horror. "I can't control myself when he takes over, but I can see and feel everything. It's as if I'm a puppet that has gained consciousness and sensation, but I can only do what the puppet master wishes. I could—" His voice cracked, and he looked away again.

She shuddered, remembering his hand crushing her throat. *He was suffering as much as I was.* She pressed his blood-stained hand between hers, but he pulled away. She wiped his blood off on her dress. "Regulus—"

"I could feel your skin." His jaw pulsed as he clenched and unclenched his teeth. "I felt your throat as you tried to breathe, your hands trying to pull mine away. I saw the fear and panic in your eyes. And I couldn't stop it. I tried. Etiros, I tried. I only stopped when he let me go. When he had gotten his point across."

She gazed at the broken man before her, at the hopelessness on his face. The man who had sacrificed his freedom to save the lives of his friends. The man who fought against the desires of this sorcerer, despite the pain he brought on himself. The man who won tournaments but recoiled from her touch in fear of himself. He didn't deserve this. No one deserved this.

Adelaide pulled Regulus' sleeve up past the mark. She thought the diamonds looked like chains as she placed her hand on it and winced. He was in pain. Because of her. Was facing a sorcerer any worse than facing Nolan? She slid her hand down and entwined her fingers in his. His gaze drifted up to her eyes, surprised.

"I see you. Your heart. Your strength. Your courage." She cradled his face in her other hand. "And I love you."

Regulus' mouth trembled as his eyes searched hers, hope and fear, joy and dread warring in their silvery depths. "You…"

"I love you, Regulus." She blinked to hold back the tears that threatened to fall as Regulus' eyes watered.

He crumpled toward her and drew her into his arms, his forehead pressing against her shoulder. "I love you." His arms tightened around her. "I tried not to, for your safety, but… I love you, Adelaide. Completely and utterly. I can't begin to express how much I love you." His shoulders shook. "I wish… I'm so sorry."

"It's not your fault." She stroked his back, her throat thick with emotion. "We should go, before he hurts you again, or worse."

Regulus pulled away, relief mixed with defeat in his expression. "You'll come willingly?"

"Yes." She had wanted to sound braver than that. If Regulus could be brave when a sorcerer could take control of his body at any moment and force him to hurt his friends, she could be brave, too. "I'll do what the sorcerer wants." Surety returned to her voice as she spoke. "We will free you. If he refuses to honor his word, we will find another way. There must be a way. And then figure out how to stop Nolan. Together."

A smile pulled at Regulus' mouth as his gaze filled with devotion and warmth. But then his expression fell. "There's something else."

What else can there be?

"The sorcerer..." His throat bobbed. "He's The Shadow. He promised not to kill you. But you should know."

The Shadow. Her lips parted. The threat she had hid from her entire life, the reason she was alone and didn't understand her magic. The Shadow that hated mages enough to murder children. Her breathing went shallow. What if he didn't keep his word?

But Regulus was in pain. He was enslaved to the evil she feared. And they didn't have another choice. She could go willingly...or she could watch the love leave his eyes as the sorcerer took over again.

"Thank you for telling me." Her voice barely made it past her lips. She cleared her throat. "But it doesn't change anything. It only makes me want you free more."

Regulus released a breath. "I don't deserve you." He reached for her face with his free hand, then grimaced at his bloody palm and drew it back.

"I hate to say it," Dresden said, "but you two need to go."

Regulus nodded glumly. "Can you wait here? I need to change."

She nodded, and Regulus trudged upstairs. She felt drained. Too many complicated emotions. Dresden still sat at the table, watching her. She stood, and he did the same, steely gaze never leaving her.

"I'm not going to run, if that's what you're thinking."

Dresden's fingers drifted to his own bruising throat. "I wouldn't blame you if you did." He clasped his hands behind his back. "I like you. Truly. But I would do anything for Regulus. Including things he might not appreciate—like knocking you unconscious if you try to run."

"I understand." She stepped forward. "Here. I can heal those bruises."

Dresden blinked. "I…okay. Thank you."

She healed his bruises, mulling over the sorcerer's words through Regulus. *The bearded one and that squire barely escaped last time.* "He attacked you. Before today."

"Yes." Dresden rubbed his healed neck, his eyes sad. "Me and Harold. Terrified Harold. But it broke Regulus. It's…taken him a long time to heal."

Adelaide looked at the shadowy stairwell, her heart aching.

"I think you're good for him," Dresden said quietly, drawing her attention back. "He felt he had to distance himself from us. He's a wolf who tried to protect his own pack by leaving it, but Regulus is at his best with others, when he feels like he has a place to belong. And you bring out the best in him."

She blushed and lowered her gaze. "He's a good man. A better and braver man than most."

"A good man?" Dresden's mouth curved into a half smile. "He's the best man I've ever known."

CHAPTER 42

REGULUS WAS SILENT AS HAROLD HELPED HIM INTO THE BLACK Knight armor. Magnus sat next to him, incessantly licking his hand. Harold moved around the big shaggy dog, cinching and straightening the layered pieces of armor. He respected Regulus' unspoken need for silence. He didn't ask about the blood Regulus washed off his hand in the water basin. Didn't question the scratches on the back of Regulus' hands as he buckled each oversized piece into place. Regulus gazed out the window, staring at nothing. Hoping against hope this was the last time he would don this armor.

He didn't want to wear it. But he didn't know where this door Adelaide was supposed to unlock was—or what might be on the other side. More importantly, he wanted to keep the sorcerer as happy as possible. Besides, if anyone spotted them, they would see Adelaide captured by the legendary Black Knight, not running away with Regulus Hargreaves.

Regulus sheathed the sword and took the helm from Harold, his heart heavy. Why couldn't he be stronger? Why was he too weak to fight the sorcerer's will? He wished he had found another way to save his men two years ago. And why couldn't he have saved them *all?* But such thoughts changed nothing. He laid a black-gloved hand on Harold's shoulder, the metal plating on the brace and gloves clinking. "Thank you, Harold."

"Of course, my lord." Concern wrinkled Harold's forehead.

"Can you pack some food and bring it out to the stables? Enough for…for two."

"Yes, my lord."

Regulus bit the inside of his lip. "If things go right, when I return, I'll be free. But if they don't—I might not come back." He held Harold's gaze and squeezed his shoulder. "You and Drez look out for each other, okay?"

Harold nodded slowly, his eyes wide, then shook his head, fast and hard. "No." He threw his arms around Regulus' armored chest. "We all need you to come back."

Regulus returned the embrace, his breath catching. "I'll try."

"Good." Harold pulled away and took a deep breath. "Be safe, my lord."

Regulus smiled weakly and headed downstairs. The heavy fall of his boots and metallic rubbing of his armor reverberated in the winding staircase. He emerged into the hall and felt surprised yet relieved to see Adelaide and Dresden sitting peaceably.

"You didn't leave," he said before he could stop himself.

Adelaide looked up, lips pursed. As she took in his appearance, he noted the slight widening of her eyes, the inaudible gasp. "You're…" Her jaw hung open. "The Black Knight. *You're* the Black Knight?"

"Oh." His face heated. "Yes."

"Several things just made a lot of sense." She shook her head, her expression softening. "As for not running away, you don't have sole ownership over the role of self-sacrificial hero." Her tone was confident and teasing but kind.

"I love you." The words tumbled out as a mix of emotions from adoration to guilt twisted his gut.

Adelaide smiled and walked to him, her hips swaying. She took the helm from his hands and examined it, then glanced at Dresden.

"You're blessed not to have borne this alone." Regulus felt a stab of guilt over how often he had shunned Dresden's help.

"Please." Drez scoffed. "We do what we can, but the fool always goes it alone."

"Not this time." Adelaide handed the helm back, then brushed her fingertips over the scar on his face. "We do this together." He still felt the lingering touch after she dropped her hand. "Shall we?"

Regulus nodded. "Together."

He led her through the hedged lane to the stables. Adelaide went to mount her horse, but he stopped her. "This way." She shrugged and followed him to the trap door. As he stepped down onto the dirt steps, Harold ran into the stables.

"You have to hurry!" Harold panted. "Nolan Carrick is here with Sir Gaius, Lord Drummond, and several knights. The gate was open for deliveries, and they just rode in, didn't even slow for the guard. Carrick says Lady Belanger is missing and he's accusing you of kidnapping her. Dresden said you're not at home, but Carrick wants to search the castle, and I don't think Drez can stop him. You need to go *now*. I'll put a barrel over the trap door. Go!"

Anger surged, but Regulus couldn't do anything about Carrick. He led Sieger down into the tunnel, not bothering with stopping to light the torch. Adelaide followed close behind, but her horse whinnied and pulled back.

"Easy, boy." She stroked his face. "Come on." The horse backed away from the tunnel, yanking on the reins.

"You have to go!" Harold's voice sounded muffled from above the tunnel.

"Let's try this." Adelaide placed her hand on the horse's forehead. A faint blue shone between her skin and the horse's forelock. The gelding calmed, and she led it down into the tunnel. Harold closed the trap door and the tunnel became pitch black. A scraping sound indicated Harold moving a barrel over the door.

"There's a torch in a nook over the steps if you can get to it," Regulus said.

"No need." A soft blue glow illuminated her face and grew to a pale blue shining orb hovering over her palm. As Adelaide lifted her hand, the orb drifted just below the top of the tunnel, above Sieger's rump.

"Right." He smiled sheepishly.

The blue-white light illuminated the tunnel. They walked in silence, the orb floating with them. At the end of the tunnel, Regulus moved aside the door and boulder and put on his helm before emerging into the space beneath the tree. No one around. Good. He went back down for Sieger, and Adelaide followed, her orb of light vanishing without a sound.

Regulus replaced the door and boulder over the tunnel entrance and turned to find Adelaide watching him, her forehead wrinkled and head tilted.

"I was right." She looked at the boulder and back at him. "You were holding back at the tournament."

He blinked. "Yes. The mark enhances my strength. You...could tell?"

"I'm used to holding back power."

"Oh." He went to Sieger's saddlebags and paused, biting his cheek. "I don't want you to take this the wrong way. And you can say no. But I think it might be a good idea if..." *There's no good way of saying this.* "If we tied your reins to my pommel and bound your hands."

"Why?" Adelaide stepped back, uncertainty flashing over her features.

"I'm not doubting you!" he said quickly. "But there's a chance someone could see us. I try not to be seen, but it happens. You know, you've heard the stories. It might be better for your rep-

utation and safety if someone sees us if they think you're a captive."
He held up a hand as she frowned. "Just a thought. You don't—"

Adelaide sighed. "You have rope?"

He pointed at his saddlebag with his thumb. "Yes."

"All right." She mounted Zephyr. "Do it."

He tied the ropes as loose as possible without them falling off.
She could get free easily, but at a glance, the binding was convincing.
He pulled the reins over Zephyr's head and tied them to his own
saddle before mounting.

Regulus kept off the roads as much as possible and listened and
watched for signs of people so he could avoid them. They narrowly
evaded a hunting party. A few minutes later, a solitary man in bright
clothes, riding a gray horse and brandishing a bow, broke through
the brush.

"Gerard, I swear if you leave—" He stopped short as he
realized they were *not* his hunting party. His wide eyes looked to
Adelaide. "My lady…" He knocked an arrow and trained the bow
on Regulus, but his hands quivered, making the arrow bounce
against the side of the bow. "Release the lady, foul villain!"

"Stand down." Regulus lowered his voice, letting it rumble in
his helm. The man released the arrow. Frightened as the hunter was,
it would have flown right past Regulus. He reached out and caught
it anyway. Both the man and Adelaide gasped.

"Run!" Adelaide screamed. Regulus looked back at her, startled
by her high-pitched outburst. "Flee!" She gave him the slightest
nod. Oh, she was clever. "Find the Drummonds and Nolan Carrick!
Find Regulus Hargreaves of Arrano!"

He pulled the reins to her horse, drawing Zephyr closer.
"Silence!"

"Tell Lord Hargreaves the Black Knight has taken Adelaide!"
The hysteria in her voice made the man turn pale. He backed his
horse up, jaw trembling.

"I said *silence!*" Regulus covered her mouth with his hand but didn't touch her.

She pulled his hand down. "Tell Nolan Carrick!"

Regulus yanked his hand free and covered her mouth for real this time. "You will be silent!" He cringed under the helm. The man turned his horse and fled. Regulus dropped his hand. "I'm sorry. Are you all right?"

She nodded. "If he does as I asked, you should be in the clear. Hopefully."

"You nearly had me convinced." He looked around and prodded Sieger forward. "We better get out of here. The rest of the hunting party might have heard you."

Other than a couple peasants out gathering firewood, who saw them, dropped their bundles of wood, and ran, they didn't see anyone else. Regulus wondered what Carrick had made of his absence from Arrano; if Dresden had convinced Carrick that he and Adelaide hadn't seen each other since the previous night when Carrick took her away. Would that coward of a hunter go to Arrano or the Drummond estate? What would Carrick make of the news Adelaide had been captured? And what about Gaius? Minerva?

He looked over at Adelaide through his helm. "What about Minerva?"

"What about—" She paled. "She doesn't know I'm safe." She said a string of what he was pretty sure were Khast curse words. Her shoulders slumped, and his heart ached. "What have I done? If that hunter goes to the Drummonds, she'll think..." She straightened. "She will think it's peculiar I told him to find you and Nolan." A hopeful look came over her face. "She's smart. She'll realize I wouldn't ask him for help. Hopefully."

"Maybe." He tried to sound optimistic, but his voice sounded harsh in the helm.

Night had fallen when they arrived at the tower. Adelaide gawked at the dead trees as they rode in the moonlight and shadow. His heart grew heavier as each hoof beat brought them closer to the sorcerer. The most dangerous man he had ever met. And he was leading the woman he loved right to him. They stopped in front of the tower and he dismounted. He stuffed his helm in his saddlebag then crossed to Zephyr's side. Adelaide looked at the bone-white trees as he removed the rope from her hands.

"What happened to them?"

"I don't know. It's like his sorcery infects them, and they just die."

He helped her down. The door to the tower creaked open as her feet hit the ground. They both looked toward the door as the sorcerer emerged, cloaked in black and red and gold, his face half-hidden under his hood as usual.

The sorcerer smiled and stroked his beard. "I knew you'd find a way, boy."

"I brought her, as you commanded." Regulus ground his teeth. "You said you would release me."

The sorcerer laughed, dark and menacing. "I said I would release you *after* she helped me." He walked toward them, and Regulus covered Adelaide with his own body. "Oh, move out of the way." The sorcerer flicked his hand, a hint of green light shooting from his fingers and forming a blast that knocked Regulus aside.

"Don't hurt—" Regulus gasped and fell to one knee as pain erupted on his arm.

"Stop!" Adelaide moved toward him, but the sorcerer raised a shimmering transparent wall that gleamed faintly with green light between them, from the base of the tower far into the trees. She looked back at the sorcerer and squared her shoulders, her chin lifted. Regulus smiled despite the pain. The sorcerer looked her up and down.

"Hm." The sorcerer turned and walked back toward the tower, leaving the wall separating Regulus and Adelaide standing. "Let's see what, if anything, you can do." He whirled around and thrust out his hand, sending several large, pointed shards that glowed green toward Adelaide.

"No!" Regulus leapt to his feet, but a shock of pain sent him back down.

Adelaide gasped and held out her hands. A shield of cobalt-tinged light flashed into existence in front of her, just before the shards slammed into it with a crackling sound. The shards disintegrated, but Adelaide staggered back, and the shield blinked out of existence. At least she knew how to defend herself. But why was the sorcerer doing this?

"You said you wouldn't hurt her!"

"And I won't, if she stops me." The sorcerer held out his hands and ropes glowing a sickly green snaked out of his wide sleeves.

Panic crushed Regulus' chest. *Not again. Etiros, please, not again.* He fought through the pain and tried to get to Adelaide through the sorcerer's barrier, but it knocked him back as the ropes swayed toward her.

Adelaide held out her hands and jets of fire enveloped the ropes. Regulus could feel the heat even through the transparent wall. The sorcerer hissed and clenched his fists, then pulled his hands back. She stumbled forward, and the flames withered. The ropes lengthened and shot toward her.

"ADELAIDE!" Regulus punched the wall, which rippled but remained intact.

She summoned another shield of blue light. The ropes bounced around the shield and wrapped around her arms, pinning them to her sides. Regulus franticly shoved his shoulder against the barrier, but it wouldn't give. Adelaide curled her hands into fists and screamed. Not a high-pitched scream of fear. A low scream that started in her chest and built. A scream of anger. A scream of strength. Not a scream at all.

A war cry.

Regulus had been in enough fights to recognize that desperate anger. Pale blue light flashed, and she pulled her arms away from her sides in a quick motion. The ropes snapped and disintegrated. Her chest heaved. A nearly imperceptible blue aura shone off her skin.

Regulus gaped at Adelaide. At the power she had kept hidden. She raised her hand and a spear of blue light materialized in her fist. She threw it at the sorcerer with fury. The sorcerer erected his own shield, which absorbed her spear.

The sorcerer applauded slowly. "Well—"

Adelaide made a sound like a growl and three sharp, shining magic throwing knives appeared between her fingers.

The sorcerer scowled. "That's quite enough." He clenched his right hand into a fist. Regulus collapsed and screamed as his blood boiled within him, burning from the inside out.

"No, stop!" Adelaide cried over his screams.

The pain subsided. Regulus looked up, his vision swimming. The magical barrier vanished, and Adelaide knelt next to him. She put her arms around him.

"Please," she said. "Stop. I'll help you. Just don't hurt him. I'll do whatever you want; don't hurt him."

Regulus wanted to tell her not to make promises like that on his behalf, but he was having difficulty getting his mouth to work, still recovering from the sorcerer's torture.

"Isn't that touching." The sorcerer smirked. "I'm impressed he's won such loyalty, even after delivering you to me. Even after you know what he is." Regulus winced.

"I'll help you, and you'll free him and let us go." She spoke with confidence, but Regulus caught the slight tremor in her voice.

"Yes, yes." The sorcerer turned toward the tower. "Follow me."

CHAPTER 43

ADELAIDE TOOK REGULUS' GLOVED HAND AS SHE FOLLOWED the sorcerer up the winding staircase to the top of the tower. Once there, the sorcerer indicated a table in the center of the room. Three gold rods laid end-to-end but not quite touching, topped with a half-foot-long oval formed of spiraling gold. A small mount was attached to the inside of the bottom of the oval, as if something was missing.

"I only need one piece to complete this staff," the sorcerer said, moving to the opposite side of the table. "An opal. I've searched for decades and finally have found its location." He glanced to Regulus. "Thanks to Hargreaves for bringing me three of the other four pieces. I spent years figuring out how to retrieve this one." He tapped the top rod. "I didn't even bother trying to find the rest until I secured it. Went through dozens of men before he walked into my trap."

"Why couldn't you get it?" she asked. Regulus squeezed her hand, quick and hard, as if warning her not to ask questions.

"Because the dolt mages who hid it hundreds of years ago put a spell on the cave it was hidden in." Irritation rang in the sorcerer's voice. "Only a good man with a selfless heart could find and retrieve the piece. When your man here traded his life to save others, I hoped I had finally found someone good enough to get it. I was right. Lucky for him."

Regulus stiffened next to her. She looked up at the hard lines on his strained face. His eyes widened. This must be the first he had heard of the sorcerer's reasons for doing what he did.

"They've done a similar rotten trick with the opal." The sorcerer tapped the mount inside the top piece of the staff. "There's a rock wall that acts like a door to where they hid the opal. But it can only be opened by," he sneered, "*uncorrupted* magic. By a *mage*." He practically spat the word. "I've read everything I can get my hands on and gone myself. There's no other way in, and no way to trick the door. It won't open for me." He looked at her. "But it will open for you."

"And if I can't open it?"

"Do you actually need me to answer that?" He gestured toward Regulus. The muscles in Adelaide's back tightened. She wouldn't listen to Regulus scream like that again. The sorcerer pulled a map out of his robes and spread it over the table. "You have to go here." He tapped the map, pointing at a spot high in the Pelandian Mountains, on the other side of the Tumen Forest where they currently were. Almost within Craigailte's borders. "You'll find a path up the mountain marked by cairns. At the top, the path will appear to dead-end at a wall of rock. That's the door."

"So, she opens the door," Regulus said, "and we just…go inside?"

"There may or may not be a guardian of some kind. The sources are in conflict."

"Great." Regulus' deadpan echoed the dread that made the hair on her neck stand on end.

"Why do you need it?" she asked.

"My business with the Staff of Nightfall is my own." The sorcerer's mouth turned down. "All that should matter to you is what will happen to you and your friends and family if you fail me."

The sorcerer folded the map and held it out. His movements cautious, Regulus stepped forward and took the map. He tucked it into his belt and turned to leave. She did the same, but the sorcerer's voice stopped them.

"Mage."

Adelaide turned back as the sorcerer slunk toward her. Regulus held his arm in front of her. Shielding her. As if that would make a difference. The intensity with which the sorcerer watched her made her feel exposed.

"I don't like needing you. And I don't trust you." His eyes glowed green in the shadow of his hood.

Regulus went rigid. He spun toward her and clamped his hand around her throat.

"Reg…" She choked as Regulus squeezed hard enough to hurt, but not enough to strangle her. She grabbed his hand as he looked down at her, his gray eyes cold as stone, his mouth set in a hard line.

"I'm not taking any chances, mage." The sorcerer grabbed her right wrist with surprising strength and wrenched her arm down. He shoved her sleeve up and put his hand on the underside of her forearm above her wrist.

White-hot pain seared into her arm. A scream rasped up her strangled throat, scraping and burning. Her vision blacked out and her stomach twisted. Right when she thought she would pass out, the sorcerer drew his hand away. The burning cooled and disappeared. Regulus released her throat, and she fell to her knees.

Harsh black lines stood out against the brown of her arm. Two touching hollow diamonds and a half diamond open toward her wrist. The same as the mark on Regulus' arm.

CHAPTER 44

REGULUS BLINKED AS THE SORCERER RELINQUISHED CONTROL. Fury and shock slid like ice through his veins. "What did you do?"

He knelt next to Adelaide. She held her right arm, underside up, in her lap. Staring at the mark on her skin. The mark that matched his own. He glared at the sorcerer. "You said you wouldn't hurt her!" His throat constricted, making his voice hoarse and scratchy. His hands hovered above Adelaide's shoulders, unsure what to do. Unsure if he dared touch her.

Her fingers trembled as she brushed them over the black lines.

"She didn't agree to this! You had no right!" Tears stung at Regulus' eyes. Her scream still rang in his ears.

"Oh, please. She agreed outside, remember? She said she'd help me, do whatever I want. Not my fault she didn't understand the weight of her words." The sorcerer turned away with a shrug, but his posture sagged and he moved slowly. "This is temporary. When the opal is mine, I'll remove both marks."

"You say that, but you said you wouldn't harm her! You said she wouldn't be in danger!"

"I said I didn't *want* to harm her. An unavoidable side effect, I'm afraid. And now she can't die, just like you. So she's not in *mortal* danger."

If Regulus could have gotten in more than a step before the sorcerer crippled him with pain or took over, he would have lunged at him. Cut his head clean off; thrown him out the window. His tongue stuck as he looked back down at Adelaide. She sat motionless, her back curved and shoulders hunched. He swallowed back his rage and guilt, but his hands still trembled as he grabbed her shoulders and helped her to her feet.

"Let's go," he whispered.

She didn't respond. Didn't look up from the ground as she blinked against tears. *I shouldn't have brought her. I shouldn't have obeyed the last two years. This is my fault.*

Regulus guided Adelaide out of the tower, across the dead ground to where their horses waited, pawing the ground and glancing around.

"I'm sorry." The words came out strained. He closed his eyes, the fright on her face too much to bear. Shame blazed across his skin.

"Regulus." The gentleness in her voice cut deeper than any wound he had ever received. "Look at me."

He forced his eyes open. Trapped breath pushed against his ribs. She looked into his eyes.

"This isn't your doing."

The breath wrenched out of him in a pathetic sob. He drew her to his chest, and she wrapped her arms around his bulky armor. "I'm sorry. I should have protected you. I'm sorry. Adelaide, I'm sorry." She quivered while his tears soaked into her dress. Her tears splashed onto his neck. "I'm so sorry." His throat was raw from trying to swallow back his sobs.

"Stop," she said. "Please."

He held her and hoped that somehow, she was finding comfort in his iron embrace. He took several deep breaths, his lungs burning. Slowly, he straightened.

"I'm—"

"If you apologize one more time, I will punch you." She smiled, although it didn't reach her eyes. "You didn't do this."

"I brought you here."

"I *came* here. I chose to come. Because I believed you were a good man. Because I loved you." Adelaide brushed her fingers over his wet cheek. "I still believe that. And I still love you."

Joy warred with overwhelming guilt. He pulled her hand down and turned over her arm to see the mark. How could she forgive him? How could he forgive himself?

"Regulus?" Doubt crept into her voice.

He leaned down, lifted her arm, and kissed the mark with the salt of his tears still on his lips. "I love you." He pulled her sleeve down. "I. Love. You."

"Great!" The sorcerer's shout drifted down from the opened window above them. "Now go before I lose my temper!"

They rode for a few hours before he stopped Sieger in the dark forest. "We'll camp here."

Adelaide's eyelids drooped. "But the sorcerer—"

"Can wait." He dismounted and tied Sieger to a low-hanging branch of a tree. "We're still on our way. We're still planning on getting what he wants. But we have to rest." She yawned. "*You* have to rest."

"Mm, fine." She dismounted and tied Zephyr next to Sieger. Regulus pulled his cloak from his saddlebag and held it out to her. Even in midsummer, the nights were chilly this close to the mountains. And winter was already on the peaks. He should have asked Harold to pack extra gear. *Idiot.* She took it, and he sat down with his back against a nearby tree. She still stood, watching him with the cloak in her hands. "You're not sleeping like that?"

"Like what?"

"In that armor."

He shrugged, the armor rasping and clinking. "I always do. Can't get it off."

"Hmph." She created an orb of light. "Stand up."

"Ad—"

"Now." The authority in her voice brought him to his feet like a scolded schoolboy. In the bluish light, she looked for the straps securing his pauldrons.

"We should sl—"

"Hush." She sounded exhausted. "I'm concentrating." The pauldron on his left shoulder loosened. She slipped it off and placed it on the ground next to him. It didn't take her long to remove it all and place it in a neat pile.

"I'm impressed." He turned to face her. "Harold does that all the time and isn't much faster."

"There was an old set of my father's armor in the cottage my mother and I stayed in." She rubbed her arm, her face downcast. "I tried to see how fast I could take it all off the display mannequin and put it back on. To pass time."

He didn't know how to respond to the loneliness in her admission, so he did the only thing he could. He pulled her into an embrace. She tucked her arms under his and hooked them over his shoulders. Her breathing deepened as she rested her head on his shoulder. Regulus wasn't sure if he was holding Adelaide together or if she was keeping him from falling apart. Maybe they both needed the other to hold them, to keep them standing. A surreal, detached calm settled over him. But as much as he didn't want to let go, they couldn't stay like that.

"We need to sleep," he whispered into her hair.

"Mm." She stepped back. Sleep pulled at her eyes as she laid down on a grassy area under a maple tree, pulling his cloak over her. He laid down a short distance away, his sword close at hand. She propped herself up on her elbow. "Where's your cloak?"

"I forgot to grab an extra. Don't worry, I'm fine." Regulus closed his eyes, then opened them as he heard grass rustle. Adelaide laid down next to him and threw the cloak over them both. She rolled onto her side, her back pressed against him. He didn't move; his breath caught. The gentle beat of her heart pulsed against his side. He relaxed as the steady rhythm of her breathing lulled him to sleep.

Light woke Regulus. He felt Adelaide next to him before he opened his eyes. He had rolled onto his side in the night, and lay pressed against her, her back curled against his chest. His right arm wrapped around her over his cloak. He blinked away the sleepiness and eased himself up on his left elbow. Mist swirled in the ethereal pale glow of early morning, and dew clung to every surface— including her dark hair. Sunlight caught in the droplets, making her hair sparkle.

The first night Regulus saw Adelaide, he had thought she looked angelic. Now, with dew drops glittering in her hair like diamonds, the peaceful, untroubled look on her face as she slept, and the sunlight highlighting her brown skin, she took his breath away.

He moved to stand, but she wrapped her hands around his arm. She grunted in her sleep and pulled his arm closer to her chest. So Regulus did the only thing that made sense. He settled back down in the grass next to her until Adelaide finally stirred. She shifted, rolling over onto her back with a stifled groan. He propped up his elbow and rested his cheek on his fist.

"What are you smiling at?"

"Has anyone ever told you," he stroked her damp hair, "that you're pretty?"

"That's the best you've got?"

"No." He gazed into her eyes. "You're spectacular. Kind. Strong. Brave. Unrelenting. You're a tigress. My tigress. My *shiraa*."

"And you're my *ekaleh hadya*." Her eyes shone with playfulness. "My lone wolf."

A pang stabbed at his chest. "I don't want to be alone anymore."

Regulus leaned over her and planted his right hand on the damp grass near her head. Adelaide gazed up at him, her chest rising and falling with each breath. Her hand drifted up to his chest and her fingers spread across his sternum. Her touch felt like the warmth of a fire on a cold night, igniting him from the inside out. He shouldn't be this close. He wanted to be closer. Her breath brushed across his face. A sudden stinging attacked his forearm. She winced, and he knew she felt it, too. He hung his head, his hair brushing the grass next to her face.

"You're not alone." Adelaide turned his face toward her. "And if we make it out of this, I'm never leaving you again." A grin broke over her face. "Marry me, Regulus."

He laughed, his elation and surprise erupting out of him. "I'd be a fool not to." He leaned down and kissed her, the pinch from the mark forgotten in the ferocity of her kiss. But the mark sent a shock up his arm, and he pulled away with an agitated sigh. He stood and offered her his hand. Her stomach growled as he helped her to her feet.

"How much food did you bring?"

"Harold packed enough for a couple days for us both." He crossed to Sieger and pulled a leather pouch of venison jerky out of the saddlebag. He took a large piece and tossed the bag to Adelaide.

"We'd better get going." Regulus grinned. "Help me with my armor?"

CHAPTER 45

THE HIGHER THEY RODE UP INTO THE MOUNTAINS, THE DENSER the forest became. Pines and firs overtook deciduous trees. Adelaide scanned the forest while Regulus consulted the map and the scribbled directions written on the back. She listened to the rustling of pine needles and creak of branches. The irregular chitter of squirrels and chirping of birds.

Regulus looked at the map, at the trees, back at the map. "All I see are trees. I *think* we're still headed in the right direction, but… these notes aren't particularly helpful."

"I say we keep going straight."

"You sound awfully confident." He cocked a brow. "How do you know?"

She shrugged. "The mark. It doesn't hurt. That means we're going the right way, right?"

"Not necessarily." He dragged his hand over his face. "It just means we're trying to obey."

"Hm." She looked around again. "You have a better idea?"

"Fair point."

They rode until her stomach twisted with hunger. Regulus pulled some jerky from his saddlebag, but they didn't stop. The dry, chewy jerky mostly tasted like salt, but it quelled the rumbling in her stomach. They rode out of the trees into a wide path, overgrown with grass. It stretched out to the right and curved up further into the mountains to their left.

"I think this is it," he said, consulting the map.

The winding trail upward narrowed the higher it progressed into the mountains until the encroaching brush forced them to ride single file. It was midafternoon and long shadows stretched across the path when they reached a fork. A dilapidated wooden sign pointed to the left branch and said only "Craigailte." The branch to the right was little more than a steep footpath over tangled roots and exposed bedrock.

"Well," she looked at the path to the right, "we're not going to Craigailte."

"No." Regulus dismounted. He pulled up the sprawling branches of a juniper bush, revealing a cairn covered in blue-green juniper berries. "We'll have to leave the horses. We'll tie them off the path, out of sight."

He made her wear his cloak. She didn't argue. The air already held a chill. She was glad she'd worn one of her riding dresses with sleeves. Regulus pulled his helm out of the saddlebag and put it on. He tied the saddlebag over his shoulder, and they set out up the footpath.

Trees and bushes caught on her dress and cloak and gravel shifted under her feet. The scent of pine and falling leaves filled the air. Regulus walked ahead of her, scanning the trees and warning her of loose and slippery rocks.

"I don't know what we'll find at the top," Regulus said as he picked his way around a sapling growing out of the middle of the path. "There are many dangerous creatures in these mountains, and the sorcerer mentioned there might be something guarding the opal. If we're attacked, I want you to run. Get to safety."

Adelaide stopped short, offended that he would expect her to leave him behind—or that she couldn't help. "You're joking, right?"

"About your safety? Never." He glanced over his bulky pauldron, but she couldn't see his eyes under the black, horned helm. "I can't die. I'll catch up."

"I can't either, remember?" She held up her right arm, even though her sleeve covered the sorcerer's mark.

Regulus turned around and took off his helm. His gaze dragged across the ground before meeting her eyes. "I've been brought back from the brink of death more times than I care to count." His voice strained. "It *hurts*, Adelaide. It still feels like dying. And the sorcerer's magic isn't like yours. There's no comfort or relief. Just pain that slowly fades."

That sounded horrible, but she wouldn't back down. "I won't abandon you." She met his gaze, challenging him. "I have my dagger and my knives. I have my magic. You know I can help."

"I don't want you to suffer if you don't have to. I don't want you to get hurt."

"And I don't want *you* to get hurt!" Emotion she hadn't even realized she had been holding in rushed out and tears gathered in the corner of her eyes. "I don't want to be here! I don't want to help this sorcerer, I don't want to have this mark on my arm, I don't want to think about my sister not knowing if I'm all right, I don't want to wonder if Nolan is threatening my family trying to find me! We don't always get what we want!" She wrapped her arms around herself and closed her eyes.

"But I *want* to help you." She looked up and whispered, "Let me help you."

"Okay," he murmured.

The tenderness and guilt written all over Regulus' face nearly broke her. She wiped her face with her sleeve as he put his helm on and started back up the path.

Regulus froze, his hand out to the side. Adelaide listened intently and leaned sideways, trying to see around him. She heard it first. A rumbling low breath that sounded more like a growl. A loud snort. Its head reared up, appearing high above Regulus. Bear. Its black nose twitched as it sniffed the air; beady eyes gleaming in the dim sunlight. Thick brown fur rippled in the slight breeze. Its front paws, held in front of its chest as it stretched up on its hind legs, were as big as Regulus' helm.

Her breath hitched as her heart thudded. Regulus eased the saddlebag from his shoulder to the ground. His hand crept toward his sword. The blade scraped against the scabbard and the bear's round ears twitched. He drew the sword faster. The bear roared. The sound vibrated through her, from her skull down into the ground, and shook the trees. Her eyes widened as she stared at the bits of bloodied fur stuck between its huge yellowed teeth. Regulus drew back his massive sword and swung. The bear swiped a paw at him, hitting him in the shoulder and knocking him to the side before he could land his swing. He fell on top of a tangle of mountain sage and juniper. The bear fell onto all fours, landing on top of Regulus. One paw landed on his chest, the other on his sword arm. He grunted and struggled against the bear's weight. She swallowed and snapped out of her momentary paralysis.

"Hey!" Adelaide pulled out her throwing knives as the bear turned its head toward her. Regulus pushed on the paw on his chest with his left arm. She threw the first knife, aiming for its shoulder. If she killed it and it collapsed on Regulus, she'd never be able to move it off him. The knife disappeared deep in the bear's fur. The beast roared and stepped off Regulus' sword arm, but that put more pressure on the paw on his chest and he groaned. The paw came down on the other side of Regulus' head as the bear turned toward her. She stepped back and threw her next knife at the bear's chest. It sank in, glinting in the mass of fur. The bear charged.

Adelaide gasped and stepped back, throwing the last knife at its head. It moved as if it saw the knife, and the blade sunk into the bear's neck where it met its shoulders. She threw up a magic shield and crouched down just before the bear slammed headfirst into the shield. She struggled to keep the shield in place as she slid on the gravelly path.

Regulus shouted from behind the bear, loud, low and guttural. The bear ignored the sound, clawing at her shield of transparent blue light. She looked up at its snarling lips, only a barrier of light between her face and its teeth. She saw the dull sheen of light on black armor as Regulus jumped on the bear's back. He brought his sword straight down, the hilt clasped in both hands above his head. The sword sunk behind the bear's head and emerged from its neck in a fountain of blood that sizzled against her shield. She dropped the shield and scrambled back as the bear fell. Its weight shook the ground as it hit the earth. She held her hands out, steadying herself and breathing hard.

Regulus stood on the bear's back as he pulled on his sword. The blade freed with the scrape of metal on bone and a sucking sound. He looked terrifying, the waning sunlight glinting off the hulking black armor and curving horns rising above his helm. Blood soaked the oversized sword in his hands and ran off the tip in a glittering stream of crimson. Now she understood why he hadn't wanted to tell her the truth.

Because in that moment he didn't look like the man she loved. The man before her was the Black Knight of whispered terrors. He didn't look kind or good. He looked dangerous. Cruel.

He looked like a monster.

CHAPTER 46

REGULUS DROPPED THE SWORD AND YANKED HIS HELM OFF, BUT it was too late. He saw the look in Adelaide's eyes. The fear. Not fear of the sorcerer. Fear of *him*. The helm slipped from his hands and clattered to the ground. *Please, no.* Her right foot inched back and his soul crumbled. He slid down the bear's side and reached toward her. "Adelaide…"

She blinked, and the fear vanished. He breathed a sigh of relief. "Why do you wear that?" Her gaze ran over his armor and her mouth twisted down. "It's not you."

"Requirement of the sorcerer's."

"When this is over, I want to burn it. Melt it down and destroy it."

Regulus laughed as the energy of the fight and tension of seeing her afraid of him wore off. "Agreed." He held out his hand and Adelaide took it. "We need to keep moving. Every creature on the mountain will have heard that. And it's getting dark."

He led her around the bear's corpse and retrieved his sword. He left the helm lying next to the body. Adelaide left her knives buried under the bear's bulk, the time required to retrieve them not worth the trouble.

Dusk plunged into night. Adelaide conjured a light to hover along the ground ahead of them, and another that hovered above their heads. Gnarled roots twisted over the rocky, narrow trail as it curved ever up the mountain. The higher they went, the steeper the trail became, but at least their exertion helped combat the increasing cold.

They walked for hours, snacking on the dwindling supply of jerky to keep their energy up. They would have to hunt on their way back.

The trees creaked and rustled and sounds of animals whispered from the forbidding darkness between trees. A few times he caught sight of a pair of reflective yellow eyes, but nothing attacked them. He kept alert, even as his attention split between the surrounding forest and listening to Adelaide's footsteps and breathing behind him. A small part of him took comfort in the mark on her arm. If something attacked—wolves, chimera, goblins, dragon for all he knew—at least she would live.

Regulus walked out of the trees onto a ledge overlooking a steep precipice. A narrow ledge curved around a sheer rock face. Had they taken a wrong turn in the dark? He scanned the ground in the illumination from Adelaide's orbs. There. A cairn sat by the rock face at the beginning of the ledge, a rock on the top shaped like a rough arrow pointing along the exposed rock. He stepped to the side. "You go first."

She peered at the ledge and her jaw slackened. "Why?"

"So I can catch you if you fall."

Adelaide swallowed, then headed out onto the ledge. The rock face seemed to stretch on forever. To their left were the shadowy tops of pines. Freezing wind blew into their faces, making his cheeks burn and his nose sting. Rock crumbled beneath Adelaide's foot and she stumbled. He wrapped his arm around her waist, pinned her to the rock face.

Her chest heaved as she caught her breath. "Thank you."

He nodded, and they continued.

Finally, the ledge widened, and the rock face curved away. They walked into an open meadow. Patches of half-melted snow littered the grass. A cairn pointed across the meadow. Tall grasses rustled around them, accompanied by the crunch of icy snow beneath their feet.

He heard a snap of branches. Heavy foot falls. He drew his sword. Adelaide froze, watching him. He scanned the trees, desperate to see whatever stalked them. A crack of snapping wood echoed as thudding moved closer. Whatever it was, it was big. Pines to their right parted and something emerged from the shadows. Cold moonlight illuminated leathery skin and reflected in huge white eyes.

Adelaide gasped. "Is that a…"

"Mountain troll."

The troll looked at them, foggy breaths puffing from its flat, wide nostrils. Regulus heard Adelaide mutter a prayer under her breath. The troll's legs were short under its colossal torso and massive shoulders. It leaned forward, black-clawed hands dragging on the ground at the end of long, hulking arms. It grunted and ran toward them, using its fisted hands to make up for its short legs. Regulus raised his sword and moved into a defensive stance, his feet planted under his shoulders as his pulse quickened in anticipation of the fight.

Adelaide gave a defiant yell and threw her hands forward. A dozen blue shards of light flew from her hands. A few whipped past the lumbering troll, but most hit. They lodged in the monster's thick hide. Regulus readied himself, waiting for the perfect moment to charge. Next to him, Adelaide punched her right hand forward. An arc of aqua light exploded from her fist and slammed into the troll. It roared and stumbled. Regulus ran forward and sliced at the troll's short, fat neck. It lurched back and blocked with its arm. His sword bit through thick hide into flesh and cracked against bone. He yanked back, slicing through more flesh as he freed his blade.

The troll screeched and lurched. Its hand hung from a strip of throbbing, blood-covered muscle and leathery skin. A spear of blue light slammed into its left shoulder and it reeled to the side. Regulus darted forward and slid under the troll, dragging his sword deep

SELINA R. GONZALEZ

across its torso. He stood, but the troll didn't fall. It stumbled toward him, roaring. He stabbed his sword into its chest, and it leaned into the sword, clawing at him with its good hand. Its weight pressed him back, and he fell to his knees as the troll reached for him. The blade sunk deeper into the troll's chest. Its claws raked over his breastplate with a jarring screech of rending metal.

Then Adelaide was there, a sword of light wreathed in flames in her hands. Her teeth showed as her lips curled back in a yell. The flames reflected in her ferocious eyes. She swung at the troll's throat. The smell of burning leather and flesh joined the stench of blood and troll as the blade of light sliced through the trolls' neck. The head rolled over its shoulder and fell. Blood splattered over Regulus. Its body fell to the side, wrenching his sword out of his grasp.

For a second, Adelaide stood over him, his cloak and her skirt swaying around her. Shoulders squared, spine straight and tall, outlined from behind by the moon and bathed in the flickering light of orange flames and the soft blue-white glow of the sword in her hands. Her eyes shone with golden light. Fierce. Powerful. Intimidating. Beautiful.

The sword vanished from her hands and the meadow fell into darkness. She created a new orb of light and knelt next to him. "Are you all right?"

"Yes… How did you do that?"

She blushed. "Honestly, I don't know. I just…did. I saw you fall and I… I stopped thinking so hard about it and did it."

"You're amazing." Regulus leaned toward Adelaide, reaching for her waist. She grimaced and leaned away from him.

"You're covered in troll blood." Her mouth curved down. "And the troll smells. I'll throw up if I kiss you right now."

He grinned. "You've got troll blood on you too, you know."

She looked at her blood-splattered dress. "Still not kissing you."

382

"Later, then." He winked and stood, then retrieved his sword. "We'd best keep going."

On the other side of the meadow, the path turned into winding stone steps that climbed almost straight up into the darkness. They climbed for an hour before reaching the top. Adelaide kept pace behind him the whole way, and when they stepped into the wide clearing at the top of the steps, they were scarcely winded. At least their bond to the sorcerer gave them extra strength and stamina, not just pain and servitude. If only it would protect them against the cold. Regulus' ears felt numb and his joints ached under the freezing armor.

The moonlight illuminated the rock wall some twenty feet ahead of them. Smooth, undisturbed snow glistened and crunched beneath their feet. Wind whistled in his ears and rustled in the pines. No other sounds filled the night. They stopped in the shadow at the base of the wall and stared up as it stretched toward the stars.

"I guess this is it." Regulus looked at Adelaide. Her nose was red, and she clutched his cloak tighter about her. "This part is all you."

"So I…" She looked at him and back at the wall. "What?"

He shrugged. "I don't know how you do what you do."

"Hm." She placed her hand on the icy rock. Pale blue light shone under her palm. Nothing happened. He tucked his hands under his arms and shifted his weight from one foot to the other, trying to keep warm. She added her other hand. Still nothing. "All right." She stepped back, and he moved back farther. She shone a bright beam of light from her hands to the wall. Still nothing. "Are we *sure* this is the right wall?"

"It lines up with his notes and description."

Adelaide blasted the wall with fire. It warmed him for a moment, but had no impact on the stone. She threw daggers of light at it. Still nothing. "Why." Another blast of fire. "Won't." Her voice rose as a glowing spear pinged off the wall. "It!" A torrent of flames. "OPEN!" She shoved her hands forward, throwing a blast of light at the wall.

A sharp crack like a lightning strike rent the air and rattled his bones. A fissure opened in the bottom of the wall and raced up some ten feet before spreading right and left. The rock in front of them crumbled and crashed to the ground. He covered his face as dust billowed. When he lowered his arm, a gaping hole in the wall opened into inky blackness. They looked at each other, then headed inside, an orb of blue light leading their way.

They stood inside a round stone room no more than six paces in diameter. In the center of the room stood a marble statue. They moved closer, and the light fell on the statue—a woman in flowing robes. The marble woman's eyes were closed, and her head lowered. She held one hand over her face, hiding one eye. The stone beneath her visible eye was stained, making her look like she had been crying. Her other hand was cupped, palm up, in front of her stomach. In her palm glittered a huge opal of black and purple with flecks of orange and red. It was polished into an oval and about as long as a little finger. Adelaide reached out and curled her fingers around the opal. Regulus held his breath as she pulled her hand back.

The statue moved.

The marble woman blinked, her lids grating over pupil-less eyes with a rasping sound. She raised her head with a creak of stone. Adelaide stepped closer to Regulus, clutching the opal to her chest. The statue's white lips parted.

"Do not seek to re-forge the Staff of Nightfall." The statue's cold voice filled the room. "The Staff brings only death and destruction. The sorceress who created it is dead, along with all her victims." She reached out her hand, the marble groaning. "You are pure of heart to enter here. The Staff's power cannot be used for good. Its desire is tainted. Return the opal and seal the door, or the Staff will bring endless night."

His heart sank. Whatever the sorcerer wanted with a staff that brought death and destruction, it wasn't good. Regardless of whether *endless night* was a metaphor, he didn't like the sound of it. *Etiros...forgive me.*

"Who are you?" Adelaide's voice sounded small in the stone chamber.

"I am the spirit of those who died by the power of the Staff of Nightfall." The statue blinked again and tears—real tears—ran from her marble eyes. Regulus recoiled.

Adelaide's fist moved from her chest. She cried out. In the same moment, a burning sensation spread from the mark on his own arm. She was considering leaving the opal. And the sorcerer knew.

"Return the opal." Tears dripped over the polished marble of the statue's face and splashed on the stone floor.

Adelaide screamed and Regulus groaned as they both fell to their knees. Regulus knew what she was feeling, because the same slicing, burning pain cut up his arm and across his chest. But he had experienced it before. Adelaide shook beside him, sobbing. He wrapped his arm around her as the pain made his head pound. She whimpered and rocked back and forth. His eyes watered—not from his own pain as much as for hers.

"Adelaide." He placed a trembling hand against her cheek.

She shook her head. "We can't, we—" She arched backward and screamed. A stifled scream ground up his own throat as it felt like his heart was being wound round and round with hot wire. The opal slipped from Adelaide's fingers and clattered across the stone.

"We don't have a choice," Regulus whispered, holding her shoulders. "He controls us."

She nodded, tears running down her cheeks and neck. "All right. All right."

The pain rushed out of his chest, down his arm, and disappeared. Adelaide leaned against him, breathing hard. After a moment, Regulus scooped the opal off the ground and put it in his saddlebag before helping her to her feet. The marble statue creaked as they walked toward the entrance, and he looked over his shoulder.

Both her stone hands covered her face.

CHAPTER 47

THE WALL CLOSED WITH A RUMBLE BEHIND THEM. ADELAIDE'S feet dragged as they stepped into the moonlight. She was too physically and emotionally exhausted to climb back down tonight. She still believed bringing the sorcerer the opal was wrong, but what could she do? He would either torture them into submission or take control of one of them. She just wanted this nightmare to be over. And she had promised Regulus she would do what the sorcerer wanted so he could be free.

They walked over to a small spruce tree several yards away from the path. The branches had kept the ground around the trunk free of snow. Adelaide used her magic to push snow off the lower boughs. They made a little pile of dead branches and needles near the edge of the dry ground so the smoke wouldn't get trapped, and she lit them on fire. She helped Regulus out of his armor, and they held each other for warmth and comfort, his cloak wrapped around them. Even the troll blood in his hair couldn't stop her from pressing as close to him as possible.

She slept fitfully, dreaming of crying statues, screaming men, women, and children, and glassy-eyed corpses. Regulus still had his arms around her when she awoke in the morning. Soft grayish light glittered on the icy surface of the snow and her breath fogged in the air. Somewhere a jay trilled a song. She buried her icy face in his shoulder, not wanting to move. Too cold.

"As much as I enjoy this," Regulus said, his voice scratchy, "how about a fire? I can barely feel my face."

Adelaide groaned as they separated and sat up. She held her hands between them and conjured a flame. It was more draining to maintain the flame than to start a fire, but she was too stiff to get up and look for kindling. Feeling crept back to her feet and nose. Regulus scooted over until his shoulder pressed against hers.

"You know what might help chase the cold away?" he whispered, his voice husky and his breath warm on her ear.

She smirked at the small fire hovering above her hands. "What's that?" He kissed her cheek, then brushed gentle kisses along her jawline. Warmth tingled over her skin and spread through her torso. "You still stink like troll," she said.

But she turned her head and kissed him. The fire faded away, and she clenched the front of his shirt. He held her close, his arms strong against her back as he gripped the back of her neck. They separated, their mouths still close.

"Warmer now?" she murmured.

"Mm, almost." He kissed her again and flames seemed to dance over her skin. She wrapped her hands around the back of his head. Tremors of joy ran down her back as she relaxed, relishing him. "Better."

She laughed at the smile in his voice. They held each other a moment longer, ignoring the rest of the world. Savoring this moment of quiet. Of being together. A slight tingle pricked the mark, making Adelaide wince. She pulled back, her hands slipping down his arms.

"Don't." He held her arms, his eyes pleading. "Not yet."

"We have to go."

His shoulders fell. "I know." He pushed her sleeve back and ran his thumb over the mark on her arm. "Let's go get rid of this."

Regulus left the armor behind, to Adelaide's relief. If the sorcerer kept his word, he wouldn't need it anymore. He kept the sword, just in case. Nothing bothered them on the way down the mountain, although she thought she saw shadows moving in the trees. She finally mentioned them to Regulus.

"Yes, I noticed. Whatever is out there probably smells the troll blood and are keeping their distance. We're either trolls, which are difficult to kill, or we killed a troll, making us more dangerous."

Once they returned to their horses, they rode straight to the sorcerer's tower, late into the night. They crossed from vibrant, living trees to blackened, lifeless trees, then naked, bark-barren trees with wood like bone. Had the decay spread further?

As they dismounted, she looked at Regulus. "The decay...was it this bad two years ago?"

He shook his head. "No. Only the vines on the tower and the trees closest to the tower were dead then."

The tower door creaked open. "Yes, well." The sorcerer strode toward them, a torch in hand. "It takes a lot of energy, keeping you alive. I have to get that energy from somewhere." He held out his hand. "Where is it?"

Regulus reached into the saddlebag and pulled out the opal. The light of the torch made the stone sparkle black, blue, purple, red, and orange. Regulus clutched the stone. "You'll release us? Both of us? And let us leave alive?"

"Yes, yes. Hand it over!"

"Now?" Adelaide confirmed.

"Yes. I'm a man of my word. Now give it here!" The sorcerer snatched the opal. He turned it over in his hand and held it up, inspecting it. Nerves and anticipation knotted Adelaide's stomach as the sorcerer rubbed his fingers across the stone. Apparently satisfied, he slipped it into his belt. "Give me your arm."

She watched as Regulus pushed up his sleeve and held out his right arm. The sorcerer pressed his hand over the mark. "I release you."

Regulus winced. When the sorcerer pulled his hand away, the mark was gone. Regulus stared at his arm, now marred only by faded scars. Adelaide pushed her sleeve up as the sorcerer approached her.

"I know you considered betraying me," the sorcerer said as he put his hand over the mark on her arm. "But you didn't. So I release you." A burning, ripping sensation coursed over her skin. She bit her tongue to keep from crying out. The feeling faded and she relaxed. "But I need a little more from you." His hand encircled her wrist.

"Wh—" Her vision went white. All the air was sucked from her lungs. She collapsed to her knees, but still the sorcerer held her wrist. Her energy drained, like when she used a lot of magic, but this felt different. Like it was being drawn out; like she was a rapidly emptying well. Regulus screamed her name, but he sounded distant.

The sorcerer's muffled voice said, "Touch me or her and I'll kill her."

Her mouth hung open, but she couldn't draw in a breath. His grip released and her hand dropped. She gasped as if she had been drowning and crumpled to the side. Muscular arms caught her before she hit the ground. She saw shadows and then smudged colors.

"Adelaide? Adelaide!" Regulus' voice sounded strange and muted. "What did you do?"

"She'll be fine in a moment. Now leave. If I see either of you here again, I'll kill you."

"Adelaide?" Regulus shook her shoulders. "Adelaide, please." His voice cut through the fog in her mind, and she blinked. With every blink, her vision cleared until she saw Regulus' deathly pale face hovering above her.

She clutched his sleeves and curled into his chest. He pulled her closer, his heart hammering against her ear. The tower door was closed, the sorcerer gone. Regulus rubbed her back.

"You're okay," he said, almost as if trying to assure himself. "It's over, we're safe. You're all right."

But she wasn't all right.

She couldn't get her thick tongue to work. She tried to speak, but only a broken sob emerged. Above them, green and yellow light flashed from the tower window. Regulus guided her arm over his shoulders, picked her up, and stumbled to his feet. He put her on Sieger, then tied Zephyr's reins to the pommel of his saddle. Regulus mounted behind her, his arms around her waist, and they rode away from the tower and the ominous flashes of light.

It took several more tries to speak past her taut vocal cords. "Regulus."

"You're safe," he repeated, his voice wavering. "It's over. We did it. I'm free. We're both free. Praise Etiros, we're free." He kissed her temple. "He won't hurt you again." His arms tightened around her middle. "I won't let him near you again."

Even with the jostling of Sieger's gallop, Regulus' racing heartbeat and deep, shaky breaths vibrated against her back. She didn't want to ruin his joy at being freed. But she couldn't keep any more secrets from him.

"He took it." Her voice cracked. "My magic. It's gone."

THE STORY CONTINUES
in
STAFF OF NIGHTFALL
July 2020

Acknowledgements

I want to thank my mom first and foremost. Thank you for reading everything I write since the beginning, often multiple times. Best Proofreader Mom award goes to you—as does Best Mom in general for your constant support and belief and your investments in my learning and life. For reading to me when I was little. For supporting this crazy idea that I could write. For reading my books even though fantasy isn't your favorite genre. I wouldn't be an author without your help.

Thank you to my dad, who is always proud of me even when I haven't been proud of myself, and whose sacrifices have allowed me the education and time to make being an author possible. I can chase my dreams because of you.

Thank you to Rebecca for always being there for me and believing in me—even if you kinda stopped reading my writing after I killed your fictional boyfriend something like NINE YEARS AGO. (Let it go!) Thank you for letting me rant to you to figure out plot holes and dead ends, for humoring me and asking questions, even when you weren't entirely sure what on earth was going on. For encouraging me when I was low or metaphorically slapping me with a newspaper and telling me to "pull yourself together!" when I needed it. For all the laughter and ups and downs and adventures. Four years apart or not, I think you're my twin. Thank you for being half of the inspiration for Regulus and Dresden's friendship.

Thank you to Alexis, my soul-sister time zones away and the other half of the inspiration for Regulus and Dresden's friendship. Thank you for understanding me even when I'm barely making sense, for laughing through the hard times, for always being down when I need to vent, for not getting annoyed when I decide to bombard you with memes and nonsense or send you the most random questions or have a breakdown, and for reading and being excited about this book and helping me make it even stronger.

Jessica, thank you for devouring my books and being my #1 fan. Thank you for the fan art and squealing, and for your support and words of encouragement and love when I've been down.

Sylvia, thank you for always enthusiastically supporting me even though you're not a big reader.

To my extended family, thank you for your enthusiastic support of my dreams—from dances to plays to Oxford to novels.

Mr. E, thank you for being one of my most faithful and helpful early readers and encouraging me to write more vivid descriptions.

Thank you to Kinsey for reading my writing attempts in high school. That early support was so important.

Thank you to Becky for loving my characters and always being willing to talk about life or writing and editing and publishing frustrations and ideas. Our conversations are the stabbiest.

Thank you, Jenni, for all the screaming and late-night convos and helping me make decisions and making me laugh and cry and supporting me, even when I'm being an irrational overthinker.

Thank you to my early readers: Heather, Verity, Janice, Claire, Cathi, Alexandra, and Becky. I am so grateful to you!

Thank you to everyone in my FB reader group—lots of love!

To everyone who has supported me and cheered me on, especially all the lovely, supportive individuals on bookstagram: thank you. I can't possibly list you all, but you are the BOMB and all your love and support makes me cry happy tears.

Thank YOU, lovely reader! Thank you for taking a chance on me and this book. Thank you for giving Regulus and Adelaide a chance. Thank you for helping me live my dream of being a published author.

Finally, to the God who gave me life, who made me creative in His image, who placed all these people in my life, who gave me stories and words to tell them with, and who is giving me a spirit of peace not of fear—who has been there comforting me and placing people in my life even in the midst of anxious thoughts and depressive episodes—all gratitude, praise, and glory.

ABOUT THE AUTHOR

Selina R. Gonzalez is a Colorado native with mountains in her blood and dreams that top 14,000 feet. She loves chocolate, fantasy, costumes, bread, history, superheroes, faux leather, things that sparkle, medieval Britain, snark, dogs, and Jesus—not in that order.

She has a bit of a gypsy soul and loves to travel. She's driven coast-to-coast in the US, visited Britain three times (once for a semester at Oxford), and moved to Maine for four and half months. She has a list of places to go as long as Pikes Peak is tall, but always comes back home to Colorado.

You can find Selina raving about books she's enjoying (or adding to her bottomless pit of a to-be-read pile) on Facebook (Selina R. Gonzalez, Author) and Instagram (@NightTooIsBeautiful) and being generally goofy and snarky as well as talking about writing, life, and the antics of her siblings' dogs in her IG stories. Make sure you don't miss any of Selina's future books by subscribing to her newsletter on her website at SelinaRGonzalez.com.

SELINA R. GONZALEZ

CPSIA information can be obtained
at www.ICGtesting.com
Printed in the USA
LVHW011721051020
667983LV00005B/1590